Praise for Abbi Waxman and
The Garden of Small Beginnings

"Abbi Waxman is both irreverent and thoughtful."

—#1 *New York Times* bestselling author Emily Giffin

"Brilliant. Simply brilliant. *The Garden of Small Beginnings* is funny, poignant, and startling in its emotional intensity and in its ability to make the reader laugh and cry on the same page . . . I loved this book!"

—Karen White, *New York Times* bestselling author of the Tradd Street Novels

"If you're looking for a summer beach read with meat, this might well be your book . . . Waxman develops and explores the characters and their relationship in depth . . . with moments of humorous writing." —*The Washington Post*

"This is my favorite kind of book—hilarious, sad, joyful. Beautifully written. *Fun*. I dare you not to enjoy it."

—Julia Claiborne Johnson, author of *Be Frank With Me*

"What a treat!! Abbi Waxman is one of the wittiest voices in the world today. *The Garden of Small Beginnings* is a beautiful book full of humor, heart, and deep insight. An intimate and hilarious journey about a young mom moving on from grief. Reading it gave me the feeling I was talking to a really funny, open mom-friend sharing secrets about life, love, loss, and gardening! Abbi Waxman's quick wit and heart shine brightly throughout this debut novel. I just loved it!" —Molly Shannon, actress

continued . . .

W9-BUV-504

"Funny and poignant. Guaranteed to make you laugh and cry. May make you want to play in dirt and grow a new life of your own."

—Wendy Wax, *USA Today* bestselling author of *One Good Thing*

"Waxman's skill at characterization . . . lifts this novel far above being just another 'widow finds love' story. Clearly an observer, Waxman has mastered the fine art of dialogue as well. Characters ring true right down to Lilian's two daughters, who often steal the show. This debut begs for an encore from Waxman."

—*Kirkus Reviews* (starred review)

"Waxman takes readers from tears to laughter in this depiction of one woman's attempt to hold it all together for everyone else only to learn it's OK to put herself first." —*Booklist*

"Kudos to debut author Waxman for creating an endearing and realistic cast of main and supporting characters (including the children). Her narrative and dialog are drenched with spring showers of witty and irreverent humor, which provides much respite from the underlying grief theme." —*Library Journal* (starred review)

"*The Garden of Small Beginnings* is a quirky, funny, and deeply thoughtful book . . . We're already dying to know if there will be a sequel." —HelloGiggles

"Waxman's voice is witty, emotional, and often profound."
—InStyle.com (U.K.)

"This novel is filled with characters you'll love and wish you lived next door to in real life." —Bustle

"Sorrow is usually an occasion for sobs instead of laughter, but Waxman manages to wring many funny and poignant moments from a sober situation." —*Augusta Chronicle*

"Lilian Girvan, the central character of *The Garden of Small Beginnings*, is an illustrator, a mother, a sister, a budding gardener, and a widow, and her perspective on how she's doing with each role doesn't always match up with what readers can see around her. But that trait makes her a more interesting and realistic protagonist, and along with the book's humor and eccentric supporting cast made it a great read." —BookRiot

"Abbi Waxman artfully tackles grief with humor in her debut novel." —Signature Reads

"It's impossible not to fall in love with Lilian, a young widow who is still trying to come to terms with the death of her husband four years later . . . If you are thinking to yourself, 'Forget it, I'm not reading a gardening book,' don't worry . . . THIS IS NOT A GARDENING BOOK! It *is*, however, a feel-good, hate-to-put-it-down kind of book!" —Chick Lit Central

Berkley titles by Abbi Waxman

THE GARDEN OF SMALL BEGINNINGS

OTHER PEOPLE'S HOUSES

Other People's Houses

Abbi Waxman

Berkley
New York

BERKLEY
An imprint of Penguin Random House LLC
375 Hudson Street, New York, New York 10014

Copyright © 2018 by Dorset Square, LLC
Penguin Random House supports copyright. Copyright fuels creativity, encourages
diverse voices, promotes free speech, and creates a vibrant culture. Thank you for buying
an authorized edition of this book and for complying with copyright laws by not reproducing,
scanning, or distributing any part of it in any form without permission. You are supporting
writers and allowing Penguin Random House to continue to publish books for every reader.

BERKLEY is a registered trademark and the B colophon is a trademark of
Penguin Random House LLC.

Library of Congress Cataloging-in-Publication Data

Names: Waxman, Abbi, author.
Title: Other people's houses / Abbi Waxman.
Description: First edition. | New York : Berkley, 2018.
Identifiers: LCCN 2017046915| ISBN 9780399587924 (softcover) |
ISBN 9780399587931 (ebook)
Subjects: LCSH: Interpersonal relations—Fiction. | Married people—Fiction.|
Adultery—Fiction. | Domestic fiction. | BISAC: FICTION / Contemporary Women. |
FICTION / Family Life. | FICTION / Humorous. | GSAFD: Humorous fiction.
Classification: LCC PS3623.A8936 O85 2018 | DDC 813/.6—dc23
LC record available at https://lccn.loc.gov/2017046915

First Edition: April 2018

Printed in the United States of America
1 3 5 7 9 10 8 6 4 2

Cover art: *house* by 3dts/GettyImages; *bicycle* by yattaa/GettyImages;
blanket by PlusONE/Shutterstock; *cat* by oksana2010/Shutterstock
Cover design by Vikki Chu
Interior art: *wooden fence* © Krivosheev Vitaly/Shutterstock.com;
neighborhood map by Julia Waxman
Book design by Laura K. Corless

This is a work of fiction. Names, characters, places, and incidents either are the product of
the author's imagination or are used fictitiously, and any resemblance to actual persons,
living or dead, business establishments, events, or locales is entirely coincidental.

To my three daughters: Julia, Charlotte, and Kate. May your lives be free of drama, unless it's really entertaining.

And to the children of my neighborhood: Eve, Hannah, Millie, Louis, Avery, Truman, Little Charlotte, Henry, Chela, Sofia, Stella, Nolan, Olivia, Rosetta, Juliette, Ruby Fern, and Nerys. Without you it would be just another place to live.

Acknowledgments

I'd like to thank everyone at LPQ, Larchmont, and The Hatchery, who give me endless cups of coffee and a place to work: Wilder, Kacy, Vanessa, Carter, Amy, Maria, and Talia. If I've forgotten your name, it's not because I don't appreciate you, it's because I'm an idiot.

I'd like to thank my editor, Kate Seaver, who says positive, constructive things about my work then deftly suggests changes that improve it immeasurably.

I'd also like to thank Margalo Chellas Goldbach, a lovely, intelligent, and highly creative child, who provided the original version of one of the more impressive tantrums in the book, and who will now, sadly, never be allowed to forget it.

Lastly, although Larchmont is a real neighborhood in Los Angeles, and many of the sights I describe are real and lovely, all of the characters are completely fictional. Any resemblance to actual people is completely coincidental and unintentional. I used my imagination, as writers are wont to do.

Cast of Characters

The Bloom Family
 Michael
 Frances
 Ava (14)
 Milo (10)
 Alexandra (Lally) (4)

The Porter Family
 Charlie
 Anne
 Theo (10)
 Kate (6)

The Horton Family
 Bill
 Julie
 Lucas (4)

The Carter-Gillespie Family
 Iris
 Sara
 Wyatt (6)

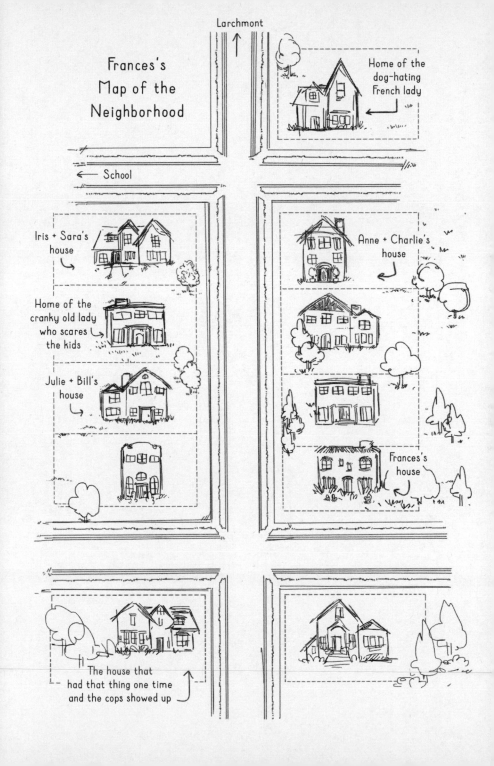

One.

$\mathcal{I}$t was amazing how many children you could fit in a mini-van, if you tessellated carefully and maintained only the most basic level of safety. Four in the very back, two of whom were painfully wedged in the space normally afforded to one child. A single lap belt over those two, a choice both illegal and stupid, but there you go—and thank goodness they were skinny. Frances Bloom always had this vague belief that, in the event of an accident, the pressure of all those little bodies would hold them in place. Ten seconds with a physicist would have cleared that up, but she didn't know any; and seeing as she rarely made it above twenty miles per hour in traffic, she might have been right. She was a careful driver, especially with other people's kids in the car, and so far she hadn't needed to put her nutball theory to the test.

In the middle, the two littlest ones sat securely in actual car seats. And next to her in the front, holding sway over the CD player with the attention to power and detail only a teenager could wield, her eldest daughter, Ava. Seven children, the genetic arsenal of four families. One big crash and the entire neighborhood would have had funeral scheduling issues. Not that it was a joking matter, of course. Frances just had these thoughts, what could you do? Rather than fight them and run the risk that they'd deepen her wrinkles, she just let the buggers run.

She'd been doing this carpool for too long, she thought. It probably wasn't a good sign that a car crash sounded like just one of several options, rather than something to be avoided. But honestly, how many times could you break up a fight over the CD player, or who had to sit in the middle, or whether they could watch a DVD, which they couldn't—and never could have, even before the in-car machine broke. When it was a full house, like this morning, it got so raucous that a tribe of howler monkeys would have fallen silent in awed appreciation. Mind you, these were professional children, the offspring of creative people and deep thinkers, who'd marveled over them as babies, encouraged them to express themselves as toddlers, and wished they'd been more consistent and mean to them now that they were old enough to sass back.

In the far backseat she had the two sibling children of her neighbors Anne and Charlie Porter: Kate and Theo. Lovely names, less-than-lovely children. Kate, six, specialized in the surprise attack, and often sat silently through the entire trip, rousing herself only to shove her brother viciously out of the van at the other end. Theo, ten, never saw it coming. It wasn't that he was thick, per se, it was just that he never saw it coming. Theo himself preferred a full-frontal physical assault, with optional screaming in the ears. God knew how that dynamic would play out in therapy.

Interleaved between them, like two all-beef patties, were her son, Milo, who was ten, and his cousin Wyatt, who was six. They weren't really cousins, they were second cousins, or cousins once removed, or something. Wyatt's mother was Iris, who was actually Frances's cousin, but it was just easier to call the kids cousins and have done with it. Wyatt reveled in the riches of two mothers—his other one was an actress famous for being America's Honey. It wasn't a secret she was gay, it was just that America apparently didn't give a shit.

Right behind her—where she could reach back and hand them stuff at the traffic lights, which she often did—were her youngest child, Lally, and her neighbor Bill's son, Lucas, both of whom were four. It was a complicated carpool that had evolved over time. At first the various parents had tried to take turns driving, but as Frances had a kid at every school, it quickly became clear it was just easier if she did it. She preferred it; she was the only parent who wasn't "working" (let's not get into the atom splitting of who's doing more work, stay-at-home parents or not; let's just agree it's a shit show for all of us, and move on), so she wasn't trying to get anywhere herself, and often did the driving in pajamas. She also hated the feeling in the house just after the kids had screamed and yelled their way through getting ready—finding shoes and losing shoes, hunting down books and bags and hats and whatever, all of which they could have gotten ready the night before, not that she was making a point or anything—and had scrambled through the door and down the path to someone else's car . . . It made her feel like she'd been picked last for a team, or left behind at a train station, or like when she'd come home to an empty house after her own days at school. *I want to go, too*, her inner child cried, and her outer adult volunteered to do all the driving and everyone was happy.

The elementary kids got dropped off first, then Ava at her school, and then finally Lally and Lucas at the preschool, where they needed to be physically signed in. She would read a story, maybe two, then pause at the kissing window for a proper goodbye with optional pretending she couldn't see her kid . . . "Where's Lally? Oh, there she is!" Jesus, did they ever get tired of that? Then she was free. Free to go to the store. Free to go home. Free to drive headfirst into the nearest wall, which was what she might have done, if she didn't have to go back in three hours and pick up Lucas and Lally. Frances wondered how many other people were overwhelmed by anticlimax but kept plodding along, taking care of their kids, picking up juice-box straws so animals wouldn't choke on them, collecting corks or buttons or whatever craft supply was needed, replacing the batteries in the smoke alarm as soon as the first *ping* of complaint was registered. Maybe this was what they meant by staying together for the children. It had nothing to do with marriage at all.

———

Frances pulled into the elementary school lot and Ava got out, sighing as if she were a fourteen-year-old Victorian child disembarking for her day down the mine. She pulled open the door and swung her arm wide.

"Medium-size children may now escape. Mind the gap, and watch out for speeding moms on cell phones."

The children had already unbuckled and piled out, high-fiving Ava as they passed her. Kate stopped, and Frances turned to see what was up. The little girl's face was a study in conflict.

"What's wrong, honey?"

Kate looked at Frances, and her chin wobbled.

"I left my toilet roll tubes at home."

"Oh." Frances looked at her eldest child. Ava shrugged, looking back inside the open minivan.

"They aren't in the car."

"Oh, OK." Frances smiled at Kate. "I'm sure the teacher will have lots of extras." She herself had, over time, sent in three thousand toilet roll tubes. For all she knew they were building a particle collider out of them, or an accurate re-creation of the New York subway system. Let's hope they didn't use the obvious choice for subway trains.

"No, I have to have my *own* ones." Kate's eyes were filling with tears, her shit-fit indicator was dropping to DEFCON 3. "It's for the class project. Everyone else will have them."

Frances weighed her options. On the one hand Kate was only six, and would not only survive but would forget the trauma of not having had toilet roll tubes. But on the other hand, she was a member of the yakuza-esque organization known as Miss Lollio's First Grade Class, whose members fell on the weakest like wolves on a lamb. Forgetting to bring toilet roll tubes and having to borrow some was a Noticeable Event to be avoided at all costs. It wasn't on the level of peeing oneself, of course, it wasn't going to give rise to a nickname you couldn't shake until college, but it wasn't great.

"My mommy put them in a bag, but she forgot to give them to me." A note of accusatory steel had entered her voice. Frances gazed at the little angel, whose mother had been heard calling her Butterblossom. Kate's eyes had gone flat like a shark's. She knew she would get what she wanted, the only question was when. *I am younger than you, old lady,* her eyes said, *and I will stand here until age makes you infirm, at which time I will push you down, crunch over your brittle bones, and get the toilet roll tubes I need.*

"Alright, Kate. I'll go back and get them after I drop Ava, OK, and bring them back to school for you." Frances knew she was being played, but it was OK. She was softhearted, and she could live with that.

"Suck*ah* . . ." Ava headed back to her seat, shaking her head over her mother's weakness, a weakness she loved to take advantage of herself.

"Thanks, Frances!" Kate beamed an enormous smile, turned, and ran off—the transformation from tremulous waif to bouncy cherub instantaneous. Behind her in the line of cars, someone tapped their horn. *OK*, the brief honk said, *we waited while you dealt with whatever mini crisis was caused by your piss-poor parenting, because we're nice like that, but now you can get a move on because we, like everyone else in this line, have Shit to Do.* Amazing how much a second of blaring horn can communicate.

Frances waved an apologetic hand out of the car window and pulled out of the gate.

She dropped the other kids and was back at Anne's house in a half hour. Having carpool duty wasn't the onerous task the other parents thought it was: All three schools were close to home, and all four families lived on the same block. As Frances ran up to Anne's door she looked over and saw her own cat, Carlton, watching her. She waved. He blinked and looked away, embarrassed for both of them.

She knocked softly on the door, but no one answered. Maybe Anne had gone back to sleep. She turned the handle and pushed open the door, peering around. Yup, there was the bag of toilet roll tubes. She grabbed it and was about to shut the door again when she saw Anne lying on the floor, her face turned away, her long hair spilling across the rug.

"Anne! Holy crap, are you OK?" But as she said it her brain started processing what she was really seeing. Anne, on the floor, check. But now she'd turned her head and Frances realized she was fine. In fact, she was better than fine. Frances had instinctively stepped over the sill and now she saw that Anne was naked, her face flushed, a man between her legs, his head below her waist.

"Shit . . ." Frances dropped her eyes, began to back out. "Sorry, Anne, Kate forgot her toilet roll tubes . . ." Stupidly she raised her hand with the Whole Foods bag in it because, of course, that would make it better, that she'd interrupted Anne and Charlie having a quickie on the living room floor. It was OK, because she was just here for the toilet roll tubes. Nothing to see here, move along.

The man realized something was wrong, finally, and raised his head, looking first at Anne and then turning to see what she was looking at, why her face was so pale when seconds before it had been so warmly flushed.

Frances was nearly through the door, it was closing fast, but not before she saw that it wasn't Charlie at all. It was someone else entirely.

Two.

Anne closed her eyes and shivered. Frances had let in a draft, along with the potential end of the world.

The younger man laid his cheek on her upper thigh and smiled ruefully up at her.

"Uh . . . I'm going out on a limb here and guessing you didn't want that person to see me."

Anne shook her head, shifting her weight and pulling her legs out from under him, drawing them up, covering herself. "No. Although of all the people who could have walked through that door, she was the least disastrous."

"Your friend, not his?"

She shrugged. "She's both of our friend, but she won't say anything to him, she might not even say anything to me." She noticed he still had an erection, bless his youthful stamina. If she'd been young herself, she would have felt an obligation to blow him—but those days were long gone.

"Are you sure she saw me?" Richard was still hoping this session could get back on track, and tried kissing her knee. Maybe he could get a consolation blow job.

She frowned at him. Stood, turned, reached for the dressing

gown she'd been wearing when he had walked in. They hadn't made it any farther than the living room floor; it had been a long time apart. If they'd gone upstairs their secret would still be safe, Anne thought, but she felt queasy about fucking this guy in her marital bed. Not that the marital bed saw much fucking, but still.

Richard, watching her face, now that her body was covered, wondered for the thousandth time what this woman was thinking. She confused and worried him; he was so drawn to her, even though he knew what they were doing was total karma suicide. The one female friend he'd told, a woman he used to date in college, but who'd turned into a much better friend than girlfriend, lost her temper with him for the first time in years.

"She has children?" Richard clearly remembered the look of disgust on her face.

He'd tried to laugh it off. "I'm not asking her to leave them. It's just an affair."

His friend knew better, and wasn't appeased. "It will end in disaster, it can't possibly end any other way. I can't believe you're being so selfish. For sex! You're not seventeen, for fuck's sake, can't you keep it in your pants?"

Richard looked at Anne now, or her back at least, as she left the room. She had twisted her dark brown hair into a knot, literally tying it within its own length. It was magical to him, watching her do things like that. He had wanted this woman from the moment he'd met her, in the fevered way he remembered from high school, when just proximity to a girl was enough to make him hard. He had thought he was long past that phase. He was an adult, he paid taxes, he had a job. He had lived with a woman for three years, bought her tampons, talked to her through the bathroom door while she took a crap, watched her dress and undress morning and night. He was getting ready for marriage, he could tell. God knew his mother was starting to bug him for grandchildren. But then that relationship had ended, almost by accident, as if they'd dropped a baton somewhere and run farther and farther apart before they noticed. The lack of emotion when she moved out was embarrassing.

But then he'd met Anne at an art store, where both of them wanted the last piece of a special handmade paper. They'd started friendly, both offering the piece to the other, then he'd prevailed and made her take it and they'd stood outside the store and talked about art . . . And when she'd smiled at him he was aroused. He was good with women, he was handsome and artistic and somewhat remote; he'd rarely been turned down. But when he'd asked for her number, she had laughed, blushed, and refused. She was married, she had kids, she'd even mocked him gently for asking out a woman who could have been his mother . . . though that was far from true; less than a decade separated them. He'd persisted and, suddenly possessed by a madness he'd never suspected in himself, told her the truth: that he wanted to take her to bed and drive her mad with pleasure, that he'd never seen a woman so beautiful before, that his apartment was four blocks away and no one would know. *No one would ever know, Anne, come with me now and give in, let me tangle my hands in your hair and make you gasp and shudder.*

And Anne, so used to being sad that she didn't even see beyond the end of each day, said yes. Walking into his small apartment had been like pushing her way through fur coats in a closet and coming out in Narnia. She left herself behind, and Richard saw an Anne no one else ever had.

For him this whole affair was unreal, a liminal period like a hangover, or the days between Christmas and New Year's. Intense sex, interspersed with long silences and days where Anne took her kids to Disneyland, bickered with her husband, made meals that everyone took for granted, tried on clothes that suddenly fit her again, decided to end the affair and then picked up the phone to call him one more time. All he knew were the sex and the silences, of course, though he wondered about the rest.

He could hear her now, in the kitchen. He reached for his clothes, scattered on the floor, and started to dress himself. Maybe Anne was making coffee, her slender fingers efficient. Maybe she was splitting open a brioche with just one twist, and getting out the jam. Or maybe she was slitting her wrists with one of those fancy ceramic knives she liked. His throat tightened, and he hopped slightly, tugging on his jeans.

In the kitchen Anne reached for the coffee and wondered what Richard was doing in the other room. Getting dressed, hopefully. Seeing Frances had thrown her so badly, all she wanted was for him to leave. She opened the coffee bag, cursing when the little wire-and-paper thing that held it shut fell off. Why do they even make that kind of bag, where the wire and paper thing was glued on? She much preferred the other kind, where the wire was part of the bag. Integrated, integral, whatever. This kind, the thing inevitably fell off, and then you couldn't close the bag. Eventually when you opened the cupboard one morning, when things didn't seem able to get much worse, the bag would tip onto the counter, flipping in mid-descent, dumping the coffee grounds onto the counter, onto the floor, where you would track them all over the house and they would work their way into the carpet like poppy seeds in your teeth. She tossed the broken bag, three-quarters full, in the trash. *Let's just avoid that disaster*, she thought to herself, her mouth turning up a little, despite the tightness with which she was holding it closed.

Richard came up behind her, his hands smoothing the silk dressing gown over her hips, his fingertips folding around her hip bones possessively. She felt different from the younger women he'd slept with. She wasn't perfect. She had broader hips, despite her narrow waist, and her butt wasn't firm from the gym. But he craved her. Dreamt about her every night, wanted right then and there to bend her over the counter and finish what they'd started in the living room.

Anne twisted away from him, gently. Pouring half-and-half into her coffee she raised an eyebrow to ask if he wanted some. He shook his head. "I guess I should be going, right? I'm getting that sense."

Anne wondered how she would explain him to Frances. Clearly, Richard was gorgeous and young and sexy, that part cliched and obvious. But that wasn't what drew her to him, although it might have been easier to explain it that way. She liked how he talked, the different vocabulary, the occasional pop-culture reference she missed, the otherness. He was interested in what she had to say, found her novel and wise, valued her experience. It didn't hurt that he constantly wanted her, that when she ran out of things to say she could lose herself in sex.

Charlie, her husband, loved her dearly, but in the way one loves a sibling, with all the wrinkles and scabs those relationships have. If she made a joke, he'd heard it, if she wore something new, he noticed but wondered if it had been on sale. Richard thought she was fascinating. Charlie thought she was competent and strong. Richard wanted to go down on her, to immerse himself in her body, to put his fingers inside her and then suck on them, grinning. Charlie was fine to wait until another night, no problem, babe, no, I understand, let's snuggle.

"I think you should go now, yeah. I'll text you or something." She held her mug of coffee tightly: WORLD'S BEST MOM.

He left by the back door, and she'd turned away before he was even out of the garden.

Three.

Frances was amazed to discover her legs were propelling her in the usual fashion as she walked down the street toward her own house. Birds appeared to be singing, the sidewalk wasn't opening underneath her, and her cat was still standing where he had been twenty seconds earlier, washing his tail. She herself felt light-headed and woozy, as if gravity wasn't working so well, or she'd accidentally had four shots of Jägermeister.

"Hey, Frank!" Startled, Frances looked up to see her cousin Iris crossing the street toward her, glowy from the gym. "Drop-off go OK? Did Wyatt behave himself?"

"Of course." Her voice worked, too. It was astounding. "He was the sweetheart he always is." She was going to be able to have a conversation without blurting out what she'd just seen. Such casual perfidy.

"For you, he is. For us, he's the spawn of Satan."

"Maybe you should have looked more closely at the donor profile."

"You think?" Iris grinned. "Maybe Nick O'Deamus wasn't the six-foot Irish-American hottie and geologist he claimed to be?"

"Yeah . . . 'My hobbies include collecting minerals like sulphur and brimstone, sharpening my scythe, and propelling souls into eternal damnation.' It's important to read the whole thing."

Iris laughed. She was tall and blond, with strong features. She and Frances had grown up together, essentially, because their mothers were sisters who lived four blocks from each other on the Upper West Side of Manhattan. When Iris and Sara, then a struggling actress making the occasional TV commercial, moved to L.A. they'd encouraged Frances to come, too. When a house on the same block was about to come on the market, Iris had called Frances and told her to jump on it. She and Michael left everything behind and made the move, and had yet to regret it. Today might be the day, of course.

"Are you OK?" Iris looked at her cousin closely.

Frances thought about telling her, because it would feel so good to just blurt it out and split the headache, but then she realized she couldn't. She had no idea why Anne was fucking around on Charlie, couldn't understand why she would threaten her entire existence by doing so, but until she'd spoken to her she couldn't tell anyone else what she'd seen. It was the *omertà* of friendship.

"I'm fine, just tired as usual."

"How can you tell?" Iris hugged herself. "Aren't you always a little bit tired?" Frances smiled tightly, and Iris added, "Why don't you go home and grab a quick nap? Don't you have a little time before you go back to pick up Lally?"

"Yeah. That's probably a good idea." Frances gave her cousin a hug and carried on to her house.

Iris stood and watched her go, wondering what was up. She shrugged inwardly—it would all come out in the end whatever it was. It always did.

———

When Frances opened the front door her house phone was ringing. The mechanical voice said, *Call from Anne Purr-tah . . . Call from Anne Purr-tah . . .*

I'll bet it is, muttered Frances, suddenly furious. *Fuck you.*

She started unloading the dishwasher, letting the machine pick up.

"It's Anne. Please come talk to me." *Click.*

Fuck you again, I say, thought Frances, calmly placing mugs upside down in the glass-fronted cabinet. *Fuck you very much for ruining my carefully constructed life in which all my friends are just as happy as I am. Where we are going to do it better than our parents did, are going to be happy and raise our kids without ambivalence and frustration. Fuck you for peeling the lid off the can of worms, you selfish, selfish bitch.*

The phone rang again. Frances clicked her tongue and suddenly picked it up.

"It's Anne."

"Yes."

"Can we talk?"

"Yes. You have to come here though. I'm cleaning up."

"OK."

"OK, see you soon." *After you shower the come off your legs, you whore.*

"Bye." Anne hung up.

Frances put the coffee machine on and checked for cream in the fridge. She pulled out cookies and put some on a plate. She swept crumbs into a pile in the center of the table and then onto her cupped palm, throwing them in the sink. She finished unloading the dishwasher and reloaded it. She put cereal boxes back in the cupboard from breakfast and wiped the counters. She straightened the chairs around the kitchen table. She checked again for cream in the fridge. She went to pee and when she looked at herself in the bathroom mirror she saw her mother's face looking back at her.

———

Anne held the mug Frances always gave her, a souvenir Anne had brought back from Venice one year. The blue and white stripes and the red scarf of the gondolier always looked so cheerful. Anne looked at the plate of cookies. "Did you make these?"

Frances nodded.

Anne reached for one, out of habit. "Drop-off go OK?"

Frances nodded again. "Apart from the toilet roll tubes incident." *Yes, let's talk about the toilet roll tubes.*

"Yeah. I put them out, but I guess she forgot to grab them. Thanks for coming back for them." *Thanks for ruining my secret.*

"No problem." *Of course, I didn't take them to your kid, yet. I sort of got derailed. I haven't decided yet whether she needs to suffer for your sins.*

Silence. Another cookie.

They'd been friends for about five years, since Iris and Sara had introduced them. They'd always gotten on well, both having the same interests—their children, their houses, their marriages, their hopes and dreams, their Pinterest boards. They weren't truly close, they were friends of proximity, friends because their kids were friends and because of the carpool. If they saw each other in the street they would stop and hug, check in, plan to have lunch, and maybe twice a year they would. They would describe each other as friends, do each other significant favors, but if one of them moved away they would promise to keep in touch,

and not. But hey, look at them now—now they were bound together in a whole shiny new way.

Frances took a sip of coffee. "So, how long have you been
sleeping with a total stranger?"

Anne shrugged. "Six months." Her tone was even, as if Frances had just asked a follow-up question about the toilet roll tubes.

"I assume Charlie doesn't know?"

"No."

"Are you in love with him?"

"Charlie?"

"The stranger."

"His name is Richard."

"I don't give a shit what his name is, Anne. Do you love him?"

"No."

"Then why, if you don't mind my asking, are you risking your
children's happiness in order to have sex with him?"

Frances's face was flushed, her eyes bright with tears. Anne
looked at her and felt irritated by her judgment, even though she
genuinely liked the other woman, trusted her completely, and
could see how much she was hurting.

"I have no idea."

"Don't you love your kids?"

"More than anything."

"Well, you apparently don't love them enough to not sleep
with this person and run the risk that Charlie will find out, be
devastated, divorce you, fight you for child custody, and make
them choose between the two of you." Frances stood up to go
refill her mug, in order not to smash it into Anne's calm, elegant,
beautiful face. Anne's serenity had been one of Frances's favorite
things about her; she'd always marveled at the other woman's
composure and wished for one-tenth the gravitas Anne had.

Francis suddenly wondered if it was a mental deficiency or sociopathic disorder. Maybe Anne looked at everyone as if they were chairs or something, unable to feel any empathy at all.

Frances turned to face her friend. "Why am I so completely upset by this and you're not? Are you having some kind of mental breakdown? I thought you and Charlie were happy together."

"We are."

Frances laughed.

The doorbell rang.

———

Sara Gillespie, the wife of Frances's cousin Iris, was sufficiently famous that people would stop her in the street. Not so famous that she couldn't walk down the street, but still, frequently recognized. She always played the slightly-ditsy-but-cute-as-a-button girl next door, doomed to romantic failure until the right knight came along, her optimism and openheartedness about to be lost forever when, *poof*, Mr. Charming realized he couldn't live without her and asked her to marry him. She was smart, and alternated blockbuster rom-coms with sharp and sarcastic indie pictures that didn't make money but won awards. She rarely gave interviews, and only went on TV to support charities or raise awareness of some atrocity somewhere. People knew she was gay, it had never been a big secret, but they were able to overlook it or something. Maybe the world accorded her the privacy and respect it wanted for itself; there was always hope. Sara just shrugged it off, and as she walked into Frances's kitchen now she was laughing at the magazine she held in her hand.

"It says here—Oh, hi, Anne—that I'm leaving Iris for this guy, whoever the fuck he is, and that I've decided I'm straight after all." She bent to kiss Anne on the cheek, and then snagged a cookie. "Am I interrupting something interesting? You both look very serious."

"No, not at all." Anne smiled at her. "We were just talking, you know."

"Oh, good. I'm glad you're here, because I came to get Frances's advice and you can chime in, too. I want to throw a surprise party for Iris, for her birthday, and I wondered what you thought." She sat on the edge of the table, one of her signature traits. She would leap onto a counter, or sit on the floor cross-legged, or flip a chair around and straddle it, but it was only under duress that she'd sit straight on a regular chair in a regular way.

Frances was making her a cup of coffee. "At the house?"

"Maybe, what do you think?" Sara rubbed a hand over her short, curly blond hair, expensively cut and tousled to look as if she'd just gotten out of bed. She spent time on her appearance, it was her job, after all, and it took a lot of money and effort to look as if she didn't.

"Why not, I think it would be fun. What kind of party? Formal eveningy, or daytime kidsy?"

Sara took the coffee Frances was holding out to her, and another cookie. "These are awesome cookies, low fat, right?" She grinned, and then answered Frances's question. "I was thinking it might be fun if it seemed sort of impromptu at first and then gradually revealed itself as a planned thing." The other two were frowning, so she clarified. "Imagine, if you will, a simple lunch with Frances, Michael, and the kids. They come over, bearing a birthday cake that Frances has deliciously baked, and I have made a plate of sandwiches and salady stuff. Trader Joe's, nothing fancy, right? Happens all the time." She grinned. "But then the doorbell rings and it's Anne, Charlie, and their kids, and hey, who knew, THEY brought some food, too, and somehow I find another plate of sandwiches from somewhere, or maybe a veggie platter, who knows, and then the doorbell rings AGAIN and it's Maggie and Melanie and they brought wine, and then . . . You get my drift? Eventually everyone would be there, and after a bit she'll realize that it was all a plot and that way I don't need to do an elaborate ruse to get her out of the house." She looked thrilled with herself.

Frances nodded. "I think it sounds great. I'm in, for sure."

Anne frowned. "But then we won't have that great 'Surprise!' moment."

Sara shook her head. "Iris hates being surprised like that. Hates it. This way I can spring something on her without worrying that she'll have a coronary or react badly. It's her birthday, after all."

"Yeah," added Frances dryly, looking at Anne with no expression. "Not everyone likes the feeling that people have been plotting behind their back."

"Right!" Sara giggled. "And I can hide food at your houses, right?"

"Sure, it will be easy."

"And I thought I'd have a bouncy house arrive in the middle, so the kids will be entertained."

"Nice."

"Yay! Good, then that's settled. Now all I have to do is prevent myself from spilling the beans in the next few weeks and we'll be fine." She slid off the table, grabbed another cookie, and hugged them both.

"How is it you eat so many cookies and stay thin? I kind of hate you." Anne was smiling as she said this. And as Frances watched Anne pretend to be normal, to have normal friendships, and to care about people, while making chatty conversation, she suddenly felt exhausted. Like, week four of a new baby exhausted.

Sara looked surprised. "I'm going to go home and vomit up the whole lot. Isn't that what everyone does?"

Frances laughed. "No, I hide them in special carrying cases I have on my upper thighs."

"Ah. Well, that's another way to go." Frances walked Sara to the door and watched her make her way down the street, her energy causing her to essentially skip. No wonder she stayed thin; her whole life was a minor workout.

Frances propped the door open to bring in some air, and went back to the kitchen.

Four.

$\mathcal{E}$arlier, after Iris watched Frances walk into her house, she'd turned and looked up the street for a moment. No Sara. Frowning, Iris had headed indoors, wondering what was keeping her wife. Sara had been gone very early, to do some voiceover fix or something, but was supposed to come home for brunch. Iris had run out after Frances had picked up Wyatt, to go to spin class and then to get the cinnamon rolls from Acme that Sara loved. Whatever. She was used to Sara's occasional flakiness. OK, frequent flakiness. She herself had a meeting at noon, but there was plenty of time. Her work was only half-hearted anyway, if she were being honest with herself. She mostly had meetings to prove she could still get people to meet with her, that she hadn't become invisible.

"Hello, Rosco." The dog was beside himself to see her, his tail a barely visible whir of excitement. She stooped to scratch his ears, smooth his small head. He was a mutt, with a comical level of mismanagement in the continuity department: a small head like a fox, a cylindrical body like a dachshund, legs like a terrier, and the tail of a golden retriever. It was a look that didn't quite work, unfortunately. It wasn't so much cute as *The Island of Doctor Moreau*. But

Iris had seen him in the pound and known immediately that this was the dog for her. He looked vaguely embarrassed that his outsides didn't match his insides, and she knew how that felt.

She paused—Was that Sara's car? It stopped short, didn't turn into their driveway, so she shrugged and went into the kitchen, Rosco at her heels. First coffee, then the dishwasher, then the laundry. The familiar one, two, three of every single morning. Like many of the lesbian couples she knew, things were at least theoretically egalitarian. They shared the work. Except that theory was one thing and practice another. When Sara was busy Iris would pick up the slack, but somehow the favor was never returned, and when Sara's schedule loosened up not all of the slack got taken back. Sara was supposed to empty the dishwasher. Iris would refill it. Sara was supposed to do the laundry. Iris would put it away. It all made sense, and yet none of it was happening these days.

Iris liked things to be clean, wanted to see uncluttered surfaces, items filed away. She worked efficiently: emptying, refilling, wiping counters, doing a sweep for stray dishes, topping up rinse aid, soap, hitting buttons, and slamming the door. Then she stood and drank her lukewarm coffee, looking out at nothing. The house was silent, so quiet she could hear a clock upstairs ticking away the hour. She supposed she looked calm and composed, but inside she was going slowly insane because she wanted another baby and Sara didn't. She'd brought it up, but Sara had shrugged and said she thought things were great right now, why fix something that wasn't broken, and the subject was dropped. Iris wasn't entirely sure why she wasn't pushing it, but she wasn't.

Iris rinsed her coffee cup, pausing the machine to put it in. Steam wafted out, along with that hideous smell of newly heated old food and salty water, so she held her breath and turned away as her hand found a space for the cup.

She couldn't stop thinking about a baby. Sara, for her part, was happy Wyatt was at an age where she and Iris had more freedom. *Thank goodness we can sleep all night now*, she would say, or, *Isn't it nice we can just leave him with a sitter and go out*. And Iris would nod and agree, because those things were nice, she did appreciate them. And yet she wanted another child with a visceral pull that however hard she tried was just getting more and more insistent.

She cried whenever she got her period, and went to the back of her closet to hold the tiny clothes she'd hoarded from when Wyatt was a baby. Sara thought she'd given them away, and some she had. A good friend of hers had gotten pregnant "accidentally" when her husband was vacillating about a third child, and Iris was bitter that option wasn't open to her. Conceiving Wyatt had been a whole *mishegoss* that took weeks of preparation, lawyers for all sides, thermometers, and doctors' offices. She had been up for the turkey baster in the bedroom method, but Sara wanted the certainty of medical intervention. Sara had been very gung ho for a child. She'd been thrilled when Iris was pregnant, and showed ultrasounds around on the set and generally looked forward to their expanding family. But now she was done, she was happy, and if she knew that Iris ached to be pregnant again, to have another baby to care for, she didn't show it.

"Rosco, do you think it would be possible for Wyatt to occasionally pick up a toy?" Rosco remained silent, though he looked supportive. Iris sat on the floor of Wyatt's room and threw toys into various buckets and baskets artfully arranged around the perimeter. Sara had hired a great decorator for Wyatt's room, and it was *Land of Nod* catalog ready, with that additional element of surprising hipness Sara loved.

Iris had grown up surrounded by mess and disorganization, her mother an exhausted working mom with four kids and a charming but feckless husband. Iris had spent a lot of time at Frances's house as a kid because there was more room for her there, with only two kids. Then Frances's brother had died at fourteen, struck down by a mysterious flu and dead forty-eight hours after he first said, *Mom, my head really hurts.* After that things reversed and Frances spent more time at Iris's house than she did at home. Frances's house had become too quiet, her parents literally struck dumb by their pain.

Iris envied her own son the many toys and clothes and space he had, the beautiful colors and prints of his sheets, the charm of his rugs and painted walls. At the same time, of course, she was happy he had it all, wanted his whole existence to be well-coordinated and whimsically decorated.

Where the hell was Sara?

———

When Sara left Frances's house she knew she'd exited some kind of scene in progress, but she couldn't work out what it was. Dismissing it as nothing to do with her, she crept around the back of her own house, hoping to surprise Iris. She spotted her through the kitchen window and ducked down behind a bush, giggling. She loved her wife so much. After nearly twenty years together she still felt glad to see her, every time. All she wanted was for Iris to be happy, for her to know how much she appreciated her.

As she peered between the leaves like a burglar or a baby deer, she was surprised to see Iris looking a little blue. Just staring off into the distance, drinking her coffee. Who knew what she was thinking? Maybe she was considering going back to work full time? She'd seemed preoccupied lately, and Sara thought maybe she was planning a return to her career. Iris had been a writer's agent at one of the major talent agencies in town, very successful and glamorous, high-profile clients and dinners every night. When Sara first broached the idea of having kids she was certain Iris wasn't going to be into it, but she'd been all for it. Once Wyatt had started school Iris had begun doing odd projects here and there, but now, of course, she might be ready to go back to work full time. Raising a kid was pretty thankless, and Sara wasn't always sure Iris loved it. She herself hadn't turned out to be as maternal as she'd expected, but hey, life is full of surprises. She briefly pondered her feelings about Iris going back to work and was surprised it made her sad: She liked being able to take everyone with her when she had to do a longer shoot. Even though she knew eventually Wyatt would need to stay in school all the time, she liked the freedom to be nomadic and artsy and bohemian. If Iris went back to work that would stop, presumably.

Shit, Iris had left the kitchen and headed off somewhere. Sara crept in through the back door and stalked her on pussycat feet. She came upon her in Wyatt's room, talking to Rosco, who unfortunately ruined her surprise entrance by standing up and waving his flaggy tail. Iris turned.

"There you are! I was starting to feel stood up."

Sara bent down and kissed her wife's hair. "You smell good. I see you and Rosco are working as a team." Rosco banged his tail on the ground, grinning up at her.

"You're joking. Rosco is taking the toys out as fast as I can put them away. He's no use at all."

Iris stood, and Sara pulled her into a hug. "Do you want to go out for brunch?"

Iris shook her head. "No, I got cinnamon rolls."

"From Acme?" Sara's tone was hopeful. Iris nodded, and Sara squeezed her. "You are a wicked, wicked woman. It's going to be pilot season soon and everyone will cast me as the plump friend."

"Well, better that than the bitter single friend. That one doesn't suit you at all."

Sara laughed and watched Iris walk away from her down the hall. She still loved looking at her, she was so strong and curvy. Maybe she could talk her into bed; there were no kids around, thankfully. When Wyatt had been young there had been months, literally months, when they didn't have sex at all. Now they had plenty of time, and often plenty of interest. But she'd missed her chance. Iris was already halfway down the stairs, and moving in a way that told Sara she was distracted. It was remarkable how much you could tell about someone's state of mind purely by looking at the way they put down their bag at the end of the day, or by the sound of a door closing, or even by how long it took for them to walk into the house after you heard the beep of the car alarming itself. You become an anthropologist studying a tribe of one, and then if you have kids, you start studying them, too; but they're harder because the little bastards are studying you right back, and changing and growing in a frustrating step function of leaps, bounds, and backward stumbles. Of course, maybe this was also an actor thing, because the semiotics of emotion were tools to her. Little hand gestures barely caught by the camera could make the difference between a visible performance and the true inhabiting of a character.

Sara looked down. Rosco was looking up at her uncertainly. He wanted to follow Iris, but it had seemed rude to do so while Sara was standing there. He waved his tail gently. She grinned at him. "Sorry, dear, I just drifted off there." She headed downstairs to find her wife.

Five.

$\mathcal{B}$ack in Frances's kitchen there was a long silence after Sara left.

"Are those the toilet roll tubes?" Anne gestured to what was clearly a bag of toilet roll tubes. *No,* thought Frances, *those are the global thermonuclear devices I was planning on planting all along Larchmont Boulevard, the ever-so-slightly twee shopping street nearby.*

"Yes. Apparently Kate faces instant expulsion from the cool kids if she doesn't have them." Frances looked at her watch, surprised to see it wasn't quite ten. How could so much be destroyed in less than an hour?

"Do you think it's too late?" Anne got up, rinsed her coffee cup, and went to pick up the bag.

"To drop them off?" Frances shook her head. "No, they have circle time first, then pointless work sheets, then lunch. I don't think they do crafty shit till the afternoon." She picked up cookie crumbs with her thumb and licked them.

Anne shrugged. "OK, then. I guess I'll run these over."

"Your boyfriend left, I assume?"

"Yes."

"I'm sorry if I ruined the mood." Frances kept an even tone as she stood and went to put her cup in the sink, although it was clear she didn't give a rat's ass about the mood.

Anne turned and walked toward the door. "No problem, he'll be back. Or he won't, who knows."

Frances followed her. "Why are you being so cavalier about it? You know you're going to get caught, don't you?"

Anne paused, searching her friend's face. "Are you going to tell Charlie?"

Frances shrugged. "No. He's not my husband."

"Are you going to tell Michael?"

"Of course. He *is* my husband."

"Do you think he'll tell Charlie?"

"I have no idea. Anne, you've been on the planet for over four decades. You read books. You watch the news. You should have anticipated getting found out, because it always happens. *It always happens*, Anne, and you knew that going in. You just didn't care."

Anne opened the door and stood there for a moment. "It's not that I didn't care, it's that I've lost my mind. I really think I've gone insane. I don't feel anything anymore, it's just a blank white sheet. And the worst part is I don't even care that I don't care. I don't miss feelings at all." She turned and looked at Frances with cool, tearless eyes. "Horny is the only emotion I've felt for the last six months."

Frances was cutting. "*Horny* isn't an emotion, Anne. It's a glandular condition of the young, which you are not. Depression isn't an emotion, either, but many people find therapy and medication a lot more effective than having sex with a college student."

"He's not a college student. He's a teacher at the art college."

"I don't give a shit what he is, Anne, it's not like I'm ever going to be his friend."

A neighbor walked by with her small dog, looking over at the raised voices. Anne and Frances both nodded and waved, and the neighbor nodded back, then paused for an awkward moment while her dog peed on the lawn. She made the classic eye roll that said, *Sorry, my dog's peeing on your grass, what can you do, I can hardly drag him off trailing piss across the sidewalk*, and the two women at the door smiled and waited.

As the lady moved off Anne suddenly sighed and walked away, and Frances turned and shut the door. Back to work, everyone, nothing to see here.

———

Across the street, Bill Horton looked up at the sound of a door slamming. Anne Porter was walking away from Frances Bloom's house, carrying a bag of something. He watched her, noting the cool way she moved, the slenderness of her figure accented by the simple jeans and loose sweater she wore. She was one of those women you couldn't help noticing, whatever the context. They came in all shapes and sizes these women, the women he mentally labeled "alluring." It was an old word, a word his father would have used, but it worked. All women could be attractive, many women were sexy, lots and lots of them were appealing and intelligent and funny and loving, but only a select few were like Anne, unreachable and, he mentally shrugged, alluring.

Now she was getting into her car, her hand on the top of the door the last thing he saw; her slender wrist torquing as she lowered herself suddenly filled his mind with the thought of seeing that wrist against a pillow as he pushed himself into her. Her car pulled away, carrying the image with it. He sat back from his desk and laughed at himself. In his forties, currently separated from a woman less timeless than Anne, but much warmer, he hadn't had sex for nearly a year and sometimes the teenage boy who lived in his dick appeared. He didn't even like Anne very much; there was something mocking that went along with her elegance, but you didn't need to like a woman to imagine fucking her. He wondered how different human history would have been had evolution selected for that.

The phone rang, and he knew immediately it was his wife, Julie. Right now they were apart, but for Bill the separation was only physical.

"Hello, you." Her voice was lovely, as ever; it might have been the thing he missed most about her. He'd always loved listening to her talk: to him, to the guy at the grocery store, to their son, even to their lawyer. Deep and melodious, with a laugh always buried somewhere inside it, it was what he'd been attracted to first. He'd heard her talking to someone else behind the library shelves, and managed to wander around in time to see her. He'd found himself staring at books about accountancy, hoping she would notice him. She had.

"Hello, yourself," he replied now, a dozen years later, still in love.

"How's today?"

Bill frowned, trying to remember. "Fine. Frances took him off to school. I'm working on twenty-four seconds of music to go behind a dancing . . . hang on . . ." He looked on his desk for a piece of paper. ". . . a dancing Danish."

"Danish what?"

"No, just Danish. The pastry."

His wife laughed, then coughed. "What is it dancing about?

Is it happily dancing because it's thrilled by its frosting, or is it drunkenly dancing alone in the liquor aisle?"

"Is your cough worse?"

"No. Tell me about the Danish."

Bill sighed. If she didn't want to talk about something, she wouldn't. That was the way with her. She was like a cat, his wife, in many ways. Mysterious. Beautiful. Happy to be alone. And totally disinterested in pleasing anyone else unless she wanted to. Not in a mean way, at all, but in a way that didn't expect anyone to do anything for her, either. He felt a mild frisson of anger, but ignored it. They'd fought hard for a long time, and now they were trying to keep the peace. He certainly wasn't going to be the one to throw the first stone.

"The people at the agency didn't give the Danish a backstory. The brief is simply this: 'The music cue is twenty-four seconds long, should have a polka rhythm, and suggest energy and happiness.'"

Julie snorted. "Well, that's plenty of background. The Danish enjoys polka music. The Danish is happy. The Danish feels energetic."

"Which is sad, seeing as, presumably, it's going to get eaten shortly."

"Not that one. That one got plucked from obscurity to star in a commercial."

There was a pause. He could hear her drinking water. "Is the cough really better?"

"I didn't say it was better, I just said it wasn't worse. It's fine, don't worry about the cough. Tell me about Lucas, what did he say this morning?"

"He repeated his request for a cat."

"That was all he said?"

"No, he said he doesn't like Cheerios anymore, then he said he wanted to wear different shoes than the ones I could find, and *then*, when he had me on the ropes about the shoes, he suddenly zigged and mentioned the cat."

He could hear her smile. "Are we going to get him one?"

"Maybe. Maybe when you come home."

A pause. "Or maybe if I don't."

"You will."

"OK." Bill heard voices in the background. "Hey, Adelaide just showed up. I gotta go."

"Busy day?"

She sighed. "Same old same old."

"Will you be able to Skype tonight? Lucas loved you reading to him last night."

"I don't know. I'll text you, OK?"

"I love you."

"I love you more."

"I love you most."

He heard her smile again, and then she hung up.

———

Lally and Lucas had apparently been hooked up to a sugar IV during the last hour of preschool, which seemed unlikely, but was empirically indicated. Both of them were in that state of little kid laughter where at any moment one of them might throw up. Frances watched them in the rearview mirror, torn between letting them laugh because, you know, children, and trying to calm them down so they didn't implode. It was unclear why they were laughing, but apparently that shit was comedy gold. They were also amused by the enormous amounts of toilet paper and paper towels on the floor of the minivan. Momma went to Costco.

Of course, by the time they pulled up in front of Frances's house, they were pale and angry with each other, and only the immediate application of an episode of *Blue's Clues* (classic Steve, on Netflix) and some goldfish crackers settled the waters. As she made them lunch, Frances answered in her head for Blue, and wished *she* had a handy-dandy notebook. This world, the world of the preschooler, was where she felt most comfortable these days. After going through this phase twice before she knew resistance was futile, and mommy-ninja'd her way through most of the challenges Lally threw at her.

With a fourteen-year-old, a ten-year-old, and a four-year-old, Frances finally felt she had some kind of paradigm for understanding her experience of parenthood: Raising kids was like warfare. Not in the "dramatic death of millions" kind of way, obviously, but in the "struggle for peace" kind of way. Babies and little kids were like trench warfare. It was physically exhausting, psychologically draining, and there was a lot of flying mud and screaming. Shit went everywhere. Your clothes were ruined. You ate when you could, slept when you could, and got interrupted at the whim of the enemy.

Elementary-age kids were like campaign warfare. You knew there would be times of stress—like forcing a child to get a shot at the doctor, or to do their homework, or to give up on the concept of becoming a Pokémon trainer in the real world—but in between those intense sessions there was a lot of boring routine. One minute it would seem as though you were making progress, with promising overtures on both sides, but then two minutes later someone chucked a grenade and everything caught fire.

The big change, however, was what happened when the hormones kicked in. Then it was a guerilla war against an unseen counterinsurgency. Everything seemed much calmer on the surface, but any minute an improvised explosive device could cut you off at the knees or a sniper could get you in the back of the neck. You could never fully relax, and there was a lot of tiptoeing about and quizzing other kids for intel.

Sighing, Frances filled three little bowls with mac and cheese and joined Lally and Lucas on the sofa. She watched Steve do his thing, and continued her inner debate about how Salt and Pepper could have managed to conceive and produce both Paprika and Cinnamon. Salt was a crystal, pepper was a seed pod from a plant, paprika was also a seed pod. OK, so yes, she could see that, but cinnamon was the inner bark of a tree. She had wondered this before, which is why she had Wikipedia'd all that stuff and had, in fact, a fairly high level of knowledge about the international pepper trade as a result. It still bothered her, and she worried that Mrs. Pepper was a little tough on Paprika, especially once the baby came.

———

Ava was angry, and Frances had no idea why. She had no way of knowing if her daughter was angry with her, or with someone else, or just furious at the world in general. Not that it mattered. Ava often came boiling out of school ready to fight, as if she'd been simmering ever since drop-off, and had planned everything she needed to say for a convincing victory and the ultimate vanquishing of the adult world. But then she just sat there, letting her silence shout at her mother instead. Could anyone emanate silence as forcefully as a fourteen-year-old? No wonder people associate poltergeist activity with adolescence; they can beat you around the head without raising a finger. Frances felt a headache starting and took a deep, cleansing breath and slowly let it out.

"Why are you sighing at me?"

Frances shot her daughter a look. "I wasn't. I was just breathing."

"Well, quit it."

"Completely?"

There was a pause.

"No," replied Ava. "Not completely. I'm not tall enough to reach the pedals from over here, and if we crash on the way home I'm sure I'll get blamed." She picked at her nail polish.

"Not to mention that you'd have to explain to Anne, Iris, Charlie, and Bill why their kids were all in the hospital."

Ava relaxed a little. "Charlie and Bill would be fine, but Anne would be pissed. She's a little bit scary."

"Anne?" Frances raised her eyebrows.

Ava was looking out of the window. "Yeah. Sometimes she looks at me as if she wants to snap my neck and throw my body on the ground."

Frances pulled to a stop at a red light and turned to Ava. "Really?"

Ava nodded but didn't elaborate, her mind already somewhere else. Frances looked in the rearview. Theo, Kate, Wyatt, and Milo were chattering away about God only knew what, and Lally and Lucas both had the thousand-yard stare of mid-afternoon preschoolers who were only a year or so out of taking a nap. None of them were paying any attention to her conversation at all.

She tried to reel Ava back in. "How was school?"

Ava shrugged. "Same same."

"Same same good or same same bad?"

"Same same repetitive, which I think is what the phrase *same same* implies." Her edge was back, like the slightly raised shoulder fur of a dog. *I don't have to fight you*, it said, *but I can and will if you keep irritating the shit out of me by merely existing.*

"Who wants to stop at the park?" Frances raised her voice, startling the littlest kids and interrupting the older ones. They all looked interested, so she started to detour toward the playground.

"I have homework," said Ava, firmly. "You need to drop me at home first."

"We'll only stop for half an hour, it will be good for you to be outside for a little while."

"No," replied her daughter. "It won't. Don't tell me what I need, you have no idea what I need." She'd shifted herself away from her mother, each incremental inch making her distaste for proximity crystal clear.

"I didn't. It will only be half an hour, and I'll buy you ice cream."

There was a pause as the Ava who loved ice cream fought with the Ava who hated to let her mother win.

Milo suddenly spoke from behind them. "If she has homework, maybe we should just go home. I don't really care about the park."

"Who are you, my agent?" Ava's tone was scornful. Frances looked at her son's eyes in the rearview. This was a new dynamic she'd noticed. He hated when she and Ava argued, so he was starting to take Ava's side; but Ava rebuffed him every time, not needing anyone's backup, thank you very much. Least of all that of a *little boy*. The little boy in question turned quickly to look out of the window, the scythe of his sister's tone surprising him to tears.

Frances felt the quick, sharp pain of empathy, which was always so complicated when the slight was between siblings. But she kept her tone mild. "Ava, he was just trying to help, there's no need to be mean."

"I don't need his help. I need to go home and be left alone to get on with my homework and, preferably, my entire life." She knew she'd just hurt her brother's feelings, and felt bad about it, but in the battle between her and her mother he was collateral damage. Unfriendly friendly fire.

Frances felt a tightness at the base of her throat that meant she was getting annoyed. She pushed it down, turned into the playground parking lot, and pulled into a space, punching the opendoor button as soon as she turned off the engine. The younger kids started unbuckling, and she turned to her oldest child and smiled. "Look, Ava, I know you're a mass of hormones and conflicting chemicals and I understand you have homework, but half an hour in the park will mean a better evening for all of us, and that's what we're doing. If you want to sit in the car and sulk, feel free."

Ava started to speak, but Frances was already out of the car and helping the little ones jump down. As Milo climbed out she gave him a quick hug and followed him to the playground, not looking back at Ava at all.

————

Frances sat on the side of the playground where a low wall ran around the equipment. In theory, this playground was well designed, with a large central play structure and the aforementioned wall going all the way around. It probably looked awesome in blue pencil on thin paper, printed out in a New York design practice. But in real life it meant you could easily lose sight of your kids. All along the wall parents would look up from their phones, scan the structure, then stand and crab walk along until they spotted their charge, sitting down again where they could see them, dropping their eyes back to their phones, and then repeating the whole dance several times. If you time lapsed it from a drone it would look like the shadows on a sundial, circumnavigating.

Frances's kids were old enough that she'd stopped crab walking. But occasionally she would scan, pausing as she waited for one or the other of them to appear, or bend to look under the structure, hunting for their shoes. When she had other people's kids, too, as now, she was more watchful. Losing her own child would be bad enough, losing someone else's would be a disaster.

Ava appeared next to her, ostentatiously carrying a textbook. She sat down, opened the book to a section on homeostasis, and did a little mime of running her finger down the page to the appropriate sentence.

"So," said Frances, "homeostasis, eh?"

"Yup," replied her daughter.

"Maintaining balance, right?"

"Yup."

"A pendulum swinging will eventually come to rest in the middle?"

Ava sighed. "That's not a perfect metaphor because homeostasis is about balance between oppositional forces, which keep pushing. A pendulum rests because it's run out of energy to swing."

Frances nodded. "Just checking."

"You wondered if you'd forgotten the meaning of homeostasis?"

"No, just wondered if we were still talking."

Ava smiled a very small smile. "Oh, we'll always be talking, Mom. I'll push from one side, you'll push from the other. You know."

Frances put her arm around her daughter and gave her a

squeeze. "I know you have homework, baby. But the littler kids need to run about a bit, OK?"

Ava nodded. "I don't know why I get so cranky with you. I'm just so tired after school, and so wound up from being nice all day." She laughed at herself. "Not that I'm all that nice at school, I must admit." Just then Lally appeared and tugged at her sister. "Will you chase me?" Ava started to frown, then suddenly nodded and got to her feet, turning to Frances. "Balance, right?"

Frances nodded, watching Ava tear away after her little sister, who was instantly hysterical with delight.

$\mathcal{S}$ix.

Michael was satisfyingly appalled when Frances told
him the news that evening.

"He was going down on her? Before nine in the morning?
Jesus."

She nodded, not sure if it was the cheating or the earliness of
the hour that bothered him, but then Lally came in. It was after
dinner, she'd had her bath and was supposed to be brushing her
teeth. To be fair, she did have a toothbrush in her hand.

"Do I *have* to brush my teeth?" She sounded like she'd maybe
identified a loophole in the tooth-brushing law, and was ready to
exploit it.

"Yes, you do." Frances was firm.

"What's up, Lal?" Michael was sitting in the big, comfy chair
in their bedroom, his laptop open on his lap. Multitasking, as
usual, although the news about Anne had almost made him
close his computer.

The little girl turned to him and stuck out her arm. "There's a
hair on my toothbrush." She pulled out her new strategy. "It
seems unsantiary . . ."

"You mean *unsanitary*?" She nodded, because that was what

she'd said. Michael took the toothbrush from her, removed the hair, and handed it back. "It's fine now. Was it your hair?"

She shrugged, turning to go, her tiny little form in elephant pajamas almost too cute to bear. "I think it might have been Jack's." Jack was one of their dogs.

"Was he using your brush?" Michael was joking, of course. The dog had his own brush, one of those items that mysteriously turned up in drawers whenever Frances was looking for something else, but which couldn't be found twice a year when she remembered you were supposed to brush the dogs' teeth. In the same class were things like chargers for SLR cameras, passport photos you hadn't sent in with the application yet, kitchen implements used only at Thanksgiving, and those tiny screwdrivers for fixing eyeglasses. Frances dubbed the whole class "occultatum," after the Latin word for *hidden*. This coinage made her feel slightly pretentious, but she enjoyed muttering it when she pulled open drawer after drawer looking for something.

Lally was losing interest. "No, but I think Milo was combing his hair with it. I'm not sure. Something."

Frances tried for clarification. "Milo was combing his own hair, or Jack's fur?"

Lally just shrugged again and wandered out. Frances turned to her husband. "Did you understand that?"

He shrugged just as his daughter had and turned back to his screen. Then he remembered what they'd been talking about and looked up again. "No, really, right there in the front room? Visible from the street?"

Frances made a face. "No. They were on the floor, not hovering in midair. The only reason I saw them was because I walked into the actual house."

"For the toilet roll tubes?"

"Yes. At first I thought it was Charlie . . ."

Her husband laughed. "You thought Anne and Charlie were having interesting sex on the floor of their living room at nine in the morning?"

Frances pulled off her boots and started taking off her clothes. "OK, maybe that isn't very likely, but it is the first assumption you make when you see a married friend having sex on the floor."

"Oh, I know that's what I think every time. Have you ever seen anyone else having sex on the floor? Is this what you get up to while I'm at work?"

Frances pulled off her sweatshirt and bra, enjoying that first scratch of tit-freedom, then put on a large pair of flannel pajamas with dogs on them. "Yes," she replied. "I creep from house to house, hunting for people having sex."

Michael smiled. "We've been married nearly twenty years, and you haven't changed a bit." He paused. "Are you going to blow the whistle?"

"Good Lord, no. Why would I do that?" She looked at her toenails, which needed cutting.

"I don't know. Because it's honest?"

She looked at him, and raised her eyebrows. "You're joking, right? Why on earth would I do that? This other guy could be just a one-time thing." She reached into her bedside drawer, hunting for her nail clippers.

"Like in a porn film? He was delivering a pizza?"

She snorted. "Yes. Because Anne Porter has pizza for breakfast every day." No clippers, what a fucking shock.

"OK, he was delivering a brioche and a venti Americano."

Jack and Diane, the dogs, came in and jumped on the bed. Frances shut the drawer and scooched back to make room for snuggling, wondering if Anne would have had an affair if she'd had a dog. *I don't have the sexiest marriage in the world,* she thought, *but I get a lot of affection and approval from my dogs, with far less negative fallout. Maybe I should persuade her to drop the extracurricular sex and get a rescue dog instead.* Then she thought about what Michael had said, and her mind wandered. "Why *don't* they deliver more interesting things in porn movies?"

He didn't look up from his screen. "Because most people aren't focusing on what the setup is, you doofus. Oh, let's watch *The Sears Guy Always Comes Twice*, it's all about the exigencies of appliance repair. The way the director sets up the tensions and potential resolutions in the first ten minutes is masterful, and the anal is all in one take."

Frances opened her mouth to reply, when Ava walked in. Michael closed his computer. Frances noticed this every time: For her he kept the screen open, just in case something more interesting popped up, but for his firstborn he shut the screen without even thinking about it. She wasn't jealous; she was reassured every time she saw the pecking order in action. She would put the kids before him, every time, and he knew it and would do the same. If he didn't take a bullet for the kids, he'd have to take one from Frances.

"Why are you guys talking about anal? And can I get a phone?" Ava asked this question pretty much every day, but so far the answer had been no. However, she had clearly studied compound interest and thought maybe bugging worked the same way: A little every day would mount exponentially. And maybe she was right. Frances could feel herself weakening.

"We weren't talking about anal, we were discussing film theory, and no," said Michael.

"But—"

Frances interrupted her. "Every kid in school has one but you, what if you get lost even though you rarely leave the house alone, you'd be able to keep your calendar on it, you'd be able to take notes in class, even though your school doesn't allow phones in class. Yes, we've heard all your arguments, Ava, and sorry, but the answer is still no. You don't need one, they're expensive, and I want you to read books rather than spend all day gazing at a screen. You have a computer, that's enough."

Ava glared at her mother, as teenagers have glared at parents since Neolithic mom first refused to get Neolithic teen a new axe. "I hate you. You guys never go anywhere without your phones, but that doesn't count, right? You just want to keep me dependent, because then you have something to do to fill your empty days and pointless existence." She turned on her heel, pretty smoothly, and stormed out.

Frances looked at Michael. "That's a new approach."

He nodded. "It's got potential."

"My days are hardly empty." Frances was a little stung, but not badly. "And how does she know about anal?"

"She uses the Internet, and don't get mad, she's full of hormones and squished on all sides by peer pressure. She'll apologize before she goes to sleep."

Frances nodded, because he was right, at least recently. Ava would pick a fight, or Frances would say something careless and Ava would get her back up, and suddenly they'd be bickering. Then, after a bit of shouting and stalking away, Ava would sit in her room and sulk for a while, then call to her mother in a wobbly voice and say she was sorry and that she didn't mean it. Frances would apologize, too. She'd also promise to herself that the next time Ava pushed her buttons she'd bite her tongue, remembering only too well the driving desire to fight with her own mother at that age, the need to lash out and bang up against something. Then Ava would cling to her and cry, reassured that she'd never drive her mother away, that Frances would always be there to fight with, make up with, take for granted, and depend upon. Frances would smooth her daughter's hair, tucking the damp strands behind her ears, knowing that in another couple of years Ava wouldn't care enough about her opinion to fight with her. The opposite of love isn't hate, it's indifference.

Michael was still on topic. "So, if you're not going to tell Charlie, why did you tell me? What if I feel obliged to tell Charlie?" He had reopened his laptop, Frances noticed.

"You don't. You wouldn't." Frances scratched Jack behind his ears, causing him to make that rumbly sound in his throat that made her smile.

"No, but what if I did?"

"I thought about that before I told you. I decided the risk of you suddenly changing completely after twenty years was smaller than the risk of me suffering a panic attack because I was keeping a secret from you." Diane had pushed Jack out of the way and was now all up in Frances's beak, demanding attention. Frances looked around her at Michael, and smiled at him.

He looked surprised. "You don't keep anything secret from me?"

"Apart from my exact weight and the location of my secret chocolate stash, no."

"A different stash from the third drawer in the laundry room?"

"Shit."

"I'm an idiot. Now you're going to move it."

"Yes." Frances paused. "Why, do you keep lots of secrets?"

"Of course. Some on purpose, and others just because you

wouldn't be interested. I'm not sure those even count as secrets." He pushed down one of his socks and scratched his ankle. "I think we need to Frontline the dogs again."

"How do you know I wouldn't be interested? I have a very quiet life, most things are interesting. Try me." She pulled on Jack's long, soft ears, gently. He let her. It was symbiotic: He let her pull on his long ears like a toddler with a baby blanket, and she fed him and told him he was wonderful. And occasionally remembered to put flea medicine on him.

Michael gave it some thought. "OK, I never told you that Bob Adams got a divorce."

A colleague from work she barely knew. "You're right, that's not all that interesting. Why?"

"His wife left him for her cats. Apparently she wasn't satisfied with the six she had and wanted number seven. He put his foot down and said it was him or the cats, and she chose Pussy Town. Either he grossly miscalculated and is brokenhearted, or he won the war by losing the battle. He certainly didn't seem all that sad about it."

"I bet his new place will be much less fluffy," Frances said.

"Oh, he kept the house. She took the cats and moved into a cat-positive commune in Northern California. When I said Pussy Town, I meant Pussy Town. That's what it's called."

Lally reappeared. "I'm ready now. You can read to me now."

"OK." Frances got up and looked over at Michael. "If that is your idea of a boring secret, I want to hear all of them."

"No, the whole point of secrets is keeping them. And none of them has anything like the human interest or feline backstory that that one did."

"I'll be the judge of that. That one was genuinely weird. I would have told you and about eight other people that story."

"Can I be the judge?" Lally took Frances by the hand, looking up at her.

Frances grinned at her. "Sure, baby."

"What *is* a judge?"

"Someone who decides things other people can't agree on. Time for bed, OK?"

Lally went to hug her dad. He pulled her onto his lap and snortled in her ear, making her laugh. She curled up and giggled, and for about the nine hundredth time Frances wished she were small enough to curl up on some big person's lap and be completely safe.

Seven.

Down the street, Anne was getting ready for bed. Outside the bathroom door she could hear Kate and Charlie laughing, as Kate explained something arcane about Pokémon, and Charlie pretended to get everybody's name wrong.

"Isn't that what Pookachoo does?" he said, causing Kate to click her tongue in amused irritation. "Isn't Claptrap a chocolate type? Or is it a popcorn type, with attacks like saltypop, and deadly kernel?"

Kate burst into giggles. "Daddy, there is no such thing as a popcorn type, and you know that! You watched the show with me THIS MORNING before school."

"Was that what that was?" Charlie sounded incredulous. "I thought that was an educational show about Japanese animals."

"They're made up!"

"They are?"

Anne used to find these exchanges endlessly touching. She'd fallen in love with Charlie for his whimsy, as much as his charming good looks. He seemed like a proper grown-up on the outside: well dressed, whip smart, a successful patent attorney and partner in his firm. But he was secretly about nine years old and still found farts, slipping on things, and silly hats hilarious. He loved to play with the kids, which was good because Anne had always had a hard time relaxing enough to enjoy it. She had found having small children utterly terrifying, convinced they were going to choke to death on something or drown in the bathtub or spontaneously develop dengue fever. Now that they were bigger and a little more robust she could relax more, but she still found herself contemplating their loss far more than she would have liked.

The affair had proved to be an effective antidote to fear, which was unexpected and, of course, ironic. When she found herself thinking about the pain of losing her children, the fear of making a mistake that led to their harm, the overwhelming sense of misplaced responsibility, she would just think about Richard. Think about his hands, his hair, his eyes, his desire, and let the physical arousal she felt blow right through her panic. She knew where she was with him; she was being naughty, she was being selfish, she was risking it all, and it confirmed her secret belief that she was a very bad person who never should have been given children in the first place.

She washed her face carefully, mixing water with some special cleansing grains she bought at the one store that carried them, the scent of roses and chalk signaling the end of the day. She enjoyed the feeling of them under her fingers, the way they held their hard edges in the water for a moment before succumbing and blooming into solution. She rinsed her face, looking for stray molecules of clay with her eyes closed, the contours of her face reassuring her. Still alive, then. Toner, again with the scent of roses, then moisturizer, firm strokes up her throat. She felt a tiny sore spot and tipped her head; the merest hint of beard burn, right under the edge of her jawline. She looked at it coldly, *why couldn't young men shave properly*, then pulled her heavy pale pink dressing gown from its hook and went to help Charlie with the kids.

Charlie looked at his wife as she came out of the bathroom, bringing the scent of roses with her, the smell he associated with her, and with her being his. He loved this Anne, the one that emerged without a scrap of makeup, without her elegant outfits and cool eyes, her pauses in conversation, her judgment. She was wearing the cashmere and satin dressing gown he'd bought her for Valentine's Day the previous year, the cost of which had made him pause for a moment before the memory of her skin against his blew his reservations away. He thought of this as the real Anne, the one that only he knew. Her eyes met his and they both smiled.

"Are you ready for bed, pumpkin?" she asked Kate, who ignored her and snuggled into her dad. He shrugged over her head, and Anne went to see what Theo was up to.

Unsurprisingly, he was on his computer, playing Minecraft. She sat on his bed, making a small stack of paperbacks slither to the floor, their irregular *thud*s on the rug reminding her suddenly of the sound of apples dropping at night, back when she was a child in Yakima County. Her children's childhood was so different from hers, she wondered what sounds would pull them back—sirens and helicopters were their nightingales and falling fruit. She asked her son what he was building.

Theo looked at her with bright eyes, happy to tell her about it. "A fortress, right now, but I just finished the gardens. Do you want to see?"

"Sure." Anne didn't really understand Minecraft, but she loved it when the kids shared their ideas and projects with her. Her own mother had never been in the least bit interested in sharing her thoughts with her children and their opinion was utterly irrelevant to her. She'd expected them to love her and follow her instructions, and they did. It never occurred to her they might want more, and they had given up waiting for more to be offered. Maybe she'd had nothing to give.

Theo navigated through the half-finished structure he was building and outside, coasting above what were apparently acres of farmland. There were serried rows of plants, separated by mere pixels, fields of digital corduroy.

Theo was listing, "Carrots, wheat, sunflowers, potatoes . . . and over here we have chickens, cows, and ocelots."

Anne raised her eyebrows. "Ocelots?"

He shrugged. "I like them."

She smiled. "Who doesn't?" She stood up. "It's time to get off now though, and go to sleep."

He looked at her, surprised. "But I still have homework."

"You're supposed to do it before you go online, you know that." Her stomach sank; she didn't have time to get angry now. "How much do you have?"

Theo looked worried and pulled his backpack closer across the floor. "I don't know. Sorry, Mom, I only meant to go on for ten minutes after dinner and lost track of time." His mom said nothing, and he found his homework quickly. "A math sheet and a chapter to read." He looked up at her hopefully. "That's not too bad, right?"

Anne sighed. "OK. No computer tomorrow at all. You have to do homework first, OK?" She walked out, saying over her shoulder, "Get ready for bed now, we'll read the chapter together and you can do the math sheet in the morning before school. It's too late to do it now, you need to get some sleep."

Behind her Theo's eyes cleared. His mom always knew what to do; she was as reliable as the sun. If he was naughty she would issue a consequence, if he was good she would issue a reward, and if he needed a hug her arms would already be open. He was by nature a worried child, concerned about unseen dangers, worried that somehow he had messed things up. His mom never seemed to worry, and she was the trellis his little vines twined around.

She walked back into her bedroom, where Kate was drifting off to sleep next to Charlie, who was on his phone and paying no attention. He looked up as Anne came in and raised his eyebrows in a question, indicating their daughter.

Keeping her voice low, Anne said, "You keep her, I'll deal with Theo, then sleep in her room, OK?" Anne and Charlie slept in the same bed maybe twice a week, moving from bed to bed as their children dictated. Both of them would rather sleep than get a chance to be intimate with each other. Charlie, at least, was glad his libido seemed to have gone into hibernation. As a younger man it would have killed him to be next to Anne but not able to reach out for her in the night, tugging at her nightgown until she woke up and came to him. But now he loved the gentle sounds of a sleeping child, the occasional foot in the face a small price to pay for the feeling of being a family. Sometimes he would wake in the night and walk from room to room, counting his blessings as they slept.

He nodded at his wife and blew her a kiss, which Anne pretended to catch and press to her lips, tossing him one in return. He turned out the light, pulled the sheet over Kate who was now gently snoring, and went back to checking e-mail on his phone.

———

Iris sat on the edge of Wyatt's bed and watched him breathe, his face smoothed out in sleep, his cheeks flushed. How could eyelids so small lift lashes so long? He held Gubby in his hand, a small rabbit that had once been soft and gray, but was now worn and torn, the cream feet and ears more like gray, the gray more like brown. *When I die*, he had once asked, *will Gubby die with me?* Iris had nodded, taking the question at face value and trying not to let him see how the thought made her feel. She prayed he'd die about eight decades after he'd forgotten Gubby, or more, maybe breaking the world record for longevity, oldest man ever.

Sara coughed gently at the door and held out her hand. Iris smiled and got to her feet, after tucking the sheet more fully around Wyatt. She held her wife's hand as they walked down the hall toward their bedroom. Sara was looking at her in a way that meant she wanted to fool around, and Iris was wondering if she could ask her, afterward, if another baby were possible. That's what it was doing to her, this longing: Everything was related to it, somehow. Every breath, every kiss, every bite of nutritious food, every baby smiled at in the grocery store, was a wish for another. She was going mad and the madness was coloring everything. She and Sara had a good marriage, a strong friendship, yet Iris was worried her request for another child would sound like a demand. What if Sara said, "It's me or a baby"? And why did Iris even think that was a possibility? Sara was never like that, had never been like that. Iris was losing her fucking mind.

———

Lucas slept horizontally, like a stave. He had fallen asleep in his parents' bed, and pretty much stretched from one side to the other. Bill had slowly moved to the very edge of the bed to make room. He folded one leg down to stop himself sliding off, and to help him balance the computer on his lap. The lights were off and he was miles away, immersed in the music he was composing. As his heart slept beside him in superhero pajamas, Bill fought dragons one phrase at a time and didn't think of his wife at all.

Eight.

*F*rances tapped the horn. Lucas was supposed to be running down the slight slope of his front yard right now. Actually, several minutes ago. She sighed, turned to Ava, and opened her mouth.

"No, honk again. Louder." Her daughter's tone was cool, but her eyes were ready to start a fight.

Frances raised her eyebrows. Ava was working on her passive resistance this morning, and had been ever since Frances had dared to suggest that something with sleeves might be a good idea.

"Here he comes," said Lally, from behind her, saving Frances from another bout with the standing featherweight champion of in-car boxing.

"Sorry, Frances." Bill had come with his son, and stood next to the car as Lucas clambered in. "I overslept. Then he didn't want to get dressed, and it took a while to compromise."

Frances looked in the rearview. Lucas was wearing pajama pants, but a regular T-shirt. She smiled at Bill. "Looks like a perfect outfit to me," she said. "He's covered, right?"

Bill smiled back, thinking for the hundredth time how much he liked Frances. She was easy, Frances was. No muss, no fuss. Just us humans here, no need to panic.

Frances smiled at him, put the car back into gear, and got ready to pull away. "See you later, Bill." She waved as she headed down the street, and Bill raised his hand in return.

Frances looked at him in the side mirror, still waving after her as she reached the end of the block. As she swung around the corner he swiveled on his heel just as smoothly, and went back into the house. She wondered anew where Julie was. Once Lally and Lucas had started at the same preschool she and Julie had begun a tentative friendship, but then, suddenly, Julie wasn't at home anymore. She'd asked Bill if Julie was away for work, and Bill had just shaken his head and said nothing.

That had been a couple of months ago, and somehow the moment for inquiry had passed. She and Iris had joked that maybe Bill killed his wife and buried her in the yard, but she'd heard Lucas talking about his mom to Lally, so presumably that wasn't true. It was strange, and the neighborhood gossips had tried Julie in absentia and found her guilty of abandonment with a side order of failing to keep them all informed. Frances hadn't known her well enough to have her phone number, and certainly didn't know Bill well enough to ask where he'd stashed his wife. Frances mentally shrugged her shoulders, and focused again on the road. People did weird shit, usually for boring reasons, and Frances tried not to judge people without knowing all the facts. She flashed on Anne's face, her eyes closed with pleasure as her boyfriend's tongue teased and pleased, and found it all too easy to judge and sentence that one.

_____

After dropping off the smallest kids, Frances circled back to the high school. She sat there with her windows down and the radio on quietly, waiting to hear the first bell. Frances had an appointment to talk to the school counselor about Ava's grades. They'd argued about it the previous night.

"My grades are fine," Ava had insisted. "A solid B is totally OK. Why are you so focused on achievement? Aren't we supposed to be embracing a growth mind-set these days?" She'd been sitting on her bed, her long legs in stripy tights folded up under her, one side of her hair shaved, the other streaked with purple. She was the cool kid Frances had always wanted to be friends with at school, but now Frances understood that the independence she'd admired had come at a price at home. The coolest girl at her school, six million years previously, had brought a pet rat to school every day, hidden somewhere on her person. At the time it had seemed bold and daring, a declaration, a manifesto. Now it struck Frances that the rat must have represented a daily argument with her mother that only got her revved up for the potential half dozen others she would have once she got the rat to school. Frances wondered what had happened to that girl. The rat was dead, of course, time being what it was.

To be honest, Frances admired the way Ava was starting to bring serious artillery to these discussions, reinforcing her arguments with actual information and well-researched ideas. Frances thought she spent too much time online, but it was clear she wasn't just watching cat videos. Ava often regaled her mother with facts Frances didn't know, sometimes casually, sometimes with enormous excitement. She had almost weekly obsessions, her future plans changing accordingly: She was going to restore old houses, she was going to breed rare lizards, she was going to be a psychologist, she was going to be president, she was going to move to Ireland, Iceland, New Zealand, New York.

Everyone loved to warn you about teenagers, particularly teenage girls. They'd raise their eyebrows as they watched your four-year-old cartwheeling about: "Oh, wait till they're teenagers, then the trouble starts," or something equally dark. Sure, Ava gave her way more attitude than she had at seven, but she also came to her full of enthusiasm about things Frances had never heard of, and asked her questions about morals and metaphysics. Frances had privately decided the world just didn't like teenagers to have fun, or to be enthusiastic and confident, so they told everyone teens needed squashing or fearing. It was the same old bullshit, and ignored the thrilling excitement of watching your child's world open up in front of them, unfurling like the yellow brick road, the emerald spires of adulthood a distant, shimmering dream. Anything was possible, they could do and be anything, they could try on eighteen different personalities a month. Frances believed in Ava, and held on tight, even as her daughter bucked and bitched and tried to throw her off.

The bell rang, and after waiting a few minutes for the kids to mill to their various rooms, Frances stepped out of the car. She believed in her kid, but that didn't mean she didn't need to go talk to the counselor. Trust, but verify.

The counselor's name was Jennifer, and she was approximately half Frances's age. She had been born perky, but had also refined her natural talents through years of pep rallies and cheer squad at school, and was now pert and energetic enough to jump-start a tractor trailer.

"Your daughter's doing great!" she said, her eyes strafing across Ava's file. "Her teachers love her, she appears relatively popular, the nurse hasn't seen her all semester . . ." Her eyes narrowed slightly. "Although, she has dropped all her extracurriculars. Did you know that?"

Frances didn't. "Like what? The school paper?"

Jennifer nodded. "Yeah, she quit that, and the orchestra. She used to go to animation club once a week, and she quit that, too." Her eyes lifted to meet Frances's. The poster behind her urged everyone not to eat the marshmallow, which was making Frances hungry. She thought back . . . Ava had definitely stayed later at school the week before for "orchestra practice." What the actual fuck?

"Well, could she just need more time for her schoolwork? I'm concerned that her grades are slipping a bit."

Jennifer smiled. "Grades aren't the only metric we look at here, as you know. They are only one of many indicators of success."

Frances hated it when neonates lectured her about things she already understood. Youthsplaining. But outwardly she smiled. "I understand that, Jennifer, but last year she got A's in English and Art, for example, and this year she hasn't gotten above a B. I just wanted to check in to make sure you aren't aware of any problems here I might have missed?"

Jennifer looked back at the file, and lifted a piece of paper. A Post-it caught her attention. "How are things with Piper these days?"

Frances was surprised. "Who's Piper?"

It was Jennifer's turn to be surprised. "Piper is a new student who arrived from New York over the summer. Ava hasn't mentioned her?" Frances shook her head. "Huh. Ava was assigned to be her buddy, you know, when Piper first got here. For the first month they were inseparable, a great pair, a good match. Then something happened, and Piper and Ava stopped hanging out overnight."

Frances frowned. "Well, couldn't that just be natural? You know, you get a buddy at a new job, or whatever, and after a week or so you make your own connections and kind of stop hanging out with the buddy . . ." Jennifer was looking at her blankly, but Frances pushed on. "Have you read *The Mezzanine* by Nicholson Baker? He talks about it, he might even give that relationship a name, it's an awesome book . . ." Now Jennifer was looking openly concerned, so Frances trailed off and cleared her throat. "No," she said, "Ava hasn't mentioned Piper at all."

Jennifer shrugged. "Well, that's the only thing her file mentions, that and the extracurriculars. Are you seeing behavior at home that concerns you?"

Frances shrugged back at her. "No, just the usual crankiness and complaints that we don't give her a phone."

Jennifer was shocked. "She doesn't have a phone?" Brief pause. "Pretty much every kid in ninth grade has a phone. What if she needs to call you?"

Frances said, "Well, apparently she could borrow one of the many phones around her. I can't believe every kid has a phone. They're very expensive and that's not including the monthly bill."

Jennifer looked genuinely concerned. "No, really, they all do." She got to her feet, the meeting apparently over. "I'm sorry, I have a staff meeting to go to." She held out her hand. "Always a pleasure, Frances. You should consider getting Ava a phone, though. Not having one really singles her out."

Frances walked down the school hallway perplexed. Had she missed a memo? Pencils, paper, textbooks, iPhone? Really? She looked up and realized she'd walked the wrong way out of Jennifer's office. A bell rang for the end of class, and suddenly the hall was filled with kids, as tall or taller than Frances. They all had backpacks large enough to support a three-month exploration of Europe, and Frances was nearly knocked over several times before she managed to find a clear channel down the center of the hallway.

"Mom?" Shit, she'd come face-to-face with Ava, who at first looked pleased to see her, then suspicious. "Is there something wrong? Is everyone OK? What are you doing here?" The other kids pushed around them, and Frances got a sudden mental image of the buffalo stampede in *The Lion King*. She really needed to spend less time with Disney.

"Everyone's fine. I had to see Jennifer about something." She looked at her daughter. "Is that eyeliner?"

"You came to see if I was wearing makeup?"

"No, I'm just asking a question. And while I'm asking: Is that lipstick?"

Ava narrowed her eyes. "Seriously?"

Frances took a breath. "Let's start over, OK?"

"OK."

"Hi, Ava, funny meeting you here."

"Not really, I'm here every day. You, however . . ."

"I'm here to see your counselor, because I had some questions for her."

"About me?"

"Of course, what other topic would we discuss?"

"Your secret desire to become a cheerleader?"

Frances laughed. "Busted."

Ava smiled, then the bell rang again. "I have to go. Mom, really, why are you here?"

"To spy on you. We can talk about it when I pick you up later, OK?" Frances went to hug her daughter, expecting to be rebuffed, but Ava hugged her back, tightly.

"I miss you when I'm at school," she said quietly in Frances's ear.

"Me, too," her mom replied.

They let go of each other, and Ava put on a believable expression of unconcern. "See ya later, Mom."

Frances nodded and Ava walked off. After a moment Frances turned to leave, so when Ava turned around to smile at her mother one more time, she only saw her back.

Nine.

*D*riving away from school, Frances called Michael, putting the call on speaker.

"Sup, dog?" His voice always cheered her up.

"Do you have five minutes to chat?" She slowed to let an extremely slow old lady cross the street, causing the person behind her to honk his horn. She raised her hand in front of her driver's mirror, the middle finger extended. What was she supposed to do, run the woman down? *We're all getting old, asshole*, she thought, *it won't be long before it's you shuffling along and peeing anxiously into your adult diapers because some dick, who isn't brave enough to chivy you face-to-face, is happy to lean on his horn. Fuck you, asshole.* The guy honked again and she rolled down the window and extended her other hand: tipped up palm, emphatic point at old person, middle finger. Frances knew that mime documentary she'd watched would come in handy one day. She tried to focus on her husband.

"Yup, as long as it's five minutes. I have a meeting at ten." He sounded busy, but relaxed, which was pretty much his default state.

Frances looked at her watch, nine forty-five. "OK. I went to school to talk to Jennifer the counselor."

Michael laughed. "And now you want to become a cheer-leader?"

"Ava said the same thing. What is with you people?" The lady had reached the other side, and stood there panting. Frances wondered what she thought about, whether she paid any attention to the world around her or just focused on making it across street after street. She suddenly hated the young guy behind her and then, as he pulled past her and honked angrily one last time, saw he was a middle-aged woman like herself.

"Ava was there, too? Why didn't you have me come?" He sounded slightly less amused.

"No, she wasn't there at the meeting. I ran into her in the hallway."

"Busted! Was she mad?"

"Not really, although she was wearing makeup that she hadn't been wearing when I dropped her off half an hour earlier." Frances wondered why this even mattered to her, why she was even mentioning it. Sometimes she was critical for no real reason she could discern, and didn't like it in herself. If it had been conscious she could stop herself from doing it, but it seemed to come from nowhere. She'd heard somewhere that a sad portion of your thoughts are just society's opinions, disguised as inner monologue. A depressing thought, or was that just society telling you it was a depressing thought? She was getting a headache.

"Well, so? She *is* fourteen. A little makeup is a rebellion I can handle." Michael sounded a little defensive. He paused and then said, "Unless we're talking full drag queen."

"No, eyeliner and lipstick. Michael, that is not the point. The point is that she's dropped all her extracurriculars, without telling us."

"School paper?"

"No, she quit. And orchestra. And animation club, which, to be honest, I didn't know she was doing, so the fact that she isn't doing it anymore isn't really a thing for me, although it's a bit sad." Frances heard voices in the background, and felt her husband getting distracted. "Are you listening?"

"No," he said honestly, "Jason just came in and I have to go. Can you call me later? Let's talk about it before we talk to Ava, OK? She is allowed to have control over her own schedule, you know." As was often the case, there was a warning note in his voice. When Frances had an issue with Ava, Michael often took Ava's side, protective of his child, which always irritated Frances. They were both on Ava's side, after all. But Michael wouldn't hear a word of criticism of his precious firstborn, or, indeed, any of the kids. He was their huntsman, and Frances was apparently the old lady with the apple. It pissed her off, and she felt her temper rising a little.

"Sure. I'm sure whatever you're doing is more important than the kids." Now, why was she baiting him? He was at work, after all.

There was a pause. Michael had known her for twenty years, and proved it by replying, "Don't get stressed out about this, Frank. It's probably nothing, and we'll get to the bottom of it without World War Three, OK?" He covered the phone and spoke to the guy in his office, then returned to her. "Go eat something, OK, you sound hungry. I'll talk to you soon."

They hung up, and Frances felt the usual combination of mollified and itchy for an argument. Sometimes one of them would pick a fight and the other one would be up for it, but more often one of them would get pissy and the other one would ai-kido that shit immediately. She guessed that was the benefit of marriage, that you could tell what was real and what was just low blood sugar. So fucking irritating.

————

Heading aimlessly home, pondering what to do about Ava, and how to approach it—unavoidable now that they had run into each other—the phone rang.

"Hey!"

"Hey!" It was her friend, Lili. Frances smiled, happy to hear the voice of someone who was completely on her side. Someone with whom she could bitch unfairly about her husband. Honestly, he could find a cure for cancer and Lili would agree that he really should have washed out all those petri dishes.

"Where are you?" Lili always sounded relaxed, regardless of what was going on. She was just one of those people who seemed to take things in her stride. Maybe she was a wreck inside, but on the outside she was the very definition of chill.

"Driving home."

"I'm in your neighborhood. Do you want to have coffee? I have about an hour to kill, and I couldn't think of anyone better to kill it with."

Frances took a right. "You mean no one else answered their phone?"

"No," Lili said. "You were the first. You had the advantage of proximity. I would have had to call Anne Porter next, so I'm glad you picked up. I like her, but she always makes me feel underdressed. Usual place?"

"Yeah, see you in ten."

Well, there you go. One minute it all seemed bleak and vexing, and the next you were going to have coffee. Thank God for friends. And caffeine.

———

The usual place was one of those Belgian chain cafés that always made Frances feel chic and European. She walked to the back room and immediately spotted Lili. Her friend was very pretty, not that she seemed to notice. She waved enthusiastically, and Frances half ran over to give her a hug.

"Dude, I was so glad to hear your voice!" Frances settled down and ordered a latte and a chocolate croissant.

"Oh yeah? Why?" Lili grinned. "Not that I don't want you to be happy to hear from me, but what's up?"

The croissant arrived and Frances took a bite. "Nothing, of course. How are the kids?"

Lili had two daughters, the eldest of whom was in the same fourth grade class as Milo. "Well, Annabel is fine, although I'm starting to see a little Mean Girl action from the other kids. Clare is as chirpy as usual, although I can see her becoming more . . . I don't know . . . normal."

Frances shook her head. "I think you're misreading. That kid is never going to be normal." Lili's younger daughter was a riot. "Who's being mean to Annabel?"

Lili shrugged. "They seem to take turns. It's all about little groups and who's your friend and who isn't." She shuddered. "It's hideous." She took a sip of coffee. "But, anyway, tell me about your whatever it is."

Frances looked around the room. There were at least two familiar faces there, which wasn't surprising. She came in maybe three times a week, and often saw the same people. They weren't at the point of knowing each other's names, but should they be caught in a zombie apocalypse or something they would naturally clump together. They nodded at each other, they would even nod at each other outside of the café context; it was only a matter of time before one of them would step forward, stick out a hand, and introduce themselves. Maybe it would even be Frances.

"Hey, Earth calling." Lili's tone was wry. "You're drifting off. Are you drinking? Is that it? Are you hammered right now?"

Frances laughed. "No, but I have noticed my mind wanders a lot. Does yours?"

Lili nodded. "All the time. The other day it went to the zoo without me."

Frances made a face at her. "I'm a little worried about Ava. Her grades are dropping and I just found out she quit a load of extracurriculars without telling me." She shrugged. "I'm used to being consulted, but maybe I've been laid off without even realizing it."

"A kind of 'once I was the student, now I am the master' kind of thing?" There was a pause, and Lili grinned. "Sorry, it all goes back to *Star Wars* for me, you know that."

"Yeah," said Frances. "But it is kind of like that. Like when you're teaching them to ride a bike and you're running along behind and then suddenly you feel them get it, and they glide away and that's something you'll never get to do again."

Lili gestured to the waitress, who came over. "Can I get another chocolate croissant? And another latte. Thanks." The waitress looked at Frances, who shook her head. Lili continued, "But you want her to be independent, right? You want her to make decisions for herself."

"Of course. She's fourteen, it's time for her to do it. I just didn't think she would take over so suddenly and completely. I'm worried that there's something going on, and now I don't know how to bring it up." She told Lili about running into Ava at school. Lili frowned at her.

"Well, it doesn't sound like you'll need to bring it up. She'll give you the third degree the minute she gets out of school." She smiled at the waitress, and took a bite of her second croissant. "Jesus, why do they make these things so delicious while at the same time offering kale salad and green smoothies? How am I supposed to pick that over this?" She paused and reached across the table, brushing at something on Frances's arm. "You have a . . . mark . . . on your arm. Doodling on yourself again?"

Frances looked at where she was pointing and smiled. "I never told you that story?" Lili raised her eyebrows and shook her head. "That's where my brother stabbed me in the arm."

"Uh, no, I'm pretty sure you never mentioned that. I didn't even know you had a brother."

"I don't really have him anymore. He died."

"I'm sorry."

"So am I." Frances looked at the tiny blue-gray dot on her inner arm. "He was younger than me and I was supposed to be helping him with his homework. He was being his usual pain-in-the-ass self and procrastinating using every trick in the book, including sharpening his pencil to the point where the lead was longer than the wood, do you know what I mean?"

Lili nodded. "Sure."

"And I kept bugging him and getting more and more impatient and eventually he stabbed me in the arm with his pencil."

"Seems a little harsh."

"Worse still, the lead was so long it just stuck there, standing straight up, as a single drop of blood oozed out and ran down onto the kitchen table. It wasn't really painful, but it was visually pretty impressive."

"What did he do?"

"Howled and begged me not to tell Mom."

"And did you?"

"Of course. And the lead broke off in my arm and left this mark which, now that I look at it closely, is starting to fade." She touched it with her finger, her skin totally smooth and soft on her inner arm. "He died a few years after that, but I always think of him when I see this." An image of her brother gazing in horror at the blood jumped into her head and she smiled. She looked up at Lili and wanted to change the subject. "Hey, I heard you're dating someone, is that true?" Lili had lost her husband in a car crash. Frances knew that, but she didn't know much more than that. It had happened before they had met, when the kids were very small, she thought. All these losses, all in the past, but still present every day.

Lili made a face. "I guess so. I don't know. Yes, I am. I think. Not really."

Frances laughed. "Well, I'm glad we cleared that up."

"It's really early, it just started over the summer. I don't know if I'm ready."

"What's his name? Tell me details."

Lili sighed. "His name is Edward. He's Dutch."

"Is he stoned all the time?"

"No. Nor does he wear clogs. He's a gardening teacher. I find him very, very attractive, but I just don't know. The kids like him."

"Well, that's good." Clearly Lili didn't want to talk about this. "What else is new?"

"Lots, for once. I went freelance, I think my sister is going to get married, and the dog has worms."

"Again?"

———

It was eleven when they left the café, and it felt as if they'd solved the world's problems, if not their own. Frances considered what she could get done in the hour, and eventually went to the grocery store. Default setting: grocery shopping.

Frances and Iris had once spent an entire afternoon planning out three months' worth of meals so that they could be sensible about shopping, and not spend so much money on food. It didn't seem right that they had cupboards full of cans and freezers full of food yet never knew what to make for dinner. Yes, a first world problem, but still, a problem. Having made these extensive meal plans they both felt fantastically free to think about more important and useful things than groceries, but fell off the wagon about three weeks into it.

Why was it so fucking hard to be consistent about anything? Literature and popular culture were full of montages of people sticking to things, working out every day, practicing in leg warmers, carrying around railroad ties, clambering over obstacles . . . yet consistently sticking to a meal plan was apparently beyond her. Drenched in self-loathing, Frances pushed the cart around the store, hating herself for picking up Oreos rather than baking from scratch, for choosing Honey Nut Cheerios rather than plain because plain was over once her kids tasted honey nut, for buying wasteful and doubtless polluting tampons instead of wearing some kind of weird internal plastic cup thing. She threw in a big container of salad then immediately took it out. It would just rot in the fridge and when she threw it away she would feel guilty for the waste of the food itself and for the wasted labor of the poor underpaid fucker who'd picked it. It was all very well educating oneself about the trials and problems of the world, but it then became impossible to just blindly go on. At some point she'd decided to swallow the red pill and the rabbit hole just got deeper and deeper.

She decided to roast a chicken for dinner, then stood over the chicken section for two minutes, trying to decide whether a vegetarian-fed chicken was better than an all-natural chicken. How could a chicken not be all natural? Artificial hips? The butcher counter guy appeared next to her.

"Which of these chickens had a better life, do you think?" she asked, one hundred percent confident he was going to think she was a fucking idiot.

Silently he took pity on her, and pointed at one marked "humanely raised." She picked it up, and smiled gratefully at him.

"It's more expensive," he said.

"That's OK," she replied. "I'm paying more so I don't feel guilty."

He turned and walked away, presumably so she wouldn't see him rolling his eyes. He probably couldn't even be bothered to do that. Frances looked at the chicken which, humanely raised or not, was still dead.

She occasionally went vegetarian for a while, usually because she'd unintentionally watched part of some hideous documentary about factory farming, but she found it shamefully hard to stick to. Instead she subscribed to the "one bad day" theory of meat consumption: As natural a life as possible, filled with open skies, fresh grass, friends and respect, and then one really bad day you were killed, as humanely as possible. She realized and recognized that this was utterly crap on her part. She loved animals so much, and would cry at those documentaries and genuinely feel grief, but it would fade. Was she callous, lame, or just lacking in imagination?

Then she headed back to the vegetable section, looking for potatoes that had been grown in earth that was free from pollutants but which retained their beneficial bacteria, or whatever the hell it was she was supposed to care about these days. *Fuck the microbiome*, she thought, *I can barely balance my checkbook, let alone my invisible flora.*

She got home, piled the bags on the counter, checked the message light (nothing), the dishwasher (needed emptying), the trash bags (needed changing), let the dogs out (needed to pee), and then started unloading. As usual, she had bought several of something she already had several of, and forgotten to buy several things she had none of. You would think after four-plus decades on the planet she'd be able to remember the difference between a kitchen roll and a toilet roll, but she invariably had none of one and enough of the other for a nuclear winter. She also tended to either have four tons of pasta or half a packet of elbows, three tins of anchovies or artichoke hearts or capers—none of which she used very much—and no tuna at all, which she used once or twice a week. She would run out of coffee filters one painful morning then keep buying them every time she went to the store, until eventually she had four large boxes and finally understood that she Had Enough. Then she'd assume she had enough of them forever, would stop buying them completely, and would eventually run out again at the worst possible moment. Why was this so hard?

Walking out of the kitchen she looked at her house as if seeing it in a catalog, and decided if it were a catalog it would be called *House Hopeless*. There were drifts of clutter in every corner, like sticks and leaves in the edges and eddies of a stream. Half-finished craft activities. Library books that had become so overdue it would have been cheaper to buy them in the first place. Invitations to parties that had taken place three years prior. Then, of course, there were the epic Pinterest fails of an actual life: a mantelpiece where she'd attempted a "curation" of photos and keepsakes, which for three days had been photo ready but then had been overtaken by school forms and Fisher-Price Little People and the registration sticker for Michael's car, which didn't need to go on for another month and would be every single place she looked until she actually needed it, at which point it would have fallen into a crevice in the earth's crust and be lost forever. And everywhere, *everywhere*, single socks and dog hair.

Oh well.

Ten.

Sara had gone to work, and Iris had the house to herself. There was only so much tidying she could do before wanting to slam her hand in a drawer with boredom, so she called her mother. Sometimes her mother was helpful, sometimes not, but she was always there at least. Her diabetes kept her largely housebound, now that her feet were so messed up. Iris's dad had died a few years earlier, and her mother's life had changed in ways she hadn't fully processed herself.

"Hey, baby." Her voice was a little tired, but basically happy to hear from her daughter. "How's my favorite grandson?"

"Your only grandson."

"True, but irrelevant. Although, if you would only give me another maybe it would take the pressure off him. Think of your child, Iris." She was joking, but only mildly.

"I'd love another child, you know that, Mom. It just isn't happening right now."

"What does Sara say?"

Iris clicked on the kettle and went to get herself a mug and a tea bag. "She doesn't. We haven't talked about it."

"Why not?" Her mother got a sharper note in her voice. "Are

you fighting?" Her mother hadn't really had a problem with Iris being gay, and was on some level relieved her daughter wasn't going to have to deal with the perfidy of men (as if women were immune from perfidy). She was definitely thrilled to be a grandmother, but sometimes she had to defend her daughter's choices to the other women at her Catholic church. It helped a lot that Sara and Iris had been married as long as they legally could be, and that their marriage was happy. Iris sometimes felt gay married couples were being held to an unreasonably high standard, as if one failure would doom the entire category. Marriage had so little to do with the bedroom, and so much to do with every other room in the house. Conversations around the kitchen table, discussions about toothpaste and toilet paper, decisions about pets and children and car insurance. How you chose to physically please each other was such a small part of it, but it got all the press.

When she and Sara had been planning their wedding, Iris had been struck by how much attention was paid to *getting* married, and how little to *staying* married. Entire magazines were devoted to centerpieces and whimsical take-home trinkets, but where were the articles about getting used to the smell of each other's poop? Where was the advice on how to end an argument about who was sicker when you both caught the same cold, or how to decide which one of you got up at night for the baby, or how to agree to put an old and suffering pet to sleep?

Similarly, when she was pregnant, there was such attention paid to labor and delivery, and so little to the first three months afterward, which made the pain of an episiotomy seem like a walk in the park. Split your vagina like a melon? Sure, but what about taking the first shit afterward? What about ninety nights with two hours of sleep and the argument all couples have in the second week when you realize this fucking baby is Never Leaving and all the help you have is That Useless Person Over There? Let's get five hundred words on that, motherfucker.

Iris realized her mother was still waiting for an answer. "Because I haven't found the right moment to bring it up. She seems really happy right now, and I guess I'm scared that if I ask her and she says no that I'm not sure what I would do."

Her mother made a noise that was hard to describe. A sigh mixed with a click of the tongue and an ageless expression of resignation. "What could you do?"

"Not sure. That's why I haven't brought it up." She poured the hot water over the tea bag, and watched the gossamer pyramid collapse.

Her mother asked, "How's Frances?"

Iris smiled. "Same as ever. Happy."

"Did she lose the weight?"

Iris rolled her eyes, but answered her mother anyway. "No, I don't think so. She doesn't look any different." She waited for her mother to comment on how skinny Frances used to be. It was as predictable as sunrise.

"She used to be so skinny, didn't she?"

"She did, yes. But she had kids."

"Sure, but we all have kids. You have kids. You're still skinny."

Iris walked over to the kitchen table and sat down. Rosco threw himself down next to her. "I was never skinny, Mom. And I only have one child, she has three."

"I had four. I kept my figure."

"You're not being very supportive. That's your favorite niece you're talking about."

"You should hear what I say about my least favorite." She laughed. "How's that husband of hers? Still drinking too much?"

"You're a horrible gossip."

"If you're talking about relations it's not gossip, it's family history."

Iris bent to stroke her dog, who never repeated anything about anyone.

Eleven.

As Lili had foreseen, Ava opened her attack before her butt even hit the front seat.

"So, why were you at school?" She wedged her enormous backpack into the passenger floor space, moving her chair back until it caused Lally to squeak.

Frances looked in the rearview. Lally was half asleep, despite the squeak. Milo, Wyatt, and Theo were in the third row, reveling in the extra space because Kate was occupying Lucas's usual seat. He had been picked up by Bill, whom Frances had only glimpsed in the distance. Dentist appointment, which Bill had alerted Frances to the week before. He was very on top of it, Bill was; maybe Julie had felt unnecessary.

Frances looked across at her daughter, whose face was calm enough. "I just wanted to talk to Jennifer about how you're doing at school."

"You'd already talked to me, wasn't that enough? Jennifer doesn't know anything." Her fingers were tapping on the seat belt, little percussive noises that belied her quiet delivery.

"Is there something to know, Ava?" In the rearview she could see Milo's eyes, watching her. He couldn't hear very much from back there, but he could read their tone. She dropped her voice, "Maybe we should talk about this once we get home? We could just sit and . . ."

"Chat about how you're invading my privacy? Sure, let's grab a cup of tea and talk it through, shall we?" Her daughter turned to face the window and said nothing for the rest of the trip.

Frances sighed. "Yes, let's have some tea."

Once they were home and Ava had walked Kate, Theo, and Wyatt down the block to their houses, and Milo had gotten Lally and himself their inevitable bowl of Pirate's Booty and had sat down with her for their regulation half hour of post-school TV, Frances carried two cups of tea up to Ava's room.

Ava looked up, apparently surprised to see her mother. "Oh, are we really going to have tea?"

Fortunately, Frances knew she'd just been sitting there waiting to nonchalantly throw out that line, in the hopes of getting first blood. No dice.

"Yeah, I thought it would be a good idea." Frances held up the tea. "But if you don't want to, it's fine." She looked around the room at the early teenage mix of old horse posters and new rock star posters (similar hair styles), the blend of dolls and books and makeup. She understood why parents who lost their children kept their rooms just as they were: Every single thing in this room meant something. Either it meant something to her or it simply meant something to her because it meant something to Ava.

Ava took the tea and resettled herself on the bed, putting her laptop to one side, keeping one of her earbuds in, just in case she needed to do that "Oh, I've just been distracted by a notification, I'm going to let my gaze drift to the screen to underscore how unimportant this conversation is" move. Again, nice try.

"Both earbuds out and close the screen, OK? I want to talk to you, and I want to hear what you have to say." Frances suddenly wondered if she should wait for Michael to come home, but it was a bit late to change tack now.

Ava rolled her eyes, but complied. Honestly, the eye-rolling thing just had to be developmental. There was no other explanation for its simultaneous appearance in pretty much one hundred percent of tweens and teens, all over the world. Three wisps of underarm hair, the first actual pimple, and eye rolling, all at once. Frances got a brief mental montage of teenage eyes rolling in the spotty faces of multitudinous nationalities, then returned her focus to the kid in front of her.

"I went to talk to Jennifer today, because your dad and I were worried that you didn't seem to be bringing the same attention to school as you used to. It's as simple as that." She smoothed the coverlet, flicking a crumb to the floor.

"As simple as 'My kid is failing, what are you going to do about it'?" Ava pulled her legs up under her, just in case her mother's smoothing hand got too close.

"No, you're not failing. You're just not succeeding."

Ava snorted. "Isn't that the same thing?"

Frances shook her head. "No, and you understand what I'm saying and what I mean, and there's no point pretending you don't. Look, lovely." She put her hand on Ava's knee, but her daughter twitched it away, frowning. "We love you, and want to help you, that's all. It's our job."

"Well, how about I fire you?"

Frances smiled. "You can't. It's a lifetime appointment. We have tenure."

Ava wasn't smiling. "I never hired you."

"We were appointed at birth. Your birth."

"How come Milo gets a pass?"

"He doesn't, but our expectations for him are different from our expectations for you. He's ten. We expect him to lower the toilet seat after peeing, eat his vegetables, and that's about it."

"You weren't that easy on me." Ava's eyes were glittering, but Frances couldn't tell if it was tears or rage.

"Yes, we were. Easier, maybe, because you were the first and therefore we didn't know how mean we could be. Poor Lally's going to be sweeping chimneys by the time she's eight."

Again, no smile. Usually humor would breach her dam of irritation, her hormonal wall of ice. Frances waited.

"Lally gets away with everything." This was clutching at straws. Ava doted on Lally, and the feeling was mutual. When Lally had been a baby Ava had been ten, and for a brief period it was only Ava who could stop her from fussing. It had been instant glory, witnessed multiple times by various members of the family, and the connection was still there.

"She's four. Are you suggesting we send her to college? Should Milo be looking for work in the financial sector?" Frances tried to touch Ava again, but she still held herself too far away. "Darling, we want all of you to be happy, and that means different things at four than it does at fourteen."

"What is it supposed to mean for me, then?" Frances could hear an actual question in Ava's voice, rippling across the surface belligerence. She really wondered what happy should mean for her, and Frances remembered that feeling well. She smiled and tried to soften her tone.

"We expect you to work hard at school, get enough to eat, get more sleep than you seem to want, and to have a social life. Not a continuous round of parties and sleepovers because that would mess with the first three, but fun is allowed and indeed encouraged." Frances looked at the face she knew better than her own, watching for clues as to what Ava was thinking. She would get a tiny indentation at the corner of her mouth when she was trying not to cry. She fisted up her hands when she was getting frustrated. She stopped blinking so much when she was about to throw a total shitter. So far her blink rate appeared normal, but Frances was ready to duck. "And we also want you to tell us what's going on with you, to keep communicating with us."

"How is that supposed to make me happy? Aren't I allowed a private life?"

"Of course you are. Everyone is. But we're here to help you, to support you, like a pit crew, but without the jumpsuits and awesome whirry wheel-changing tools. We can't do that if you don't tell us what you need."

"What if I don't need anything?"

"We all need something. No one gets out of here alone, babe." Why was this so hard, why was her child resisting her so much, so furiously? When she was small Frances had been her everything, and now she seemed to resent her mother's very existence.

"But what if what I need is to be left alone?" Ava's tiny indentation was there now, at the corner of her mouth, but so was the reduced blinking. The teenager was fighting herself for control.

Frances tried something else. "Have some tea."

"I don't want any fucking tea."

Pause. Crap, now Frances needed to make one of those snap parenting decisions that she so frequently got wrong. She should have waited for Michael. Should she get angry at the cursing? Should she not? Two milliseconds, three milliseconds, four milliseconds . . .

"Then don't have any fucking tea."

Ava rarely heard her mother swear, except occasionally in the car, and this was startling enough to provoke a small smile. Frances doubled down, as this seemed to have been successful. "How about some fucking cocoa?"

Ava's smile widened. "Nah, tea's fine." Her nascent tears seemed to be under control, and she took a sip and blinked at a normal rate. Frances cheered inwardly, and was tempted to get up and walk away while she was ahead, even though she hadn't done anything except get her daughter to smile and drink tea. Seriously, some days that might be as good as it got. But then she remembered her conversation with Jennifer, and decided to press on.

She softened her tone, tried to sound open and nonjudgmental. "Jennifer said you've dropped your extracurriculars . . . What's up there?"

In the blink of an eye the smile was gone. Ava scowled. "What's up? Nothing's up. The extracurriculars were (a) boring and (b) time consuming, and now I'll have more time to do my precious homework. Isn't that what you want?"

Frances shrugged. Maybe it was contagious. She'd be rolling her eyes next. "If you need more time to do your homework then it's good you gave yourself that time."

"Because I'm too stupid to do my homework in a regular amount of time?"

Oh, for fuck's sake. "No, you were the one who mentioned homework."

"Because that's all you care about."

"No, all I care about is you. I thought you liked working on the newspaper."

"They got a new editor. It wasn't me. I quit."

Frances was surprised. "Because of that?"

Frances could tell Ava wanted very badly to look at her computer screen and feign indifference; her hand even drifted toward the laptop. "No, I just didn't enjoy it anymore."

"And the animation club?"

"Flip-book shit. It was stupid."

"And the orchestra?"

There was a pause. Frances watched her daughter's face. Ava was clearly trying to remember if she'd said she was doing a rehearsal the previous week, which she had, and wondering whether or not Frances had realized she hadn't been. It was quite the little opera of facial expressions, and in the end the teenager decided to roll the dice.

"Yeah, that, too. I went last week, but I'm not going to go anymore."

Frances pondered. Should she call her on the lie, wait for Michael to come home and discuss it with him, or let it slide right now but come at it another way?

She plunged on. "Oh yeah? Jennifer thought you'd stopped a couple of weeks ago. But you told me you were at rehearsal last week, right?"

Ava shrugged and frowned. "Did I?" She reached for her tea, took a sip.

"Yeah, I'm pretty sure. What did you do instead?" There, that was straightforward. You know and I know that you said you were at rehearsal and we both know you weren't, so tell me the truth. Good, right? Right?

"Nothing. Hanging out in the library I guess. I forget."

Ah. Fuck. A sideways bluff, a teenage classic. Maybe I was doing something you wouldn't like, maybe I wasn't, I don't remember. How much do you want to push this, Parent? We can both walk away at this point, the pothole covered over, appearances preserved. Wouldn't that be the easier choice? Go on, let it go.

Frances didn't want to let it go. Her own parents had been masters of the "everything's fine here, move along, nothing to see" while at the same time being so incredibly miserable and fucked up they could barely breathe. They'd never recovered from losing her brother, but everyone in the neighborhood thought they were doing really well, so brave, an inspiration.

"I don't believe you. If you quit a couple of weeks ago then you've been 'at rehearsal' at least twice since then, and I'm pretty sure you stayed late at least one other day." Frances raised her eyebrows. "What's going on, Ava? I'm not angry. I just want to know what's up."

Ava looked at her mother, a momentary look of hurt almost immediately replaced with anger.

"My private life is none of your business."

"Yes, it kind of is. I don't need color pictures, a verbal overview is fine. Are you seeing someone? Are you doing drugs? Are you counterfeiting money under the bleachers?"

Which was when the gasket blew, and all the way off. Ava sat up and pointed her finger, her face flushing. "You think you're funny, don't you? You're always so ready to make a joke, to make it seem like we're all so cool and relaxed here, sharing goals, working as a team, whatever theory you've gleaned from whatever parenting book or podcast you've listened to recently." Ava looked at Frances with a more than reasonable facsimile of disdain. "You're no different from anyone else's parents, Mom, just a prying, fat old woman whose own life is essentially over and who needs to run their kids' lives to distract themselves from imminent menopause." She swung her legs over the side of the bed and stood up, physically escalating the conflict while giving herself space to swing.

Frances took a breath and stayed down. At moments like this she felt sorrow in a way she never experienced in any other context. Sorrow for herself because, let's face it, that shit was hurt-ful, and sorrow that she had failed at parenting so badly that her child was capable of such cruelty. She knew Ava saved her harsh-est words for her, she knew that intellectually, but she also knew that those feelings were real, that at points like this Ava genu-inely didn't like her very much.

"That's not true, and it's very mean. I just asked you a reason-able question. There's no need to make a federal case of it. Just tell me what you were doing, and why you're lying to me about it." Frances really hadn't wanted this conversation to go this way. "I don't think of you as a liar, Ava. Please just tell me what's going on with you."

"Nothing. I already told you. I hung out at the library and did my homework. There's nothing."

"Why did you tell me you were at rehearsal?"

Yet another shrug. "Because it was easier than explaining why I wasn't."

"Which you still haven't explained. And who's Piper?" *Don't get angry, Frances. The minute you get angry, the minute you raise your voice, you lose the argument and everyone ends up in tears and the emotional hangover the next day is such a bastard.*

Ava crossed her room to sit in her scruffy, oversize armchair, a fixture since she'd been born. She'd been nursed there, rocked there, read to for years and years. Now it was her own nest, and as she pulled her legs up tightly, Frances could see her thinking hard and trying not to lose the fight. Winning mattered so much to her because she hadn't yet realized that she and Frances were on the same side. "Piper is nobody. Just a girl at school who liked me and doesn't like me anymore."

"'Liked' in the romantic sense?"

Ava deepened her scorn, if that were possible. "You'd love that, wouldn't you? If I was gay like Iris? It would be so easy to look cool then, you could just be like, 'Yeah, my kid's gay, it's fine, as long as she's happy.' You'd be so accepting and right-on about it."

Frances felt her temper rising. "And that would be bad? I should throw you out of the house instead?"

"No." Ava tossed her head, looking momentarily like the piebald in the poster above the chair. "Oh, never mind, Mom. You don't even know what you don't know."

Count to three. "And what about the orchestra?"

"I quit because I wanted to have more time. I want to have some space, for crying out loud. I need time to myself, time that is just mine." Suddenly, she had tears in her eyes. "Everyone knows where I am and what I'm doing all the time. I have a schedule on the wall. I have organized activities. I have about as much freedom as someone on death row and that's pretty much how I feel. I just want to have something private, something only I know, and a little fucking room to breathe." She turned and buried her face in a pillow that said "No Bad Days" on it in fluffy letters. "I just want you to leave me alone!"

Frances reached for her. "Ava, I . . ."

From the pillow, desperately, "Mom, I'm not speaking hypothetically. I want you to leave me alone now. Just go away. I hate you!"

Frances got up and walked out, almost in tears herself.

That went well.

———

To add insult to injury, even though it wasn't needed, Michael was annoyed with Frances for going ahead without him.

"I thought we agreed to talk to each other before talking to Ava?"

Frances was sitting on their bed, surrounded by dogs as usual. She nodded. "I know, it just . . . I should have waited. I didn't think it would go that badly, that quickly." They kept their voices low, but Michael wasn't one of those people who needed volume to make his displeasure felt. He wrinkled his eyebrows at her.

"Do we even have a theory about why she dropped her extra-curriculars? Do we know anything about this Piper girl? Has she ever mentioned her?"

"Maybe. I don't remember it, but that isn't cast iron. Those first weeks of school are always such a clusterfuck. Three different schools this year, all new names, I'm surprised I remember who's teaching which kid."

Michael looked at his wife, who was hiding behind Jack and Diane. He loved her very much, but he found himself increasingly mystified by her relationship with Ava. For his own part, he found the teenage girl living in his house as confusing as the ones he'd gazed at as a teenager. He hadn't understood them then, and barely any of them would even deign to talk to him. When his kids brought home friends he could never tell them apart. They all looked like critters to him, just fast-moving blurs of hair.

"Was that Bella?" he would ask, and Frances or Ava would roll their eyes and say, "No, that was Quinn, they're completely different!" and he would shrug. He knew his own kids at a vast distance, or from the corner of his eye, and that would just have to do. He loved them unreservedly, especially Ava, who was the most like him. But his conversations with her were completely different from the ones she and Frances had.

Early on Frances had told him something he'd taken very much to heart. "You," she'd said, "are the alpha man in your daughter's life. You are the model. Every other man in her life will be measured against you, and her relationships will be measured against ours. If you speak to her disrespectfully she will accept that level of shit from a future boyfriend." She'd paused and smiled at him. "No pressure." He tried hard, and largely spoke to Ava about neutral things, or things they both agreed on, or sometimes he would just listen to her rattle on about whatever she wanted to rattle on about. He would be sitting there and suddenly that conversation with Frances would pop into his head, and he would get anxious: *Am I being supportive? Am I understanding her and encouraging her to share her thoughts? Would I be OK with a future boyfriend treating her this way . . . ?* But then he would get so irritated at the thought of some future dickhead treating his daughter badly that he would drift off, and suddenly Ava would be looking at him silently with one eyebrow raised. D'oh.

But Ava always cut him slack, something she was apparently never prepared to do for Frances. Any tiny error, any thoughtless word, and Ava would be all over Frances like white on rice. He could see how much it stressed Frances out, but then he could also see how her stress made it worse, how caring about Ava too much was preventing her from letting that shit wash over her.

He went over and sat on the bed next to her, stroking the dogs' heads and reaching for Frances's hand. "Honey, you just need to back off a bit."

"I try!" Frances pulled her hand away. "It doesn't matter what I do, I get into trouble every time we speak. It's like walking blindfolded through a field of, I don't know, exploding things in the ground."

Michael frowned. "A minefield?"

There was a pause. "Yes, a minefield. Jesus, it doesn't help that I'm clearly developing a brain tumor the size of a fucking tangerine." She rested her head on her husband's chest, over the head of Diane, who stuck her nose up and tried to lick their chins. "You'd be much better at this than I am, so maybe that would be for the best."

Michael hugged her. "Look, I get to be the guest star, the occasional cameo appearance. And, unlike on old episodes of *Columbo*, I don't always have to be the bad guy."

"I miss *Columbo*."

"I'm sure they have it on Netflix."

"What if it isn't as good as I remember it?"

"Few things are."

"I love you."

He grinned above her head. "I know."

———

Anne was in the bathroom, washing her face, the grains dissolving as they always did. Charlie was sitting in the bedroom watching Theo and Kate playing some game or other on the iPad. Anne could tell from Kate's tone of voice that things were about ten minutes away from going supercritical. She'd take eight of those minutes to finish in the bathroom and then walk out and pull the irons out of the fire just in time. What a heroine she was. She made a face at herself in the mirror and heard Theo's voice in the other room say, "Who's Richard?"

She clutched the side of the sink and her hand slipped in the water she was washing her face with. Lurching forward she almost cracked her head on the mirror. Her blood turned to ice, a phrase she'd never understood until that very second, and she heard Charlie say, "No idea, is it something in the game?" He didn't sound all that interested.

Theo sounded puzzled. "No, he just texted me."

Please, God.

"What did he say?"

"'Are you there?'"

"That's all he said? Is that my iPad or Mommy's?"

"I don't know."

No, really, please, God.

Charlie sighed. "Show me."

Anne looked at her reflection and listened to the last seconds of her old life ticking away. She looked so old stooping over the sink, her ratty kitten pajamas—a Mother's Day gift from the kids—a little damp on the front, her quivering arms barely holding her up. She looked like a dog about to vomit, hunched, fearful. *No one will ever know.*

Charlie's voice again. "It's Mommy's iPad . . ." He raised his voice. "Hey, Anne, did you know you're getting texts on the iPad? Does that mean you're not getting them on your phone?"

She could speak. "No idea, babe." She sounded totally normal. "Who is it?"

"I don't know, some guy named Richard?"

"Huh . . . I don't know anyone called Richard. Maybe it's a wrong number." *My voice couldn't sound more innocent and disinterested.*

"Can I have it back, Dad?"

There was a tiny pause, and Anne could almost see the small frown on Charlie's face, followed by the usual microshrug and casting aside of worry. It was his way. She loved him for it, ironically enough.

"Sure, here you go." Another pause. "Nearly time for bed, though, OK?"

Anne rested her forehead against the mirror in the bathroom and willed herself not to smash it there, killing the selfish monster who threatened her family.

Instead she reached for her dressing gown and walked out to lie to their faces.

Twelve.

Wednesday morning at five o'clock as the day begins . . .

Frances had a Beatles song stuck in her head and sang it under her breath as she blundered into the bathroom, everyone else still sleeping. The dogs followed her, wondering if this morning they would get fed in the bathroom; it paid to keep an open mind.

She looked at herself in the mirror, naked and sheet-marked. *Not too bad*, she thought, turning. Yeah, OK, there were definitely thirty extra pounds, but first thing in the morning it all tended to hold together, and not . . . fold so much. By the end of the day, having been squeezed into jeans and a bra and sitting and standing and driving, she looked like a transit map, lines intersecting pinkly in hubs and spokes. She'd been very slender as a young woman, and clearly remembered looking at herself in a mirror at the age of twenty-four, not an ounce of fat, not a hint that gravity operated on her the same as everyone else, and pledging that if she ever saw even the first hint of cellulite she wouldn't ignore it, but would work that shit off right away.

Frances made a face, remembering the idiocy of her younger self. She'd stayed slender until she had kids, then she'd gained with each pregnancy and not completely lost, and now she was overweight in her midforties, with a muffin top that rivaled any artisanal bakery in town. And did she give a fuck? No, zero fucks given. Except for every thirty or forty minutes, when she would catch sight of herself in a store window or mirror and scowl inwardly, scolding herself for being lazy, fat, unattractive, old, past-it, unsexy, uninteresting, invisible yet glaringly, obesely obvious as she lumbered around the world, an insult to the media and good women everywhere. Yeah, apart from those punctuating moments of vicious self-criticism, zero fucks given.

But so far this morning, she felt fine. She had the opposite of body dysphoria, maybe. She looked at herself and basically thought she looked good. Body euphoria? It didn't feel *that* good . . . The dogs loved her regardless, as they told her continuously, pressing their heads under her hands, gazing up at her . . . *You're fantastic*, said their liquid eyes, their waving tails, *we just can't get over how terrific you are in every way, we're so glad to have chosen you as our leader.*

She pulled on her jeans, looked at her mom-butt in the mirror—seriously, how did she suddenly have such a wide ass, what was wrong with her—then pulled on a sweatshirt which covered it. See? No mom-butt here. Just a cool hoodie. Suck it, internal critic. Suck it all the way.

She headed down the stairs, the dogs apparently attempting to kill her at every step, pushing behind her in a clattering fall of fur and claws. She saw the cat sitting on the sofa, waiting. *Ah*, his smooth outline said, *I see the servants are awake.*

Frances put on the coffee, humming, then pulled the dogs' dishes from the dishwasher, having let them both out the back door to take a shit she could step in later. Carlton the cat sauntered in, timing his arrival perfectly with Frances putting fresh kibble in his bowl, up on a counter where the dogs couldn't get it. She loved this cat. He was old and predated everyone in the house except Michael. His purr was rusty and only for her, his fur slightly thicker and more matted than it had been when she'd brought him home from the shelter sixteen years earlier. The dogs were scared of him, his orange tiger stripes conveying danger just as they should, and he sauntered around the house unmolested.

The dogs came back in, the coffee dripped into the pot, the lights were on, she could hear Ava moving around upstairs, facing her own reflection in the bathroom mirror. Frances hoped her daughter saw how beautiful she was, but doubted it. She herself, like every woman she knew, only recognized her own youthful perfection in retrospect, with deep regret not for losing it but for not seeing it at the time. Frances tried to remember this every time she criticized herself—one day she would be eighty, God willing, and she was ready to bet she'd look at herself then and long for the strength and bone density of forty-six.

Frances thought of Anne. A few houses away she was also wandering around her kitchen, packing lunches (although she could be *that* mom, the one who assembled them the night before and only did the sandwich at the last minute, to prevent sogginess), drinking coffee, singing Beatles songs under her breath. Or maybe she was doing a light yoga workout, from memory, wearing strappy bamboo yoga wear that didn't leave a mark on her flesh because she didn't have any fat, because she worked it all off fucking a teenager and darting around like the cheating cow she was. Frances chided herself for being a bitch, and Ava came in.

"Morning, lovely," said Frances.

"Yello," replied her daughter, which was a neutral to medium-friendly response. Frances looked sideways at her, trying to gauge her mood. She'd left her alone the previous night, falling asleep herself before Ava had, which was a pretty common occurrence these days. Had she gotten over her bad mood, or was Frances still on her shit list?

Ava had the fridge door open. "Are you going to the store later?"

"Does the day have a *Y* in it?"

Ava smiled. "Can you get some more string cheese with the stuff wrapped around it?"

"Prosciutto?"

"Yeah." She pulled out from the fridge, shutting the door. "I'm about to eat the last one."

"Sure." Frances made a mental note. Those particular snacks came from a different market from the usual one; she'd have to make a special trip. None of her family noticed the various efforts she made on their behalf, hunting for new foods for them to try, picking up their favorite flavors of this and that, pouncing on the rarities they favored, the Japanese candy, the artisanal brand of root beer, the slightly nicer-than-usual wine she picked out for Michael, though she didn't like red wine herself.

Before there was Pinterest there were magazines that showed happy women providing beautiful things for their families to enjoy, and despite her intelligence she was just as much a sucker as anyone else. She wanted a bright yellow pitcher of wooden spoons on her white marble counter, she wanted tall French windows that looked out over green valleys, she wanted a pair of strappy ballet flats that ribboned up her slender calves as she romped about town in artfully shabby dungarees that somehow took twenty pounds off her. Instead she had a jar of dog-chewed wooden spoons, windows that hadn't been washed since the first Obama administration, and if she'd put on a pair of dungarees she would have been mistaken for a plumber. A male plumber. However, she did maintain a world-class snack cupboard.

Ava came close, leaned over to be kissed, and went back upstairs. Frances listened to her footsteps as long as she could hear them.

Stepping outside she is free . . .

Anne's kids were younger, so maybe she didn't think about losing them as frequently as Frances thought about life after Ava was gone. As her eldest had turned into a teenager Frances and Michael could feel her getting ready to leave, all her energy pivoting toward the exit. It was palpable, the change in attitude. Sometimes it hurt to think of Ava picking a college, picking a boyfriend, picking a city to move to, and other times it filled them both with pride to think of the young woman she was turning into. *Mind you*, Frances thought, as she heard Lally calling her from upstairs, *a stick of cheese for breakfast wasn't going to cut it out in the real world.*

————

Actually, Anne wasn't doing yoga, she was throwing up and trying not to let anyone hear. She'd filled the toilet with toilet paper and draped a towel over her head to muffle the retching. She'd woken at 4:00 a.m., the universal hour of regret and recrimination. She knew she'd come dangerously close to being caught, to losing trust she didn't deserve to have, and she knew she had to break it off once and for all. She'd tried before, and failed, but that was when she was only fighting her own willpower. Now she knew she was fighting Karma, and that bitch carried a big stick and forgot nothing.

Light was starting to come through the skylight above her head as she lay on the floor, the cold tiles flecked with bile. In a moment her morning alarm would go off, and she needed to get her ass off the bathroom floor and go prevent it from waking Charlie. She had to gather herself, wake the children, make the lunches (she'd been too freaked out to do it the night before as usual), put on the kettle for her morning coffee, check the backpacks for things she was supposed to sign, hunt for shoes. She must pretend it was all OK, that there was no possibility at all that her heart would burst and kill her where she stood. What if she died? What if Richard showed up at her funeral and the children turned to Charlie and asked who the tall crying guy was? This thought propelled her to her feet, and as she shuddered one last time over the toilet, a cold sweat spreading the smell of burning metal through the room, she prayed this was the last day of this part of her life.

———

Lucas wanted to know what made Fruity Pebbles change the milk all rainbowy. Bill said, "Chemicals," but Lucas wasn't satisfied.

"Which ones?"

Bill picked up the cereal box and read the label. "I spoke too soon, it does say natural colors here, so it's just colors from fruit juices and stuff."

"It does have fruity in the name." Lucas was nothing if not fair minded.

His father nodded.

"Is Mom coming home today?" Lucas carried his bowl carefully to the sink, spilling it only at the last minute. He looked at his dad, but Bill just smiled. He didn't give a shit about the floor.

"No, honey. But we can Skype her later, maybe. Do you know where your shoes are?"

Lucas nodded and went to get them. He came back with two almost identical shoes, but both were the left foot. Bill sent him to find another pair just like it, and then sat on the bottom of the stairs and leaned his head against the wall. He closed his eyes and thought of his wife, of the year she'd done this morning routine without him knowing any of it. She'd never told him footwear was such an issue. No wonder she'd left; the shoes were just too much.

"I'll text your mom," said Bill, as Lucas stomped down the stairs, carrying two more shoes, neither of which matched. "We'll set a time, OK?" He got up and looked under the sofa, rewarded by a shoe that matched one of the four Lucas had harvested. He crouched down in front of his little boy who leaned his head forward until it touched his dad's head, and kept it there. Bill felt tears well up in his throat, the sweetness of the gesture surprising him. It should be Julie's head that felt this little touch, it should be Julie's hands stretching the Velcro straps. But it wasn't, and that was how it was. He straightened up and stood, towering over Lucas, who looked up at him trustingly.

"Promise?"

Bill smiled at him. "I promise I'll text her. I can't promise she will be able to talk. Sometimes she's too busy, remember?"

"This work is taking a very long time, Daddy."

Bill picked him up. "Yeah, baby. It really is."

———

Ten minutes later, with Lally, Lucas, Wyatt, and Milo already in their spots, Ava with earbuds in, backpacks kicking about on the car's messy floor, Frances pulled up outside Anne's house to get Kate and Theo. Anne stood there, her arms folded across her celadon T-shirt and smiled a small smile at Frances.

"Thanks for taking them," she said, her eyes expressing a different gratitude. "I took your advice," she added, "and stopped doing that thing we talked about the other day."

Frances paused for a moment, listening for the clunk of the sliding door finishing its slow groove, and looked wide-eyed at her friend. "You did?"

"Yes." Anne nodded. "I decided you were right and it wasn't a good idea."

"Uh, great," said Frances. "We can talk about it later." *Later when I don't have seven bat-eared children in the car, children who ask questions as they occur to them, context notwithstanding.*

"OK." Anne smiled, her face calm.

Frances pulled away, strangely uncomforted by this exchange. She looked at Anne standing there in the rearview, still with her arms folded, unmoving. There was no outward sign of her recklessness; she just looked normal. Frances pulled her eyebrows together, and flicked the indicator.

Something inside that was always denied
For so many years. Bye, Bye.

Thirteen.

After drop-off there was a PTA meeting at the elementary school, so Frances was heading back there once she was done at the preschool. Preschool drop-off took time, though, what with book reading, multiple hugs, and a surreptitious glance at today's snack.

Frances was now old enough to resist what she referred to as The Tyranny of Snack. It started innocently enough, when your first child started preschool. For the first week or so the school would offer the kids goldfish crackers, fruit, whatever, and put together a roster of parents who would bring in a snack in the future. Then a hunting horn sounded and all hell broke loose, but in a very progressive, mutually respectful way, of course.

First blood would be drawn by those parents who baked. Frances had had the misfortune of Ava being in a preschool class with a world-famous chef, who would send in tiny tartlets, each one folded like origami, filled with fresh figs and mascarpone. For three-year-olds, who took one bite and declared them "yucky." Others sent in baby chia muffins, or curated granola bars, baked from scratch and containing at least four grams of omega-3s per serving. One time Frances reached out to snag a homemade cheese straw and realized it was literally the best cheese straw in the history of the world. There were two little boys using them as light sabers, crumbs flying everywhere, and it was all Frances could do not to confiscate them.

Then there would be a murmuring about gluten intolerance, and baked goods would give way to fresh fruit, washed and presented artistically. Sometimes there would be a confit of some sort to dip things in, other times the fruit would be cut into shapes. Generally, it was a no-no to just buy a fruit platter at the grocery store and dump it on the table. The fruit had to be decanted into artisanal bowls of indeterminate national origin. "We're teaching the children to appreciate presentation," one mother had explained to Frances. "We're raising their aesthetic bar." Seeing as that mother's child had another kid in a headlock around the corner and was forcing sand down his pants, Frances wasn't sure aesthetics was going to be his primary challenge, but she let it go. She also simply stopped signing up for snack once Milo started school, and now that Lally was there she just went to Costco and bought Cheez-Its in bulk instead. If it was a banner day she would find the ones with letters on them, and consider herself ahead of the game.

Anyway, elementary school was a different arena. In that one, fights were held at PTA meetings. Frances kissed Lally goodbye and drove to the school. There she donned her full-body armor, grabbed her pepper spray, and headed into the auditorium.

Hunting for a familiar face and somewhere to sit, she spotted Lili Girvan. Tiptoeing around the other parents she sat next to her and hissed, "What did I miss?"

"Not much," replied Lili. "So far there's just been the naked human sacrifice and the lamb-shearing contest."

"Oh, thank God," said Frances.

Miss Delgado stood at the front, clutching a sheaf of papers. She was the assistant head, and nominally in charge of the *T* part of the PTA. The *P* section was represented by Erica Feinberg, a dermatologist and professional viper, who'd served time for lasering off someone's entire head, on purpose. That wasn't true, but she was a bitch. She'd started out as secretary, then treasurer, and now had attained the highest office possible in a medium-size public charter school: president of the PTA. It was heady stuff, apparently, because Erica's eyes were gleaming.

Lili leaned closer. "Could Erica's pupils be any wider?" She paused. "Do you think she did cocaine this morning?"

"Before school?"

Lili shrugged as Miss Delgado began to speak.

"Thank you all for coming, we certainly appreciate your time. We'll try and move through the agenda as quickly as possible. I know you all have places to be."

"Although," put in Erica, "I know we all consider this our most important job."

"Not me," said a voice from the front, and everyone laughed. Natalie Clements was the mother of a sixth grader, and she'd been at every PTA meeting Frances had ever attended. She was a comedy writer on a TV show and couldn't keep her mouth shut. Some people came to PTA meetings just to enjoy Natalie. Erica hated her, which was a huge point in Natalie's favor.

Miss Delgado, who regularly faced hundreds of children with nary a hint of mortal fear, kept moving on.

"Our first item is next semester's after-school enrichment offerings. We have a couple of new options, in addition to the standard arts and crafts, yoga, and drumming circle." She looked again at a piece of paper, as if to check the words hadn't changed.

"First off, we are adding knitting and crochet, because we discovered Miss Mariachi can knit and crochet and I caught her at a weak moment." Another laugh came from the crowd, who were clearly overcaffeinated. "The other new offering is gardening, which has been generously funded by an anonymous donor, including the building of brand-new raised beds and a new gardening teacher." There was a small round of applause, and Miss Delgado could be seen blushing. Apparently, the new gardening teacher was handsome. Frances turned to Lili.

"Is that your Dutch guy?"

Lili shook her head. "He may have had something to do with the anonymous donation, and it's possible my kids guilted him into it, but the teacher is a young guy who just graduated from college."

"Why is Miss Delgado blushing?"

"He's young, attractive, single, and multilingual. Entirely blushworthy."

Miss Delgado cleared her throat. "We also have a couple of suggestions from Erica, based on feedback she's received from other parents." There was a pause. "Apparently."

The room grew watchful. It was extremely rare for Miss Delgado to throw shade. Something Was Afoot.

Erica stepped forward and smiled a cosmetically enhanced smile that nonetheless managed to look natural, which is why she made the big bucks. "Esther Avilar has offered to teach Reiki after school this year, which would be great." Someone raised a hand, but Erica anticipated. "*Reiki* is a healing modality dealing with the redirection of life energy." The hand went back up. "A healing modality is just a method of treatment." And up it went again. "And *life energy* is precisely what it sounds like."

This time the hand waved and Erica snapped out, "Yes, Elliott?"

Elliott Schaefer had twin boys in the fourth grade. They had plenty of life energy. "Doesn't Reiki involve the laying on of hands?"

Erica shook her head. "No, it involves the hovering of hands just above the body, to rearrange the chi."

"Well, putting the chi to one side, I'm not sure that's a good idea. My kids aren't ready to master hovering."

"So, don't sign them up. You are your child's best advocate, remember."

Elliott started to add more, but Erica called on someone else. The mother of a girl named Araminta asked, "What about personal boundaries and space issues?"

The mother of a boy named Ronin: "Would these classes be in gender-specific groups?" And then, adding quickly, "Organized by the gender the child identifies with, of course, not with their gender at birth." A chorus of "of courses" could be heard rippling across the room. This crowd was nothing if not intersectionally aware.

Erica coughed. "We're just opening up discussion at this point, and these are all good points for further evaluation. Another suggestion is cooking, but obviously not with actual heat or anything. Children would be encouraged to use fresh vegetables to make delicious dishes."

"A salad-tossing class?" Natalie asked incredulously. "What could possibly go wrong?"

"Finally," Erica was not to be deterred, "junior cotillion."

And there it was. The hand grenade they'd been waiting for. Miss Delgado had her eyes down, admiring her bright, white Keds. Frances flicked a glance at Lili, who had closed her eyes to appreciate the moment. You might think cotillion, which is basically a class where kids learn to be overly polite, to use the right fork, and where boys learn to open doors for girls, is a trivial offering, but you would be wrong. It is a fulcrum of dispute between two parenting paradigms, at least in Los Angeles.

One approach holds that kids need to be taught good manners, that they are an Important Life Skill. The other believes children shouldn't be forced into the societal norms of the hegemony, and should be encouraged to express themselves authentically. The vast majority of parents, of course, have no real opinion either way, try not to use the word *hegemony* at all, and are just stumbling through the day trying not to get banana smeared on themselves. Frances had noticed that both opinionated camps had fierce devotees who were primed and ready to sound off about them. She looked around. About two-thirds of the room were slowly slipping down in their seats, getting comfortable; while the other third, the true believers, were sitting up and sharpening their shivs.

Later that evening Frances told Michael about it.

"Elodie Keene opened the fight by standing up and saying cotillion reinforced the patriarchy."

Michael was pulling off his shoes. "A nice opener. Simple, to the point."

Frances nodded. "I thought so. Erica came back that she didn't need to enroll her kid if she didn't want to, and Elodie responded that she wouldn't enroll her in a chapter of the KKK, either, but it didn't mean she'd accept one on campus."

Her husband's shoe dropped at the same time as his jaw. "She did not."

"Oh, she did. Jessica Artessian—I know, she has too many *s*'s in her name, we've covered this before—stood up and said learning good manners was not in the same league as burning crosses, which is true, generally speaking."

"Yes, but she still has too many . . ."

"Which produced the response from David Millar that cotillion belonged in the same drawer of history as burning crosses, and then it all got out of hand."

"Brilliant. Why don't I come to these things?"

"Because we rock, paper, scissored for it and I lost."

Lally wandered in, deeply aggrieved. "I have my finger stuck in an aardvark."

"If I had a dime . . ." said Michael, as he reached out for his daughter. "I see the problem." There was a Littlest Pet Shop head on Lally's pinkie. "Where is its body?"

"In the dog."

"OK." He wiggled the toy, and eventually managed to squeeze it hard enough that the neck hole got bigger and she was able to pull her finger out. He handed it to her, she said, "Thanks," and ran off to do it again.

"Those are the skills they should teach in the prenatal class, along with diapering."

Frances laughed. "Finger removal?"

"That sounds dark. Finger release?"

"That sounds dirty. Finger extraction?"

"OK. They also need to teach Toddler Hiding Techniques. It took me a while to realize if my keys were missing that I needed to check doll purses first."

"Yeah. And in the oven."

"The toilet."

"The back of the diaper they're currently wearing."

"Exactly. So how did the meeting end up?"

"Stalemate. A show of hands revealed parents were split three ways."

"Three?"

"Ten for, ten against, and the rest no opinion."

"See, this is the problem with parents today. No commitment."

He sat down in his favorite chair and opened his laptop. Yes, it was the start of another evening that was just like every other evening at the Bloom house. "You managed not to sign up for anything, right?"

"Well . . ."

He closed his laptop—success—and frowned at her. "Frank, you made me promise to prevent you from signing up for anything. Last year the Walk-A-Thon nearly killed you."

"I know, I know. I walked out of the elementary meeting completely unscathed. However, I did agree to go to a meeting about the High School Spring Fling."

Michael made a disgusted noise and opened his computer. "You're beyond help."

She gazed at him. "Are you seeing someone else?"

He closed his computer. "This is about Anne?"

She didn't say anything. On the one hand they had such a low-sex marriage that she could understand if he was having an affair, or getting blow jobs from hookers, or whatever, but on the other hand she was certain her heart would stop beating without him. "We don't . . . you don't want to have sex with me anymore." She swallowed. "It wouldn't be impossible for you to be sleeping with someone else. You are human."

He put his computer to one side and stood to walk over to her. For a split second she was genuinely terrified. Oh God, he was seeing someone and he's about to confirm it, and it's all going to come crashing down just like it did when Alex died, just as suddenly and irrevocably as a giant Acme safe through the roof. Michael sat next to her on the bed.

"Frank. I love you very, very much. I'm not having sex with anyone, including you. Sometimes I worry that you're seeing someone else. We used to have a lot of sex, remember?"

She smiled at him, holding his hand. "I remember."

"But then we had kids, and dogs, and started working longer hours and using our free time to sleep instead of fool around, and here we are. I'm happy, Frances. No sex on the planet is worth losing our life together."

"Not even a blow job from Angelina Jolie?"

He frowned at her. "We agreed Angelina was the only exception."

She nodded. "For both of us, if I remember rightly."

He looked relieved. "OK then."

Frances looked into his gray-green eyes, his long lashes, his face that had softened and widened with age, his hair that was largely no longer there. "She called the other day, you know."

"Again?"

"She sounded upset."

He shrugged, leaning forward and kissing her on the lips, firmly. "I've tried to let her down gently, but she takes these things so seriously."

"Actresses."

"Right?" He stood up. "We're OK, Frances, don't worry. Just because Anne can't keep her pants on doesn't mean anything to us, OK?"

Frances nodded. But as he opened his laptop and went back to work, she wondered.

Fourteen.

Lucas was talking to his mother on Skype as Bill made dinner in the kitchen. He could see his little son, or at least the top of his head, over the laptop screen. And he could hear his wife. He could tell she was tired, just by the way she was asking Lucas about his day. He frowned to himself. If she had him to help her, she wouldn't be so fucking tired.

"And did you have fun?"

The top of Lucas's head bobbed. "Yes, it was awesome."

"Did everyone from class go?"

More bobbing. "Yes, except for Alison, she's sick. So, she didn't come. She was at home. Sick."

"OK. And did you see lots of spiders?"

"Lots!! Some of the girls were scared, but I wasn't. Why are girls scared of spiders?"

"It's not just girls. Lots of people are scared of spiders."

"Are you?"

"No."

"What are you scared of?"

There was a pause, and Bill looked over at the back of the screen. He knew she'd be wondering what to tell him. She wasn't scared of much, his wife. She was a tough woman who'd grown up in near-poverty in the rural Midwest, made it to college, and didn't talk about her childhood much. They had met randomly in the library, fallen deeply in love after a week, and been together ever since. He'd never met her mother. Her father was never mentioned.

"I don't like being cold."

Lucas peeped over the top of his screen at his dad. "No one likes being cold. But are you *scared* of it?" His dad looked at him and smiled, thinking of the possibly hundreds of times he'd brought Julie a blanket, a sweater, his jacket, a hot water bottle. She really didn't like being cold. He hoped she wasn't cold right then, and then realized there was nothing he could do if she was. She didn't want his help anymore.

"I guess not. I'm scared of sharks."

Lucas made a snorting noise. "My teacher said more people are killed by cows every year than are killed by sharks."

"Really? Maybe I should be scared of cows."

Bill could hear she was running out of energy. There was a time difference, it was later where she was, and he knew she'd had a busy day. "Come on, kid, it's time for dinner. Say goodbye to Mommy, and come eat." He called out, "Bye, Jules, I'll call you later."

"OK," her voice floated back, and then dropped as she murmured good nights and much love to her son. Bill knew what she was really terrified of was never seeing Lucas again, but they didn't need to talk about that.

They never talked about it, in fact.

———

Ava was also on Skype, as it happened, that service's ethereal wires humming with bedtime chatter between parents and kids, grandparents and kids.

"So, how's your mom?"

Ava shrugged and smiled at her grandma. "She's fine, I guess. She's always fine, right? She's the most even-tempered person on the planet, which is so annoying. Was she always like that?"

Her grandmother laughed. "Oh yes, she was a very stable kid." She dropped her voice. "One might even say boring, except that she was also very sweet and friendly and most people liked her a lot." She looked sad, fleetingly. "I think I left her alone too much."

Ava snorted. "Well, she hasn't repeated your mistake, unfortunately. She's always up in my beak."

"She loves you."

"I know."

"She worries about you."

"There's no need. Everything's fine."

Her grandmother snorted, the original that came down through time and genetics to her granddaughter. "Please, Ava. There is nothing fine about being fourteen. It's a total mess."

"It's OK. Parts are OK."

"The whole period from eleven to fifteen is pretty much a yawning chasm of pain."

"A catastrophe of confusion."

"A maelstrom of unrelenting hormonal surges and storms."

"OK, you win, Grandma. I don't want to talk to you about hormones, please. That's weird."

"Why?"

"Because I can barely get my head around them in the peace and quiet of my room, let alone discussing them openly." She looked at her spotty socks and flexed her feet, wishing she had longer toes. Just one more thing that wasn't perfect about her.

Grandma sighed. "Your generation is far more prudish than

mine. You get naked online, you send topless self-chats, or whatever you call them, but when it comes to having a private conversation about basic biology you get all squeamish."

"Kids these days," said Ava. Her mother's voice floated up from downstairs. Dinner was ready. "I've got to go, Grandma, dinner. We'll talk soon, yeah?"

"Of course. Give your mom a hug and kiss from me. And your brother and sister, please. When are they going to get on this thing?"

Ava got up, carrying the laptop over to her desk. "I don't know. Milo has a laptop. I'll help him put it on. Lally doesn't have anything, but she could use mine, I guess."

"That would be nice. Go eat your dinner, baby."

After Ava had folded the screen down she stood there for a moment, her hand resting on her computer, a smile still in her eyes.

———

Wyatt and his mom were having dinner alone that night. Sara was shooting a commercial and was running late, as usual.

"Will Mommy be home in time for bed?" Wyatt was talking with his mouth full, but Iris didn't care. Mommy was Sara. Iris was Mom.

She shook her head. "I don't think so, sweetheart. She wants to be, but sometimes these things take longer than you'd like."

Wyatt nodded wisely. "Directors."

Iris smiled. "Exactly."

He turned up his hands, one of which was holding a carrot. "And don't get me started on the studio."

His mom laughed out loud and he joined her, thrilled to have pulled off a comedy bit. It was a relatively new skill, and he was crushing it. Iris leaned across the table and stroked his cheek where it grinned, a petal-soft swelling of happiness. She was blown away by him, then as ever. When he was small he'd basically gotten his words from Iris and Sara, so although she would sometimes hear her wife in what he said, she rarely heard anything surprising. Then he started watching TV and things from shows cropped up, little references from *Dora* or songs from *Sesame Street*, tiny nuggets of cultural exchange. But once he'd started school, and started listening more carefully to the conversations of adults, suddenly a whole new lexicon opened up and for the first time he brought fresh material to the table and, more thrilling still, ideas of his own.

It reminded her of his first smile at six weeks, that moment when the beauty of nature revealed itself by producing a smile at *exactly the right moment* to prevent parents from taking their irritating little blob and exposing it on a hillside. *Hello, parents*, said the smile, *look, I am an actual human being, I will make all this exhausting trouble worth it.* And your heart pulled a total Grinch and expanded three sizes. Now, looking at her son doing comedy bits he'd learned from his other mother, the woman she loved so much, she thought there might come a time her ribs wouldn't be able to hold it all.

———

Anne was sitting with Kate, later that same evening, reading to her. They were lying next to each other on Kate's bed, Anne on her tummy, propping the book in front of her. Kate was curled up, holding a knitted bunny, lifting her head whenever Anne said there was a picture.

"She's naughty, isn't she?" asked Kate. They were reading *Junie B. Jones*.

Anne smiled. "She's just a kid. She's not really naughty, she's just full of beans."

"Would you be mad at me if I cut the dog's hair?"

"Well, we don't have a dog, so I would be confused rather than mad. You'd have to go get a dog and then cut its hair."

Kate giggled. "It's a lot of trouble."

"Right." Anne leaned on one elbow to free her other hand to stroke Kate's hair. Kate gazed at her, still amused by the idea of the dog. Anne could see Charlie in Kate's bone structure, but saw herself in her daughter's eyes. Each child was such a blend of history, of influences forgotten generations ago, but saved in DNA to confer height or a sense of humor or green eyes. Anne suddenly thought back to the aborted conversation she'd tried to have with Richard that day. She'd called him several times, but he'd never answered, and only texted back at the very end of the day that he'd been monitoring exams and hadn't had his phone. Did she want to meet up? Was Charlie away? He wanted her.

No, she'd texted back, we'll talk tomorrow.

I love you, he'd said, and she'd deleted the conversation.

"I love you, Mom," said Kate, snuggling into her shoulder. "Keep reading."

So, Anne turned back to Junie and the unfortunate Tickle, and tried to pretend her biggest failure as a parent was not getting her kids a dog whose hair they could cut.

Fifteen.

The next morning Lucas had a fever, so Bill texted Frances not to pick him up. Thank God for cell phones. Frances frequently listened to Ava bitch about not having one, watched her classmates all sitting with their heads bowed over their devices like penguins with their eggs, and wondered if they were destroying an entire generation's ability to have a regular conversation. But then something would happen—she'd be able to coordinate an entire carpool, or arrange last-minute babysitting, or order something from Amazon—and she would sigh at her own reliance on her shiny little oblong. She wondered if parents watching their kids picking up books back in the eighteenth century had worried that they were going to rot their minds. And then she wondered if she was too fat, and should she download a tracking app of some kind.

"I'm sorry, Anne, did you say something?" She was suddenly aware she'd been gazing at Anne as her kids clambered into the back of the car and that it was possible the other woman had said something to her.

Anne smiled, although she looked anxious and uncharacteristically messy for once. "Yeah, but it was only good morning."

"Good morning," replied Frances automatically.

There was an awkward pause. Fortunately, the kids helped by starting a squabble in the back over who sat where, so Frances was able to turn away from Anne to take care of it. By the time she was ready to pull away from the curb Anne had already gone back inside.

"Mommy didn't say goodbye!" wailed Kate.

This was really A Thing. Kids who seemed mature and capable of many irritating things were thrown to the floor when their parents failed to say goodbye. To discover a parent had left the house without the correct handoff could ruin a whole day. Proof, if proof were needed, that children were masters of magical thinking. Frances knew better than to breeze through it. She started to dial Anne's number but then just punched her seat belt and got out, jogging up Anne's path to knock on the door.

Anne opened it, holding her phone and looking worried. "What?"

"You forgot to say goodbye," Frances said, already turning and heading back to the car.

"Shit, sorry." Anne followed her and there was a sweetly sentimental goodbye scene, as if she was putting her kids on the Kindertransport, rather than sending them to public school for a few hours.

Eventually it was done, everyone felt emotionally ready to face the day, and Frances was able to pull away. Ava had gone temporarily blind from excessive eye rolling, but apart from that, all was well.

———

Anne went back inside, determined to end the affair she'd been having for six months, and making a mental note to not forget to say goodbye in the future.

Charlie was still wandering around upstairs, so she took him a cup of coffee.

"Thanks, babe," he said, pulling her close and smelling roses in her hair. "What are you doing today?"

"Not sure. Not much." *Breaking up with my boyfriend.*

"Do you want to have lunch?"

"Sure, that would be nice. Where?" *Assuming I stop feeling nauseous long enough to eat.*

He named somewhere they'd been before, close to his office. She nodded, and went to get herself more coffee, too. *I can barely see for panic.*

Charlie watched her turn the corner of their bedroom door, and smiled all the way down to his toes. He was a lucky man. He turned around and sat down on the edge of the bed to put on his shoes. Maybe he'd stop at the little hipster jewelry store Anne loved so much, and pick her up a gift he could give her at lunch. She was a sucker for pretty things, always had been. When they'd first met she'd not been all that interested in him. She was an art student, he was a law student, they couldn't have had that much in common. She was a free spirit but, it soon became clear, a free spirit with a serious penchant for silk underwear and vintage jewelry. He blandished her with gifts until he could charm her into falling in love, and here they were, a decade later, still together.

Charlie tied his shoelaces, and stood, shaking his suit into place, satisfied with his lot.

———

It turned out that breaking up really was hard to do. Anne called Richard and explained the situation. As soon as she heard his voice she'd stopped feeling anxious and sick. She was going to end this, and she was going to be free of it. End of story.

"But nothing has changed," he protested. Why had she never noticed how whiny he was?

"Yes," she said, firmly. "You texted me the other night and my kid saw it and I suddenly realized I don't want to do this anymore. It's very simple, Richard, it's over. Please just accept it." She was in her underwear in the bathroom, choosing an outfit to have lunch in. She wanted to make an effort for Charlie. She needed to turn this ship around. She looked at her body briefly; it was still good. The best side effect of infidelity, it turned out, was improved core strength and muscle tone. Young men were so energetic. Her particular young man was still talking, so she dragged her attention back.

"I'll be more careful. I won't text you at all anymore. Please come see me. I miss you so much." He was in his office at school, having gone in early in the hope of talking to her before his day began. He woke up thinking of her, went to lunch thinking of her, held his dick and peed thinking of her, washed his hands thinking of her. He knew it was getting dangerous, he could feel himself losing control, knew on several levels that payback was going to be a bitch. He just couldn't handle it being over *now*. He needed more.

"No, Richard. I'm not going to see you again. It's been fun, but you knew it was never going anywhere. I never wanted to leave my family. I never lied to you." Everyone else, yes, but not you.

"I know." Silence. "I'm coming to see you."

"No."

"Please. Let's go to bed. We can talk about it after I make you come like a million times."

She wrinkled her nose. "No. This is it, Richard. We're done. Goodbye." She hung up and went back to her closet. The celadon dress, which said elegant woman of a certain age, or the overalls, which said hip young mother who still gave blow jobs? Such a tough call.

Three miles away in his office, Richard put his head on his desk and sobbed.

———

It just so happened that when Sara walked into the restaurant where she was meeting her agent for lunch, the first person she spotted was Charlie, the guy who lived up the road and was married to that cool drink of water whose name she couldn't remember right away. He saw her, too, because he was watching the door. He raised his hand in greeting.

"Hey, Charlie, how's it going?" Sara leaned down for a kiss, and suddenly remembered his wife's name. Anne, her name was Anne. They didn't really know each other, but they had a kid in Wyatt's class . . . ? Iris took care of all of that stuff.

"Hi, Sara." He was pleased he'd remembered her name. "Everything's good with me, how're things down the street?"

She smiled. "Good. Are you meeting Anne for lunch?" Look, see how casually I display my knowledge. I do know you, we know each other, we are friends and neighbors, and I didn't just screw up the social contract.

He nodded. "Yeah, although she's late. Mind you, she's always late, so that's not a big deal. Are you meeting Iris?" Five points for remembering the other lesbian's name. He didn't consciously think of them as "the lesbians," but that was one of their many tags: neighbors, parents, women, hot women (this one in front of him, the other one not so much), famous people (again, this one, not the other one), parents of a son, a friend of Milo's, people in the kids' carpool, people one saw at the holidays, people one saw at soccer practice . . . It was a long list of tags.

Sara shook her head, and then made eye contact with her agent, whom she'd spotted at a table in the back. "No, I'm here for work. I see my person. I'd better go."

"Sure, well, see you in the 'hood." He smiled, pleased to have navigated their little exchange without messing up anyone's name. Anne took care of all that stuff. As he thought that, Anne walked in the door and his head turned, along with several others. She had her own set of tags in his head, of course, but the most important one was Best Friend, and he was pleased to see her. He stood up as she approached the table and she smiled her incredible smile, the one that touched him to the core, the one that made him think of the birth of his children, the first time he'd kissed their little wet heads and then looked up into Anne's eyes and felt that nameless connection nothing could explain or express sufficiently. Nothing would take that away; that was in their bones.

"Hey, babe," she said, sliding into the chair across from him. "Did you order?" She looked around at the beautiful room, the cream walls, the open fireplace, the open French windows into the garden. L.A. was so beautiful, now that her conscience was clear.

He shook his head. "I just ran into Sara whatshername from up the road."

"Iris's wife? Frances's cousin?"

He frowned. "Is she?"

"Is she what?"

"Frances's cousin?"

Anne smiled at him. "She's not. Sara's not. But Iris is, her wife. Iris is Frances's cousin on her mother's side."

"Oh yeah?" Charlie was always surprised at how much information about other people women knew. He didn't think he was being sexist, it was just not something he ever heard from his guy friends: Hey, did you know that Arthur, who is Danny's cousin by marriage, and the one who did that thing at Christmas, do you remember? Anyway, did you know that Arthur has diabetes, which is not all that surprising seeing as his grandmother died of it. Nope, that was not a typical guy conversation, although maybe he was just hanging out with the wrong guys.

"Yes. Frances and Iris basically grew up together. Her brother died, you know."

"Iris's?" He was getting hungry, and this was now edging into boring.

"No, Frances's." She could see he was losing interest, and to be fair, it wasn't all that interesting. She wasn't one of those women who was fascinated by other people; she just maintained the most basic database. "Are you hungry?"

He nodded, and opened the menu. "What appeals to you?"

"Apart from you?"

He looked up in surprise. She was smiling at him in a way she hadn't for a while, that slow smile that said she wanted him. He raised his eyebrows. "Have you been drinking?"

Her grin deepened. "No. You just look sexy today, is that a problem? You are my husband, after all, aren't I allowed to find you attractive?"

He felt himself stirring, and reached across the table. "Of course, it's just been a while."

"Maybe it's been too long?" He heard a soft *thud*, and then her bare foot started moving up his leg, pressing.

Charlie was taken aback. Not in a bad way, necessarily, but still. Anne was flirting with him in a way she hadn't in a long time. A very long time. There wasn't so much need for foreplay and seduction when you were sure of someone, when you knew their body so well, the order of their lovemaking, the process that worked. When couples complained that the romance was gone from their marriage this was what they were missing. The insecurity, the tension, the subtle but powerful question and answer of seduction. Maybe this time I won't get her into bed . . . But after buying that bed, washing the sheets, maybe having a case or two of flu in it, it was pretty much a given.

He crossed his legs, trapping her foot. Then he reached down and started tickling her arch, watching the color mount in her face as she tried not to laugh. His fingers moved higher, and she stopped laughing.

He looked for the waitress, and called for the check.

———

Later that afternoon, after Charlie had left her half asleep in bed and had gone back to the office, Anne decided to purge her clothing. If Richard had ever seen it, it was going in the trash. Clothes he'd seen her in, underwear he'd taken in his mouth and tugged down her thighs, all of it was going. Then she showered, dressed, went to the store, and bought six new sets of bras and panties, all of it in a size smaller than she'd purchased last time. She hadn't been this slim since her twenties; the affair had given her back her body. And now that body was just for her husband, and everything was going to be fine.

She thought about his face earlier, when she'd slowly undressed for him the way she had when they'd first been together. He'd looked younger, too, hot eyed with desire, and it had been very, very good. She was still pleasingly aware of herself, a slight soreness in her muscles and skin. She was filled with triumph as she handed over her credit card, smiling at the assistant. She'd pulled it off, and Charlie would never know. She'd successfully rebooted her marriage and everything was OK. She looked at her watch. Time to go home and get ready for the kids.

Sixteen.

*I*t was nearly four, and Frances was herding Theo and Kate down toward Anne's house just as Richard pulled up in front of it. He got out and started toward Anne's door, not seeing the kids until he was nearly on top of them. His arrival at the end of Anne's path coincided to an almost comical degree with theirs, and both parties came to a polite halt. The front door opened and Anne called to the kids, not seeing Richard until the words were out of her mouth. To add to the general Marx Brothers–ness of the moment, Charlie's car pulled up in front of the house and parked behind Richard's, and his kids started bouncing up and down and calling, "Daddy!" in amazed tones, as if he'd just returned from several years in exile, rather than eight hours at the office. Anne went pale and turned to see if Frances was there. She was, and she was moving. She was pretty sure the guy on Anne's path was her boyfriend, and she was one hundred percent confident Charlie was about to run into him. *But don't worry, sister,* said her swift, sneakered footfall, *the cavalry was on the way.*

Charlie got out of the car and walked around, grinning at the kids, his eyes only on them. They threw themselves at him, presumably overcome by the surprise of seeing him *in the street*, rather than *in the house*. *What the hell?* their little faces said, *we didn't see that coming!* Kids were like dogs in this way: happy to unexpectedly see you. Although, unlike dogs, they were also just as likely to hate you and blame you for everything, including the weather and the physics of bodies in motion. Lally and Lucas, who had been left to clamber out of the car alone, started bleating after Frances, sensing that something interesting was going on. Ava, of course, had already gone into the house, earbuds on, head down.

Had Charlie's car pulled up ten seconds later, or had Anne opened the door ten seconds earlier, or had Richard known anything at all about the public-school timetable, this situation would never have happened. But, you know, life is hilarious that way.

Richard was halfway up Anne's path when Charlie noticed him. Richard was looking at Anne, and suddenly put it all together. Until that split second he'd thought she'd opened the door for him, and that the adorable kids were just local color and not two tiny horsemen of the apocalypse. The realization that they were her kids, and that therefore the man they were hanging on was almost certainly her husband, made him freeze in place like a rabbit. This inability to multitask and improvise is why women are just better.

"Hey, wrong house, doofus!" called Frances, smiling widely. "Hey, Charlie, how's things?"

"Good," replied Charlie, frowning and trying to parse the scene. Frances moved past him and hailed Richard again.

"We're one forty-two, not one thirty-two, goober." She had reached Richard and gave him a hug. "It's just as well I caught you before you embarrassed yourself by going to the wrong house, right?"

"Right," said Richard, struggling to catch up. He looked over at Anne, who looked, if anything, slightly annoyed. "Sorry."

Kate and Theo blew past them and hurtled into the house, telling their mother about how bizarre it was their own father showed up outside their own house. Charlie was behind them, and paused politely for an introduction.

"Charlie, this is Phil. Phil, this is Charlie, my neighbor." Richard stuck out his hand, automatically, and he and his lover's husband shook hands politely. Fortunately, Anne missed this cosmic ridiculousness, having already turned blindly to follow her kids and shake some crackers into a bowl. She'd turned her life and fate over to the gods, in the earthly form of Frances. Besides, nothing could go wrong now, she'd already fixed this problem, hadn't she? She'd done the right thing.

"Nice to meet you, Phil," said Charlie with his usual easy charm, and then he paused again. "How do you two know each other?"

"School," said Frances.

"Work," said Richard.

There was a pause. "Both," amended Frances. "School for me and work for him. He works at the art college, and Ava was thinking of applying. We know each other through a mutual friend, and he came over to chat with us about the application process." This sounded utterly lame to her, but it was what she had at that moment. Fortunately, Charlie wasn't considering the possibility of her lying to him, as she'd never done it before, and took it at face value.

"Wow," he said, "you're way ahead, aren't you?" He laughed. "What's next, visits from Harvard and Yale?"

"That's next week," said Frances. "Come on, Phil, let's let Charlie get on with his evening."

"Of course," said Richard, pale but pulling it together. "I could use a cup of coffee, it's been a long day."

"I bet," said Frances.

"Well, see you around," said Charlie, heading in to his wife, a small jewelry box hidden in his suit pocket. He'd spent more than usual, still reeling from the sexy Anne who'd appeared that afternoon. The door closed.

There was a pause, and then Frances turned and started walking away, followed by Richard, Lally, and Lucas, like a gaggle of goslings.

They'd reached Frances's house before she gathered herself enough to turn and face Richard. "We don't really need advice on art school applications. You can go home."

Richard stared at her.

"Don't start crying, please," she said, keeping her voice low. "Lally, you and Lucas can go inside, OK?"

"Is Lucas going to play?"

"Yes, honey, for a little bit until his dad gets home."

"Can we watch TV?"

"Yes, sweetie." Once the door closed behind the kids she turned back to Richard. "Look, I realize you don't know me at all, but . . ."

"You're the one who walked in on us the other morning." His voice was deep and sexy, but to Frances it just sounded sad. "It all started to fall apart after that."

Frances was firm. "Yes, that was me, but I'll be blunt, it was never together in the first place. You just nearly destroyed Anne's life, and whether you agree she deserves it for having an affair in the first place, I would hope you agree that her kids don't deserve to see their lives unravel in real time, before they've even had an after-school snack."

"I didn't realize they would be around," said Richard.

"School gets out at three."

"Art school doesn't. I'm sorry."

Frances shrugged. "Go home. She doesn't want to see you anymore."

Richard turned and walked away, the set of his shoulders as depressed as anything Frances had ever seen. She kept watching until his car turned the far corner, and then she sighed. What a fucking shit show. And now she was part of it.

———

Inside the house everything was as usual. There might be a storm brewing down the street, but here the leaves weren't even rustling. Frances sighed and walked into the kitchen, realizing when she saw Ava that she'd been smug too soon.

"Who were you talking to outside?"

"What?"

"Just now. I wanted to ask you a question, so I stuck my head out of the door and you were talking to some guy."

"Some guy who needed directions." She paused. "What was the question?"

"Are you cheating on dad?"

"Was that the question?" Frances looked at her daughter. Her tone was cool, but her mother could see a telltale stiffness in her shoulders. Ava was freaked out.

"No, the question was about tea, but then I saw that guy and your face looked weird, not like someone giving directions."

Frances turned away from Ava, and walked over to the cupboard above the kettle where she kept the tea. "Which tea were you looking for?"

"Why aren't you answering me?"

Frances opened the cupboard and scanned the many boxes and tins of tea. Maybe one of them would have the answer printed on it. "Because it's a ridiculous question. Of course, I'm not cheating on your dad. If you must know, that guy was a friend of Anne's, and he and I were just chatting for a moment." Silence. Frances put the kettle on and went to the refrigerator to see if someone had crept into the house earlier and made dinner. Sadly not. Over her shoulder she said, "You're making too much of it." She leaned on the fridge door and suddenly spotted two pounds of ground beef hiding behind a wilting head of lettuce. *Nice try*, she thought, *it might have been a good spot before your little green friend gave up the ghost and got smaller.* She reached in. "Spaghetti and meatballs for dinner, OK?"

"Is Anne sleeping with that guy?"

Oh, for fuck's sake. Frances sighed. "Ava, it's an adult thing that's complicated and private, so, if I can quote something you say to me all the time: Stick to your own lane."

"Adult things are complicated? What do you think my life is, paint by numbers?"

OK, good, thought Frances, her daughter's teenage narcissism had dragged the topic back around to herself, so maybe we can move away from talking about Anne. She waited for what felt like inevitable follow-up questions, but when she looked up Ava had already left the room.

———

Lucas ended up staying for dinner because Bill got stuck in a meeting. As Frances watched him eat his spaghetti, chattering away to Lally about God only knew what, she marveled at the mystery of other people's children. It didn't matter how many children you had of your own, other people's children seemed alien. Well, to Frances anyway. Lucas was bigger than Lally, and moved differently. He was a boy, but she'd raised a boy. It wasn't that. He was just unfamiliar, and that made him appealing. He seemed nicer than her kids, better tempered, easier to deal with. Even though she knew this was completely untrue, she enjoyed the illusion.

The way children behaved with adults who weren't their parents was interesting. They were more polite, more accommodating, less inclined to bridle at the smallest thing. She knew this was true because other parents would tell her how well behaved her own children were. At home they would balk and kick up a fuss if a green vegetable even approached the table, whereas other moms would open the door to Frances after playdates and say things like, "Wow, Lally is such a good eater! She packed away the broccoli like a champ! I wish I could get TiddleyWink to eat vegetables like that!" or "It's always such a pleasure when Ava babysits, Frances, she's just so interesting to talk to. So chatty!" It was one of the paradoxes of parenting that the children you wished you had were actually the versions of your own children that other parents saw. The secretly much nicer versions. *Thank God parents talked to each other,* Frances thought, *or we'd all be circling the drain wishing our kids were like everyone else's.*

However, Lucas was, even his own parents would admit, a nice kid. Four was a difficult age, or had been for all of Frances's kids, but it seemed to suit him. He was ready to argue the toss over everything, like every four-year-old, but somehow it just came across like good-humored independence. As she knelt down and wiped the spaghetti sauce off his face, Frances could see Julie in his eyes, and wished she had gotten to know her better before she went wherever it was she had gone. And maybe she'd misjudged Julie, seeing as she was apparently able to leave this perfect child and her lovely husband to go off and follow her star, wherever that was. Maybe she was a selfish cow, and Frances had dodged a bullet by never becoming close with her. She doubted it, but everything she'd thought was true was turning out not to be, so why not that?

When Bill came to pick him up, full of unnecessary apologies, Lucas and Lally were both sleepily sitting on the sofa, being read to by Milo. As an older brother, Milo was frequently guilty of neglect, albeit benign, but he enjoyed being the bigger boy and after dinner they'd all played Legos until the littler ones got tired. Lally had asked Milo to read and Frances, tidying up in the kitchen, had reached for a dishtowel to dry her hands and take up the task, but Milo had surprised her by saying yes. For a moment she'd stood and listened to the soft questions he asked, determining whether they wanted a picture book or a chapter book, and the sounds of all three of them getting settled on the sofa together—*Do you want your blankie, Lally? Are you warm enough, Lucas?*—and her eyes suddenly filled with tears, remembering the feeling of her own brother's head against her shoulder, the soft ear of his stuffed bunny in his hands, folding and refolding as she read him *Mrs. Piggle-Wiggle.*

You grew up in a family, you left that family and then, life permitting, you built your own family using much of the same material. She would hear herself saying things to her children her mother had said to her, re-creating moments she hadn't even realized she'd treasured at the time. She did Christmas stockings the same way her parents had. The birthday child got to pick whatever meal they wanted. The tooth fairy left a silver half-dollar, inflation be damned. You give them the best eighteen years of your life, if you can, and you think about their health and happiness and choices and future and then they become adults and all that effort becomes a single line in their life story: *My mother made lunch for me every morning.* Or, *My dad was away a lot.* Or, *Yeah, my parents divorced, but it was cool.*

Frances had friends whose child, as a baby, had spent weeks in intensive care recovering from heart surgery, whose brief life had hung very much in the balance. Her friend would have slit her own throat to give that child life; she would have done anything at all to make it better. She'd cried and prayed and clutched her husband's hand in terror, and that whole experience would be related by her daughter as: *Yeah, funny story, I had heart surgery before I was even a year old! Crazy, right?* Frances remembered sitting with Ava as a baby, nursing at 2:00 a.m., looking down at her milk-drunk child and suddenly understanding that her mother had loved her like this, and that she loved her daughter more than her daughter would ever love her, and *that was how it was supposed to be.* You're supposed to walk away with only the very occasional backward glance, and only appreciate years later, as you hold your own child, how painful that was for your parents. As Vonnegut so elegantly said: "So it goes."

Bill came into the kitchen while Milo finished the book he was reading. Frances looked sad, which was unusual for her. But then she saw him and her face changed, smiling away whatever inner concerns she'd been contemplating.

"He's a nice boy, Milo." Bill smiled back at her, shaking his head at the offer of coffee. "I wish Lucas had a brother."

"He's welcome to borrow mine," said Ava, who was sitting at the kitchen table doing her homework. The dogs thumped their tails on the ground, hearing her voice.

Bill looked at Frances and smiled. "Thanks for being so helpful, Frances. I needed to stay at that meeting."

"Of course." Frances smiled. "What are friends for? He's very easy company, and he and Lally get on so well. It's our pleasure." She wanted suddenly to ask him where Julie was, but then Milo finished the book and the moment was gone.

Bill carried his son across the street, the little head nestled into the curve of his neck, and wished his wife wasn't so far away. They tried to Skype to say good night. "Maybe she was out, Lucas, or maybe she was already asleep. Tomorrow morning, for sure."

Bill put Lucas to bed, ate a ham sandwich standing over the sink in the kitchen, and went to bed himself. Maybe tomorrow morning would be better.

$\mathcal{S}$eventeen.

The next morning Anne watched Frances drive her kids away up the street then turned and went back into her house. Walking only a little way into the kitchen she picked up her phone and jabbed at it.

Hey.

No answer, no little dots letting her know he was writing her back. Anne got herself a second cup of coffee, listened to the silence of the house. Charlie had left for work, the kids were gone, she was queen of her domain. She looked at the phone . . . dots. Then his words appeared, and she could see the familiar planes of his face as he thought of her.

Hey, you.

What the fuck were you thinking yesterday?

Sorry. I have to talk to you.

No. It's over, please leave me alone.

I need to talk to you.

                                        Stop, Richard. It's over.

No. You can't end it over text,
we're not teenagers.

                                        I can, and I did. No more, Richard.
                                        I don't want to hurt my family.
                                        I'm blocking your number.

No, I love you.

                                        You don't. Don't contact me again.

Then she ended the conversation and put down her phone. Her face was wet with tears, unexpectedly, and she put her face in her cupped palms and wept. With grief because she would miss him, with fear because he wouldn't go away, and with relief because it had to be done and she had done it.

Then she heard a sound in the kitchen and looked up. Charlie was holding the iPad in a trembling hand, and his face was almost green it was so white.

"What the fuck, Anne?"

She looked at him. "I thought you left for work."

He shook his head.

"I didn't know you were here."

He frowned. "Are you suggesting you're cheating on me because I don't go to work when you expect me to?"

"I'm not cheating on you." Her voice was firm, despite the hot tears still dampening her palms, mixed now with cold sweat. She should have blocked Richard the other night when the world had nearly ended. Instead, she'd forgotten and now it really was ending.

"Yes, you are." Charlie waved the iPad. "I just watched your entire conversation with Richard, someone you previously claimed not to know. How long has this been going on?"

The iPad started ringing. Charlie looked at it. "He's calling you."

Anne opened her mouth to say she'd blocked his number, but of course she hadn't yet. Only in her head and heart, not in the real world.

The device stopped ringing, but then almost immediately started again. Charlie was shocked, but his decency remained. "Will you answer it, or shall I? Maybe I should. Both of us just got fucked over by the same woman."

Anne said nothing. She had nothing to say, no appropriate vocabulary for the end of the world. This wasn't supposed to happen, it was supposed to be over now, it wasn't going to harm her children, she had fixed it. And yet the jarring sound of an old car horn was filling the room. The kids always fucked with the ringtones; they found it hilarious. Suddenly her husband hit speaker and answered.

"Richard?" he said.

There was a pause. "Hello?" Anne felt faint at the sound of her lover's voice in her kitchen, just like the other day when Frances had signaled the beginning of the end, the first tear in the veil. She looked at her husband, but he was looking at the iPad, a bewildered smile of confusion and shock on his face, struggling to make sense of what the fuck had just happened to his life. It wasn't even 9:00 a.m. yet. He had been sitting on the toilet swiping through the headlines when the conversation had popped up on his screen, presenting him with a newsflash he hadn't expected. He was reeling, but he was pulling it together.

"This is Charlie, Anne's husband. I'm afraid I just discovered what was going on at the exact moment my wife was trying to break up with you."

"I was breaking up with him," Anne said.

Charlie ignored her. "We should have a drink or something to celebrate the incredible weirdness of this moment."

Richard sounded like he was crying. "I'm sorry. I'm in love with your wife."

Charlie snorted. "So am I. Doesn't seem like she's interested in either of us, though, does it?" He was looking at her, his eyes cool. "She can be remarkably unfeeling, you know. Once she's done with someone she's really done, I'm afraid. If I were you I'd cut your losses and find someone nicer. Are you young? You sound young."

"I'm twenty-seven."

Charlie looked at his wife, who had started to tremble. "Robbing the cradle, Anne? You should be ashamed of yourself. I know I am." He was pulling on the well-cut jacket of his courtroom persona; Anne had seen it before. In this mode he could handle anything and she was suddenly afraid. "Well, Richard, sadly for you I'm not going to divorce my wife because she owes my kids another decade of service even if I never want to lay a hand on her again."

"I love her . . ." Richard dissolved into tears, and Anne suddenly hated him for his weakness, despised the person she'd welcomed into her body over and over again. She gazed at her husband, recognizing him as the strong, capable, fully adult man he was, about five minutes and six months too late. He was still speaking to the iPad, holding it up in front of him like a book.

"Well, that's unfortunate, Richard, you have my sympathy. However, I want to make something clear, OK? I'm going to block your number, and if you call my house or come anywhere near it I'm going to beat seven shades of living shit out of you. Do you understand me? I'm about to throw Anne out of the house, so please feel free to slobber over the ice queen somewhere else, but come near me or my children and I will literally break your arm."

"Anne?" Richard said. "Are you there?"

Charlie waited, but his wife said nothing. "Nope, Richard, she's gone. Good luck to you, and I sincerely hope one day your beloved wife and the mother of your children fucks around on you so you can enjoy the sensation of having your balls fed into a meat grinder the way I am now." And he hung up, took ten seconds to block the number, and then smashed the iPad on the corner of the counter repeatedly, until it was just shards on the floor. Then he looked at Anne, his mouth curved into a ghost of the smile she'd seen on it every day of their life together, and told her to get the fuck out of his house.

Eighteen.

Frances was heading home when the phone rang. It was Iris.

"Oh my God," she said, sounding half horrified, half giggly. "Are you sitting down?"

"Yes," said Frances. "Because I'm driving, and it's not a chariot. Is something wrong?"

Iris took a breath. "Yes, but not for us. I just walked out to go to the store and found Charlie and Anne Porter having a knockdown, drag-out fight in the street. She was demanding he let her back into the house so she could get some clothes, and he was refusing to let her in saying she had rescinded her membership in his family and should ask her boyfriend to loan her his hipster flannel." She laughed. "Honestly, he was hilarious and cold and terrifying, and she was a total wreck." She paused. "I realize I shouldn't laugh, and I honestly don't think it's funny, but what the fuck?"

Frances felt swoony, and looked briefly in the driver's mirror before pulling across two lanes to take a shorter route home. "Did you just stand there and watch?"

"No! I backed slowly into the house and then took up a position by the window, ready to get involved if it got physical. But honestly, every time she got closer to him he'd step back. It was remarkably effective body language. Sara would have loved it."

Frances asked, "Is she still out there?"

"Sara?"

"No, Anne."

Iris paused, presumably while she peered between her curtains. "No, the street is empty. I guess the show's over." She waited. "I think I saw a car slow down as it went by, and I'm pretty sure there was a third-grade parent driving it."

"Great. That'll be around school by lunchtime."

"Did you know she was fucking around? She's your friend, right?"

"Yeah," replied Frances. "She's my friend. I'll be home in a minute, let's talk then. Do you have coffee?"

"Of course," Iris said, and hung up.

Frances hit speed dial for Michael, but his line was busy. Then, a second after she hung up, his call came through. This happened all the time, they would call each other at the same moment, or she would think of him and then the phone would ring and there he was. Either they were growing alike, like dogs and their owners, or they really didn't have an original thought between them.

"Did you hear?" His voice was low, so presumably he was at work.

"Are you at work?"

"No, I'm still at home. I was about to leave, but Charlie and Anne were fighting in the street so I hid indoors until it was over."

Frances could hear the jingle of a dog collar in the background and knew her husband was bending slightly to scratch his beloved behind the ears. "Jesus, I leave to do carpool and all hell breaks loose. Iris just called me, she saw the fight, too. Were they selling tickets?"

Michael laughed, his voice still low. "No, they didn't need to, you could hear it up and down the street. Who knew Charlie had so much lung power?"

"He is a lawyer, maybe they learn projection, like actors. Why are you whispering?"

"I'm not whispering, you're going deaf. Anyway, it seems to be over, but clearly the shit has hit the fan and you might want to call Anne and see if she's OK."

"Did she drive away?" Frances looked involuntarily into the cars around her, as if she might see Anne making her getaway.

"Yes and no. Charlie literally wouldn't let her take the car, said it was the family car and she was no longer in the family. He called her an Uber, and when she asked where it was going he said he'd told it to go downtown to city hall, so she could file for divorce. Then *she* said *he'd* said on the phone he wasn't going to divorce her, and then *he* said he'd changed his mind and how did that feel, being blindsided by a decision someone else had made that was going to fuck up your life." His tone shifted suddenly. "It sucked. Anne was a total mess, sobbing and begging and he was all business. It wasn't the finest moment for either of them."

Frances frowned, turning onto her block. "I'm nearly home, but I'm going to Iris's. Do you want to meet me there?"

"No, I want to go to work. Don't fuck around on me, OK?"

"OK, babe. Ditto."

"Like I have the energy."

"And again, ditto. I love you."

He hung up, and Frances pulled into the driveway at Iris's.

Iris already had two cups of coffee sitting on the table, and was cutting slices of banana bread as Frances walked in. She turned to look at her cousin, reading her face.

"You knew."

Frances nodded. "Yes, but only for a couple of days. I think it had been going on for a while. I wasn't quite sure what to think about it yet, to be honest."

Iris sat down, sliding a piece of the sweet bread across the table. Frances broke off a corner and ate it, noting the chocolate chips. "You're not going to tell me this is healthy, right?"

"It's full of fruit, of course it's healthy. The chocolate chips are for antioxidants. Who was she sleeping with? Anyone we know? Please tell me it was Mr. Carerra from school."

"The math teacher? Why?"

"I hate him. He's mean to Wyatt."

Frances shook her head. "Some young guy she met somewhere. No one we know."

"How young?"

"I don't know. He looked in his twenties, but I only saw him for a second or two, and it wasn't that good an angle, to be fair."

"When did you see him?"

Frances explained her discovery, and Iris literally sat there with her mouth open, a piece of banana bread held in midair, a crumb clinging to her finger, a fleck of chocolate on her upper lip. Once Frances was done, Iris popped the treat in her mouth. "That is the best craft supply/infidelity story I've ever heard," she concluded. "What a bitch."

Frances was surprised. "'Bitch'? Why? Because she cheated? I think she was going to break it off."

"That doesn't stop her from being a bitch. You don't agree?"

Frances shrugged. "I don't know. I think maybe she's having some sort of breakdown or depression or something."

"I think the statute of limitations on postpartum runs out long before your kid is six, sorry."

"There are other forms of depression besides postpartum, you know."

Iris looked severe. "Look, I don't care how shitty you feel, you get married with a commitment to not cheat, and you keep it. Sleep around *after* the divorce, not before."

"Don't lesbians cheat on each other?"

"Of course. All the time, just like anyone else. Now that we've gained marriage equality we're making just as much a mess of it as straight people have done for centuries. We cheat, we run off, we lie, we insult each other's families, we get drunk at Thanksgiving and blurt out terrible secrets . . ." She popped her last chunk of banana bread into her mouth, and grinned around it.

"Wow, remind me to avoid your house at turkey time. Although," added Frances, "your family secrets are also my family secrets, so you know . . ."

Iris got up to get more banana bread. Raising her eyebrows questioningly, she sliced another piece for Frances, too, and carried them back. "Do you think Anne and Charlie are going to get divorced?" She swept some crumbs onto the floor for Rosco, who snuffled them up.

"No clue. Would you divorce Sara if she cheated?"

"Maybe. Probably. Don't know. She's away a lot, you know, filming, and I imagine it's pretty tempting when it would be so easy. If she told me, I guess I'd have to."

"What happened to 'stand by your woman'?"

Iris looked at her plate. "I think it went away with 'my country, right or wrong.' Too much wrong to overlook, you know what I mean? Also, I think women used to stand by their men because they had to. They didn't have fuck-off money, didn't have legal status, were worried they would lose their kids. Those days are gone, mostly."

"For us middle-class chicks, sure. I'm sure there are millions of women trapped in shitty marriages." Frances started on her second slice of cake. "I always felt it would be easier to kill Michael as he slept than divorce him. Less paperwork, certainly."

"You're a practical woman. I like that about you. Always have." Iris grinned at her. "I'll help you hide the body."

"Nah, you're good," replied Frances. "I think he and I are beyond the murdering stage anyway. We're like conjoined twins with two separate brains but one heart, you know, one spine. I couldn't kill him without simultaneously eviscerating myself." She looked at Iris, who was putting down her fork.

"You've put me off my cake with your hideous imagery."

"Wow. Sorry. You're really not going to eat it?"

Iris shook her head, then slid the plate across.

"Thanks."

———

Two hours later, in a coffee shop frequented by elementary-school parents.

"Did you hear Anne Porter was fucking around?"

"No!"

"Yes. With a much younger man."

"No!"

"Yes! Her husband threw her out. He found her sucking him off in the baby's room."

"She doesn't have a baby."

"Oh yeah. Well, must have been some other room then. But still."

———

Two and a half hours later. Different coffee shop. Similar parents.

"And I heard she came in and found her husband fooling around with her boyfriend, and stormed off."

"That doesn't seem likely, does it?"

"Well, he did wear a pink shirt to the school picnic last year, remember?"

"Wasn't it an Easter theme? Didn't everyone wear pastels?"

"Everyone that *had them* . . . My husband couldn't find anything that wasn't black, gray, or navy."

"Oh . . . *oh* . . . I see what you mean."

———

Three hours later. Grocery store. Produce section.

"Those poor children."

"Exactly. What are they going to think? They're going to come home and 'Hey, no Mom.' How's he going to explain that?"

"Doesn't Frances Bloom carpool Anne's kids? Maybe she's supposed to make something up."

"Saint Frances? Good luck."

"I thought you liked her?"

"I do. I just wish she were a little less pleasant and helpful. I'd like her more."

"She does always seem to have it together, doesn't she? Bitch."

"No wonder she and Anne are friends. She's probably fucking around, too."

———

Four hours later, just before pickup. School gate. Early-bird parents with not much else to fill their lives.

"Hey . . . is that Charlie Porter?"

"Where?"

"There, heading into the office. Maybe he's here to talk to the principal."

"Well, that didn't take long, did it?"

"Is Anne here, too? I'm not sure I'd even know her. She doesn't do drop-off, does she?"

"Nah. Gets Frances Bloom to do it for her. Lazy, cheating cow. I guess she doesn't care about her kids at all."

"I think Charlie Porter is kind of hot."

"Definitely. And now he's single . . . and brokenhearted . . ."

"You're a terrible woman."

"I know."

Nineteen.

Charlie waited in the outer office for Mrs. Garcia to be ready. Her assistant, Jillian, watched him surreptitiously from under her lashes, occasionally reaching for another Werther's caramel from the dish on her desk. She went through a bag a day, and her back teeth ached in the evenings. She made a mental note to buy flossers. The candy was supposed to be for the kids, but they were all too scared their parents would find out they ate sugar. Those same parents always helped themselves, of course. Assholes. She loved the kids and despised the parents, like every other member of staff at the school.

Charlie had finished the caramel she'd pressed on him when he arrived, and now his mouth felt dry. He was about to ask her where the water fountain was when the inner door opened, and a small child exited the principal's office. The kid looked fine, so clearly not a punishment-type visit. Maybe he was just going in for a hug; that was the kind of principal Mrs. Garcia was: sweet and friendly, unless you transgressed in the drop-off line, or sent your kid in without the correct PE kit or whatever, at which point she turned twice on the spot, reverted into her basic demon form, and released the kraken.

She smiled at Charlie, and for a second he thought he saw pity in her dark eyes. *Impossible*, he reminded himself, *nobody here knows anything about Anne.*

Once in the office he took a seat, still warm from the kid. Mrs. Garcia was a larger woman, but she moved elegantly around her office, lowering herself into her chair with a smile for the parent across from her. Mr. Porter was handsome, she thought, and wondered how long he would stay single, assuming he was finished with his wife. She *was a cold fish*, thought the principal, but sometimes the coldest fish was the most compelling catch. She'd seen husbands take wives back far more often than they didn't. Men got lonely easily, she concluded. Fragile little fuckers.

"Mr. Porter, what a pleasure. What can I do for you?"

Charlie cleared his throat. "I just wanted to let you know that there's going to be some upheaval at home over the next, you know, little while, and I wanted you to know in case Theo and Kate seemed, you know, upset or something."

Mrs. Garcia looked concerned. She wanted to say, *Yes, I heard already, your wife has been cheating and you threw her out and now your children's lives as they knew them are going to be over, and let's face it, that's going to be like a total volcanic explosion and pyroclastic flow of white-hot shit rushing down the mountainside toward their little heads.* But instead she said, "Oh? Nothing too serious I hope?"

Charlie reddened. "I'm not sure. Just some . . . issues between their mother and me . . . She's moving out . . . Hopefully we will all be adult about it and they won't feel too unsettled."

Again, the internal voice of Mrs. Garcia, who had seen divorce and domestic violence and abuse and starvation and all manner of bullshit aimed at kids in her three decades of public service, wanted to say, *Well, if you were being adults in the first place none of this would have happened, but, as always, we're all just human beings with the frailties and failures that implies.* But her audible voice said, "Oh, I'm sorry to hear that. Would you like some advice?"

Charlie looked at her, and for the first time since walking in felt like he was truly seeing the woman across from him. Her face was kind and patient, although she doubtless saw this all the time. He clutched at the straw she offered. "Yes, please."

Mrs. Garcia sat back in her chair and steepled her fingers. "For your children, this will be the worst day of their lives so far. They will always remember where they were when you told them their mother wasn't at home anymore. You need to be very clear this is not because of them, that you both love them more than anything, and that the adults will be working to make things better. You don't need to tell them any details, and they understand that people fight and disagree, they do it all the time. But up until now it has never occurred to them that their parents would separate. They've heard of divorce, they know parents can break up, but it's like I leaned across this table and told you that everyone but you can talk to animals. You've heard of the concept, you've seen it in the movies, you've seen it on TV, but you never thought it was real. From today onward they will never feel completely secure again, and I'm afraid that will just have to be OK. That's life, life can change in an instant, we all know that. Today is just the day your children find that out."

Charlie stared at her. "That's advice?"

Mrs. Garcia smiled. "Yes, sorry. Don't think about what you need to say, Mr. Porter, think about what they need to hear, OK?" She frowned at him. "Will Mrs. Porter be there for this conversation?"

Charlie shook his head.

"Then you should wait until she can be. They need to see her to understand she's not leaving them."

"I don't know where she is right at the moment."

Now Mrs. Garcia looked stern. "You need to know that, Mr. Porter. You're very angry with her right now, as your wife, but she will always be the mother of your children. You need to be able to reach her in case anything happens to them, or in case you need her help. You may end up divorced, but you can never be truly separated, because of Kate and Theo."

Tears suddenly welled up in Charlie's eyes, and the principal pushed a box of tissues across the desktop. It was already half empty, and Charlie fleetingly wondered how many of those tears had been those of parents. "I don't want to see her."

Mrs. Garcia shrugged. "I'm afraid you don't have that option. Or at least, you do, but if you'll take my advice and put your children's needs uppermost, even at this truly difficult time for you and your wife, you'll put your pain aside and make things calm and friendly for your kids."

Charlie felt his chest constrict, and the tears came hot and fast, curling him over in his chair, stealing all sense of time and place from him. Mrs. Garcia sighed and hit a button on the phone. "Hold my calls, Jillian."

Then she got up, circled the desk, and put her arm around Charlie Porter, comforting him just as she had the little boy who'd sat in that chair not ten minutes earlier. Of course, a splinter was easier to deal with than a stake to the chest. Mrs. Garcia sat there for a while, patting Charlie as he cried, wishing she had a caramel.

———

Frances got a text from Charlie just as she was leaving for pickup.

I'm picking up Theo and Kate, thanks.

> OK. I heard what happened.
> Here if you need me.

Keeping it real. Practical. No judgment here, no comment, just a reminder she was here to help.

> OK.

Frances stood in the street looking at her phone, thinking about what she needed to say to her own kids that evening. She wanted them to be aware of what Kate and Theo were going through, wanted them to look out for their friends, to make sure they weren't floundering. They would be floundering, of course, everything just went to shit. She looked at her watch and thought of Kate and Theo finishing class. Going to get their backpacks, a drink of water, their jackets. Both completely certain they were going to walk outside, clamber into Frances's car like every day, go home, have dinner, go to bed with a story and a cuddle. They'd step outside and see their father and some very basic instinct would tell them something was wrong. Frances's mouth tightened in sympathy and relief that she didn't have to face what Charlie had to.

Twenty.

*A*va was uncompromising, which was typical. Her younger siblings had been sympathetic, immediately worried their own parents were divorcing, and generally over it in
two minutes. Ava on the other hand was sitting at the dinner
table holding forth on the perfidy of adults.

"Honestly, grown-ups are forever talking about how important it is to be honest, and not to lie, and to think about others,
and all that crap, but they're always lying and cheating." She was
spinning her knife, the little noise apparently pleasing her.

Frances was emptying the dishwasher in order to fill it again
with the dinner dishes, and she looked over at Michael. He and
Ava were still at the table, the younger kids having bolted as
soon as possible, and he was on his third glass of wine. He was
looking at Ava sadly.

"We try not to, just the same as you try not to. But grown-
ups are just as fallible as kids, Ava."

She looked scornfully at him. "Then why do you make such
distinctions between kids and adults? 'You're too young to do
this, too young to do that, you'll understand when you're older,

you can do this when you're older' . . . Meanwhile, you're behaving worse than children."

"I'm sure Anne didn't intend to wreck her marriage. She just made a bad decision."

Frances was torn between continuing to clatter dishes, or going over and joining the conversation. There would always be a dishwasher to empty, so she joined Michael and Ava at the table.

Ava was glowingly self-righteous. It was always about her; her smooth prefrontal cortex wouldn't allow her to think otherwise. "Well, when I make a bad decision you remind me that I should have thought it through, right? Consider the consequences of failure, you always say, think about both outcomes, make a plan for both. You're apparently expecting more of me than you do of grown-ups."

Frances shook her head, helping herself to a glass of wine. "No, we expected that of Anne, too, but it's not our place to tell her that we're disappointed in her, right? We're not raising her."

"Why not? Why is it OK to tell a kid you're unhappy with their behavior, but you guys give each other a pass all the time." She looked genuinely annoyed. As she stood up to get herself another glass of water, Frances looked over at Michael and made the face that meant *Should we change the subject, talk about something more neutral*, but she could see he was interested in what his daughter had to say. She sighed inside. She felt danger, Will Robinson, land mines ahead.

Michael tried another tack. "Maybe Anne and Charlie were unhappy. You never know what someone else's marriage or family is really like. We don't always get on, right? Your mom and I argue and you and I argue. Maybe they just argued more."

Ava shook her head. "No. Charlie is nice. I think Anne was just selfish and narcissistic and a bitch." She watched her dad's face to see if he was going to protest the use of the B word, but he didn't flicker. "I never liked her." She turned to Frances. "Didn't I just say that? The other day?" She sat back down with her water, and started unlacing her sneakers. It was getting dark outside, time to relax into the evening.

Frances took a sip of wine and nodded. "You did. But I think what your dad is trying to say is that it's not a good idea to judge people when you don't know all the facts and maybe not even then. You know the whole glass houses thing, right? None of us is perfect. You lied to me the other day for example."

There was a pause. Crap. Frances hadn't meant to bring that up, it just came out.

Ava looked at her, and shot from the hip. "And did you tell Dad you were talking to Anne's boyfriend in the street only yesterday?"

Michael looked at Frances, and saw this strange accusation was true. Being who he was, he covered for her and came to her rescue. "Of course she did. However, she has consistently lied to me about the location of her chocolate stash since we were first living together. Humans keep things from each other, and most of the time they're little things that really don't matter."

"And other times," Ava said scornfully, "they're things that really do matter and everything gets ruined." She dropped her second high-top on the floor and Frances knew she'd be hunting for them the next morning.

Michael coughed. "You sound like you're speaking from experience . . . Did someone tell you something that ruined things? What's going on, Ava?" His voice was gentle, his eyes as he looked at his daughter so full of affection and so devoid of judgment, that Frances marveled again at the love they shared. She'd carried Ava, used the calcium from her own bones to build the child's, ached and screamed to give birth to her, but it was her father who knew her best.

Ava gazed back at him and both her parents saw her eyes fill with tears, and saw her struggle to keep them there. She shook her head and stood up. "No, Dad, it's not all about me, you know. Or so you keep telling me, anyway."

She pushed her chair roughly back under the table and strode to put her plate in the sink, leaving the room swiftly enough to cause the dogs to stand up and follow her, concerned. Or maybe thinking she was leaving the house and might be up for taking them, too, who knows? Michael turned to Frances and frowned.

"What was she talking about?"

Frances sighed, and got up to go hide her face in the dirty dishes. "Yesterday Anne's boyfriend showed up just as I arrived with the kids. Two seconds later Charlie showed up, too. It was a clusterfuck."

Michael frowned. "But why did they wait to fight until this morning? I'm confused."

Frances turned on the faucet to rinse the dishes she was putting in. It bought her a little time, but once she'd turned it off she replied, "Charlie didn't find out about it then. I sort of covered for her." She turned and looked at her husband. "Like you just covered for me, with Ava."

"How did you manage that, exactly?"

"I pretended I knew him, and that he was heading toward Anne's house by accident." She watched Michael's face, but it was difficult to read. She frowned. "I think it was stupid, but I couldn't help it at the time. She's my friend, and the kids were there, and I didn't want it to all . . ."

"Blow up?"

She nodded. "Not that it helped."

"Nope. And now you've involved yourself in someone else's marriage. Or rather, the end of it."

Frances finished with the dishwasher and shut the door. She waited until the reassuring swishing sound began. "Maybe it won't ever come up."

"It's a bad habit, Frank."

"How do you mean?" She was about to head back to the table, grab herself another glass of wine, but there was a coolness in his expression that made her stop halfway and lean against the kitchen island instead.

"I mean your obsession with getting involved. You always want to be part of what's going on. You offer to help other people not just to help them, but because it satisfies some weird childhood desire to add to the list of people who need you."

She looked at him and thought about what he was saying. Suddenly she was annoyed. "I think you're full of it. I'm not forcing anyone to do anything. I have my own kids to take care of, plus the neighbors' kids, plus the occasional kid from school. It's not an international network of children requiring constant care and feeding."

Michael was filling up his wineglass again, for the fourth time. This was usually the point at which things went downhill. He was generally a genial drunk, but after three glasses he could be critical, like now, and four or more usually brought out his inner dickhead. Frances got ready to concede and withdraw; she had too much shit to do to argue with Michael, who would be hungover and contrite in the morning.

Sadly, Michael wasn't at that point. "Occasional? How many people have you as their emergency contact, Frances?"

"It doesn't matter. You're right, I'm too nosy." She turned to leave the room, but he repeated his question.

"No, really, Frank. How many?"

She shrugged. "Several. Why does it matter? It's not like anyone's ever called me in an emergency." She started angrily tidying, which was one of the more effective methods of countertop clearing.

"Last year you were the backup emergency contact for seven other families, not counting the ones in your carpool. And here's the thing: You love it. You love feeling needed, you love being involved. You sign up for this thing and that thing, you know everyone." There was a hint of disdain in his voice, a mockery Frances felt very sharply.

The dogs had wandered back in, having discovered Ava was only heading to her room to sulk. They could sense tension in the kitchen, and they both started slowly wagging their tails in a "Let's all calm down" kind of way. Frances reached down to pet them, but her anger was growing rather than fading. "Why is that bad? I don't have a job-type job. This is what I do. I'm a mom, a parent. I take care of my own kids, and I help other parents take care of theirs. I have time. They don't. When I don't have time, one of them will. It's a fucking village, right?" She thought, but not for long enough: "It's not like you're helping all that much, is it?"

"I help."

"When? When was the last time you did a load of laundry?"

"The other day, before my trip to San Francisco."

Frances snorted. "Yeah, you went through and picked out a basket of your own clothes and washed them. You didn't do anyone else's, you just took care of your own shit."

The fourth glass was nearly gone. The dogs were backing out of the room. Other men might have raised their voices, but Frances's husband lowered his. "At least I take care of my own shit. You put everyone else first so you don't have to look at your own life. You're way too busy to go to the gym, or get a part-time job, or even get a fucking haircut. We haven't had sex for nearly six months, we haven't gone out to dinner, we haven't had a conversation that wasn't about the kids, we haven't done anything that wasn't to do with the mundane quotidian details of existence. It's so fucking boring, Frank, it's all so fucking boring." He tipped the bottle but it was empty. "At least Anne Porter generated a little heat and light while she burned her fucking house to the ground."

Frances turned and walked out before she said something she would regret, and her husband almost certainly wouldn't remember.

———

Despite her deep irritation with Michael, Frances still had things to do. She pushed the argument to the back of her mind, where it wedged itself in a mental closet full of such things, and went to give Lally a bath. Ava was sulking in the bedroom to her right, Michael was sulking in the kitchen downstairs, and she was going to hide in the bathroom and form her daughter's hair into soapy devil horns. Fuck them.

Lally, who was completely unaware that anything was going on with her mother at all, said, "So, will Anne still be Kate and Theo's mom?"

Frances nodded. "Yes, you can never not be someone's mom, once you've started." That wasn't the best way to put it, but it was what she had at that moment. "Once your baby is born you're its mom, and that's forever."

Lally had contrary information. "But what about babies who are adopted? They get new moms."

Frances sighed inwardly; she should have seen this coming. Fuck Michael, he was putting her off her game. Her knees hurt from kneeling next to the bath, so she shifted to her butt. Much better, although now she could feel soapy water seeping through her pants. "Yes, but the lady who was pregnant with them is still their mother, she just isn't the person who's going to be their everyday mom. And the person who adopts them is going to be their mom or dad just as much as if they had been pregnant with them, right?"

Lally wrinkled her nose and looked up from under her horns. "Two moms? Like Wyatt?"

"No," said Frances, running the sprayer water, making it the right temperature. "Turn around, baby, and tip your head back." She started rinsing the little head, shielding Lally's eyes as best she could with her left hand. The sprayer was broken and one clogged hole directed water down her sleeve while another generously watered her left nipple. She ignored them both. "Wyatt has two mommies at the same time. Adopted children have an original mommy, who they often don't know very well, but sometimes they do," this was getting confusing, "and another mom or dad, who adopted them and is their everyday mom or dad."

"Soap! Soap!" Lally jerked her head forward and stuck her hand back for a towel, which Frances handed her. Once she'd dealt with that, Lally tipped her head back again, trustingly.

"So even if someone has two dads, like Molly"—a kid at school—"they still have a mommy somewhere."

"Exactly." Frances wondered if she could just leave it there. Had she given enough information to satisfy, and not too much? She felt herself guilty of over-information all the time, explaining too much, going into too much detail. Michael was better at this. When a younger Ava had asked where she came from, and Frances had opened her mouth to start explaining the intricacies of sexual reproduction, Michael had said, "New York," and Ava had nodded and walked away.

"It was like the joke, right?" Michael had said, reacting to Frances's laughter. "You know, the kid who asks his parents where he's from, and they go into all the details about sex and pregnancy, and then he says, 'Oh . . . Billy's from Chicago.'" Frances had just shaken her head and leaned over to kiss him. She wished he were in the bathroom to handle this line of questioning, and not downstairs being a self-pitying dick.

As Lally climbed out of the tub, and was wrapped in a hooded towel that made her look like a dinosaur, she said, "But if Kate and Theo's mom and dad get divorced, then she won't be their mom anymore, right?" She thought for a second. "Or will their dad not be their dad?" She looked suddenly worried. "Or do they have no mom and dad at all?"

Frances picked her up, which was getting harder, but Frances wasn't ready to stop. She carried her down the hall, holding her tight, and sat down with her on their big bed.

"OK, here's how this works." She paused. "Do you want chocolate milk?" Lally shook her head, not ready for cocoa yet. "Do you need pajamas?" Lally shook her head. "OK, so, you know that Daddy is my husband, right?" A nod. "And I am his wife, right?" *Currently*, she thought, *assuming I don't stab him in the throat later.* Another nod. "OK, so a *husband* and a *wife* can get divorced, but if they have kids and are also a *mommy* and a *daddy* to someone, that is forever."

"You can't divorce a kid?"

"Nope." Frances looked up and saw Ava leaning in the doorway. "Once you're someone's mommy you're their mommy forever, and you never stop loving them or taking care of them or wanting them to be happy. That's just the way it is." She was looking at Ava as she said this, and saw her daughter about to challenge pretty much everything she'd just said, citing child abuse, death, drug addiction, et al., but then Frances frowned slightly, indicating Lally, and Ava just rolled her eyes. There would be time for brutal honesty later. For now Frances was determined to let Lally think the best of the world, and apparently Lally's older sister was OK with that, too.

"Unless the kid is really bad, right?" There was a pause, and Lally tipped her head back to look at her mom. "What if the kid is really bad, can you divorce them then?" Whether she was planning some terrible crime, or just wondering how bad refusing to eat vegetables was, legally, Frances didn't know. She kissed her daughter on her clean little forehead, and shook her head.

"No, baby, it doesn't matter how naughty a kid is, you still love them forever."

"Even if they poo on the floor?" This was a question based on experience.

"Yes, even then."

"Or if they steal your hat?"

Frances grinned. "Or even then. There is NOTHING you can do that will stop me loving you. I might not like what you do, but I will always love you."

"Promise?"

"Promise."

Frances hugged her littlest child, and looked up at her eldest. Ava was just looking back at her, impossible to read. Then she turned away and headed off to her room.

Twenty-one.

Wyatt was already asleep when Sara came home from work, still in makeup and looking gorgeous. Iris was wearing an old-lady flannel nightgown, lying in bed reading the *New Yorker* and eating ice cream. She was happy to see Sara, of course, but inwardly cursed that she hadn't gotten more ice cream in the first place because now getting seconds would look greedy. Bad planning.

Sara threw herself down on the bed next to Iris, kissed her hello, then sat back up again. *Such energy,* thought Iris, closing her magazine and smiling.

"I like your nightie," Sara said, half smiling. The granny nighties were a running joke between them because Iris shopped for them compulsively on eBay, hunting for genuinely old, worn flannel gowns that genuinely old, worn ladies had possibly died in. She liked how soft they were, found the patterns and cuts comforting. Sara thought it was funny, and secretly adorable.

"Thanks. How was work?"

Sara shrugged and leapt up to go wash her face. Her voice drifted from the bathroom. "It was fine. I kind of rushed out of there, but I think it went well. David Rapelli turns out to be a nice guy."

Her costar. He was a hunky handsome guy, the dude next door, the fuckable-husband type. He and Sara were married in this movie, but that was about as much as Iris knew about it.

"Oh yeah?" Iris reached for the magazine again, but was thwarted by Sara suddenly reappearing, her face bare. She had the common actor's ability to put on and take off makeup in about three seconds. Ten thousand hours of anything makes you an expert, presumably. Iris patted Rosco instead, as if that had been her intent the whole time.

"Yeah. He's married, two kids, not the brightest bulb on the tree and knows it, mostly grateful for the lucky break he had genetically, followed by the lucky break he had temperamentally, followed by the lucky break he had professionally."

"So, grateful then?"

Sara nodded. "Largely. He started to be a dick about craft services, but he picked the wrong day for it, so that didn't last long."

"How do you mean?"

"Lynsey was first AD."

Lynsey was a woman they both knew socially, after Sara had become friends with her through work. A dedicated and gifted multitasker who could have been directing enormous movies or captaining some industry or other, she was instead a first assistant director on made-for-TV movies so she could earn enough money and have enough working flexibility to care for her younger sister who was slowly but surely dying of cystic fibrosis. Lynsey had incredible empathy, maybe as a result of watching someone you love fight to stay alive despite a life filled with pain, which made her a pleasure to work with unless you were rude, at which point she would flay you alive and you'd never be hired again.

Sara pulled off her clothes and clambered under the covers, snuggling up to Iris. "Ooh, you're so toasty." She wrapped her long legs around her wife, who shrieked and pulled away.

"Your feet are like ice cubes. What were you shooting, a scene on an iceberg?"

Sara laughed. "Yeah, because in this story the young married couple are going on vacation to the Grand Canyon and an iceberg comes floating down the Colorado."

"Global warming. It could happen."

"Well, this isn't the dystopian vacation rom-com you seem to be imagining. I just have cold feet. You married me for better or worse, let me tuck my cold feet under your warm legs." She did so, and continued. "Anyway, Lynsey pulled him briefly aside and said something and after that he behaved himself impeccably. I think you'd like him."

"Is he incredibly short?"

"No, he looks like he does on-screen, pretty tall." Most actors were shorter than you'd think, Iris had discovered, with big heads and large features and an overwhelming tendency to look at themselves in mirrors, windows, other people's sunglasses. She had never been very comfortable with "industry" people, and largely kept away. But they did have some friends from Sara's work, like Lynsey.

"How was your day?" Sara's feet were warming up, and her arms stole around Iris's waist and tugged her closer, rubbing her face into her neck, smelling the clothes soap they used, feeling secure and loved. She could give David Rapelli's gratitude a run for its money.

Iris shrugged. "It was good." Then she suddenly gasped and sat up. "Oh my God, I can't believe I didn't tell you this as soon as you walked through the door! Anne Porter has been having an affair and Charlie found out today and threw her out. They had a huge fight in the street, I saw the whole thing, it was awful."

Sara rolled away from her wife and sat up. "No way."

"Way."

"Seriously? She was cheating? How long had that been going on?" Sara looked genuinely shocked and surprised.

Iris shook her head. "No idea. Frances said she thought several months."

"How did Frances know that?"

"She talked to Anne about it."

"She knew about it before Charlie did?"

"Yeah, but only for a few days." Iris told Sara the craft supplies/infidelity story.

Sara sat there and gazed at her. "Holy Fucking Shit. Those poor kids. What a disaster. Do you want more ice cream?"

Iris nodded. Sara grabbed her bowl and headed downstairs. The dog followed her, and Iris sat in bed and listened to the two of them having a conversation. Or at least, Sara had a conversation, but Rosco was apparently jotting his answers down on a pad because Iris couldn't catch his responses at all. When Sara came back she had two bowls with her. One contained her own ice cream, which was vanilla and about the size of a walnut, and the other was for Iris, which had two flavors of ice cream, whipped cream and chocolate sauce.

"We're out of maraschino cherries," Sara said, as she helped Rosco get up on the bed again. "We weren't, but I gave Rosco the last one."

"That explains his pink nose. Are maraschino cherries good for dogs?"

"No idea. I give him them all the time, and he's never complained."

"You do?"

"Yeah, that's why we're out. Anyway, tell me more about Anne and Charlie. What's going to happen?" She sat down, still naked, put the bowl in her lap, screamed at the cold, got up, put on a T-shirt, and tried again.

While watching this pantomime, Iris half-heartedly picked up her magazine, then put it down. "I don't know. It's just happened. I doubt they even know themselves." She looked at Sara. "Would you divorce me if I cheated on you?"

Sara nodded. "Of course. If I knew. If I didn't know I'd be fine about it." She frowned. "You're not cheating, are you?"

"Of course not. Not that I'd tell you."

"Right." Sara tipped her head on one side as she thought about it, a habit she had that impersonators often mocked. It was natural, though, she'd always done it. "I guess it would also depend on what kind of cheating."

Iris turned onto her side, facing her wife. "How do you mean? Isn't there one basic kind, the kind where you sleep with someone you're not married to?"

"Yeah, but there are so many variations on the theme."

"Please explain, Professor."

Sara sat up in bed and curled her legs under her, counting off on her fingers. "One, the wham-bam-thank-you-ma'am school of cheating, where you hook up with strangers in bars, hotels, nightclubs, and simply have sex. No information is exchanged, no follow-up is expected or desired."

Iris nodded. "I've heard of this, continue."

"Second, the kind that comes up on sets or on vacation or on temporary assignments of one kind or another. This kind is mostly about sex, but it's also about re-creating the first few days or weeks of a new relationship. You're both slightly nauseous, you lose ten pounds in as many days, you start wearing nicer underwear . . ."

"Or NO underwear . . ."

"If you're that way inclined, and you flirt in front of other people and generally toy with the secrecy and excitement of illicit romance. However, it is always understood that this is a fling, nothing more, and although it can be passionate and personal and intimate, it is not intended to develop into anything."

"OK, check." Iris was suddenly enjoying this conversation less. Sara had clearly thought this through.

"Third—and this is where it starts to get sticky—is the kind that starts as one of the above, usually the latter, and then gets out of hand. This can happen anytime, to anyone, which is why infidelity is such a dumb idea if you love your spouse. One minute you're having a giggle with the wardrobe girl, and the next she's boiling your rabbit, if you get my reference."

"To *Fatal Attraction*, yes, I get the reference. We don't have a rabbit, thankfully."

"True. And finally, you have the worst—or best—kind of infidelity, the one where you fall in love with someone else and your marriage ends."

"Is that always what happens? Your marriage ends?"

"No. Sometimes you fall in love with someone else and are grown-up about it and change jobs, or do something else so you don't see that person anymore, and never take it beyond the confines of your own head. Other times you both know you're in trouble before you get into it, and you have a very sad conversation where you agree that if you lived in a different world you'd be together, but you don't, see earlier reference to changing jobs. And other times you acknowledge the attraction, have one very steamy make-out session, and end it there." Sara suddenly sighed.

"But that choice is a very dangerous one, in my experience, because once that physical bridge has been crossed, it tends to fall down behind you like a chase sequence in an action movie and there's no going back."

Iris looked at her wife, who wasn't even seeing her anymore. She cleared her throat. "In your experience?"

Sara looked up and correctly read Iris's expression. "Not in MY experience, but in my experience of other people's experiences, my knowledge of the world, and my extensive watching of movies and reading of books."

Iris frowned. "Are you sure?" Her heart was curling at the edges, her palms suddenly sweaty.

Sara smiled at her. "Yes, idiot. Besides, this is why I like it best when you and Wyatt come on location with me, then I don't need to worry that you're screwing around with some other hot mom. Or delicious coed babysitter who wants to be taken in hand by a gorgeous older woman and shown the ropes."

"You watch too many movies."

"It's my job."

Iris shook her head. "Wyatt's going to be in middle school soon, and then it won't be so easy to take him out of school, you know. What then? What if you're on location for months and the starlet is irresistible?"

"We'll get a tutor. This is L.A., schools are used to it. This is because of Anne Porter, isn't it?"

Iris thought about the second baby she wanted so much. What would that do to her marriage?

Sara suddenly put both bowls of ice cream aside and straddled her wife. She pinned Iris's arms down as she kissed her. "Why." *kiss* "Would I." *kiss* "Ever risk." *kiss kiss* "Losing one second of your happiness for hours of anything else?" *kiss kiss kiss*

"Anytime I'm not actively doing something, anytime I'm not doing my work or driving a car or making a sandwich or anything, in fact, at all, I am thinking of you, of your face, your hands, your waist, your sweet, sweet smile." Sara leaned closer and gently licked the end of Iris's nose. "And your delicious, incredible nose." She let go of one of Iris's hands, and slid her own down under the covers and started gathering the hem of Iris's nightie. "My biggest problem with these ridiculous nightgowns is how long it takes to get them off . . ."

———

Later, as Sara was drifting off to sleep she muttered, "Plus, what if Anne had gotten pregnant . . . It could have been even more awful and complicated." She yawned, squeezing Iris's hand where it lay beside her on the quilt. "At least we can cheat secure in the knowledge that that particular outcome isn't going to catch us out." Her breathing slowed, her grasp loosened.

Iris lay there in the dark, gazing up at the ceiling, her heart suddenly constricted again. "Yeah," she said softly. "Lucky us."

Twenty-two.

When Frances got home from drop-off the next morning, Anne was sitting on her front step.

"Can I talk to you?" She looked awful, cold and pinched despite the typical warmth of the day. As Frances nodded and opened the door she thought she saw Charlie coming out of his house up the street, but wasn't sure. She hoped not; she really didn't want to take sides. Well, apart from the side of the kids, that side she would always be on.

The dogs greeted Anne in their usual enthusiastic fashion, because (a) they didn't know she was a cheater and (b) they're instant forgivers, dogs, it's just the way they roll. They also sensed deep misery, and followed her into the kitchen and sat next to her while she lowered herself into a chair. While Frances pulled the usual mugs from the cupboard and looked to see if there was any coffee left, Anne petted the dogs and felt like death warmed over.

In the distance, Frances could hear the shower running. "Michael's still here, you know. Is that OK?"

Anne was still petting the dogs as if it were going out of fashion. She nodded. "It doesn't matter. I just wanted to talk to you." She looked up suddenly. "Does he hate me?"

"Michael?" Anne nodded, so Frances shook her head. "No, or at least, he hasn't said so. It's not our place to hate you, is it? You didn't cheat on us." What she didn't say was that she and Michael hadn't spoken yet that morning, so who knew what he thought? She'd been giving him the cold shoulder, and had been a little vexed that his car was still out front when she got back from drop-off. She'd hoped he'd be forced to reach out to her from work, maybe send her flowers, or leave her apologetic voicemails. That way she could nurse her resentment in solitude, whereas if she saw his face she would find it hard to stay mad. Their relationship was basically a deep, deep friendship at this point, and flares of anger usually just fell into the darkness and burned out. They frequently ignored the advice to never go to bed angry, but it took too much effort to stay mad past the following lunchtime.

Anne got a flush of color. "I'm not sure everyone will be as understanding as you two."

Frances had started making a fresh pot of coffee, and was reaching for filter papers as she answered. "I don't think it's understanding. You know how I felt about you cheating, after the other day. But the fact that I was right, that it ended really badly, doesn't make me happy in the least. You know that. I wish I had been wrong, because now things are all fucked up."

Anne looked at her. "I don't know what's going on with me. I felt so lonely and empty and suddenly Richard was there and he saw a totally different side of me, not even a side that I knew existed. I was a different person with him."

Frances was leaning against the counter, listening to the gently puffing efforts of the coffee maker. She noticed the laundry was done and moved it over to the dryer, dumping the dry clothes into a basket. "Well, who are you now? Are you seeing a psychiatrist?"

Anne frowned. "Do you think I should?" She kept crossing and recrossing her legs, and Frances wondered idly if she had a urinary tract infection.

She said, "Well, let's look at the face of it, shall we? You just destroyed several lives, including your own, over a brief and meaningless relationship. You're mystified as to why you did it, and you find yourself adrift now, not sure how to get back to normal. I would think a psychiatrist might be helpful. You're depressed."

"Am I depressed, or am I just responding appropriately to a disastrous situation?"

"It wasn't disastrous until you made it that way. Go get help, Anne." The coffee maker was done. "Usual?"

Anne nodded. "Will you help me?"

"I'm not a shrink. I'm not any kind of doctor, and you need professional help." She added half-and-half, hesitated as she tried to remember if Anne took sugar in her coffee or not, decided she could use the extra calories and added some. Anne was still talking.

"I mean with Charlie. Will you help me with Charlie?"

Frances carried over the coffee, then turned to get cookies. "Did you have breakfast?" Anne shook her head. "Eggs?" Anne shrugged, so Frances pulled out a pan, butter, and eggs. Food before anything, always. Her mother had always been a good cook, and after Frances's brother died she became almost fanatical about it. Frances would eat three meals a day, under the watchful eye of her mother, because she knew it was three times a day her mother felt like maybe she had some control over the shit storm that was life. *If this child was fed*, she seemed to radiate, *then maybe she won't suddenly die.* Frances had inherited this belief, and now she was making eggs for Anne because it

was what she could do. Ava had once joked that on her mom's headstone it was going to say, "I'm fine, but when was the last time you ate something?"

Frances cracked a couple of eggs while the butter melted, whisking them together with a fork, adding a pinch of pepper. "I don't honestly know what I can do for you, Anne. You need to fix this, if you can. How are the kids?"

Anne shrugged. "We told them together, because that was what Charlie thought we should do, but they seemed confused about it. I stayed and helped put them to bed, but then I left."

"Are you staying at your parents'? They're in Santa Monica, right?"

"Yes, but no. I haven't told them yet."

Frances put a plate of eggs in front of her friend, and felt herself standing over her, just like her mom had always done. That was creepy, so she sat down.

Anne ate, her usual color returning. "These are so good, thanks."

Frances smiled. "You have to take care of yourself. If you want to save your marriage you're going to have to fight for it. You'll need your strength."

"I don't think Charlie will forgive me."

"Would you forgive him, if he'd been the one who cheated?"

Anne shrugged, cleaning up the last of her eggs. "I have no idea." She looked at her neighbor. "Will you help me? Will you help me talk to Charlie?"

Michael walked in, his hair still wet from the shower. He opened his mouth to speak to Frances, but paused when he saw Anne. Two seconds passed, then he glided onward. His unflappability was one of the things Frances enjoyed about him. "Hi,

Anne, sorry to hear things are all fucked up right now." And his honesty, Frances enjoyed that, too.

Anne blushed. "Yeah. I messed up. Sorry."

Michael grabbed a travel mug from the cupboard and filled it with coffee. "Don't say sorry to me, dude, no need. We all make mistakes." He added cream, put on the lid, and said, "Last night, for example, I behaved like a total dick to my lovely wife, who has punished me terribly by simply not smiling at me this morning." He stood in front of Frances and added, "I am such a phallus, I am so sorry, please smile at me again so I can go on with my life."

Frances narrowed her eyes at him. So. Fucking. Annoying. He would behave badly but then apologize magnificently, so she would have to forgive him. She smiled a small smile, which broadened once he'd bent down and kissed her. "Go to work, total dick," she said, and he turned to leave. As the front door closed Frances could smell her shampoo in the air. He bitched about her "fancy" Aveda shampoo that cost too much, but used it himself, the hypocritical swine. She felt a sudden swoon of gratitude that she wasn't in the same boat as Anne, that she and Michael were making it OK, despite hating each other from time to time, and not having enough sex, and not having much to talk about besides the kids. It wasn't a sexy marriage, it wasn't a fun-filled romantic romp, but it was solid. She felt a flicker of concern at the back of her mind that if a few glasses of wine were revealing Michael's real feelings about her, then maybe they were in more trouble than she realized, but she couldn't face thinking about that now. She had other people's lives to think of. And yes, she was aware of the irony of that.

"I'll help you if I can, Anne," she said, reaching across the table for her friend's hand. "But I don't know what I can do." She paused, treading carefully. "Were there problems between you two before?"

"Before?"

"Before you started the affair?"

Anne looked out of the window, noticing how untidy Frances's backyard was, wondering why Frances had no standards at all. "No, things were fine. Just the same as ever. Richard just made me feel young again." She turned to Frances suddenly, her face flushing. "You know that feeling you had when you were twenty-two and you met someone and fell in lust and spent days and days in bed, fucking and talking and laughing and fucking and it felt like there was only the two of you? It was like nothing I'd experienced for years. It was wonderful."

Anne laid her head on the table and cried, her fingers curling around Frances's. *OK,* thought Frances, *well, this I can do.* She squeezed Anne's hand and sat there thinking about what her friend had said and how scared she suddenly was that her husband felt that way about someone else.

———

The store was called Please Come Again, and it was on Hollywood and Western. Frances had driven past it a thousand times, idly reading the list of offerings: bedroom toys, massage lotions, DVDs, fun bedroom wear. Every single time she read the list she'd gotten an image of her husband on a scooter, naked, rolling gleefully across the bedroom with a jester hat on his head. She'd never seen this in real life, of course, but the combination of the words *toys* and *fun bedroom wear* met up in this way in her imagination. Clearly her imagination was nine-tenths of the problem.

The lady inside the store was a middle-aged Latina with a friendly face and a surprisingly vanilla approach to sex. She liked it straight down the middle, missionary, with her husband and no one else, no need for anything more exotic than an extra Dos Equis on Friday nights. However, there was nothing she hadn't heard or seen in her twelve years in the store, and as she saw Frances walk in she knew she could sell her a vibrator, a self-warming massage oil, and maybe, just maybe, a pair of fur-lined handcuffs. She further knew that Frances would maybe use the vibrator once or twice, the self-warming oil the next time she had a sore neck, and the fur-lined handcuffs never. Then she would ignore them in her bedside table for a year or two until she suddenly realized the kids could find them and would struggle to think of a way to dispose of them without scaring the cleaning lady. She'd put it all in a paper bag and drop it in a trash can on the high street somewhere, thinking as she did so of the surprise of the next homeless person who'd hoped for a half-eaten sandwich but ended up with so much more. But all this was in the future. Araceli was ready to focus on today.

"Good morning, how can I help you have better sex today?"

Frances was unable to stop a nervous giggle. "Does it have to be today?"

Araceli nodded and smiled a smile that suggested they were talking about knitting, rather than sex. "It should be every day."

"Really?" Frances felt tired suddenly.

Araceli nodded. "It is like any form of exercise: A little each day is better than a lot once a week." She turned her attention to the cabinet she was resting on. "Can I show you some toys? A vibrator, perhaps? Pleasuring yourself is the first best step to pleasuring someone else."

Frances nearly bolted right then. The word *pleasuring* always made her laugh, she wasn't really sure why. "Uh. I guess so. Nothing too . . ." She stepped forward and looked through the glass lid. ". . . extreme." There were things in the cabinet she could only hazard a guess at. Basic penis-shaped things she recognized, but there were also things with multiple ends and extra flaps and ribbed surfaces and bobbled surfaces and movable parts that would surely increase the risk of embarrassing hospital visits? (Well, I was walking along and I fell on it . . . Yes, in a seated position, Doctor.)

"How about this one? It's very popular." Araceli held up a seven-inch silver bullet–looking vibrator, shiny and smooth.

"It looks a little high tech for me." She also knew someone small would be using it as a lightsaber within two seconds of finding it, God forbid. Shit, where was she going to keep all this stuff?

Araceli reached for another. "This one is maybe more familiar." It was basically a realistic looking penis. Araceli turned it on, and it hummed in a friendly way. Frances nodded, feeling she could get her head around that one. So to speak.

She looked over at a rack of lingerie, and Araceli followed her gaze. Without the other woman noticing she quickly scanned her figure, gauging what she had to work with, and stepped out from behind the counter. "Are you interested in something sexy to wear? We have many lovely things."

Frances could see nothing but string on hangers, but she gamely went with Araceli to take a look. Black and red featured prominently, although animal skin was also a common motif. She thought about the nature documentaries she'd seen, and got sidetracked by images of baby pandas. Maybe she'd forgotten how to be sexy. She had been sexy, as a younger woman, sexy and free and uninhibited. She'd had many lovers before Michael, and felt pretty good and liberated about the whole thing. But she'd also felt anxious and slightly crazy and out of control, and the safety and warmth of her relationship with Michael had felt like a safe harbor, not a dry dock. And then came the kids. Adorable little passion killers, each and every one.

Araceli was holding up a black . . . item . . . that seemed to be constructed of three lacy doilies held together with boot laces. She thought about looking at herself in the mirror, the doilies gamely holding on for dear life, the boot laces disappearing into her little folds and curves, and shook her head. "My husband prefers me naked," she said, without thinking, and then started giggling uncontrollably. It made her sound like some acolyte, and Michael stood tall in her mind, ordering her washed and brought to his tent. She lost it completely. Araceli waited patiently, shifting her weight from one foot to the other, thinking about what to make for dinner.

Once Frances calmed down she paid for the vibrator, some warm massage lotion, and a pair of fur-lined handcuffs, which she'd thrown in completely on impulse. If Araceli had been surprised by the choice she certainly hadn't shown it.

———

That afternoon Frances called her mother, amazed at herself for thinking of it, and further amazed that she thought of it at a time when she had access to a phone and time to place a call. The kitchen was empty, the dogs were outside, the washer and dryer were both humming, there were flowers on the counter, sex toys in the bedside table . . . She was on top of her game and nothing bad was going to happen to her. Her mother answered the phone, thousands of miles away in New York.

Frances said, "Hey, it's me." She pulled her cup of tea closer, listening for the children. Normally the best way to get them all to appear was to try and place an important phone call. They would then instantly materialize, often in tears, and always with demands of some sort. It was a kind of magic. Shitbird magic, but effective.

"Hi there, sweetheart. How are you doing? What's new in your neck of the woods?" Her mother sounded just the same as always, the cadences of her voice familiar on a cellular level. Frances loved her mother dearly and also felt very sorry for her, which hadn't been that great a combination when she was a teenager, but worked now. More or less.

"Nothing much."

"I heard your neighbor has been sleeping around. Is that such a normal occurrence it's not worth mentioning?" Her mother laughed, and Frances heard the click of a kettle being turned on. She could see the kettle in her mind, see the kitchen counters with their countless red jars and mugs, a little color being what her mother loved. Anything red. Made her very easy to shop for.

"How on earth do you know that?" Frances took a sip of tea, debated whether she wanted a cookie enough to get up for it.

"Ava told me."

Frances was surprised. "When did you speak to Ava?"

Her mother laughed again. Clearly, she was in a good mood. Or maybe she was as high as a kite, who knew? "Yesterday. We talk on Skype, you know. You should look into this Internet thing. I think it's going to catch on."

"Funny. That's nice. I hadn't realized you two were in touch so much." Her tea was sweet enough without a cookie.

"It's not that much, maybe once or twice a week. She likes to talk, I like to listen, it's good." Her mom sighed suddenly. "I wish I had listened to you more, when you were her age. I have no memories of that time at all. I'm sorry."

Frances raised her eyebrows. "That's OK, Mom. It was a hard time, right? Because of Alex. I don't know how you kept going, honestly."

"Is that why you called?"

"What?"

"Tomorrow is the anniversary, you know. I thought maybe that was what you were calling about."

Frances got up and grabbed the cookie jar, which was shaped like an elephant. "No. Or at least, I don't think so. Maybe on some level I remembered, but I just wanted to hear your voice."

"He'd be the same age as Michael, you know."

She bit into a cookie, which truly was delicious. "Yeah, I know. Their birthdays are even close."

"Little May babies. Both Taurus, strong and calm. I think about Alex all the time, do you?"

A second cookie. "I do. I think about what a great uncle he would have been. I think about the cousins the kids might have had, the nieces and nephews, the grandkids. Of course, he might have married someone we didn't like, there's always that chance. Like that girl across the street."

"Isabel? She ended up marrying a proctologist from Long Island."

"Serves her right."

"Who knows, maybe she and Alex would have been happy together. When you lose a child, you lose the life they would have had, too. Right? Don't you look at the kids and wonder what kind of adults they're going to be, who they're going to marry, that kind of thing?" Her mother's voice faded in and out as she bustled around her kitchen, all those miles away.

Frances laughed ruefully. "Mostly I just try to make it through the day alive, but sure, sometimes I think about the future. Mostly trying to imagine what life will be like once they've moved out and I finally have enough storage space."

Her mom sighed. "I used to pretend Alex was just away, you know. Sometimes when it got too hard, I would just decide he was at camp and I would write him letters in my head, or imagine him climbing on ropes and riding horses and having a wonderful time. I would tell myself it was good I hadn't heard from him in so long, it meant he was busy and happy."

"Wow, that sounds . . . delusional and painful." Would a third cookie lead directly to diabetes, or was it OK?

"Yeah," replied her mother, dryly. "I think it's generally understood that outliving your child is horrible."

"And now?"

"Still horrible. But bearable, because time really does, as they say, heal all wounds. It's also easier because none of my friends have kids at home, either. The first few years it hurt so much because of this constantly nagging sense I was forgetting something, then I'd remember he was gone and there was nothing I could do. And the other mothers in his grade knew it, too, and I knew that every time they saw me dropping you off they remembered Alex and felt sorry for me and guilty for being glad it was me and not them. Did you ever have those dreams where you forget you have a child?"

Frances shuddered. "Oh my God, not as much as I used to, but when the kids were babies I'd have them all the time. I'd dream I'd left the car seat on top of the car and driven off, or that I'd forgotten they existed and they'd been at home for days without anyone feeding them, and I'd rush home and they'd be crying and dirty and hungry, or not there at all because someone had taken them away from me. It was horrible. I still get them from time to time, but not so much."

"Well, it was like that, but I was awake. That pit-of-the-stomach-panic feeling, combined with a terrible physical pain and emptiness. I'd forget for a second or two, then it would come slamming back and knock the wind out of me. Your father and I didn't talk about him for nearly a decade. I think we each thought it would kill the other, just the act of physically shaping his name with our mouths."

"How is Dad?"

Her mom laughed. "He's addicted to meth and having an affair with a forty-year-old."

"No! You're joking."

"Yes, I'm joking. He's fine, he's working on a book, he's teaching, he's happy. He has a cough that won't go away, and in the middle of the night I think it's cancer. But hopefully not."

"Has he seen a doctor?"

"No. He just tells me not to worry, so I don't."

Lally came in, wearing a swimsuit and bunny ears. "Who are you talking to?"

"Grandma."

Lally took the phone. "Hey, Gramma. Did you watch the show?"

A pause.

"No, just her."

Another pause.

"Yes, but . . ."

And another.

"I don't know." Lally handed the phone back to her mother and rolled her eyes. "Gramma doesn't get *Littlest Pet Shop*." She walked away, then stopped. "Can I have some chocolate milk?" Frances nodded, and pointed to the fridge. Lally wandered over and hung on the big door with all her weight. It suddenly swung open, nearly knocking her over. Never not funny. Frances started to ask about the swimsuit, but remembered in time there was no point. She turned back to the phone.

"What don't you get about *Littlest Pet Shop*?"

"So many things," her mother replied. "Why would someone leave a chameleon at a pet boarding service? Do all those animals belong to people who've just abandoned them? Do they have lives outside the pet shop? Is Blythe the only one who can talk to them, and why is her head so big? Who looks after her while her dad is away flying airplanes? Is the old lady who runs the shop on drugs? Why do those rich twins who are so funny go to a public school, and not a fancy private one?"

"Wow, you do have a lot of questions. I had no idea."

"Don't you watch it?"

"Not if I can help it. However, I like the idea of you sitting in your nice Riverside Drive apartment, watching *Littlest Pet Shop*, taking notes."

Her mother laughed. "I like to talk to Lally about these things, although she was no help just then."

Frances's mind jumped back. "So, tomorrow is thirty years? Is that possible?"

"Not only possible, but inevitable."

"Is it hard every year?"

"Yes."

"It doesn't get easier?"

"Yes, it's easier, but if something starts out as the most difficult thing in the world and then gets progressively easier each year, it's still pretty hard at the end, right?"

"I guess so. I hope I never find out."

"Me, too."

"I'm so sorry, Mom." Frances drank her tea, and watched

Jack the dog rolling in a patch of sunlight in the garden. Hope-fully it was just sunlight. "I see him in Milo, you know. Milo has his hair, and his ears."

"He does? Send me a picture." There was a murmuring in the background. "Your dad is here, do you want to say hi?" More murmuring. "No, wait, he says we have to go. We have tickets to something."

"OK, Mom. I love you."

"I love you, too, Frances. Kiss everyone for me."

"I will." She hung up and sat and looked at the phone until Ava came in and asked about dinner. She surprised her daughter by pulling her onto her lap and hugging her, very tightly. After a moment, Ava relaxed, and for a blissful minute they just sat there, together.

Then they parted and Frances stood to get dinner ready.

Twenty-three.

*I*t was late, easily past ten, as Charlie walked slowly upstairs to bed. He paused, hearing a noise. Then he turned
at the top of the stairs and went into Theo's room.

"Daddy?"

Charlie sat on his son's bed, his weight tipping the child
slightly toward him. Theo completed the small fall, curling
around his dad and resting his head near Charlie's legs. In public
this boy was slightly standoffish, but in private he had always
been a cuddle bug. Charlie rested his hand on Theo's head,
smoothing back his hair.

"Yes, buddy? Can't you sleep? It's really late, and you have
school in the morning."

"I know." Such a small voice.

"What's up?"

"Can I ask you something?"

"Sure."

"You promise you won't get mad?"

Charlie nodded, and meant it. "I promise. Ask whatever you
like, but then you should go to sleep."

The little boy nodded. A beam of moonlight slid through a

gap in his dinosaur curtains and illuminated one ear. Charlie looked at where he assumed his son's eyes were, trying not to notice the similarity between Theo's ear and his mom's.

"Why isn't Mom living here anymore? What really happened? Someone at school said she cheated on you."

"Who said that?"

"I don't remember," lied Theo.

Charlie sighed. "Well, I'm afraid that's kind of true. Your mom met someone else she liked more than me."

There was a silence.

"I don't know what you mean."

Charlie shrugged. "It's hard to explain, chief. You know when you've had a toy a very long time and you get something new? For a while that new toy is so much better than the old one, right? It's exciting, it's shiny, it does new things . . ." He trailed off, wondering if Richard had done new things with Anne, things he'd never tried. Maybe he just had new jokes. Maybe he went to the gym more. Or at all. Maybe he loved different things about her than Charlie had loved. Still loved.

Theo wasn't satisfied. "Yeah, I get that. But some toys are so good you never stop liking them, right?"

"Like?"

"Like Rotten Corner." Rotten Corner was the name he'd given a piece of baby blanket he'd carried around since he was a toddler. "Does your blankie have a name?" Anne had asked, as he'd sat on her lap, sucking his thumb and curling and uncurling the piece of baby blanket, its blue and red stripes still bright from the hospital. He'd told her it was called Rotten Corner, two words she'd had no idea he even knew, and clearly the name had stuck. Now RC, as it was more familiarly known, was a pale piece of blanket about a foot square, all the color washed out, but the magic still intact. It was folded under Theo's pillow now, just in case.

"Yeah, some things are like that."

"You're like that for me, Dad." Theo reached as far as he could around his father and moved his head onto his dad's lap. "I won't ever want a newer dad."

Charlie felt his throat tighten. What if Anne ended up marrying this asshole? What if he tried to be a dad to Charlie's kids? For a moment he felt light-headed with a mix of anger and fear, then he unclenched his fist and spoke softly.

"Buddy, no one could love you and your sister more than I do. And your mom loves you both just as much as she ever did. The problems we're having are between us, just grown-up stuff. It doesn't mean anything about you guys, OK?"

Theo turned his head and looked up at his father. The moonbeam was now falling on the back of his neck, and Charlie could see the bones of his upper spine sticking up against his pajama top. "If she loves us so much," he said in a voice as pale as a whisper, "she wouldn't want to play with anyone else. We'd be like Rotten Corner, the best forever. The best *because* it's old, not new." He started to cry a little, and tried to cover it, pushing his voice through the lump in his throat so he'd seem tougher than his dad might think. "A new one might be shiny, but it wouldn't know anything. RC knows everything about me, it's been everywhere. Why doesn't Mom care about that?" His hand tightened on Charlie's leg. "Is she going to have new kids, too?"

From down the hall Kate cried out, and Charlie was saved from answering a question he didn't have an answer to.

"Let me go see what's up with Kate, OK? I'll come back in a minute."

Theo watched his father go, and reached under his pillow.

Kate had had a bad dream, and wanted to sleep with Charlie. He picked her up, her head already lolling on his shoulder and carried her into his bedroom. He had no idea nighttimes were so active in the house; he'd always been the one who slept through. After placing her on Anne's side and covering her up, he sighed and went back to Theo's room. His son was sleeping, too, his cheek pressed against the damp piece of blanket he loved so much.

Charlie went back to bed and lay there for an hour or two, wondering if Anne was going to have new children.

Twenty-four.

AYSO, which stood for something Frances could never accurately remember, and which was also described as peewee soccer, was Frances's least favorite thing in the world. She also felt pretty strongly about eggplant, but she fucking hated little kids' soccer. It started in the fall, which in L.A. is still really hot, and involved several painful rites of passage. When she and Michael had been considering a third child she had said out loud, *No, wait, we'd have to do soccer again* . . .

For some reason it was a blight that hit every family hard. It started with the application form, which was only slightly less detailed than the forms for getting into one of the city's charter schools, which were currently heading the field of Forms That Are Complicated Beyond Belief. Then there was the day, which started at some ungodly hour like seven on a Saturday, when the teams got picked. You'd see groups of experienced parents herding their kids together as swiftly as greyhounds rounding a track corner; while other, less experienced parents ended up wandering around with wobbly chinned kids looking for a group that "had room." Shockingly painful, especially when your kid ended up in a little clump of other kids whose parents didn't understand the process. It was the sporting version of the Island of Misfit Toys, and if you think five-year-olds haven't seen that movie, you're drunk. Then there was Team Parent and Snack Mom and Volunteer Coach, all positions that went to parents who'd just gotten off the turnip truck, soccer-ly speaking.

She personally hated Team Parent, but Coach was also a disaster. She'd seen world-famous directors in bright jerseys made of nonbreathing material reduced almost to tears by the challenge of getting a dozen six-year-old boys to run in the same direction. Get a thousand horses to come over a hill at once, sure; get precious actors to emote on cue, no problem; wrangle a set of producers who don't understand the importance of using real butterflies, damn the cost, all in a day's work. But stand in the blazing October sunshine getting Tarquin, Samson, Argo and Aero (twins) to stop kicking the ball at one another's heads, impossible. Snack Parent sucked ass, too: She once saw a mom who published a well-known mommy blog about finding the joy in every moment, handing out Tic Tacs from the bottom of her purse as the postgame snack. Thank God the bottle of Xanax was in her other bag.

On this Saturday Frances had drawn the short straw because Michael had some work thing he "needed" to do. She was marginally bitter as she stood on the sidelines being grateful she wasn't Snack Mom this time, when she heard her name being called. She turned and smiled, while inside her head she said, *Fuck, fuck, fuckity fuck.* She braced herself.

Shelly was a mom in Milo's class, and Frances hated and feared her in equal measure. She was a "cool mom" on the surface. Casual shoes that cost a fortune, leggings on toned legs under vintage kaftans, jewelry personalized with her many children's names, a commitment to veganism and alternative medicine, a firm belief in the joy of a childhood lived free of electronics and sugar, and a tendency to gossip about other parents with the rapier knife of a trained assassin. She specialized in concern, and as she got closer, Frances could see the small eyebrow furrow that indicated she was about to ask about Anne Porter.

"Frances, how *are* you?" Shelly cooed, embracing Frances and, as always, making her feel momentarily guilty for doubting this woman's good intentions. "How are the kids?" She turned and looked at Lally, who was running in the wrong direction, but grinning like an idiot. "Lally looks like she's having a good time." She kept watching as the referee came over and turned Lally around, sending her heading in the right direction without apparently realizing she'd been turned. "And that's all that matters really, right?"

"Of course," said Frances, correctly reading the implied comment on Lally's lack of athletic coordination. Shelly's kids were naturally good at lots of things, which, to be fair, was hardly their fault. Otter and Persimmon, both girls, and Gin and Arable, boys. Shelly liked to question gender-normative naming conventions because, as she had memorably put it at one early birthday party, names carry such weight in our society. Frances often wondered how much weight being named after a water mammal, a fruit, a clear alcohol, and a farming term carried, but as the kids themselves were very nice and easygoing, she'd never posed the question.

"I heard the news about Anne Porter, it's terrible." Shelly looked at the ground, almost conjuring a tear, and radiating Genuine Concern. She looked up in time to catch Frances's raised eyebrow, and added, "Not that I know her very well, of course. Not like you."

Frances wondered if Shelly was suggesting that Frances was

somehow complicit in Anne's cheating, but decided to give her the benefit of the doubt. "Yes, it's sad. I hope they're able to work it out."

"For the children."

"Sure, but also for them. I imagine divorcing someone is very painful, even if you're both ready to leave the marriage."

"And Charlie presumably isn't ready, seeing as he wasn't the one cheating."

Frances shrugged. "You'd have to ask him. I'm trying to stay out of their business."

"How do the kids seem?"

Frances nodded her head at a distant field. "Theo's playing goal, and hasn't let any in yet, so he's presumably fine right now. Kate is sitting with her dad over there, doing stickers. I expect they're sad, but they'll be OK. Kids are resilient, right?"

Shelly looked at her and tipped her head to one side. "You know, Frances, you don't need to be defensive. Friends rally around at times of crisis, it takes a village, right?" She smiled sweetly. "It's interesting when other people's pain brings up issues . . . Are you and Michael having problems?"

Frances resisted the urge to punch the other woman in the throat. "I didn't think I was being defensive, Shelly. I'm sorry if I gave you that impression." She felt herself starting to sweat, hating any kind of conflict. "If you're so worried about the Porters you should go and speak to Charlie, he's right there." She wasn't even going to touch the comment about her own marriage. She herself never felt she was intimate enough with someone to ask about their marriage, unless they were, like, friends for a decade or related by blood or thrown together on a sinking cruise liner or something. You came across this false, fast intimacy all the time in the circles she moved in. People who loved to talk about their feelings, their fears, their colonic irrigation, their therapy, their children's therapy, their sex life, their new car. Frances barely had room in her head for her own feelings plus a running grocery list. She felt like the Mad Hatter: No room! No room!

She looked around, hoping the soccer game was nearly over, or that Lally had been mildly concussed, or something that would end this stupid conversation. But no, Lally was now running in a different direction, still wrong, but different. Over on a nearby pitch Milo was playing a real game of soccer, as the difference between four and ten years old was significant when it came to rules and balls. Ava had loved soccer. Frances suddenly had a vision of the little trophies she used to bring home proudly, the slices of orange making her wrists sticky, the bouncing ponytail as she pelted across the grass. That nine-year-old was long gone now and Ava seemed to barely remember her, or even care about the things that used to matter so much. Dinosaurs. Doll clothes. Horses. Legos. Drawing was the only one that stayed, the one passion that had yet to wane.

"Frances?" Shelly was still looking at her, a deeper wrinkle between her eyebrows. Shit, apparently she'd drifted off there for a moment. She looked at Shelly and smiled vaguely.

"Sorry, Shelly, got distracted. What were you saying?"

But Shelly herself was suddenly distracted by something behind Frances, and the way her eyes widened suggested it was way more interesting than Frances's apparent descent into dementia. Frances turned, guessing before she saw her that Anne Porter had just arrived.

―――

Anne realized as she got closer that this was a major mistake, but she had told Charlie she would show up and there was no turning back. She couldn't have chosen a more public place to appear, as pretty much everyone she knew was there, or at least enough of them that everyone she knew would get a firsthand account.

She felt like crap. Apart from the eggs at Frances's she'd barely eaten in the last few days. She still hadn't called her parents: Her mother didn't enjoy bad news. Or maybe she did enjoy it, but whoever brought the bad news lived to regret it. Anne decided to wait until she had a better story to tell. Rather than, "Hi, Mom, I fucked up massively and now my life has shattered into a million pieces," she wanted to be able to lead with, "Hi, Mom, Charlie and I have been having some problems, but it's all better now. How are you?" It might take a while, but she was going to wait for that. Her mom preferred to parent the good parts of her children only.

Now Anne was standing in the heat of the soccer fields in the park, looking around for her kids and trying very hard not to make eye contact with the parent body of her school. It was hard because although a generous third of them were doing her the courtesy of pretending she wasn't there, the other two-thirds were avidly watching and hoping she was either drunk or insane. Some of them were looking behind her, hoping she'd brought the eighteen-year-old she was supposedly sleeping with.

Suddenly she saw Frances, and instinctively started walking toward her. Frances was looking at her, but with a question in her eyes, rather than judgment: *Are you OK?* Anne walked toward her resolutely, avoiding any other eye contact. As she got closer, though, she realized Shelly was standing with Frances and nearly stopped. Shelly was absolutely the worst possible person to run into, but fortunately Frances was stepping around her and walking to meet Anne in the middle, curving her body as she walked to suggest a bench off to one side as a meeting point. It was like semaphore: *Don't panic, we're heading for that bench, we're going to make it, keep going.* Anne had started to feel tingling in her hands, and pulsing nausea; she was going to have a panic attack.

"You're fine," was the first thing Frances said as they got close enough to hear each other. "You're fine, just sit down on the bench. I'll get out the taser and keep the bitches at bay, OK?"

"OK." Anne's voice was a whisper.

They were now walking together, and Frances added, "Lili's here somewhere, and so are Jim and Andy, and between us we will create a human shield if we have to."

They reached the bench and sat down. Anne was breathing rapidly, her color very bad, her nausea worsening.

"I'm going to throw up."

Frances shifted her purse on her shoulder and let it fall to the ground. "Oh dear, I dropped my purse. Quick, bend down and help me pick up my shit. Keep your head lower than your knees."

Anne did as she was told. Frances, it turned out, had a great deal of stuff in her handbag. Toys, sweets, coins, a pack of cards that spilled helpfully across the grass, a little Hot Wheels car, a bottle of bubble solution, several pens, several pen lids, none of which went together, and so on and so forth.

Frances knelt on the grass in front of the bench, shielding Anne while they picked up the contents of her bag. "Feeling better?"

Anne kept her head down, and a sob escaped her. "No."

Frances made a soft noise of support, such as one might make to a child, and touched Anne on the knee. "Anne, you messed up, but you're here now for your kids, and you need to pull it together. You are not going to throw up or freak out, you are going to let the blood flow back into your extremities and once you're able to stand up again we'll find the kids and you will be good once you see them, alright?"

"If they want to see me. If Charlie will let me."

"He told you to come here, right?" Frances looked worried, suddenly. "You're not just turning up unexpectedly?"

Anne shook her head, gathering the playing cards together and searching for a rubber band or something to keep them together. Frances handed her a black-covered hair elastic, which worked just fine. "No, I'm invited."

"Excellent." Frances looked relieved.

"He's coming," Anne said and suddenly sat up, the blood restored, the nausea subsided, the inner anxiety reduced just by seeing her husband, even though he hated her now. She tried a smile. He'd always loved her smile.

Charlie didn't smile back. Instead he spoke to Frances. "Nice to know whose side you're on, Frances."

Frances sat back on her heels and looked up at him. He was barely holding it together. "Don't be silly, Charlie. She looked like she was about to pass out, and rather than give the local witches something even juicier to talk about, I helped. I hope you would do the same for me."

He shook his head. "Not if you'd cheated on your husband and ruined the happiness of your children. You'd be just as big a bitch as she is." He looked at his wife with disgust. "I'd have let her fall, personally."

Frances stood up. "I'm glad to see you're handling this so well. I'm going back to my kids now, before I say something we both have to live with for years." She turned back to Anne and smiled. "Sorry, Anne. I hope you feel better."

Apparently soccer was over because behind them they heard

Kate and Theo happily calling to their mother, and thundering in their direction. Frances walked away, and the kids passed her going top speed. Her own kids were waiting for her, watching her come with trusting expressions. There were juice boxes in their future, and possibly ice cream.

"Is Anne OK?" Shelly had stepped into her path, looking concerned in a way that suddenly pissed Frances off. Shelly barely knew Anne, she just wanted to be the One Who Knew the Scoop.

"Sure," replied Frances, not slowing down very much.

"Can you believe she cheated on Charlie? He's so nice. Those poor kids. So selfish, right?" Shelly made a little clicking sound with her tongue. Frances still didn't slow down, but she looked at Shelly and raised her eyebrows.

"You know absolutely nothing about it, Shelly, and you should keep your ill-formed and unwelcome judgments to yourself. Maybe your life is a well-orchestrated series of elegant vignettes, with perfect photo opportunities every ten minutes, but if you're anything like the rest of us then you're lurching from one near-disaster to the next, crossing your legs every time you cough so you don't pee your pants after having had four children."

Shelly just stared at her, her mouth open.

"That's what I thought," said Frances, walking by and farting silently as she went. She was opposed to chemical warfare on principle, but sometimes you just had to go with what you had at hand.

Twenty-five.

Theo and Kate were beyond excited to see their mom, which wasn't surprising, thought Charlie. He had felt the usual warm feeling, too, for a nanosecond. Habituated neurons firing as they always had. It takes a while for the head to catch up with the heart, it would seem. He was so incredibly angry with Anne it took all he had not to scream at her or slap her, something he had never, ever even been remotely tempted to do to her, or to anyone. But he didn't, because his kids were beaming and hanging on her and she was smiling down at them as if she hadn't just thrown away their happiness for a fuck.

Two days earlier, after he had spoken to the school principal, he had forced himself to call his wife.

"It's me."

"I'm so sorry, so sorry, Charlie, I really never . . ." She had started crying as soon as she saw his name on her phone, "ICE Charlie Porter." Would he even come in an emergency now? She'd have to change that along with every other single aspect of her life.

He couldn't have been further from tears. "Save it. We need

to tell the children together. I just met with the principal. She persuaded me that it's better for them."

There was a pause. "What are we going to tell them?"

"We're going to tell them that we're not being very good friends right now, and that you're going to move out for a while so we can stay friends. That we love them just as much, that we are still their mom and dad, and that it has nothing to do with them."

"You're not going to tell them about what I did?"

"Not today. Today we're going to just tell them what's going to happen. Are you able to do that? Mrs. Garcia said it's better if we both do it, but if you're going to fall apart I'll do it alone."

For a split second Anne remembered how cold he had been on the phone, as she hugged her children on this hot Saturday afternoon, and looked up at him. He looked like he could punch her any minute, and although she had never been afraid of him before, not even fleetingly, now she dropped her gaze.

"Where do you want to go, my loves?" *Focus on the kids, Anne.*

Kate shouted out for ice cream, but Theo looked confused. "Aren't we just going home?"

His dad's voice came from behind him. "Mommy isn't living there right now, remember?"

Theo frowned, and turned to face his father. "But she can still visit, right? She's still our mom." He turned back to Anne and tugged on her hand. "You can come to my room, Mom."

"And mine!" Kate said, jealously. "We can play Littlest Pet Shop."

Theo was scornful. "She doesn't want to play that."

Anne would have given her right arm to play Littlest Pet Shop with Kate as if nothing was wrong, but she tried not to show it. She waited for Charlie to give her permission to visit her own house, a house that was half in her name, a house she could choose to forcibly occupy if she wanted.

Charlie was wrestling with competing desires: On the one hand he wanted Anne nowhere near his house, but he also wanted his kids to feel safe, loved, and on his side. He was so ashamed of this feeling that he immediately said Anne could come. Of course.

"I want to ride with Mom!" Kate said, jumping up and down. "Did you get a new car?"

Anne shook her head. "No, I walked here, we can all just go home together." The words came out smoothly, but she suddenly needed to use the bathroom, her gut twisting at the thought of walking into her house.

But her face showed nothing, and together they all walked to their car, just like it was any other Saturday.

————

Walking into his house behind his wife, Charlie nearly lost it when Anne went to hang her keys on the hook, then realized she didn't live there anymore. Like a sound wave her pain passed back from her to him, the whole moment lasting maybe half a second. He wanted to cut out this connection to her like a tumor. He wanted to wind back his arm and throw a ball of shared history arcing out over the ocean, an unheard splash, unrecoverable. But he couldn't forget loving Anne any more than he could forget a second language spoken every day for a decade. She was in the curls of his brain. His eyes had recorded and decoded her tiniest expression. They'd seen and codified her fear, her caution, her passion, her childbirth, her laughter. His hands had touched her intimately, aroused her, held her hair while she threw up, carried her into their first house, wiped her brow in fever, handed her diapers and wipes, brought her coffee. He'd smelled her perfume, her blood, her hair, her bad morning breath. He'd heard her voice, possibly every word and tone her larynx was capable of. She was talking now, asking the kids if they were hungry, as if she was still their mother, which of course she was, and always would be. Suddenly he hated her with each and every one of the senses that had loved her so thoroughly for so long.

"I'll get them a snack," he said roughly, pushing past her, aware he'd made her step sideways, knowing by that brief touch that she'd lost weight, that she was barely holding it together. *Get out of my head,* he wanted to scream, *disappear from the earth and never have existed, all of you.*

"Is there raisin toast?" Kate asked. He smiled at her and nodded. For a moment he had the mad thought he was cheating on his children by pretending to be OK when, in fact, he was clinging to sanity with only the tiniest sliver of fingernail. He wondered if this was how Anne felt, if the distance between her inside and her outside had been that yawning a chasm. Well, he was holding it together for the kids and she should have, too, the bitch.

He pulled two pieces of raisin bread from the bag and put them in the toaster, pushing down the lever hard enough the first time, rather than having to do it over and over as so often happened. See? Broken on the inside, capable on the outside.

The kids had run upstairs to change out of their soccer stuff, and Anne watched her husband standing by the toaster, apparently guarding the little machine from attack. He'd made it stay down the first time; she could never do that. It was fussy, that toaster, maybe the fifth one they'd had in as many years. How come they couldn't make toasters that lasted anymore? Her grandparents had had the same toaster her whole childhood, one with enamel sides with blue flowers on them, drawn by what must have been a drunken artist with a shaky hand, his blue pencil wavering as he drew those long stems and petals.

Charlie was angry, she could see it in his shoulders, and she ached for him more than she'd ever ached for anything. The toast popped and she watched him butter it for Kate with quick, efficient movements, getting the butter to the edges, no further. He loved his kids so much, and he would never love her again. He turned and carried the toast past her, the cool breeze of his passing sweetened by the smell of raisins.

"Charlie," she said, her voice breaking.

"Toast," he replied, walking out of the room.

———

She waited for him in the kitchen, but he didn't come back. Looking around she noticed how much tidier it was now that she no longer lived there. Who would have guessed she was the messy one? She went upstairs but her bedroom door was closed, so she went to Kate's room. Kate was out of her soccer uniform, but had clearly been interrupted by the arrival of the toast, because she was wearing leggings and socks, but no top. Anne brushed toast crumbs from her daughter and pulled a little sweatshirt over her head. Then she sat down in the glider where she'd rocked this child from birth, and pulled Kate onto her lap.

"How's school? Anything fun happen?"

Kate nodded, her smooth hair brushing Anne's chin. "Ella got a kitten. We wanted to call it Yellowy, but her mom called it Butterscotch." She pulled her head away from Anne and looked at her. "Isn't that a dumb name? What does that even mean?"

Anne was surprised. "It's a kind of candy. And kind of a color, too, sort of a browny yellow."

"Ohhhh . . ." Kate nodded again, light dawning. "I get why it's a good name then." There was a small pause. "Why can't you be living with us anymore?" Kate's voice was soft. "Daddy can go away and you can come back."

Anne was still thinking of the kitten and scrambled to catch up. "I can't baby. Daddy and I aren't friends right now, and . . ."

"You told me it's not nice to stay mad when someone said sorry already. You told me that when Liesl at school melted my Easter chicken and I was so angry and she was crying, remember? I remember that."

Anne remembered. "Yes, that's right, it's better to forgive someone when they . . ."

"And you said sorry, right? You said sorry, didn't you?" Surely her mother wouldn't forget this very basic first step.

Anne nodded. Mindlessly she noticed Kate's bedroom was as tidy as the kitchen. He'd had the cleaners in. It wasn't her bad influence; it was his readiness to throw money at a problem.

"Well then, Daddy should let you come home and be friends again." Kate started to squirm off Anne's lap. "I'll go tell him, maybe he didn't hear you."

Anne held her hand. "He heard me, sweetheart, but he's just still really mad. I did a bad thing, and it might take more than sorry."

Kate frowned at her. "There is no more than sorry."

Anne swallowed. "Do you remember when I told you that when you say mean things it makes little holes in people, do you remember that?" She'd read this analogy on Facebook or something, about nails in wood or some such thing, some deep thing that made her nod thoughtfully and feel a tiny pain in her heart.

"And that when you say sorry it's like covering those holes. It helps, but it doesn't make the holes go away forever, remember?"

"Yes."

"You broke a plate." Theo's voice came from the doorway. Anne looked up, and Kate turned to face her brother.

"I did?" Anne didn't remember that. You'd think she'd remember that.

Theo nodded. "Kate wasn't there. It was after Ollie and I got into a fight at school, and you had to come in and see Mrs. Garcia, remember?"

It came back to her.

"You were super mad, and you took a plate out of the cupboard and you said that when I said hurtful things to someone it was like breaking a plate, and then you smacked the plate on the counter and it broke in two and then you put both pieces together and said, 'Look, see, it's fixed but there's still a crack. There will always be a crack,' you said."

Anne frowned. Shit. When she'd performed this magnificently meaningful symbolic piece of parenting she hadn't considered this outcome.

"But the plate still worked, right?" Kate looked anxious. "Even if you and Daddy are cracked you can still be together, right?" She looked at her older brother, whose face was so still it might have been porcelain itself. "They can be together again, if she says sorry and he says thank you and lets her come back, right?" Her brother shrugged at her, ten so much more resigned to ambiguity than six.

"I did say sorry, honey, but Daddy's still really angry, and he needs some time apart. Like when you get mad and you want to be alone in your room for a while to calm down, right?"

Kate was visibly struggling, and Anne suddenly wondered if

all these allegories and examples and parallels were helping her understand, or if they were just things Anne could say in the face of inexplicable pain. If the people of Pompeii had built a baking soda and vinegar model of a volcano as schoolchildren would that have made their sudden, disastrous demise more . . . relatable? Would they have been like, *Oh, hey, we've seen this before, we know how this is working. Yes, we're all about to die in an instant of suffocating heat that cooks our lungs and roasts our beating hearts in our chests,* but we get how it works, so, you know, that's something. *We know* how, *even if we are still blaming the gods for* why. Kate didn't look like she was understanding any of it, and her expression said her heart was running the show because, let's face it, her brain was letting things *go to serious shit around here.*

The little girl suddenly left the room. As Theo and Anne looked at each other, she realized the expression on her son's face was pity.

Down the hall, Kate was tearful but optimistic. "Mommy says she's sorry, Daddy, she's really sorry OK?"

Anne got to her feet. She reached her own bedroom in time to hear Charlie say, "I know she is, babycakes, but I think it's too late for that."

Kate stamped her foot. "It's never too late for sorry, you told me that last week when you found the pudding."

"That was different."

"No. Mommy did something bad, she didn't tell you, just like me and the pudding, and then when you found out, she said sorry. And I helped you clean it up, didn't I? Even though it was all sticky, I helped you, and I said sorry and you said it was OK." She started to cry. "So why is it too late for Mommy to say sorry?"

"Mommy did more than make a mess, honey. It was a grown-up thing, it doesn't matter what she did, it's done and it can't be cleaned up." Charlie looked up at his wife standing in their bedroom doorway and all he wanted to say was: *Please come home and let's never, never talk about this again. Let's pretend it never happened; let's rip the pages out of the fucking calendar and move to another state and start over.* But that couldn't work because the knowledge would linger under his skin like a keloid and he'd rub it absentmindedly during every silence that fell in their marriage from that moment on.

Anne saw all this on his face, even as she noticed he was wearing the boxer shorts she'd given him for Christmas many years before. Reindeer on skis. She couldn't see from here, but she knew the flannel under his balls was wearing thin, had thought a few months earlier that new holiday boxer shorts should be under the tree this year. Her stomach twisted at the thought of Christmas. Oh my God, his parents.

"She said she's sorry!" Kate was losing it, her voice clogged with tears and her un-blown nose. "You have to accept her apology, you have to! You're the one being mean now, you're the one who's doing the bad thing! You have to say sorry! You both have to say sorry!!" She fell, sobbing, to the floor, literally pulling on her own hair, her tiny fingers so furious at herself for not being able to make this right, not being a big enough girl to fix this, until her brother pushed past his parents and joined her on the ground, pulling her onto his lap and rocking her, smoothing her hair and holding her fingers, letting her pinch him so hard, letting her punch and smack at his face—the only person in her life left to safely get angry at. He looked at his father, his eyes cold and unblinking. Ten years old. Battlefield promotion to adult, first grade.

Anne turned and walked downstairs, unable to handle their pain. Coward. As she turned at the bottom of the stairs and stumbled out she could hear her husband closing the bathroom door above her. She walked away from the house blindly, the door left open behind her, her children sitting alone on the bedroom floor where they'd opened birthday presents and run for hugs and crossed for bad dreams in the middle of the night, totally alone. She was every bit the bad mother she'd always known she was, and had a car driven along the street at that very moment she would have thrown herself in front of it with relief.

Twenty-six.

When Frances had come boiling back from soccer, full of ire at Shelly and a certain amount of pride at being able to fart on cue, Michael had been surprisingly unsupportive. He had simply made a face at her and kept watching the football game on his computer.

Frances frowned at him. "You don't think I was right to get annoyed at her?"

Her husband shrugged, still keeping his eye on the ball. "I think you were judging her as much as she was judging Anne, to be honest. The farting I support completely."

Frances sat on the bed and looked at him. "But Shelly doesn't even know Anne."

"You don't know her all that well yourself. It's not like you and Iris. You and Anne were always, you know, different from each other. I would call you politely warm acquaintances."

"Aren't you friends with Charlie?"

"Not really. I'd go get a beer with him. I'd definitely do a playdate or something with Theo and Milo, but would I confide my concerns about erectile dysfunction? Nope."

"Do you have concerns about erectile dysfunction?"

"Nope."

"Well then."

"Not the point. I'm clarifying degrees of friendship." He sat back from the computer, and regarded his wife thoughtfully. "There are those friends we're friends with because our kids are at school together. We are happy to see them at school events, birthday parties, etc. We hang out preferentially with them at stuff like that, because we like them better and have more in common with them than other parents. Right? But you'd never invite them to dinner because you have about forty-five minutes of conversation and that's about it."

Frances frowned. "Like who?"

"Tracy and Arthur? Andrew and John? Dahlia's mom and dad, whatever their names are?" Michael was clearly master of this material. Frances thought about it. He was right. People she liked, but had no real desire to know any better than she did already.

"But Anne and Charlie are different than that."

"Because they're neighbors, and because that means Theo and Milo could potentially be friends outside of school, ergo, not a time-limited friendship. Plus, carpool, therefore a relationship of dependence." He was about to steeple his fingers like a professor, but chose to scratch his armpit instead. Keeping it classy.

"Since when did you get a degree in anthropology?" Frances pulled off her sneakers, wondering if that was mud or dog shit. She threw the shoe under the bed, either way. A doctor friend of hers had once told her the entire world was covered in a fine patina of shit particles, so why worry?

Her husband answered easily, "Since I spend so much time in traffic and my mind wanders in circles." He looked back at the game. "Anyway, then you have real, actual friends, like Sam and Cory, or Mark and Dana, who we became friends with when the kids were at preschool, and are still friends with. Not friends we see all the time, but friends we hug and love and are always pleased to see. And, more importantly, friends we would call in an emergency, friends where we could show up in the middle of the night with our asses on fire and they'd run and get a bucket of water without asking questions. Friends where you could pull up in front of their house, dump the kids, and know they'd mind them no problem until you got back from evading the authorities, or whatever." He smiled lazily at her, sure of himself. "You wouldn't necessarily leave the kids with Anne, she's just too damn coordinated." He corrected himself. "At least until now. Now she's just a hot mess." He giggled suddenly.

Frances looked at him. "Have you been smoking pot while I've been out?" There was a pause. She narrowed her eyes. "You have, haven't you?"

"It's legal in California, you know."

"I know. I'm just reframing this whole conversation and it's making a lot more sense. I don't give a shit if you had a hit or two of pot—you're not going anywhere, it's Saturday afternoon, you're still in your boxer shorts. But I'm paying less attention to your grand, overarching taxonomy of friendship." She tugged off her jeans and threw them at him. He reached up and caught them in midair.

"See? Not so stoned I've lost my catlike reflexes."

"That's not as reassuring as you might think." She tugged on her sweatpants and slippers, not planning on going anywhere herself. "Have you seen Ava?" A thought occurred to her. "Please tell me she didn't see you smoking pot. I'm having a hard enough time as it is."

He shook his head. "No, I took the dogs for a walk and had a quick puff while I was doing it. No big."

"You're a horrible example of a parent, and I'm going to see how she's getting on with her homework."

"She's done," Michael replied. "I already checked." Then he made finger guns at her, and she rolled her eyes.

"You're a goober."

"Maybe," he countered. "But when this game is done I promised Lally I would play My Little Pony with her, and thanks to my en-gentled state, I'm even going to enjoy it." He blew on his finger guns, and holstered them.

Frances couldn't argue with that. Game, set, and match, Poppa Pot Head. Even if *en-gentled* wasn't actually a word.

———

Ava was indeed finished with her homework, and seemed in a good enough mood for Frances to risk sitting on her bed. "What've you got planned for the rest of the day?"

Ava pulled her earbuds out and smiled at her mom. "Nothing really, got any suggestions?"

Frances considered. "Want to go to the bookstore? Art supply store?"

"Yeah!" Ava got up and went to find shoes. Frances felt elated momentarily; score one for Mom and the offer of art supplies. She ran over her usual checklist to make sure she could leave the house. Lally was taken care of, the dogs were fed, dinner was going to be pizza . . . She went to check on Milo.

Milo was lying on his bed reading, which was unusual enough for Frances to utter a noise of surprise. Her son looked up and grinned.

"I'm not always on the computer, you know. I'm too hot after soccer." He still had his cleats on, Frances noticed, with little perforated sheets of mud gradually drying and dropping onto his bed. She quite enjoyed these pieces of mud, the ones from cleats, because they looked as though they'd been crocheted by Mother Nature, like beach stones with holes in them, naturally occurring things that looked like they'd been made by people. Amusing. She stepped forward and tugged his shoes off his feet.

"What are you reading?" she asked, between tugs.

He turned the book to show her. It was some graphic novel about a middle-school kid, one of several series he loved and read and reread over and over again. Sometimes she would sit by his side at night and read them to him, even though you'd think a graphic novel wouldn't be a good read-aloud. But they were, and whether the kids were wimpy, big, heroic, or whatever, he loved them all and she loved them because he did. She'd preorder them as soon as they were announced, sure of a moment of shared excitement. God bless books.

"I'm taking Ava to the art store. Do you want to come?"

"Nah, I'm good. Dad's here, right?"

His mom nodded. He made a "well then" noise, already back to his book. She looked at the curve at the back of his ear, the way his hair grew there, echoing the shape of Michael's hairline. The color was hers, but the thickness and wave were like her brother, Alexander, long gone and never had a chance to be a favorite uncle, which he would have been. Milo was the child she understood least, even though in many ways he was the most like her. He was quiet, stable, pleasant, reliable. Precisely because he was so equable she worried he got taken for granted at school, that he would suddenly blow a gasket, that he was hiding deep sadness or rage or something.

Sometimes she would sit and talk to him for ages about Pokémon or Minecraft or *Star Trek* or whatever the heck it was he was obsessed with at that moment, and hope he might take the conversation in a more personal direction. But he rarely did. Had her brother been alive he would have been her bridge to this child, but now she was on her own. Milo and Michael were easy companions, spending time building Legos or going to baseball games or any number of the classic father-son activities. Anytime she worried aloud about their son, Michael would look at her and roll his eyes. "He's fine," he would say. "Stop forcing yourself to worry about something that isn't broken."

She squeezed Milo's shoulder, which he barely noticed, and left the room.

Twenty-seven.

The art store was surprisingly busy, although Frances wasn't sure why it was surprising. This was not her store, not one of her regular haunts. She knew the people at the grocery store checkout by name, the Trader Joe's, the bookstore on Larchmont Boulevard, the coffee place, the juice place . . . Those were hers. This was Ava's, so she followed her daughter as she confidently moved around, looking for the little things she needed and the other things she wanted.

A young man stepped out of her way, and then, a moment later, appeared around the corner of an aisle. He cleared his throat, and Frances looked up at him. *Oh, for fuck's sake.*

"Don't I know you?" he asked, half frowning. He knew her face was familiar, but these days his sadness was confusing him; he often forgot what he was doing, or where he should be. Not a student, too old for that. Another teacher?

Ava was looking from her mother to this totally hot guy, and for a split second wanted to giggle. Like her mom would know him. But still, maybe if she did . . . Ava grinned at the young man, and he smiled absently back, noticing the teen for the first time, and therefore starting to run through his rolodex of students.

Maybe this woman who seemed so familiar was just a mom he'd seen at the art college.

But Frances was now literally backing away, shaking her head gently. "No, I don't think we know each other, sorry." Ava hadn't seen his face the other day; she had no reason to learn who he was now.

But Ava hadn't turned, and the guy was insistent. "No, I'm sure I've seen you before. I'm Richard Seitz. I'm a teacher at Otis?"

"The art school?" Ava had taken over the conversation. Frances had started to sweat, and now she took her daughter's sleeve and literally tugged.

"Come on, Ava, we've got stuff to get." She turned back to Richard and her expression suddenly said, *Look, go the fuck away, we definitely know each other and either you're pretending not to know me, in which case I will fuck you up if you continue this charade, or you really have forgotten me, in which case you're in worse shape than I thought.*

He stepped back. "Sorry, my mistake."

"I've sometimes thought about going to art school, and that's a good one, right?" *Oh my God*, Frances thought, Ava's flirting with this guy because, let's face it, he's cute and closer to her age than he is to Anne's, but there is simply no way this is happening.

Richard was still not getting it. "It is. I'd be happy to show you around sometime, if you like. We have open houses all the time." He pulled out his wallet. "I'll give you my card, you can e-mail me."

That's when Frances turned to look at him with an expression of extremely explicit warning and Richard suddenly remembered who she was, where he'd seen her, and why she was tugging her cute little daughter away from him down the clay aisle.

———

Ava was pissed. "Why wouldn't you let me talk to that guy?" She was sitting in the front seat, the art store bag on her lap, clearly simmering.

"He was too old for you," Frances replied, eyeing the ice cream store across the street. She wanted a milkshake so badly, no wonder she was overweight. She ate whenever she felt bad, which was more frequently than you might think. Also when she felt good. And sad. And angry. OK, she ate whenever she fucking felt like it, and having run through the familiar "I want to eat that, no, you're too fat, no, I'm a feminist and I reject your body-shaming bullshit, but what about your health, what *about* my health, like you care about my health, you just want me to conform to some cultural norm, I'm talking about a milkshake and I'm a grown-ass lady and fuck you" thing, she suddenly turned the car off and got out. It was more than a milkshake, it was a political stand, and she was going to add malt. Ava didn't move, so Frances leaned down to the window.

"Do you want ice cream?"

"He wasn't too old for me, one. And two, ew, he was like thirty—you shouldn't even be thinking about him like that—and I was only asking about school. I thought you wanted me to go to college?" Ava went to open the car door and Frances stepped back to put money in the meter.

"I do want you to go to college, but I didn't want you talking to some strange guy in an art store. He'd be asking you to pose nude next."

"Which would have been reasonable if he's an artist, right?" Ava wasn't as mad now, because ice cream, and because she was finding this conversation amusing.

They entered the store, with its high ceilings and metal tables and chairs and familiar faces.

"Chocolate malted?" The guy at the counter had seen Frances so many times, and she never wavered. She didn't let him down and nodded. Unbeknownst to her they called her Mommy Malted. Not that she would have cared. "And for you?" The guy looked at Ava, and his expression altered, subtly. Not so subtly that Frances missed it, and it struck her that the days when she got that "Hey, I see you, attractive young woman" look, were long gone. She got friendly, she got recognition, eventually, but she no longer got physical awareness. She didn't mind, although she knew many women who hated it, who hated becoming slowly invisible, fading away. Like Marty McFly in his family photo.

"I'll get a shake, too, but cookies and cream, please." Then Ava smiled at him, the smile that said, "Hey, attractive young man, I see you and I see you seeing me and it's nice that we see each other, ciao babe." Then they turned away to wait. So much communication, so little time. Ava turned her back on the cashier and spoke again to her mother.

"Like, if he's an artist and wants to draw me that's a different getting nude than any other kind, right?"

Frances shook her head, looking at the cakes and cookies in the case. There was a blue velvet cake that perplexed her, even as she wanted to try it. "No, and you know it. You're fourteen. You shouldn't even be thinking of getting nude." She paused, struggling to be honest. "Actually, that's not true. At fourteen you probably will be thinking about it a lot, but you shouldn't be doing it." She wrestled a little more, thinking back to her own teen years, her virginity lost at fifteen, quite happily, with a fellow fifteen-year-old she still knew on Facebook, and whose two sons were around the same age as Ava. "Or at least, not with a man twice your age."

Ava laughed. "You just revised your position, like, fifty times in one sentence." She looked at her mom's face, pondering. "You did know him, though, didn't you?" She made the connection. "Was he Anne's friend from the other day?"

Frances shrugged. "Maybe he's a parent, or maybe I see him at the café a lot or something. You must have people like that, kids you see at school a lot but don't know. You'd recognize them on the street, but you don't *know* them."

"Sure." Their milkshakes arrived, and they headed back outside.

Richard was standing there, clearly waiting for them. "I need to talk to you," he said to Frances, starting to cry.

———

Ava had been sent back to the car, where she was doubtless sorting through her throwing stars collection, waiting for her mother to get back within range. She had Very Much Wanted to stay and hear the conversation, but Frances had been firm. Now she and Richard were standing on the street, twenty feet away. Out of throwing star range, but Frances kept one eye on the car windows, making sure they stayed closed.

"Is Anne OK?" Richard had stopped crying for a moment, but he didn't look all that composed.

Frances shrugged. "She's alive. Her life is fucked, but I guess you know that."

He shook his head, and Frances realized he was both young

and not as young as she had thought. He had to be thirty, maybe a little less. He wasn't a child, he was a man, a grown man who could easily be a father, a husband, even an ex-husband. Suddenly she felt bad for him. Who knew what Anne and he had had together? It had been a bad idea, in her humble opinion, and not worth the price in any way whatsoever, but that didn't mean it didn't have *some* value.

"She's not talking to me. I haven't spoken to her since I spoke to her husband." His voice was full of tears, though his eyes were dry.

"You spoke to Charlie?" Frances was confused.

Richard looked at her, noticing the kindness in her eyes, feeling his own eyes fill with tears in the face of such obvious pity. "Yes, he answered her phone and told me to fuck off. He threatened to break my arm if I came anywhere near him and the kids."

"He did?" Frances suddenly grinned, unable to stop herself. She covered her mouth and tried to get it together. This was so very awkward.

And just as suddenly, Richard grinned, too, close to hysterics. "Yes. He was very articulate. I'm ashamed to say I had never really thought of him as an actual person, you know. I didn't know what he looked like. He was just the Other Man."

Frances stopped grinning. "To be honest, he was the First Man, the Husband Man, but I get it." She looked over at the car, and caught Ava staring at them. Great, God only knew what she was making of this. Better wind up this weirdness. "Didn't you realize this was going to happen? You're not a teenager."

Richard wiped his face with the back of his hand and Frances fought a desire to hand him a tissue. "I guess so, but I love her so much. I want to marry her. She won't speak to me." He started crying again and stepped into Frances, blindly, someone else's son, but someone's child nonetheless, however tall he was. She put her arms around him as he rested his head against her shoulder and cried and cried and cried. Frances patted his back, murmuring little mommy sounds as she had so many times in the last fourteen years. She looked over at the car and saw Ava watching them with a surprisingly sympathetic expression. Next to her Frances's chocolate malted was slowly melting in the heat of the car. God fucking dammit.

Twenty-eight.

*Y*et another day dawned bright and clear. Sometimes Frances looked through the curtains and suspected Mother Nature of phoning it in. Really? Sun and blue skies *again*? Birds sang, flowers waved their frilly skirts and wafted perfume into the noses of homeless and hypocrite alike, and Frances hoped today would be less exhausting than yesterday.

She scratched her boob and farted thoughtfully, which unfortunately alerted the dogs that she was awake and available to feed them. Jack stepped on her stomach in his enthusiasm and she cursed, struggling to sit up with a comic level of arm flailing. Life was full of such inelegant moments, and Frances felt she had far more than her fair share of them. She made it to standing without snapping a bone, and headed to the bathroom.

She'd gained three pounds. How was that even possible? It couldn't have been that third slice of banana bread. Or the ice cream. She stepped off the scale and decided it must be sabotage by a foreign power. They were clearly after her, there was no other satisfactory explanation.

She headed downstairs, followed by the dogs who'd put on tap shoes, judging by the shocking noise. She stood in the kitchen doorway and thought for a moment they'd been robbed: Every drawer and cupboard door was open, packaging was scattered on the counter, a half-empty milk carton stood insultingly close to the apparently locked refrigerator. Surely it hadn't been this bad the night before? Ava must have been up in the night, making herself a snack. Coffee, let's just get to the coffee, people. Face reality in ten minutes.

Frances pulled the jug from the coffee machine, dumped the old grounds in the trash, and went to fill the jug with fresh water. It didn't start well. She inserted the faucet into the wide sleeve of her dressing gown and filled that instead of the jug, an experience that was so much less pleasant than you might think. She rolled up her dripping sleeve and tried again.

That achieved, she fed the dogs and, while the coffee machine did its work, swept off the counters, closed all the drawers and doors, stepped in cold pee of some kind, swore, put down layers of paper towels, put half-and-half into a cup and wrote *half-and-half* on the shopping list. Then she put the pee-soaked paper towels in the trash, washed her hands, and couldn't find anything to dry them on. She used the nearest dog, wrote *paper towels* on the shopping list, and poured her coffee.

It can only get better from here, she prayed, and headed back upstairs, with her coffee, to wake Ava. She made it far enough into Ava's room to open a single curtain before getting yelled at, inarticulately. Ava was not a morning person, so Frances had created a system of repeated, darting attacks not dissimilar to poking a bear with a stick. First step, curtains. Second step, lamp. Third step, insertion of cup of tea. Usually that did it. It was in no way guaranteed, and every morning was Russian roulette—optimal outcomes were sulky silence or grudging conversation, less optimal would be full-on screaming and door slamming. It was really a great way to start each day, and Frances was beginning to understand why parents were so relieved when their kids left for college.

She went back down to get hot chocolate for the other two, feeling momentarily grateful for nonteenage children. Milo and Lally both woke up like little buds unfurling, smiling and reaching for their mom. She gave them each their hot chocolate, and went back downstairs to fetch Ava's tea, pausing on the way to run in and turn on a lamp. She was yelled at again, this time with discernable words. It was working.

After she'd delivered the tea (this time just muttering from under the duvet, which was progress), Frances went to get dressed herself. She took her time, flipping through the racks in her walk-in closet, spinning her shoe tower, and steaming her face to open her pores and maximize the effectiveness of her skin regime. None of that was true: She pulled on the same pair of jeans she'd had on the day before and the hooded sweatshirt she found under them. Look, if they hadn't wanted to be worn a second day they would have run away, but instead they just lay there overnight, asking for it.

She leaned over Michael who, like his daughter, was not a morning person. "Hey there . . . coffee?"

"Go away, woman. It's the middle of the night!" Her husband groaned, sticking his head under his pillow and reaching behind himself to try and bat her away.

"It's after seven."

"No."

"Yes." Frances patted the pillow where she thought his head must be, but he just shuddered. He'd explained to her once that he and Ava slept more deeply than other people and that, for them, waking up was physically painful. He'd said, "You know that bit in science-fiction films where the crew of the spaceship wakes up from hypersleep and they're all throwing up and shivering?" She'd nodded, but frowned skeptically. "Well, it's like that for us."

"Every morning you wake up feeling like you've been traveling through space for several years in a state of suspended animation?"

"Yes. And with a feeling of terrible dread, like you've woken us up to go investigate a distress beacon from some alien planet or abandoned spaceship." He'd looked pretty serious. "It's terrible."

Nonetheless, Frances had continued to wake them up, but she did try to do it gently and with caffeine in hand. When she got downstairs again Milo was already dressed and sitting on the sofa, eating Cheerios and watching *SpongeBob*. No one ever really saw him get dressed anymore, it was so quick. If you passed his room at the right time you might hear a zipper, or the *whoosh* of a sweatshirt passing over his head, but that was it. Then he'd make his way downstairs and get his own breakfast—Frances wasn't sure he was her child at all.

Taking Michael his coffee, she checked on Ava and found her half dressed, hunting through her drawers for some specific pair of socks that were almost certainly not where she was looking for them. Frances backed out before she could get blamed, and went to help Lally.

Lally wasn't a morning person, either, but in a different way. She woke up filled with joy that another day had presented itself for her amusement, and would wander about naked for a long time if you let her, playing with her toys and singing to herself. It was charming, but it was also deeply irritating when you needed to be somewhere, like school. And she resisted clothing as if she were a cat you were trying to get into a wet suit: Not only did she not like the garment itself, she was convinced putting it on was only the beginning of her problems. However, Frances wheedled and cajoled and then threatened and bribed, and eventually she was dressed.

Frances looked at her watch. Fifteen minutes until departure. She went and checked on Michael, who was sitting up in bed looking like a baby chick who'd just gotten coldcocked with a cricket bat. Wide eyes. Staring. Sheet marks. He looked at her and asked why the dog was wet. She explained. He nodded, cupping his balls under the sheet in case someone ran through and tried to take them. It could happen.

OK, time to make lunches. Peanut butter and jelly for Lally, cheese for Milo (this year, second grade was a no-nut classroom). Frances threw in individual Tupperware containers of cherry tomatoes, secure in the knowledge she and they would meet again that evening. It was the same with the banana, but half the time she was making lunches for the teachers, imagining them looking into the lunchbox and nodding approvingly at her appropriate and healthy choices, and ignoring the Jell-O and the chocolate chip granola bars—which were the only things that ever got eaten.

Ava appeared. She was wearing a sleeveless T-shirt that read: "Feminism is the radical notion that women are human beings" and Frances clucked her tongue at it. Ava frowned.

"Go back upstairs and change. That is in no way dress code, and you know it."

"Because of what it says?"

"No," Frances said. "Because it shows your shoulders." Ava opened her mouth to argue, but Frances help up her hand. "I know. It's bullshit, it's patriarchal overreach, it prioritizes the primacy of the male gaze over the individual right to self-expression, and it's a kick-ass T-shirt. I get all that, but last time they made you put on a Justin Bieber oversize hoodie and someone posted it on Instagram and you were miserable."

Twenty minutes later they all left the house. Kate and Theo were ready, standing outside the house with comb marks in their hair. Charlie was clearly Bringing Order to Chaos, the poor sod. Then came Wyatt, who was holding a piece of toast in one hand and his shoes in the other. Then finally Lucas, who was carrying a plastic bag of Cheerios. Frances realized it was just the inner bag from the box of cereal, which she admired as an efficient choice.

Right then. Time for school.

———

At recess Kate was cornered by some of the other girls in her class.

"Hey, is it true your mom left?"

Kate frowned and looked around. There were four of them, all of them girls she'd known since kindergarten. Alison, Jemma, Becky, and the other one whose name she could never remember. She nodded, but then shrugged.

"I guess so. She's not living at our house right now. She's coming back soon."

Alison shook her head. "She's not coming back." Alison was one of those kids who was always very definite in their opinions. Often wrong, but always definite.

"Yes, she is," Kate said, no wishy-washy kid herself. "They said they're having a problem right now. When that's over she'll come back."

Alison sighed. "My dad was supposed to come back, but he

didn't. And Leo's mother went away and was supposed to come back and didn't. They always say they're coming back, but it's not true."

"Maybe this time it's true."

Another sigh. Ah, the innocence of youth. "No. It never is. Maybe you can go and live with her instead? That happens a lot, right?" She looked around for support. One of the other girls, Jemma, piped up.

"My mom lives in a much nicer house than she did when we were all in the same place. She said now that she doesn't need to pay for my dad she can afford a better place. I have a cat at her house. And a bike."

Kate considered this. Jemma had more details. "But when I stay with my dad he lets me stay up late and watch TV with him on the sofa, and then I get to sleep in his bed."

"Where does he sleep?"

"On the sofa. I guess he likes it."

"Why can't you both sleep in the bed?"

Jemma shrugged. "It's not big enough. It's just a regular bed, like I have at home. Not a big parents bed."

"Where is your mom living?"

A ball came flying toward them, but Becky deftly returned it, displaying the superior reflexes of a seven-year-old. A clump of boys scattered as the ball plowed through them, like pigeons evading a toddler. One of them hurled insults at the girls for no reason, and Becky flipped him the bird.

"I don't know where she is," Kate realized suddenly, a feeling of panic starting in her tummy.

The bell rang for the end of recess, and the girls turned to go inside. Suddenly Becky put her arm around Kate and hugged her. "Don't worry, Kate, everything will be fine. Hardly any of the kids in school have both parents at the same time. It's not that big a deal."

It felt like a big deal to Kate, but she smiled anyway.

———

That night at dinner, Lally was incredibly bent out of shape. She wanted a different plate. A different spoon. A different pasta shape. Frances tried to convince her they all tasted the same, but Lally considered that a ludicrous argument and Michael unhelpfully agreed with her.

"I think the thicker shapes, the penne, the rigatoni, the farfalle . . . they definitely taste different from the thinner ones."

"Like what?"

Ava chimed in. "Spaghetti and angel hair."

"No." Frances felt pretty strongly about this. "They taste different because of the way in which the sauce interacts with them."

"Is *interact* the right verb? I think of pasta as pretty passive, I'll be honest."

"Yes, Michael. It takes both pasta and sauce to make a taste, otherwise we would just eat them on their own."

"But I do want to eat them on their own." Lally felt this conversation was getting away from her. "I just want spaghetti with butter and cheese."

"But you like meat sauce."

"No. I've never liked it."

This was a lie, but suddenly Frances didn't care anymore. She put a fresh pan of water on to boil, and gave Lally a bowl of strawberries in the meantime.

Milo had been steadily eating during this whole exchange, and now pushed his plate away. "I'm done, is there dessert?"

Frances nodded. "There's ice cream in the freezer, like always. But you can't have it until everyone is done eating, like always."

Milo sighed. "May I be excused?"

Frances sighed back. "You can't just stay here with your family for more than the time it takes to eat? Maybe we have exciting news."

"Do you?"

"No."

"OK then. I have homework to do."

Frances nodded and her son got up and headed out, putting his plate down for the dogs as he did so. There was only the faintest smear of sauce left on it, but the dogs took their pre-rinse responsibilities seriously, and became worried if you didn't put your plate down. Apparently, they lived in fear of being replaced by, what, a running faucet?

"I have news," said Lally, around a strawberry.

"Oh yeah?" asked Ava, who was in a relatively good mood for once.

"Yeah. Treasure is getting a puppy." She turned to her mom. "We should get a puppy."

"No puppy," Michael said, automatically.

But Lally was insistent. "Jack and Diane are old now, we should get them a puppy."

"That's not how it works," explained her father. "They won't look after the puppy, your mom would look after the puppy, and she's got enough to do right now."

"No, I would help . . ."

"Lally, I really have my hands full enough, OK?" Frances said, maybe a little more sharply than she'd intended.

Lally looked at her mom, and suddenly subsided. "OK."

There was a short silence.

"That's it?" Ava couldn't keep it in. "You're just giving up?" She reached over to her sister and felt her forehead. "She's not hot."

"I don't want a puppy, it's OK."

Frances frowned. It was most unlike Lally to stop bugging them this quickly. There had to be something deeper at work.

"I don't want to make Mommy mad."

Michael looked over at the stove. "I think her water is boiling."

Frances got up to put the pasta on.

"It's fine, Mom, I can eat the penne." The four-year-old started eating her pasta, which was now sitting cold in front of her.

"It's not a problem, Lal, honestly." Michael reached across the table and touched her arm. "Mom's already making spaghetti."

But Lally was upset about something, and her chin was wobbling, even as it was getting covered in spaghetti sauce. Suddenly Ava spoke, her connection with her baby sister helping her put the pieces together faster than the rest of the family.

"She won't leave, Lally. It's not that big a deal. Mom's not going anywhere."

Michael looked at Frances, who had just dropped a handful of spaghetti into the water and was about to stir it to stop it from clumping. The spoon was in the air.

Lally started crying, putting down her fork and wiping her face.

"But she might."

"She won't." Ava was firm. "Good luck getting her to leave just by asking for a puppy or a different dinner. I've been driving her mad for my entire life, and she's still sticking around."

Lally sniffed and looked at her big sister. "Really?"

"Really. Honestly, I've been terrible. You're a rank amateur compared to me."

Milo had wandered in during this, having heard the commotion from the other room. "Plus," he added, "what about that time I set fire to the curtains in the front room?"

Lally's eyes grew round. She hadn't been alive for that one, but it was part of family lore. It was alternately referred to as The Curtain Incident or That Time the Dog Saved Our Lives. Jack had been a lone dog at that point, and a heroic one at that.

"If she didn't leave over an actual fire, then she isn't going to leave over pasta."

Lally looked trustingly at Milo and nodded. But then her face clouded. "But Kate and Theo didn't do anything at all and their mom left."

Michael cleared his throat. His turn. "Well, Anne left for reasons to do with her, not because of Kate and Theo. Mommies and daddies never leave because of something their kids did, or at least, only very, very, very rarely." He got up and came around to Lally's side of the table. He knelt down next to her, and turned her little face to look at him. "Listen to me, Alexandra. There is nothing, NOTHING, you could do that would make your mom or me leave you, do you understand? We have been a family for a long, long time and we're going to be following you around the grocery store when you're at college, got it?"

"That's creepy," said Ava. "You'd better not do that to me."

"I'm not promising anything."

Finally, Lally got up the nerve to look at Frances. "Are you going away?"

Frances was stirring the pasta, letting Michael and the kids sort this one out in their inimitable way. Her heart was breaking for her baby, but she kept her outside calm and measured, nothing to panic about. She smiled at Lally and shook her head. "No, baby. Your dad is right, there is nothing you can do to get rid of me. You're stuck with me forever, I'm afraid."

"Seriously," said Ava. "She's like a genetic disorder."

"Or a birthmark," added Milo, turning to head back to his homework, this crisis having been averted.

"Or termites," concluded Michael. "You might not always be able to see them, but they're nearly always there."

Frances threw a piece of spaghetti at the ceiling, where it stuck next to the one that had been there since before Lally was born. She waited, but it stayed.

Twenty-nine.

*I*t was Saturday again. There was a kids book Frances liked, where the alphabet decided to wing it for once and go in a different order from usual. *A* started it off, but then one of the other letters got pissy and they all ran about and picked their own places. It got completely out of hand, but Frances often wished things could be more like that in real life. Let's throw Tuesday out completely one week, and have two Thursdays instead. Tuesday is a pointless, soul-destroying day, the day when you're brokenhearted that the week still has so much to go, and none of this work is going to do itself. Tuesday is the day you stare at the wall and wonder if you should have chosen a different major. A different husband. A different haircut. Wednesday you get your shit together emotionally because, let's face it, you've been doing days in this order your whole life, and what's the point of fighting the system? At work, however, it's touch and go all day. But Thursday? Thursday you can see the weekend ahead and you get a second burst of steam and plow through everything so you can leave early on Friday. Frances gave this kind of thing a lot of thought, and if there were a "Random and Totally Useless Thoughts" category on *Jeopardy!*, she would crush it.

Frances was back at AYSO again, having thrown scissors against Michael's rock. They used rock, paper, scissors to settle everything, and it had reached the point where they would throw the same thing for about six turns, then one of them would throw scissors and the other would throw rock. She wondered if when they were eighty it would take them thirty identical throws to get to a decision, which was another question for that *Jeopardy!* category, if Alex Trebek ever called. Occasionally she would play "crazy" rock, paper, scissors with Lally or Milo, where they would throw nutball things like shark (one hand making biting movements), spider (obvious), flames (upside-down spider), or rabbit (again, if you need a diagram this isn't the game for you). She'd tried this against Michael one time and he'd vetoed it instantly.

"How can you say for certain that shark would beat scissors?" he had asked, incredulously.

"Oh, I don't know," Frances said. "Could it be that sharks are one of the world's most efficient killing machines, with super tough skin and teeth that constantly replace themselves, and scissors—even if they're incredibly, surgically sharp—are still just scissors? PLUS you would need to be very close to the shark to deploy them, and then it would just eat you. Particularly if you had just stabbed it with a pair of scissors, which it would probably consider unfriendly."

"Yeah, that's true," he'd said. "But if we start going outside the norms of rock, paper, scissors I think we'd be playing a dangerous game."

"Rather than a childhood game?"

"Yes. Who knows where it could lead. You could throw karate chop and I could throw finger guns and all of a sudden it's a Tarantino movie."

Suddenly Frances got hit in the head with a soccer ball, which jolted her out of her pleasant replaying of Idiotic Conversations with My Husband, a channel she watched a lot in her head.

"Sorry!" A small boy ran up to her and retrieved the ball. "Sorry, Frances!"

She looked down. It was Lucas. She smiled. "No problem, sweetheart, I wasn't using my head for anything right then anyway." He ran off. Frances waved at Bill, who was standing on the goal line of Lucas's game, and then looked over to see if either of her own kids was injured. She wasn't asking for a broken leg or anything, a badly skinned knee would cut this shit short.

"Hey, Frances, anyone injured yet?" It was Lilian, clutching an enormous cup of coffee.

"Hey there, no, sadly, all hale and hearty and running around this morning." Frances looked around. "Did you bring Mr. Edam?"

Lilian nodded, pointing one finger from her coffee-gripping hand. "He's over there, watching Clare. Her team are the Pink Dolphins. He's holding a Pink Dolphin. That's how you'll pick him out."

Frances spotted him. "He's very tall."

Lilian nodded. "Yup."

"And quite broad in the shoulders."

Lilian sighed. "Yup."

"And handsome and all that stuff. I can see why you're ambivalent."

Lilian clicked her tongue. "But look at him waving a stuffed dolphin! Isn't that questionable behavior in a grown man?"

Frances shrugged. "I think it's cute. I think he's cute. I think Clare likes him, judging by the way she's clutching him around the knees."

Lilian smiled. "Yes, the kids like him a lot. Annabel wasn't sure at first, but now it's like he was her idea all along. I don't know why I'm reluctant about him, he's really nice."

Frances shrugged again. "Because you're as nuts as the rest of us? Because why let yourself be happy when you can get in your own way and question it? Because you feel guilty for being happy when there is so much misery and suffering in the world?"

"Sure," said Lilian, after taking a thoughtful swig of coffee. "All of the above. Plus, he's amazing in bed, and who needs that?"

"Never mind," consoled Frances. "That will fade. I promise."

Lilian looked at her. "Sex life not what it used to be?"

Frances shook her head. "Actually, much as it used to be, if you only go back a decade or so. My mother once memorably told me if you put a coin in a jar every time you had sex the first couple of years of a relationship, and then, once you'd been married a year started taking one out every time you had sex, you'd never empty the jar."

Lilian frowned. "I'm not good enough at math to understand that."

"Me neither, when she told me. I thought she was wrong, and told her so. She laughed, and I think now I understand why. You don't have very much sex after you've been married twenty years. Or at least, we don't." She coughed. "How on earth did we get onto this?"

"My hunky Dutch guy."

"Oh yeah. Well, anyway, get it while you can. Enjoy."

"I have two little kids. There's not all that much time for chandelier swinging."

"Get a room."

Lilian suddenly looked animated. "Oooh, like Anne Porter? Is that all true?"

Clare came running over, with the dolphin in her hand. "Mom, can you hold this for me?"

"Wasn't Edward holding it?"

"I was." The tall Dutch guy had shown up behind Clare. Frances looked him over surreptitiously. Jeez Louise. He noticed her and smiled, holding out his hand. "Hello, I am Edward."

"Hi there." Frances shook his hand, enjoying Lilian's obvious discomfort. She was dying to say, "Hey, Lilian says you're great in bed," but decided to save it for when there wasn't a child present. She looked at Lilian, who clearly saw the internal debate she was having. "Are you having dolphin problems?"

He cleared his throat. "The game is over, and Clare wanted to go to the playground. Is that OK?"

Lilian nodded. "Sure, knock yourselves out. Annabel's game will be over in another fifteen minutes or so. I'll hold Pinky and meet you down there."

"It's not Pinky," said Clare.

Lilian looked at the dolphin. "It's not? Who's this then?"

"That's Dolphy." Edward kept a straight face. "Pinky used to be her name, but she changed it."

"Why?"

He opened his mouth to answer her, but Clare was tugging on him. "Mom," she said, "can we just go? We can talk about names later."

Lilian raised her palms and nodded.

"See, Edward?" Clare took his hand and dragged him away. "You just need to be firm, then she can understand anything!" Edward looked apologetically over his shoulder at Lilian and Frances, then turned back to the child at hand.

"Yeah," said Frances. "He's awful."

"So, is it true, about Anne?"

"The cheating part or the getting divorced part or both?"

"All of it. Tell me all of it."

Suddenly Frances was tired. "Do I have to? I'm bummed out about it and I just can't get excited about it as a piece of gossipy news. I'm sorry, but you're an actual friend, so I'm being honest. I realize I've talked about other families like this many, many times, but for some reason now it's my life, so to speak, or at least this close to my life, and it feels wrong to talk about it. It may ruin gossip for me permanently. You know Anne, you can ask her directly."

Lilian looked at her. "Are you OK? I'm sorry, I didn't realize how upsetting it would be. You're right, when it's someone else it's all fun and games, but when it's your own life it's not the slightest bit funny." She sighed. "After my husband died people I didn't know very well suddenly became very interested in me. They wanted to chat, wanted to know stuff, wanted to make inquiries, do you know what I mean? Most of them meant well, wanted to help. But after a few months you start to hate the smell of dropped-off rotisserie chicken and the obligation to make coffee and rehash your pain for someone else's vicarious experience." There was a silence. "Everyone brings a fucking rotisserie chicken." Another silence. "I call them The Birds of Grief."

There was a short pause, then Frances said, "Have you tried the rotisserie chickens at that weird little place on Eighth and Western?"

"The one with all the wood piled outside? The one that looks like it might be condemned at any moment?"

"Yeah. Those chickens would help you get over your rotisserie chicken issue. In our house we call it Bacon Chicken, even though there is no bacon involved. It's that good."

Lilian grinned suddenly. "This is what I like best about you, Frances," she said. "You're the most comforting yet most unsympathetic person I've ever known."

"Is that good?" Frances was a little taken aback.

"Yeah. Oh, look, Annabel's finished, thank GOD." Lilian drank the rest of her coffee and gave Frances a hug. "Thanks for being you, and thanks for respecting Anne's privacy. I'll go get the gossip from someone with lower standards of friendship."

"OK, no problem. Next week?"

"I'm afraid so. Only five weeks until the end of the season!"

She walked off to meet Annabel, her older daughter, whose face was looking more and more like her mom's every day. Lucky girl.

Milo flung himself against Frances's legs, nearly knocking her over. "I'm done! We won!!" He was grinning up at her like a puppy, all skinny legs and bad coordination, hair flopping around, the sweet smell of kid sweat still enjoyable before the inevitable change to puberty and sports clothes that walked out of gym bags on their own.

Lally wandered up. "We lost. I think. Not sure. Don't care." She sat on the grass and tugged off her shoes, too impatient to undo the laces. "Can we have ice cream now?"

Bill arrived. "Hey," he said. "We were thinking of going for an early lunch and ice cream. Any interest?" Lucas was sporting a new Band-Aid, and looked pretty stoked about it. He was limping, but on the leg that didn't have the Band-Aid. Still, a strong effort.

As the kids whooped and jumped about, Frances nodded and then looked around at all the other families gathering themselves to move on to the next section of their day. She could see Iris and Sara in the distance, she had Bill and Lucas in front of her, and somewhere on the playground were Lilian and Edward. All these families, all struggling against one thing or another, doing their best, or maybe just pretending to be interested, or maybe actively trying to destroy each other, who knew? All of them united momentarily around fucking peewee soccer, brought together by the twin desires for healthy children and something to do on a Saturday. Inwardly Frances shrugged, because it doubtless meant something significant and deep, but all she could think was that the whole thing was incredibly tiring and she needed more coffee. Sometimes life is just what it is, and the best you can hope for is ice cream.

————

Back at home, Ava was just waking up. The house was very quiet. It was Saturday morning, so . . . AYSO. That's right. She turned over, and buried herself deeper in her covers. Her mind flickered to that guy, Richard, the guy it turned out Anne Porter had been sleeping with. She had to admit she'd been impressed, but Anne was good-looking for an older woman. Piper was sleeping with a senior at the local catholic boys' school, the five-year age difference too big to tell her parents about, but not so big it made him unfuckable. Ava hadn't met him, but she'd seen his feed, which was essentially the same thing. She'd seen what he wanted to be seen. Piper said he was nicer than that, and Ava certainly hoped so. Too many pictures of his friends, and just enough shots of him holding animals to ensure a steady supply of blow jobs from a girl who only just got her braces off.

Ava hadn't slept with anyone yet. She'd been felt up the year before, at someone's bar mitzvah, and the kid had gone for her underpants, but she'd stepped back in time. Her friends told her about getting fingered, which didn't sound all that good. When you'd watched that same hand slap a dozen high fives and throw inaccurate gang signs with other pubescent boys . . . ew. Also, she hadn't yet been able to put in a tampon, because it hurt, so presumably getting fingered would hurt, too. Piper had told her if you didn't want them to stick their hands in your pants all you had to do was blow them, and then "they can't think of anything else." Apparently it was the ultimate distraction tactic, but shouldn't sex be less of a defensive battle? Her mom had given her A Talk that was mostly about not doing what you didn't want, and feeling OK about wanting to do stuff you did want to do, but it hadn't been all that helpful as Ava had spent most of the time trying to sink through the floor.

She understood why Piper liked the seniors. Boys her own age had voices that were deeper suddenly, but they still ate sour straws for breakfast and pushed each other for no apparent reason. Older boys, boys her mother called "young men," were focused on getting into your pants, knew how to get there, and knew what to do once they were there, which was good when you had only the vaguest idea yourself. Sometimes that meant you ended up doing things you hadn't anticipated, but Piper said a lot of those things were amazing. She also said it turned out you knew how to give a basic blow job all along, it just came naturally. Ava frowned into her pillow, while feeling the increasingly familiar tug of arousal when she thought about sex.

She was fourteen, and she wished she had a boyfriend she could fool around with. The senior boy had a friend who'd apparently seen Ava's pictures on Piper's feed and thought she was cute, but now that she and Piper weren't talking anyway it hardly mattered. She couldn't approach Piper and say, "Hey, I know we aren't friends right now because I called you on some shit and you told everyone I hit on you, but I'm getting increasingly horny so I was wondering if your boyfriend could hook me up with someone who would deflower me without spreading it over the Internet?"

She pulled the sheet up over her head and groaned.

Thirty.

*T*he children kept coming in and out, of course, as they will. They genuinely don't give a shit about what the adults in the room are up to until it gets in their way, at which point they'll whine about it.

Theo was trying to get Charlie to go outside and play with him, which was causing the usual Gen-X parent cognitive dissonance: I want my kids to have the awesome free-range childhood I enjoyed and develop independence and grit, but I also want them to feel 'seen' by me, and not just benignly neglected. However, my fucking life is falling apart here and I might suddenly lose it and run around the kitchen stabbing appliances with a fork, so maybe now's not the best time to play Frisbee.

"Now's not the best time, Theo, sorry. I'm having a conversation with Michael."

Theo shrugged and wandered outside, ending up on a swing, but not swinging. Charlie and Michael watched him go.

"So, he's not taking it very well?" Michael kept his eyes on Theo, who had started swinging, but only to the extent of his own lower legs, back and forth.

Charlie shrugged, an echo of his son. "I don't think so. It's been a fucking shit show, these last two weeks. If I didn't despise Anne so much I'd be giving her a medal for all the crap she's been taking care of without me. I had no idea how much mind-numbing, repetitive detail went into just keeping them alive. I've upped the cleaners to three times a week."

Michael smiled a small smile. "Grocery run getting you down?"

"It was fine for the first week. I decided I would run the whole thing like a Swiss Army Hospital . . ."

"I thought the Swiss didn't have an army?"

"They don't?"

"I don't think so. I could be wrong."

"Well, like some super-efficient type of organization, then, which doesn't sound as good, but I defer to your greater knowl-edge of international defense. I had the kids up early, I made full cooked breakfasts, I bought a thing that lets you write their names in pancake batter, I did laundry at night, I folded clothes and put them away . . ."

Michael made a "wow" sound.

"Right? Anyway, after a week I had a total nervous break-down in the bathtub after they'd gone to sleep. Sitting there with a beer in my hand, crying into the bubbles as quietly as pos-sible, totally fucked in every possible direction. I am barely clinging to sanity. I really don't know what to do."

Kate came in. She had a Barbie-type doll in one hand, the hair of which was cut short, not very stylishly, and a roll of tape in the other. She came over and dumped both on the table. Then she reached into her pocket and pulled out all the hair from the doll.

"I need you to put this back on again." She looked at her Dad. "I got the tape and everything."

Charlie looked at her, seeing Anne in her face, but loving her regardless. "Uh . . . I'm not sure that's going to work, honey."

Kate frowned. "Yes. Just help me tape it on."

"It won't look the same as it did before."

"That's OK. Tape it."

"You'll be able to see the tape. And it might keep coming off."

"Tape it, Daddy." Your injection of reality is not needed here, old man. I have a vision and I am here to see it executed.

Charlie sighed, shared a quick glance with Michael, who tried to look supportive, and pulled out a long piece of tape. It kept curling. Michael reached over and held one end, and told Kate to hold the other. They held it taut and Charlie carefully applied the hair to the tape, chunk by chunk. It wasn't completely successful, it must be said. The individual hairs that touched the tape would stick, but the ones above would fall off. So then he tried spreading the pieces, which ended up working better, but then they looked like spider legs, which apparently wasn't what she was going for.

It was Michael who solved it. He held up a finger (not from the hand that was holding the tape down) and suggested they make a sandwich of tape, putting the hair in between, and then use additional tape to reattach it. The team voted, this approach was adopted, and it worked ever so slightly better. It still wasn't winning any awards, and in the distance you could hear the whirring sound of Vidal Sassoon spinning in his grave.

Finally, after winding the "hair tape" around Barbie's head, and then applying a metric ton of additional tape to hold it on, which ended up making Barbie look like she'd lost a fight with an industrial thresher, Kate held her up and evaluated.

"She's perfect!" She ran off, calling back to Charlie. "Thanks, Dad!"

Charlie got up to get more coffee. "Want some more?"

"Sure, because it's too early for beer, right?"

Charlie looked at the clock, hanging over the doorway to the garden. It was 3:00 p.m.

"Do the normal rules apply on the weekend?" He put down his coffee cup and opened the fridge instead, grabbing two bottles of Anchor Steam. "Anne wouldn't approve, which makes it even better." Sitting down, he popped the caps with a bottle opener that was already lying on the table, and held up a bottle. "Cheers."

They drank, and Michael idly pushed the remaining Barbie hair into a pile. He looked out at the garden. Theo and Milo were now both out there, sitting on the swings and shooting the shit.

"Do you think Frances would cheat?" Charlie wasn't looking at him as he asked, but gazing out at the kids.

Michael shrugged. "Probably not. When would she have time, for fuck's sake?"

Charlie made a face. "Anne found time."

"Anne worked. She wasn't trailing kids around all the time. She had agency. Frances has about two hours of empty space in the morning and that's usually filled with trips to the vet."

"You do have a lot of pets."

"She likes animals, what can I say? I tried protesting, early on, but there was no point. She likes taking care of things."

"But what if some other guy is taking care of her, right? I mean, clearly Anne wasn't getting what she wanted from me." He finished his beer, rose to fetch another.

Michael was still nursing his. "Well then good luck to both of them."

Charlie looked incredulous. "You wouldn't care?"

"Of course I would care, but it clearly isn't substantially affecting the quality of my marriage, right? If she's managing to get a little on the side while still making everyone else happy, then congratulations. She's even more competent than I thought. If she's worked another guy into the mix, maybe she should be running a company, not me."

"And you?" Charlie stepped out onto the deck a little, frowning. The boys were swinging properly now, and he could see the swing set flexing to a nerve-wracking degree.

"Do I cheat?"

"Yeah."

"I don't even have sex with my wife, why on earth would I have sex with anyone else?"

Charlie turned to him and grinned. "Because you don't have sex with your wife? You are a human being, after all."

"Yeah, I guess. I just don't get that horny anymore. I find women attractive, I watch porn, I whack off, but that driving, confusing level of desire that filled my twenties just went away. Maybe I'm happy, maybe I'm just too fucking tired. I'd rather lie in bed next to my comfortable, gentle wife and watch Netflix than go to a bar and hunt for fresh flesh. No contest." He laughed. "I think I'd rather do that than almost anything, especially if in the distance I could hear my kids being thoroughly entertained and taken care of by someone else. But hey," he took a final swig of his beer, "maybe I just haven't met the right woman."

"Or maybe you already have. And married her."

Michael raised his bottle. "To my wife."

"To Frances," replied Charlie, "a faithful friend."

Michael raised his eyebrows. "She's not a dog."

Charlie smiled. "What was she like when you first met her?"

"She was just the same. She's nice, you know, a warm, loving woman who cares about other people. Maybe a bit too much, but that's not the worst thing in the world. I was kind of an asshole, and she sorted me out." He put down his beer bottle, wishing he'd had more coffee instead.

Charlie hesitated. "Was she always . . . you know . . . curvy?"

Michael laughed. "She's overweight, Charlie, I can handle the truth. No, she was skinny. She always had big tits, but she was skinny everywhere else. Then she had three kids and filled the fuck out." He indicated himself. "As did I, without the excuse of three pregnancies."

"Does it bother you?"

"What?"

"That she let herself go?"

Michael looked at him curiously. "I don't think she let herself *go*, Charlie. I think she just lets herself *be*." He shrugged. "Do you know my friend Jason?"

Charlie nodded. "The one with red hair who bikes everywhere?"

"Yeah, the bike guy. Well, I met him around the same time I met Frances. He's lost most of his hair and his ass kind of dropped, despite the cycling. Does anyone expect me to give a shit about that? Does anyone wonder if it affects our friendship?" He waited, but Charlie didn't say anything. "It's the same thing. I can't expect Frances to do all that she's done in the last twenty years, including simply aging twenty years, and not look different from the twenty-five-year-old I fell in love with. If she's comfortable carrying extra weight, fair enough. If it bothers her enough, she'll change it." He drank some beer, and waved the bottle at Charlie. "I don't get it when guys are like, 'Oh, my wife isn't like she used to be.' Why would she be? Don't you expect to change as you get older? I mean, I'll look at a twenty-three-year-old as happily as the next guy—they're pretty and their bodies are gorgeous—but what the fuck would we talk about? Juice cleanses and YouTube?" He made a face. "Besides, having daughters has ruined young women for me. All I can see is someone else's daughter."

Charlie thought about it. "Yeah, but what if they start out nice, like Anne, and then turn into selfish cheating cows?"

Michael shrugged. "No clue. But was everything else about her still good? Did she love your kids, take care of you, make you laugh, turn up when she said she would . . . ? If it was only sex then, you know, was that the only thing you loved about her? Is that the one thing that makes all the rest worthless?"

Kate came in, still carrying her Barbie, who'd given up the fight with the tape. "Dad, will you take me to the store? Barbie needs a hat."

———

Out in the garden, Theo and Milo were swinging on the swings. They would try and stay in phase, but then one would pump harder and pull ahead.

"You have to stop pumping, idiot," Milo said. "If you pump harder the swing goes higher."

"I know how it works, buttface," replied his friend. "But I'm bigger than you, so even if I only pump half the time I'm still going to go higher."

"I don't think that's how it works, dorkasaurus. I might be smaller, but I'm stronger. I do Tae Kwon Do."

Theo made a snorting noise. "Huh. I play soccer."

"So do I."

"I weigh more than you. It's like if you throw something bigger, it goes farther."

"I don't think so. I think things go the same farness."

Incredulous snorting noise, followed by the dragging of feet through the gravel under the swing. "Really? So if I throw a feather it's going to go as far as if I throw a rock? Doofus."

More dragging. "My dad told me if you drop a ton of feathers and a ton of stones they're both going to hit the ground at the same time."

There was a pause. "Watch and learn, sensei." Theo picked up a small piece of gravel and a stick.

"*Sensei* is the teacher, you loser."

Theo paused, his arm back. "You're right, whatever. Watch and learn, wormbrain."

He threw the piece of gravel, which arced over the garden and landed somewhere unseeably distant. Then he threw the stick, which landed closer.

"No! You didn't throw it as hard. Watch."

Milo picked up a rock and a stick and demonstrated. He had slightly better physical coordination than Theo, and managed to get the two things closer together.

"No way! You did that on purpose. This won't work unless you throw them the same." Theo looked pissed, suddenly. "I don't want to play this anymore." He turned back to the swings, but hesitated. "You're not supposed to throw stones anyway."

"I think," responded Milo, judiciously, "you're not supposed to throw stones AT things or people or dogs or something. You can throw them into space."

"How can you throw them into space? You'd have to be Iron Man or something." Theo sat on his swing. "Do you know what time it is?"

Milo shook his head. "I don't have a phone. Do you have a phone?"

Theo made a face. "As if."

Milo's face brightened. "Maybe now that your mom and dad aren't in the same place you could get a phone? Like, what if you were here and you needed to ask your mom something you could call her. Or FaceTime or something." He tried to look modest. "My big sister might be getting a phone." He looked rueful. "But she won't let me use it. She's a teenager. She doesn't like me anymore."

"Why?"

Milo shrugged a bit. "No idea. One day she just stopped liking me."

Theo started swinging. "Maybe she'll start again."

"Maybe."

Theo swung higher. "My dad doesn't like my mom anymore. One day he did, then one day he didn't."

"Why?"

"I think she cheated on him."

Milo looked at his friend, puzzled. "What's that?"

"I think she kissed someone else. That's what Eloise said at school. She said sometimes dads kiss other women and then they have to go live somewhere else. That's what happened to her dad, and she thought maybe that was what happened to my mom."

"Another dad kissed her? But then isn't that the dad's fault?"

Theo swung really high, and his answers dopplered in and out to Milo. "I don't know. I don't know why it matters. I kiss Grandma all the time, no one says I have to go live somewhere else."

Milo started swinging. Lally suddenly appeared at the kitchen door. "Theo! Your dad says it's time to go."

Theo stopped pumping and drooped on his swing, reaching out with his toes for the gravel.

"Are you seeing your mom today?"

Theo had slowed the swing, and now jumped when it was still going pretty high. He landed well, then bent down and picked up a handful of gravel. He pulled back his arm and let it rip, sending the gravel all the way across the garden, into the hedge on the far side.

"No," he said shortly. "Not today."

Thirty-one.

Tuesday morning Ava watched her mom talking to Iris as Wyatt climbed into the back of the car, their bare early morning faces equally familiar to her. Iris was cooler, though, Ava thought. Her mom was nice, she loved her mom, but she was overweight and dressed like a scruffy teenage boy. Iris was tall and slim and more stylish, and Ava felt bad inside for even thinking it. When she'd been younger her mom was the most beautiful woman in the world. The eight-year-old Ava had gazed up at her mom's warm brown eyes and soft hair and marveled at her good fortune in having a mom so lovely. Then she'd heard a friend of hers describe Ava's mom as fat, and even though the friend had suddenly noticed Ava and added quickly, *Not very fat, you know, just a little bit fat* . . . it was too late. Ava had watched her mom walk into the playground that afternoon and noticed for the first time that she was bigger than the other moms. After a while she decided it didn't matter, that she liked her mom's soft lap, her hugs and warm skin, everything about her gentle, not a hard edge anywhere. But as she got older, and started paying attention to the opinions of other kids, to pictures in magazines, to shows on TV, she realized it was OK to be a bit ashamed. Everyone was a bit ashamed of fat people, even fat people.

She went through a phase of encouraging her mom to buy new clothes, suggesting they go on walks together, but then her own hormones had arrived and she'd stopped worrying about anyone's appearance but her own. Now, at fourteen, she knew her discomfort about her mother's appearance was a cultural norm, and called bullshit, while at the same time wishing her mom would drop her a little farther from the school gates. Then she hated herself for that feeling, and resolved to hug her mom more and spend more time with her, but then she would come home from school and her mom would ask about homework and Ava would hate her again. She was so *irritating*; her little habits of singing as she cleaned the kitchen, of talking to the dogs as if they were people, her endless supply of hooded sweatshirts and unfashionable jeans. Lots of moms at Ava's school were super hip; it was that kind of school. Sharing clothes with their kids, going shopping together, getting manicures and whatever the fuck it was you did at nail places. Ava didn't want to be one of those girls, she really didn't, but sometimes it was hard not to want to fit in. It was easier to let the current carry you along.

Then, of course, there was the other Ava, the one who got overwhelmed at school and needed her mom so badly it was all she could do not to cry. She ached for her mom's voice, her calm demeanor, her air of unflappability. If she saw her mom unexpectedly, as she had at school the other day, she was filled with love and surprise and joy. *My mother!* Her heart would sing, *There she is!* Their eyes would meet and her mom would smile that smile . . . the one that made her feel hugged across any distance, and then some hand inside would reach up to her heart and poke hard and remind her she was a teenager now and Ava would dampen her smile and her mom would raise her eyebrows in question, and the moment would pass and they would be squabbling again.

Ava felt lately that she was on a moving sidewalk, like those things in airports, slowly gaining speed and carrying her in one direction while she walked faster and faster just to stay in one place. She re-read *Alice's Adventures in Wonderland* and somehow it was a whole different book than it had been at nine. Then it had been a book about smiling cats and fairyland; now it was a book about the world where everyone is mad and you're likely to lose your head for the most capricious of reasons.

Still, books remained her favorite place to go. Orwell confirmed her nihilism, Steinbeck made her cry, Saroyan made her homesick for a time she'd never known. She would disappear into these novels and emerge blinking into a life she wasn't entirely certain of. Every day was like leaving a movie in the middle of the afternoon, strange and heightened, the light alien, the voices loud. Then her mother would appear with a cup of tea and remind her of being a child and she would feel such a storm of confusion it made her giddy. She'd read somewhere that hurricanes had winds so powerful that a piece of straw could pierce an oak, thrown so hard it became deadly beyond its weight. She was the straw, pushed by forces she only barely understood.

As her mom dropped her off at school then headed off with the little ones to preschool Ava turned and watched her go, wishing for a mad moment she could run after her, throw herself against the fence and go back to preschool with the others.

—————

Frances watched her daughter in the driver's mirror, standing irresolutely outside the school. She wished she could read her as well as she'd used to. Ava used to be an open book to her, but now she was not only closed, but written in a language Frances wasn't familiar with. It was so difficult. Frances wished she could help her, but she also knew the whole point of being fourteen was learning how to do it without help. What a fucking disaster. Thank God she still had little kids whose needs were more binary.

Thirty-two.

*T*uesday night is traditionally adultery night, but on this particular evening Anne was determined to save her marriage. She'd chosen clothes she hadn't worn in years, clothes from when she and Charlie were first married. Now that everything fit her again she had yards of clothes to choose from, although if she kept not eating they would all be too big. She waited for Charlie at the restaurant, fiddling with the cutlery and sipping her wine a little too fast. She'd been early. He was late. Eventually he arrived, bringing the scent of the almost-frosty air in with him. He'd clearly been in court; his suit was impeccable. Anne felt anxious around him, as if they'd only recently met. She knew every inch of his skin, but the expression on his face was of very recent vintage. He'd never looked at her like that before.

Anne tried to make conversation. "Who's got the kids?"

"Shirley."

"The wonderful Shirley."

"Yup. She's awesome. Super reliable." *Unlike some people.*

"Yup." *Unlike me.*

"Are you hungry?" Charlie picked up the menu, and Anne noticed his fingers curling around the edges of it, the nails bitten for the first time since they'd met. *You did that*, she thought to herself. *You made this man unhappy enough to revert to a childhood soothing behavior.*

"A bit," she replied, picking up her own menu. "Maybe just a salad."

"You look like shit, maybe you should eat something more substantial." He lowered his menu and looked at her. "Or are you working off more calories than you're taking in?"

She paused. "With Richard?"

"Is that his name?"

"You know it is. You spoke to him more recently than I have. I haven't seen Richard since you threw me out."

Charlie lifted the menu again. "Poor sod," he said, from behind it. "You really are coldhearted, Anne."

"No," she said, evenly. "I'm brokenhearted. I destroyed my marriage, my family, and I'm doing everything I can to fix it. I won't ever see him again. I will wait every day of my life for you to forgive me."

"Well, don't hold your breath." The waitress came over, and Charlie smiled at her, his full wattage, judge-persuading smile. The waitress blushed. "Hi there, I'm going to get the steak frites, and the lady across the table will have a small salad and a glass of water."

The waitress looked over at Anne, who raised her eyebrows. "No, I'll have the steak frites, too, thanks. No salad. And another glass of Cabernet, please."

The waitress looked back at Charlie. "Wine for you, sir?"

"No thanks," he said. "I'm driving."

The waitress stepped away, wondering what the fuck was going on there. Handsome guy, pretty woman, but tension for days.

They sat in silence for a moment. A busboy brought bread

and butter, and Charlie tore into a roll. Taking it out on the baked goods, apparently.

"How are the kids?" Anne tried to keep her voice neutral.

"What the fuck do you care?"

"Charlie . . ."

"They're shitty. Kate has been wetting the bed. Theo got into a fight at school that he won't tell me about, but I can imagine it felt pretty good to smack the shit out of someone when you're so angry with your parents you can barely look them in the eye."

"He's still mad?"

"He hasn't smiled at me in nearly three weeks."

"What are you doing about Kate?"

"Changing the sheets. I dug out the plastic bed thingies we had when they were toddlers. I double sheet with the plastic thingies, just like we used to. It's fine. She'll get over it. We'll all survive."

"I miss you all so much."

He popped bread into his mouth, and spoke around it. "Should have thought about that before you sucked someone else's dick."

"I'm so sorry, Charlie. I fucked up so badly, but I really . . ."

"Shut up, Anne. We're here to talk about how to end our marriage, not rehash it."

"Can't we try and work it out? I love you . . ."

"Not enough to stay faithful. Wasn't I good enough for you, Anne? Not enough fucking, was that the problem? I tried. You never wanted to."

"It wasn't that."

"I'd ask what it was, but I don't care. I can barely sit across the table from you, Anne, without wanting to punch you. I've never felt physically violent in my life, but I would happily beat you to death for what you've done to our kids." The waitress had come back during this speech, and was pretending not to have heard it.

"Your wine," she said, placing it in front of Anne.

Anne's hand trembled as she picked up the glass. "I'm so sorry, Charlie."

"Fuck off, Anne."

He watched her drink, suddenly wanting to cry. He was angry, he was furious, but he was also so lonely and sad it was all he could do not to beg her to come home. He wanted to stay angry, though, so he looked away, not wanting to watch her large gray eyes fill with tears.

"I've never stopped loving you, Charlie. I really think I've been having a nervous breakdown, some kind of mental illness."

"I don't care about this, Anne. Let's just work out a schedule for the kids."

"No, Charlie. Please listen. I've been seeing a psychiatrist. I've started medication. I've found us a marriage therapist— Will you go with me? Please, please can we try and work this out? I don't want to divorce you, I want to make it right, I want to come home and be there forever. I made a mistake, a terrible mistake, but I was sick, Charlie." Her hands were shaking. She put down her wineglass before she spilled it.

"Then why didn't you ask me for help, Anne? Why didn't you go see a psychiatrist months ago? Why did you sleep with another man instead? Why did you creep around for months behind my back, behind the kids' backs, cheating on all of us instead of doing something about your supposed misery? I don't think you're sick at all. I think you're a selfish, narcissistic bitch who wanted to fuck a younger, good-looking guy who thought

you were special. I hate you, Anne, I really fucking hate you."
For all the fury in his words, his tone of voice was cool and de-
tached. Anne felt herself eviscerated.

He held up his hand, and the waitress came over. "I lost my
appetite. Can I get the check, please?"

Anne protested. "But we haven't worked out . . ."

Charlie shook his head. "Look, Anne, I'm not ready to do
this, clearly. Did you drive here?" The waitress brought the
check, and he threw his credit card down.

"No, I took an Uber."

"I'll drive you home, we'll talk in the car, and then that's it. I
can't sit with you for an hour and make small talk." His voice
was tight and she could hear the tears in it. Suddenly she remembered that same tone one night years before, when baby
Kate had run a sudden fever of 104, and Charlie had rushed her
to the ER. He'd called Anne to let her know—as she sat at home
with toddler Theo—that they'd had to do a lumbar puncture,
that they wouldn't let him stay in the room, that he could hear
his little girl crying. She knew this man so well, had loved him
so long, and now she had ruined it all.

They walked silently to the valet, waited silently for the car, sat
silently as they drove back to the apartment building where she was
living. Anne tried several times to speak, but Charlie said nothing.
She turned to him in the car as they sat outside her building.

"What about the kids?"

"Did you sign that release thing?"

"Yes, it's inside. I'm sorry, I forgot . . ."

"Go get it. I need it to change my name to primary parent,
otherwise the school will call you first for everything, and you're
just not reliable, Anne. Who knows where you'll be if the kids
need you?"

"Charlie." For the first time Anne felt a little flare of anger. "Charlie, I know you're angry with me, but for God's sake I made a mistake that thousands of married people make all the time. I'm incredibly sorry, but I never let anything get in the way of taking care of the kids. You're pissed, but even you have to admit that."

Charlie shut off the engine and stepped out of the car. "Whatever, Anne, let's just get this piece of fucking paper and sort out a schedule."

They went inside to Anne's apartment. There was a pile of paper on the desk, and she sorted through it. "It's here somewhere. I signed it earlier." She looked at him. "They'll still notify me about everything, right? They'll just call you first if there's an emergency?"

He was right behind her, impatient. "Yes, it's just a legal thing, I guess."

She handed it to him, and impulsively touched his arm. "Charlie . . ."

He looked at his wife, the angles and planes of her face as beautiful at that moment as they had been at the altar so many years earlier. He felt himself get hard and hated himself for his weakness. It was such a physical habit to want this woman, his brain apparently had very little say. Look at her now, tipping her beautiful face up to his, wanting him to give in.

Suddenly he pulled her closer, kissed her roughly, twisting her long hair in his hands as he had done hundreds of times before. Anne lost her mind for a moment, swooning with relief as the familiar edges of his mouth roamed over her throat, her arms going around him, pulling him tightly against her, making it clear that she wanted this, wanted him, wanted to make it better if she could. He turned, still holding her, and they stumbled to the bed, half falling onto it. His hands were at her waist, tugging her shirt off, her hands were at his waist, tugging his belt off, and then suddenly he pulled back.

"Anne . . ."

"Please, Charlie . . . I miss you so much." Her words were mixed with kisses as she tried to pull him back down to her, her hands undoing the buttons on his shirt. "I'm your wife, please be with me . . ." She touched him where he liked it, she knew him so well. *Come on, baby,* her body said, *I know you want me because I know what you feel like when you want me.*

"I hate you." His voice broke. There were tears on his face, and she lifted her head to lick them off, still overcome by optimism and desire. "I hate you." He sighed, his voice soft.

"I'm so sorry . . ." Anne pulled his face down to her breast, arching her back to press herself against him. "Please forgive me."

He paused, his hands still in her hair. Something inside him gave way, and he bent his head to kiss her again. *Twenty minutes of oblivion, God, that's all I ask.*

———

Afterward he turned away from her. She lay silently, curled into a ball next to him.

He cleared his throat. "I'm sorry, Anne. That was a mistake." His voice was dry as dust again, the lawyer back in control.

She turned to him, trying to twine herself around his body. He stiffened, but she pressed against him. "It wasn't a mistake. We're married. Please forgive me and let me come home. I promise things will be different."

He turned sharply. "It was fine before, Anne, as far as I knew. I had no idea there was a problem, and that's why you can't come home. How can I ever be sure you're happy? How can I ever trust you again?"

Anne reached for him, but he evaded her. "I miss the kids so much. I miss you."

Charlie sat up, turning to sit on the edge of the bed. She wanted to touch his back, unwind the stiff muscles around his neck and shoulders, but she knew she wasn't allowed to. That moment had passed. "They miss you, too, Anne, and so do I. But you're not the same person we thought you were. They don't know that you chose fucking some other guy over protecting their happiness. They don't know that you pretended to still love me . . ."

"I do love you. I never stopped loving you. I was just so . . . lonely. My therapist says I was depressed."

"Could you not have seen a therapist before you got into bed with someone else? Could you not have chosen what other people choose? Medication and a thorough and almost certainly ineffective rehashing of your childhood?" He stood and started hunting about for his clothes, scattered on the floor. She'd seen him do this so many times, in many houses, many hotels, over years and years, she could predict the order in which he'd dress himself, the point where he'd sit down, the point where he'd no longer be tempted to get back into bed. "And why were you lonely? I was there, the kids were there, you have friends. What the fuck, Anne? Are you like the kids, requiring constant entertainment?"

He was disgusted with her—and with himself for sleeping with her. He had sunk to her level, maybe even lower. He felt nauseous; this whole thing was killing him from the inside out. He suddenly stopped dressing and flared at her. "Do you know I've lost ten pounds in the last two weeks? I've had to leave meetings and go cry in the car. I can't cry in the bathrooms at work in case someone hears me and thinks I'm losing it. Yesterday I told them I had to leave early to pick up the kids and one of the other partners asked if maybe it was time to get a babysitter. I told him to fuck off, which maybe wasn't the best choice, so maybe I'll lose my job and then we'll all be homeless and your destruction of our family will be complete. Maybe then you and your boyfriend can move back into our house and take the kids from me and then I'll just wander the fucking streets like the total loser I am!" His voice had risen so much that by the end he was screaming, his face red and wet with tears.

Someone banged on the apartment wall, and Charlie banged back, furious, his vehemence knocking a picture down and breaking it. "We can't go back, Anne, there's no back to go to. See that picture?" He pointed. "We can no more fix our marriage than we can fix that glass. It's fucked. We're fucked. It's done. And it's your fault."

She was still curled on the bed, sobbing, when he slammed the door. The breeze moved her hair across her cheek like a kiss.

Thirty-three.

The day of Iris's birthday dawned bright and fair, as it usually did. Not just her birthday, of course, but most days in Southern California, with their dulcet winds and spangled sunshine. There's a reason every other major city in the U.S. looks down on Los Angeles and makes fun of its supposed lack of culture, and it rhymes with bellousy. The reason Los Angeles doesn't care what other cities think of it? It's too busy looking at all its pretty girls in sundresses and happy people living out their dreams and eating well. Never mind, San Francisco. You can keep the fog.

Anyway, Iris's birthday was another of those lovely days. Rosco the dog had given Iris a cashmere dressing gown, as soft and silky as a newborn's earlobe, Wyatt had given her a chew toy in the shape of a birthday cake, and Sara had given her a hand-painted mug with MOM on it.

There was a pause as Iris unwrapped it.

"Uh . . . I like the colors you chose," she said gently. "But I'll be blunt: I just have the two hands."

Wyatt went off into gales of laughter. "That's MY present! I made that! It's a sword!" He grabbed the mug from his mom and pointed at the third arm. "See? It's a sword, and you have a helmet on."

Sara also looked confused. "I thought that was her hair?"

Wyatt snorted. "No! It's gray! She doesn't have gray hair! It should have been silver but they didn't have silver." He looked at Iris, crestfallen. "They didn't have silver, sorry."

She hugged him close. "It is so perfect and awesome and I love you so much. Silver would have been too much, this way is more realistic. I look like a real knight this way, ready to fight and a little bit grubby."

He smiled gratefully at her. "They probably did get pretty messy."

"Of course! Fighting dragons is sweaty work."

He was still concerned. "I put the names on the presents. I guess I put the wrong ones on. Rosco picked out the birthday cake toy."

"It's a very good choice, although I suspect he'll enjoy it more than I will." She took an experimental nibble on the chew toy, which made a sad noise. "It tastes like cake." She looked at Rosco with new respect. Rosco wagged his tail and offered to take it off her hands, if it was bothering her.

Wyatt needed reassurance. "Do you like the mug as much as the pink coat thing?"

"More."

"Really? You seemed to really like the pink thing."

"I hadn't seen the mug yet, and I thought it was from Rosco, remember? He doesn't usually get things like that, his funds are so limited. I wanted to be encouraging."

"Can I go watch TV now?"

Iris turned to her bedroom window, which looked out onto the treetops that surrounded their house. From her bed she lived in the forest. "Why don't you have some breakfast first, and then you can call the other kids and see if . . ." Her phone pinged, and she reached for it.

Happy Birthday, you old fart, read a text from Frances. Does Wyatt want to come up here for pancakes? You can have a birthday breakfast in bed.

Yes! she texted back. That would be awesome!

Sending Milo. Have fun.

"Put on some clothes and go downstairs to wait for Milo, baby, you're going to your auntie's for pancakes." Wyatt yelped and sped off, happy to spend time with his older cousins. They often let him on their computers, and were teaching him Minecraft.

Iris looked at Sara. "Is there any coffee?"

Her wife reached for the birthday mug in Iris's hand. "Yes, AND fresh cinnamon rolls from Acme."

Iris snuggled back under the covers. "You spoil me."

"Well, now that Wyatt's gone," replied Sara, "I plan to spoil you some more." She did a dramatic stripper slide around the bedroom door and nearly fell down the stairs. When they were done laughing, Sara went to get breakfast.

———

Once the rolls were finished, and the icing had been licked off of fingers, Sara rolled over onto her tummy and regarded her wife thoughtfully.

"I want to talk to you about something," she began.

Iris nodded. "Me, too," she said. "But you can go first."

Sara laid her head down on the sheet for a moment, and Iris frowned. "Is something wrong?"

"No," Sara replied. "But this stuff with Anne is making me think." She looked at Iris. "And the other night . . . you seemed worried. Of course, it could have been a brilliant double bluff and you're already cheating on me."

Iris grinned. "I assure you, I'm not sleeping around. And if you are, please don't tell me, because then I'd have to smother you with this pillow." She picked one up and shoved it at Sara, who snatched it away, tucking it under herself. Iris watched her wife's shoulders move, the angles of her collarbone, the curve of her lower back, and decided that whatever Sara had to say better be quick, because she really wanted to take advantage of this time alone. "Go on then, what's up?" She mock frowned. "Am I too old for you now?" There were three months separating their ages; it had become a running joke.

Sara didn't answer, just raised an eyebrow and waited for Iris to be quiet. "Look, I didn't mention this before because it wasn't settled, but I've been offered a film."

"A film?"

"Yes. A movie. A good one."

"When?"

"Soon."

"Where?"

"China." Sara laughed, briefly. "All the money's in China right now, and somehow the money for this film came attached to principal photography over there. It's fine, it's good, it's a real studio, real people, it's going to be great."

Iris sat up and pulled another pillow onto her lap, holding it tight. She leaned over and picked up her coffee cup, only to find it empty. "Is it a good part?" She needed more coffee, although maybe she'd had too much already. Her heart was really loud.

Sara sat up, too, and knelt in front of her wife. She watched the way Iris held her cup, saw the tremor in her wrists, knew she was upset. Dammit, she should have waited till after the party.

"Baby, this is what I'm saying: I want you and Wyatt to come with me. It'll be three months. He's only in first grade, he can easily catch up, you're not doing anything."

"I'm not?"

Sara shook her head. "You're taking care of Wyatt, you're taking care of me, you're treading water waiting for something, I don't know what. Come with me to China, it'll be fun." She waggled her eyebrows. "The studio's paying for a house. I put it in the deal."

Iris thought about it. Why did she feel so angry? She was married to an actress, a successful one. Traveling for work was par for the course, and had always been fun even if it wasn't quite as fun as Sara thought it was. A lot of waiting around for her to be finished for the day, a lot of taking care of Wyatt without any of her usual equipment or surroundings. But a big movie would be great for Sara, for all of them. "What does Anne have to do with this?"

Sara looked confused. "What do you mean?"

"You said, 'this stuff with Anne is making me think' . . . ?"

Sara smiled, relieved. "Just that it reminds me how important you are to me, you and Wyatt."

Iris sat very still, trying to get a handle on what she was feeling, and what she wanted to say.

Sara frowned at her, "What's wrong? I'm just saying it would be nice to be together. You've never been to China, Wyatt's a perfect age to go . . ." She studied her wife's face, a little lost about why this wasn't being greeted with the enthusiasm she had expected. Iris had always loved to travel. "We can get a tutor there, if that's what you're worried about."

"How long have you known about this?" Iris felt wrong-footed, as if something had just been sprung on her, but she also knew that was a ridiculous reaction. Why couldn't she just be happy for Sara? Why couldn't she feel good about this?

She'd wanted to bring up the baby, wanted the discussion this weekend to be about her, about them. It was her birthday; it wasn't fair.

Sara shrugged. "I don't know, a week or two, maybe. I talked to the producer a month ago and forgot about it, mostly, you know what it's like. It came back last week, we had some back-and-forth, I have to give them an answer on Monday."

"You didn't say yes yet?"

Sara leaned forward and looked closely at Iris. "No, sweetheart. Why are you freaking out? Talk to me."

Iris took a deep breath. "I want to have another baby," she said. "And I want to do it soon."

———

An hour or two later they'd reached the silent stage. Sara was open to a baby, after China. Iris was open to China, after a baby was begun. They'd argued all through getting dressed, and now they were sitting out on the deck trying not to start the argument up again when the front door opened

Frances's voice floated through the house. "Hey! Where are you hiding?"

Iris called out to her, and Sara got up to go greet her.

"I brought your kid back," said Frances, who had also brought her entire family. "And a cake. I heard it was someone's birthday."

Iris raised her eyebrows and turned in her comfy wicker chair to see the cake. "That's enormous!"

Frances grinned and put it down on the table. "I lost two pounds last week. I need to gain them back as quickly as possible."

"I like your methods."

The doorbell rang. Sara looked at Iris and shrugged a question. "Are you expecting someone?"

Iris made a face. Sara went to open the door and reappeared with Bill and Lucas. Lucas was carrying a present.

"Oh," said Bill, looking around. "Are we interrupting something? We just wanted to drop off a present."

Iris stood up looking surprised. "How did you even know it's my birthday? That's so nice of you! Come on in!" Lucas looked a little lost, but then Wyatt ran up to him and they sped off upstairs, presumably to begin disassembling something.

"Would you like a cup of tea?" asked Sara, trying to pull her shit together. All she wanted to do was pause time so she could work things out with Iris, but, of course, time was as uncooperative as it always was. You had to *stay* married in the brief pauses between *being* married, and those pauses so often had to be rescheduled.

Bill smiled, oblivious to any undercurrents in the room. He was in on the secret, of course, and was enjoying his job as first surprise guest. "That would be great."

The doorbell rang again. Iris frowned at Sara, who was looking a little stressed. A vague suspicion started in her tummy, but it was just Charlie and the kids. Theo immediately disappeared upstairs, but Kate stayed with her dad. She was also carrying a present, and Charlie appeared to have brought a case of champagne.

"Hi," he said, putting the cardboard box on the table. "I thought you guys might like this. I got it at work for something, can't remember what . . ." He trailed off. "Hi, Michael! How's it going?" He went over to chat and the doorbell rang again. When Sara left to answer it Iris turned quickly to Frances and lowered her voice.

"What's happening?"

"How do you mean?" replied Frances, determined not to be the one who ruined the surprise.

"Frances, Sara and I are having a horrible fight because I want another baby and she wants to go to China and if you don't tell me what's going on I'm going to fucking hit the roof." She took her cousin by the arm. "Spill it, Frank."

Fair enough. Cousins first. Frances leaned in. "Sara is throwing you the world's gentlest surprise party, and I don't care what you two are fighting about, she's been planning it for weeks and Wyatt is about to shit himself with anticipation, so put your argument on hold and make it work, OK?" She pulled back a bit and fixed her cousin with a firm look. "I realize it's your party, and you can cry if you want to, but wait until afterward, OK?"

Iris looked at her and nodded.

"This block needs a good day," added Frances. "And I pick today."

Iris nodded again, and poured herself a glass of champagne.

This time the guests were Lili and her daughters, Annabel and Clare. Kate was excited to see Annabel, and the two of them ran off to play. Clare came over to Iris and smiled up at her.

"Hi, Iris! I'm Clare, do you remember me?"

Iris smiled. "Yes, Clare, I've known you since you were very small. How could I forget you?"

"Well," said Clare, "you're old. My mom calls me Annabel all the time, and she GREW ME IN HER STOMACH, so, you know."

"A good point." Iris drank some champagne. "Did you bring a present?"

"Yeah," said the little girl. She paused. "But don't tell Sara because I think it's a surprise. It's not a very good present, I don't mind telling you, because Mom picked it. I wanted to get Sara a Game Programmer Barbie, but my mom got her a stupid jug or something." Clare rolled her eyes. "And a piece of paper for a massage, which is just ridiculous." This was a new word for Clare, and she was enjoying it. She said it again, with emphasis. "Ridiculous!"

"Adults!" agreed Iris, making a face.

"Right?" said Clare. She sighed a tiny little sigh, then added, "Still, I got the Game Programmer Barbie, so, you know, that was good . . . She has a headset for her cell phone and a laptop of her own. But you can't take it off her hand I don't think, which is weird. I mean, you'd need to put it down to pee, for sure." She looked thoughtful for a moment, as if running the logistics of peeing while holding a laptop, but then shrugged and ran off. Iris caught Lili's eye and shook her head and grinned as Lili mouthed *Sorry* and rolled her eyes.

Someone had clearly propped the front door open, because now a steady stream of friends with food and presents were arriving, and Sara's Grand Plan was revealed in all its genius. Iris caught her eye across the kitchen and smiled tightly, raising the second glass of champagne that had miraculously appeared in her hand. Sara looked back at her for a moment, then looked away. She'd wanted so much for this day, and now she just wanted it to be over.

An hour later the party was in full swing. Two different sets of people had brought very small babies, who were being passed around like sleeping loaves of bread. Iris had one on her lap at that moment, but wasn't sure whose it was. It appeared to be a girl, based on the pink bunny cap, but you could never tell with newborns. A small roar came from the front room as someone showed up with an even more exciting small thing, a three-month-old dachshund puppy, and Iris was starting to feel a little bit tipsy. She could see Frances's cake on the table and resolved to go get herself a piece.

Sara came over and knelt by her chair. "Are you having fun?" As far as everyone else was concerned the hostess was having a fantastic time, but Iris could see her wife was very much a working actress.

Iris nodded, and was about to try to make peace when suddenly they heard raised voices from the other room. A glass shattered. Anne had arrived.

———

As Sara and Iris came into the front room, Charlie was hissing at his wife, "You shouldn't even be here."

"I was invited," she replied, from where she knelt on the floor, picking up the pieces of the glass he'd dropped. "Iris is more my friend than she is yours."

"I think you forfeited all connection to the neighborhood when you slept around, Anne," said Charlie, who'd clearly had more than a few glasses of wine. Several people were trapped at the far side of the living room, where they had been chatting in a small group before Charlie and Anne had collided at the front door. They looked plaintively at Sara, hoping for an airlift.

Sara stepped between them. "Hi, guys, how about you take this outside?"

Anne looked apologetic, but Charlie was past it. "How about this bitch just leaves, if her legs come together sufficiently for walking?"

"Wow," said a voice from across the room, although it wasn't clear who had said it.

Sara firmed up her voice a little. "Charlie, this isn't the place for this. We're all here to celebrate Iris's birthday, and there are lots of little kids here, including yours, so let's just table this discussion for now." She touched his arm, but he shook her off.

"You broke my heart, Anne." He leaned forward and poked his wife in the throat, making her step back. "I've loved you ever since we met, and we have kids, and they love you, too, and you just. Don't. Give. A. Shit. Do you?"

"I do," Anne whispered, her face pale, as she turned to leave. "I'm so sorry, Sara, I shouldn't have come."

"It's OK, Anne," said Sara. She turned as she felt Iris's hand on her elbow. Her wife was right behind her, not a hell of a lot less drunk than Charlie. "What the heck's going on?" she whispered in Sara's ear. Sara turned up her palms, watching Charlie's face carefully.

"It's not OK. It's so fucking messed up, it's beyond comprehension," he said loudly, grabbing Anne by the arm.

Bill showed up, having just diverted a set of children who were heading in this direction. "Hey, guys, you can be heard in the garden, and the kids are getting worried."

"Fuck off, Bill. Your wife left you, too, right? Maybe there's something wrong with the water on the street. It turns wives into whores." Charlie wavered slightly, but wouldn't let go of Anne. "Hey, Anne, maybe we could go home for another guilt fuck like the other day, before I found out why you were suddenly so hot for me." Tears came into his eyes. "I was so happy."

"Let me go, Charlie," said Anne, pulling away. "You want me to leave, and I want to go. We'll talk later when you sober up."

"No, let's talk now," he said, and started dragging her out of the front door. "I want to talk now."

Bill looked over at Michael, who had appeared with Frances, and all of them followed Charlie and Anne out into the street, with Iris in tow. Sara closed the front door behind them, although several faces appeared at the windows. Now all the neighbors were outside, with all their kids inside. What could possibly go wrong? Sara and Frances both kept looking back at the house, torn between competing responsibilities.

Bill tried to reason with Charlie. "Charlie, let her go for now. You guys can talk another time. Come in and have some coffee, and something to eat."

Charlie turned on him. "You're such a nice guy, Billy, why did your wife leave, eh? Why did Julie run off? Maybe we're too nice, that's our problem."

Bill ignored him. "Yeah, we're awesome, Charlie. Let's go get something to eat, yeah?"

"No, but really, where did Julie go, Bill? She was here and then she wasn't. Is she fucking some other guy, Bill, is that it? Or some other woman? Or two other women? Or did she just get sick of the same old cock, was that the problem?"

"Jesus, Charlie, get a fucking grip," said Michael, who could see Bill was starting to get angry. "You and your wife are having a problem right now, don't drag us into it."

"Shut up, Michael. Just because you and your fat wife have it all together, everything perfect. Of course you never have sex anymore . . ."

Anne pulled away from Charlie, suddenly, and started down the street, tears streaming down her face. Frances walked quickly after her. "Anne, let me drive you home."

"No!" shouted Charlie. "Let her walk! Let her stumble into traffic right under a tractor trailer! I wish you were dead, Anne. I really fucking do." He turned to Bill. "Don't you wish your wife was dead, too, Bill? Better dead than in someone else's bed, right?" He began to laugh. "That rhymes."

Bill suddenly stepped forward and punched Charlie with enough force to lift him right off his feet. He landed on his back and lay there, stunned and suddenly sober.

"My wife *is* nearly dead, you asshole," hissed Bill, his fist still clenched. "My wife has been in another state for three months getting treated for cancer and it's killing her." He was furious. "And I'm stuck here, trying to hold it together for Lucas, because he's only four years old and Julie wanted to go face her shit alone, because she thought he needed me more than she did. He thinks she's working on a movie somewhere, and twice a day she drags herself into clothes and puts on a fucking wig and props her ass up on a pillow and Skypes him so he knows how much she loves both of us. We're doing our fucking job, like you should be. Don't you think I'd rather she was with some other man? I would give my fucking arm for Julie to be having an affair, instead of fighting for her life all alone in fucking Minnesota . . ."

"Daddy?" A small voice came from the doorway, and they all turned to see Lucas heading out of the house. "You said the F word!" He looked shocked, but had clearly only heard the last few words.

Bill looked at his son. His face relaxed, and those close enough could see the effort it took. Lucas had no idea. Bill held out his hand. "Hey, chief. What's up?"

"Nothing. I just wanted to see you."

"Do you want to go home?"

"Can we call Mommy? I want to tell her you said the F word." He noticed Charlie on the ground and hesitated. Then he went over, as little children will. "Did you fall over?" He stuck out his hand to help, but Charlie just looked at him for a moment and then lay back down on the grass.

Lucas frowned and turned to his dad, who picked him up and held him close. "Charlie's fine, Lucas, don't worry about it. Shall we go call Mom so you can tell on me?" They started to walk away, skirting Charlie where he was on the grass, shamed and silent.

"That was a great party, Daddy," Lucas's little voice piped back. "Did you see me eating cake?"

"Yeah, buddy. Was it good?"

"Yeah. Mommy's going to be so mad with you for swearing." The little boy giggled, resting his head on his father's shoulder, his hand gathering up the fabric of his daddy's T-shirt and holding it tight.

They crossed the road and walked away. Charlie sat up, wiping his mouth and weeping. Anne pulled open the car door and Frances went around to the driver's side. Iris, Michael, and Sara just stood there. Iris wasn't feeling so good.

A short man walked up, pushing a large trolley.

"Are either of you Sara?"

Sara nodded.

"I've got your bouncy castle," he said. He made an apologetic face. "I know you wanted Spiderman, but some studio exec threw a fit and got the last one. What you have here is a deluxe." He stressed the word *deluxe*. "Elsa's Frozen Castle." He paused, aware that this might not fly if this was a boys-only party. "With a giant Olaf thrown in gratis. No charge for the six-foot snowman."

Iris suddenly leaned forward and threw up on the grass.

There was a short pause, then the bouncy castle guy said, "Fine. No snowman, then."

Thirty-four.

*F*rances woke up the next day with an emotional hangover. She closed her eyes and lay in bed for a moment, not ready to face the day. Driving Anne home had turned out to be the last straw. She'd lost patience for the other woman, maybe at the worst moment to do so. But hey, Anne's husband had just told the neighborhood she was fat and had no sex life and that was, you know, awkward.

Anne was temporarily staying at the Palazzo, an apartment building across the street from the park where the kids played soccer on Saturdays. The Palazzo was in many ways the secret long-stay hotel Angelenos never told tourists about. Some people lived there year-round, sure, but a large part of its business was during pilot season, and in general it served the Industry. Studios owned apartments there and would put up actors and directors when they needed to. People would rent furnished apartments for three or four months while shooting a pilot, or some other short-lived project. The building was also across the street from the Grove, a big outdoor mall, and was painted the kind of ochre normally seen in hotel paintings of the Italian Riviera. It was a color not found in nature, yet somehow it worked.

Anne had basically lost her shit all the way from Iris's party to the Palazzo. The security guard waved them into the parking lot with not even the slightest flicker at the sounds of distress coming from inside the car, having seen it all several times. Anne's apartment was a two bedroom on the ground floor, dark and cool and decorated in timeless and faceless style. She'd barely made a mark on it.

When Frances had looked in the fridge hoping to make Anne a cup of tea or something, she found literally nothing. The cupboards were also entirely bare.

"What on earth have you been eating, Anne?" she asked.

Anne had reached the staring portion of her distress, and turned her head toward her friend. "I go across the street when I get hungry." She'd stopped crying, but her eyelids were puffy and for the first time that Frances could remember, she looked like shit. "Farmer's Market, you know."

Frances nodded. "Are you hungry now?"

Anne shook her head. "I think I'm going to be sick." She went into the bathroom and Frances heard the toilet seat hit the tank, but then there was silence. Frances went and stood at the window, looking out through the manicured greenery. It was quiet out there, the occasional and distant *ping* of the elevator the only sound to be heard over the ever-present hum of pool pumps. A slender girl in sweatpants and furry boots came out through a door, leading the world's smallest dog on the world's thinnest leash. It looked like she'd tied a cotton ball to a piece of dental floss. Frances watched the dog poop a lentil, then sit and snooze while the girl conducted a lengthy operation on her cell phone.

"I've got nothing to throw up," Anne said, returning. "I can't breathe properly. Do you think I should go to the ER?" She sat on the edge of the overstuffed coral sofa.

Frances turned and looked at her. "You're having a panic attack, and your blood sugar is zero. Go get something to eat and ask for a paper bag to put it in, then you'll have something to breathe into." She turned to go.

Anne said, "Please don't leave me."

Frances said, with more than a hint of exasperation in her voice, "Look, Anne, I don't want to kick you when you're down, but you need to get it together."

Anne's eyes filled with tears. "You're angry with me."

"I'm angrier with your husband, but seeing as you're the one that put him into this filthy mood then I guess I'm a little angry with you, too. But now I need to get back to my kids, and I can't stay and hold your hand. Call your mom. Call your brothers. Pull it together, Anne."

She'd walked out knowing Anne wasn't going to pull it together, and comfortable with the fact that she really didn't give a fuck.

Now, the next morning, Frances felt exhausted. She turned her head to look at Michael and found him already awake and looking at her.

"'Jesus wept,'" she said. "You scared me."

"Score," he replied, smiling.

"Why are you awake? Are you OK?" She pulled her hand out from under the sheets and stroked his head. His face was so dear to her, and so familiar.

"Yeah. Yesterday sucked. I had bad dreams about it."

She nodded. "Yeah. Let's not do that to each other. Let's grow old and be boring together forever." She paused. "It was a bit embarrassing."

"The massive revelation that we don't have a lot of sex?"

She nodded.

He shrugged. "I'm happy, are you happy?" She nodded. "Then fuck the neighbors, who gives a shit what they think?" He looked closely at her. "Do you think Charlie knew there was a problem before?" Frances said nothing, so he continued. "What if you're really cheating on me this whole time, and just doing a really good job of hiding it?"

She laughed. "The idea of willingly taking my clothes off in front of another person is absurd. If you and I divorced, I would sew my vagina shut, get fifteen cats, and let myself go completely."

Michael laughed. "That seems extreme. You're wonderful. I expect you would be a hot commodity on the open market."

Frances rolled her eyes. "Yeah, because an extra thirty pounds and three kids is what all single men want. I can read the dating profile now: Single man seeks overweight, middle-aged woman to ignore his input while raising her children. Willing to share school run and homework duties in return for annual blow job (not guaranteed)." She sat up and threw back the covers. "And *Playboy* called me the other day hoping I could make time for a centerfold shoot." She stood and faced him, naked and smiling. "Because this"—she indicated her gentle rolls—"is incredibly hot."

"I love looking at you."

"You're used to it."

"That's true. I'm used to it and I love it."

Frances sat back down and leaned forward to whisper in his ear. "I went to a sex shop the other day and bought a vibrator and some fur-lined handcuffs."

Michael burst out laughing. "My penis isn't good enough for you?"

Frances reached under the covers. "It's totally fine, but I don't feel it vibrating." There was a pause, then she smiled. "That isn't vibrating."

"Look, it's movement. Give me a break."

"Mommy!!!" Lally's voice rang down the hall.

"And . . . that's you," said Michael, snuggling under the sheets. "Good luck hiding that shit from the kids, by the way."

———

Down the street Charlie was horribly hungover and ashamed of himself. It was not a good combination, and he was wondering if he would ever feel like eating again, or be able to face the outside world. Sadly, sheltering in place was not an option in this particular battle.

"Hey, Theo," he said to his son, gently shaking the sleeping child. "It's time to get up for school." Theo grunted and pulled the covers over his head. "Come on, buddy, time to shake a leg. Do you want some OJ?" The lump shook its head.

Charlie wandered down the hall to Kate's room, and found her already dressed and sitting on her floor, playing with her sizeable collection of little animal figures. There were ponies, weirdly big-headed animals of all varieties, and the obligatory elongated dolls with odd makeup on. He didn't know what they were called, and thought they looked like extras in a German fetish movie, but who was he to judge?

"You're already dressed," he said, surprised. Kate nodded, but didn't say anything. "Do you want some breakfast?" She shook her head. "Toast?" No. "Eggs?" No. "Cheerios?"

Finally, she turned to look at him, and frowned. "No thanks, Daddy. I'm not hungry. I woke up really early and got myself something already."

"You did?" She nodded, already back at her game. "OK, well, great. Time for school in twenty minutes or so, OK?"

She looked back at him. "Are you taking us?"

"Do you want me to?"

Back to the dolls. "No. I like when Frances takes us."

OK. He heard noise from Theo's room, and went back there. Theo was sitting on the edge of his bed pulling on his socks, more or less dressed. His eyes were swollen, and Charlie stepped over to feel his forehead. Theo ducked his head away, and frowned at his dad. "I'm fine," he snapped. "How long until school?"

"About twenty minutes."

Theo went back to his socks, ignoring Charlie for the thirty more seconds he stood there wondering how to reach his kids, and why he was suddenly the bad guy when Anne was the one who cheated. As if reading his mind Theo suddenly looked up and said, "You know, you could just forgive Mom and let her come back and everything would be just like it was before."

"No, it wouldn't. It won't ever be the same."

For a moment his son looked at him blankly. Then he pulled on his shoes and stood, pushing past his father and closing his bedroom door behind him, leaving Charlie standing there alone.

————

Lucas wasn't awake yet when Bill Skyped Julie. He told her about the day before, and she surprised him by laughing out loud. He hadn't heard it in a while, and it was worth some bruised knuckles.

"You punched him? Really?" She was in bed, of course, the tablet propped up on her arm, and her face was so close it was almost easy to pretend she was in the same bed as Bill. She smiled, her warmth undimmed by weeks of chemotherapy, even as it robbed her of her eyelashes, pubic hair, and immune system. "How very macho and unexpected of you."

He grinned. "It was unexpected even to me. I didn't know I was going to do it until I did it, if you know what I mean. I just got pissed off with his fucking whining."

"Oh, come on. His heart is broken."

"No," Bill said firmly. "His ego is broken, and he's sad as shit that his wife let him down, but he'll recover."

"Don't be a dick, Bill. What about his kids? I'd be fucking devastated if you did that to me. To Lucas."

"How do you know I'm not doing it right now? I could be sleeping with a wide variety of lovely young women while you're out of the picture."

She laughed. "I assume you are, because I know how much free time you have. It's easy to take care of a small kid and work full time, right?"

"Yeah, it's a walk in the park."

She stopped laughing. "See, this is why . . ."

He interrupted her. "Don't even go there, Jules. I wanted you to stay here for treatment, and I still think you were wrong. I'm your husband. I want to take care of you."

She was firm. "I need you to take care of Lucas, and I need to take care of myself. This way is easier."

He sighed. "For you."

"And for you. And most of all for him."

Then they just looked at each other until Lucas appeared sleepily behind Bill, his hair sticking up at all angles.

———

Iris was talking on the phone to her brother Archie.

"Mom said you guys are fighting." Iris could hear Archie's kids yelling in the background, thousands of miles away. Her brother lived in Ireland, married to a gorgeous woman somewhat like their father had been, charming and dreamy and un-ambitious and exhausting. He loved her, loved their four kids, loved the green grass of Ireland, and hated the rain. Of all her brothers he was the one she was closest with.

"Did she?" Iris slowly pulled her coffee cup across the table toward herself. "What did she actually say?"

"She said you want another baby and Sara won't let you have one."

Iris made a face. "That's not true."

"Which part?"

"The not letting me part. Sara is open to having another baby, she just got offered a movie and we're trying to work out the de-tails." Her brother waited, hearing the unspoken in her voice. "And yes, I want one and she wants one less."

"Didn't you discuss this years ago, when you had Wyatt? Pre-sumably you did."

"Sure, but like you do when nothing is real or binding. We said we were going to have a dozen kids. We didn't mean it."

"But you'd like another."

"Yes. But not if it costs me my marriage."

She waited while he settled a dispute over a ball, sipping her coffee and watching birds peck about on her lawn. She wondered if birds thought anything of the people they saw milling about below them. Probably just wondered what was keeping them on the ground, lazy bastards.

"I'm back. Kieran felt strongly that the one who scored the goal should be the one who got to throw it back into play, but Jenny disagreed."

"She's in goal?"

"Exactly. She pointed out she didn't get to really kick the ball at all . . ."

"She has a sound point."

"Yeah, but she illustrated it by kicking her brother in the ankle, which undermined her position."

Iris smiled. "Maybe you could just send me one of yours."

"I'd be thrilled." He had a drink, too; she could hear him sipping. "So, what's going on now?"

"Now we're stepping around each other carefully, both trying not to be the one who starts it up again."

Archie made a surprised noise. "That isn't like you two. Normally you guys can't stop talking."

Iris sighed. "I know. It's weird. I should have just mentioned it like a year ago when I first realized I wanted another kid, but I got nervous for no reason that she was going to flip out, and then I waited a little longer, and a little longer, and then it turned into a Big Thing in my head, even though it wasn't. And then one of the neighbors had an affair and her marriage blew up and suddenly that seemed like a far worse outcome than just having one kid."

"You're losing it. Sara's always been very laid back, and you pretty much always get your way, right? And she's not the cheating sort and neither are you, or at least, neither of you used to be."

"Yeah, but nobody thought this neighbor was, either." She stood to go empty her cup. "Do you and Carol fight a lot?"

"Of course. Everyone fights. But mostly we talk about the kids, or about moving back to the States, or about what's for dinner. We're sort of in a holding pattern right now, I don't know."

"Why don't marriages just wheel along on their own? Once you've given them a good push at the beginning they should just keep trundling along."

She could hear a shrug in her brother's voice, and got a mental image of his tall frame, his angular face, and missed him. "If the path was always smooth then maybe they would, but, if we can stretch this metaphor too far, it isn't smooth and all those bumps slow it down and send it off course. I think of it more like one of those old-fashioned hoops you see in Victorian illustrations, you know?"

"The ones with the stick?"

"Yeah. You have to keep it going by poking and prodding, and marriage is like that, maybe. Basically wheeling along, but needing a poke from time to time."

"You need a poke."

He laughed. "That's a true story. OK, I gotta go." The noise in the background had changed to the dull roar of actual warfare. "Someone's crying and I'm not sure who."

"Got it. Talk soon?"

"Yeah. Love to Sara and hug Wyatt, OK? Stop fighting and sort your shit out."

"You sort your own shit out."

"OK, babe."

He hung up. Iris thought about him, about his wedding, about her other brothers, about her father and now her mother, all alone. Then she got up and went to find Sara and sort out her shit.

Thirty-five.

After dropping all the kids at school Frances had a high school committee thing to go to. She found herself wondering about the future. Next year Lally would be in kindergarten. Maybe it was time to get a job outside the family. It would be nice to bring in extra money, but she knew—because she wasn't an idiot—that she would just be adding to all the shit she had to do, because everyone knows the division of labor between couples isn't equal. She daydreamed a meeting between herself and Michael where they shared out the domestic duties, carefully writing them all on a whiteboard.

"Pet care?" she said in her daydream, holding a green marker.

"What's involved with that?" Michael asked, looking up from his increasingly long list. His pencil wavered; he liked pets, this might be one for him.

"Feeding, walking, pee/poo/vomit clean up, minor first aid, flea medication and deworming, vet visit scheduling and attending, and anything else that comes up."

He was shaking his head. "Nah, that sounds more like a you kind of thing. What else you got?"

"Laundry?"

"What goes with that?"

"Well, you pick up all the clothes on the floor and sniff them to see if they're clean. Then you wash them, dry them, fold them, and either leave them in a giant pile somewhere to be rummaged through, or you carefully put Lally's away and deliver Milo's and Ava's to their rooms, telling them to put them away themselves, only to discover them lying on the floor the next day, unworn. And you spend time pairing socks, time that could easily be spent doing pretty much anything else. Plus, every so often, you have to field the desperately delivered comment that 'nothing is clean in this house' or hunt through the dirty laundry for some particular piece of clothing a child wants." She remembered something else. "Of course, soccer uniforms are bundled in there, too. I like to do that at nine o'clock on Friday evening in a panic, but you can do it on a Sunday morning and feel smug if you like."

And then, when the meeting was over, she'd drop a folder the size of Poughkeepsie on the desk in front of him. "What's this," he would ask and she would reply, "It's the contents of my head from the last fourteen years of taking care of everything."

She found a parking space and sat there smiling for a moment. Then she sighed, rolled some "calming" essential oils on her wrists, ineffectively, and headed into the café.

———

Like childbirth, volunteering to organize a school event was way more painful than you expected it to be, but the minute the event was over you forgot how awful it was. It's the only possible explanation for why those lovely but exhausted women do it every year. This year Frances had decided to join the Parents Spring Fling Committee at Ava's school. The Spring Fling was the school's major fund-raiser. It had a theme, a silent auction, a raffle, and a tendency to produce the kind of drunken behavior that kept the school gate gossips warm for the rest of the year. Three minutes into the meeting Frances was already kicking herself, and it hadn't even officially begun.

Sitting in a coffee shop, around the large central table, were a half dozen women who mostly wished they were somewhere else. Frances knew only one of them, and had already forgotten the names of the others.

One of them was clearly new to this game because she was talking about her daughter. Rule number one when meeting school parents you don't know? Never talk about your child. Think about Fight Club, and double down. Whatever you say will get back to the other kids and be spread around school in no time. One time Frances had mentioned Ava was getting braces and by the time Ava got home *that same day* everyone in her class had asked her what color bands she was going to put on.

"Why do they even care?" Frances had asked, bemused.

"I don't know! But why did you tell them?!" Ava had been deeply annoyed and went on and on about feeling violated until Frances had had to drift off into her mental happy place just to survive. In her happy place there was a gentle hum of bees and birdsong, and no one Ever Said Anything. But anyway.

"So," this mother said, innocently enough, "Flora-Grace just got shortlisted for the art museum's painting contest, isn't that fun?"

A tall blond mom turned to another and said, "Didn't Butterfly Absinthe win that last year?"

"Yes," her crony replied, "I think she did. It was before the drug thing, of course." She turned to the innocent mom. "Does your daughter know Anglepoise Whateverthefuck? In eigth grade?" The innocent one, slowly realizing she had transgressed in some way she didn't really understand, shook her head. "Well," continued the other mom, "I think she got shortlisted, too, and she's super, *super* talented. We should introduce the two of them."

"We should!" said the tall blonde. "I'm sure they'd have a lot to talk about!" Having taken ownership of this topic, she then turned to Frances. "So, how's Ava enjoying eighth grade? I hear she's doing much better."

Fortunately for Frances, this was not her first rodeo, so she merely smiled and nodded. The best defense against aggressively competitive parents is a simple one: silence. Followed by a definitive changing of the subject. To whit:

"So, the Fling . . . What's the theme this year?"

"Well," said the tall blonde, pulling out a stack of glossy magazines. "I was thinking classic seventies spank rags. Winged hair, split beavers, and a disturbing amount of pubic hair compared to today's sanitized Internet porn."

"Great idea!" said the woman next to her. "And we could have an S&M raffle to bring in the *Fifty Shades* folks! Maybe we can get a ball gag in school colors?"

None of this happened, of course, but imagining it kept Frances sane throughout the rest of the meeting, and she managed to get out without volunteering for anything more onerous than coat check.

After that she had to pick up medication for one of the dogs, who had developed a skin condition only slightly more expensive to treat than the aforementioned braces had been, and go to Staples for printer paper. She came out with the paper, a blank composition book with kittens on the front (Lally), a pack of monster pencil toppers in a variety of colors (Milo), and several "to do" list pads with humorous headlines (Ava). She forgot the ink toner cartridge she also needed, and had to go back, of course. It never failed. She resolved to keep one of the "to do" pads for herself.

Then she went home for an hour, during which she emptied and loaded the dishwasher, moved laundry through the system, scheduled a doctor's appointment for Milo whose birthday was coming up, rescheduled an orthodontist appointment for Ava, and sat and gazed into space for nearly ten minutes trying to remember what it was she'd forgotten. Then she went to pick up the preschool kids.

———

Lally was in a good mood that day, and Lucas was open to being in a good mood once he'd had some lunch and watched a show. After lunch he surprised Frances by pulling an iPad out of his backpack.

"Look!" he said. "Dad got me a thingy so I could talk to Mom and today he let me bring it to school for show-and-tell."

"Does it have games?" asked Lally, ever practical.

Lucas frowned. "No, does yours?"

Lally shook her head. "I don't have one." There was a pause, and they both looked at Frances.

"Don't look at me," she said. "I don't have one, either."

"Do you want to see my mom?" asked Lucas.

Frances frowned. "It's OK, she might be busy right now."

He shrugged. "She won't answer if she's in a meeting or something, that's the rule. I only call once." He'd already hit a shortcut on the screen, and a window had opened up placing a call.

Suddenly Julie's smiling face appeared. Frances hadn't seen

her in several months, and she was shocked by how pale she was. Clearly Lucas didn't notice, in that callous but useful way children have of seeing adults without really seeing them.

"Hey, Mom!" he said, grinning and waving the iPad. "Frances is here, look!" He turned it around and handed it to Frances. Then he and Lally turned and ran off to play, presumably. Or to cook meth in the upstairs bathroom, who knows?

There was an awkward moment. "Hi, Julie," said Frances. "He took the iPad in for show-and-tell, and he was just . . ."

"Showing and telling?" asked Julie, smiling. "Hey, Frances, how the heck are you?"

"I'm good, how are you?" Frances held the tablet awkwardly, not sure if she was supposed to stand still. She needed coffee, so she began walking very slowly toward the coffee maker.

"I've been better, but I've also been worse." She paused. "Why are you walking like the queen?"

Frances laughed and stopped. "I'm trying not to wobble you."

"You realize you're not really carrying a tiny me in your hands, right?"

"I need coffee," Frances replied. "I'm having my early afternoon brain cramps." She propped the tablet on the counter and made coffee.

Julie asked, "Is Lucas still there?"

"Uh, no. He just handed me the thing and ran off."

Julie sighed. "Can he hear us?"

Frances shook her head.

"Do you have time to chat? I'm bored out of my mind right now."

"Sure." Frances took her coffee outside onto the deck and sat down, propping the iPad on her lap.

"So, I hear my husband is punching the neighbors." Julie didn't seem shocked, more amused than anything.

"Yup. He's turned into a total liability since you left. The neighborhood watch association had a meeting recently and it was all about his roustabout behavior."

"I'll bet. So, I guess you also heard I got cancer."

"Yeah, that came up just before the punching. I'm so sorry. That sucks."

"Yeah. I'm bald all over."

"Wow."

"Yeah. It's not as sexy as you would think." There was a pause. "I'm sorry I didn't tell you. It was . . . weird. I found out, then I came here for treatment really fast, and the whole thing just . . . happened. I didn't want to make a big thing out of it, and have people being super helpful or anything."

Frances suddenly laughed. "Yeah, that could be really annoying."

Julie said, "We let you be helpful, though. We couldn't have done it without you, literally. Bill is only able to keep working, which means keeping our insurance, because you help with Lucas. You have no idea how much we appreciate it."

"You could have told me, it wouldn't have made me more helpful, I promise."

Julie nodded. "I know. I just wanted to tell you in person, and then the moment never happened. I'm sorry."

"Yes, please apologize to me for getting cancer. That's entirely reasonable. Are you doing OK?"

"Not really, but I seem to be responding to treatment, so that's good." She shrugged. "It's too soon to tell."

"Can I ask you about it?"

"Sure, if Lucas isn't there."

"Hold, please," said Frances, getting up to check on the kids. She soon came back. "They're upstairs playing a version of My Little Pony that somehow involves storming a castle."

Julie nodded. "OK, ask away."

"What kind of cancer?"

"Boob."

"What stage?"

"Stage three. Pretty bad."

"Did you cut your boob off?"

"Both of them, in an overabundance of caution and a desire to be able to wear thin spaghetti-strap tops for the first time since puberty." Julie had been pretty busty, one of those women who were slender but curvy, irritating but hardly blameworthy. "I kind of yearned for a smaller, French-style breast, you know, tiny pink or brown nipples, able to go topless on the beach, able to wear sundresses without a bra, you know. I'd had big tits since I was fifteen. It was time for a change."

"So, cancer was a lucky break?"

"Fashion wise, yeah."

"OK, so, how did you find out? Did you find a lump?"

Julie nodded. "Yeah, it was pretty classic. I knew as soon as I felt it that it was cancer. It was just . . . wrong. I went to my OB/GYN that day, got scans, a biopsy, and was in front of an oncologist the same week. Thank God for excellent insurance."

"Wow." Frances took a sip of coffee. "What did Bill say?"

"He said, 'Oh shit.' Then he cried. Then he stopped crying, and said, 'OK, what's the plan?' I wanted to come here for treatment, he wanted me to stay there, so we fought about it solidly for a week. It sucked."

Frances was confused. "I'm sorry, which part were you fighting about?"

Julie sighed. "Like I said, he wanted me to get treatment in Los Angeles, so I could stay home and he could take care of me. I wanted to come to Minnesota so Lucas didn't have to see me so sick, and Bill could focus on him. I felt like it was as if I were in the army, do you know what I mean?"

"Not really, continue."

Julie sighed. "Well, I was going away to fight and either I was going to come back in one piece or I wasn't. Bill said he'd married me in sickness and in health, and that it was his job to take care of me. It got really quite heated, but then I pulled the 'I'm the one dying of cancer' card, and he gave up. He's still pissed, though."

"And how is it?"

"A fucking nightmare. The treatment makes everything taste bad, like metal. I can't eat hardly anything because the mouth sores are just the worst, and what I *can* eat tastes like WD-40 smells. I miss Bill and Lucas all the time, but I would hate it if they were here because then I'd need to worry about them, too. Do you know what I mean?"

"What does Lucas think is going on?"

Julie shrugged. "He thinks I'm working on a film. He was used to one or the other of us going away for work, so we just told him I was on a work trip, and I'd Skype every day if I could, and it's been fine." Julie was a script supervisor.

"Did the surgery hurt? Do you have small boobs now?" Julie was wearing a hooded sweatshirt, so it was hard to tell.

"It hurt so fucking much, honestly, but after those mouth sores I could handle anything. And yes, small boobs, but they're still pretty messed up." Someone had clearly come in the room because she smiled at them, and then looked back at Frances. "I have to go. But I'm really glad I got to talk to you."

"Me, too. Try and come back soon. We miss you, and your husband is clearly going to the dogs."

"Not to mention that I turn my back for five minutes and Anne is porking some random guy. What the actual fuck is going on with that?"

"Call me another time, I'll fill you in," said Frances. "Go do something relaxing. You should get one of those coloring books for grown-ups."

Julie made a hacking noise. "Oh my God, you have no idea how many people have sent me those. They're very kind, but honestly, if I see another fucking mandala I'm going to scream. On the positive side, I have enough sets of colored pencils to keep my kid stocked until college." She sighed. "Let's hope I see him get there."

"Positive attitude, Julie."

"Sure, OK." Julie rolled her eyes. "Talk to you soon." She hung up.

Frances took the iPad and tucked it back into Lucas's backpack. Inside she found a drawing of him and his dad. Julie was in it, too, talking to them through a window. All of them were smiling.

Thirty-six.

Soccer that weekend was particularly irritating. There was something in the air, like a giant cloud of irritation, that doubled the usual number of sideline tantrums—and the kids were pretty bad tempered, too.

Lally was in especially fine form. Michael had dug himself a hole by telling her, in the car on the way there, that she could grow up to be anything she wanted. He was getting out of the car, congratulating himself on his right-on girl-empowerment fathering, when she suddenly asked, "Can I be a toilet?"

"I'm sorry?"

"Can I be a toilet when I grow up?"

He made a face at her. "No, you can't be a toilet. You can't grow up to be an object, you're still going to be a person." He anticipated the next question. "And you can't change species either, you're stuck with human."

"But you said I could be anything I wanted." Lally had had a bowl of Cheerios for breakfast, about three hours earlier. He had tried to give her a granola bar in the car, but failed. He understood low blood sugar was a factor here, but seriously, a toilet?

He was firm. "Yes, you can be anything, but anything that a

person can possibly be in real life, not like, you know, a tree or something."

"But I *want to be a toilet.*"

Milo was waiting to get out of the car. "Dad, just let her be a toilet, what does it matter? She's not applying for toilet college, is she?"

Michael saw the wisdom of this. Frances was good at this, letting the small stuff slide over her; he would be like Frances. "OK, whatever. Sure, honey, you can be a toilet."

Then they got out of the car and headed to the game. Michael had remembered orange slices in a Ziploc bag and two water bottles. He had remembered shoes to change into after the game. He had remembered his phone and car keys. He was crushing it.

"So," continued Lally, as they wandered through the crowds of parents strung along the perimeter of games that were in progress, or about to start, or about to end. "If I was a toilet, where would people poop? Would people poop in my mouth?"

As Michael told Frances this story later, he emphasized that this had been the moment he could have headed off the whole thing. "I should have just ignored her," he confessed. "I should have simply pretended that I didn't hear, but, you know, I was distracted by finding the right little field, and looking for other kids on the team . . ." His voice trailed off. "I just didn't . . ."

But in that moment, he didn't ignore it. Instead he absent-mindedly said, "I guess so, baby."

They found Lally's team, the Glitter Marlins, and Michael left Lally there for a moment to take Milo to his team, the Raging Robots. As he made his way back he paused for a moment to say hi to Lili Girvan and meet her boyfriend, but he wasn't away for long. Really, maybe two minutes. Three, tops.

As he got closer to the Glitter Marlins field he could see

something was going on, and quickened his pace. A crowd of kids was gathered around the coach, but they seemed to be gazing at something on the ground. Maybe someone was injured already?

"I want you to poop in my mouth!" Lally was yelling. "My daddy said people would poop in my mouth!" She was lying on the ground screaming. "He said so!"

Which was precisely when Michael joined the circle of adults, all of whom slowly turned to look at him.

———

"They threw her off the team?" Frances was half horrified, half thrilled. "We don't have to go back?"

Michael was sitting at the kitchen table with his forehead on the wood. "Milo is still on his team, so we have to go back until his season ends."

"But Lally's done?"

"As far as the Glitter Marlins are concerned, she is no longer welcome."

"All because she said a bad word?"

"No." Michael started rolling his forehead back and forth on the table. "All because she insisted people were going to poop in her mouth, then became enraged when it was suggested they wouldn't. Then she kicked the coach in the knee."

"Really?"

"Yes. Hard. While shouting, 'My daddy said people would poop.'"

"No."

"Yes. Would I make it up? Who could have seen that coming? Who could have seen an innocent statement like 'you can be anything you want to be in life' would end up in peewee soccer disgrace." He lifted his head. "Lili Girvan said she's never heard of anyone being thrown off a team before. Not a girls team, anyway."

"Lili saw all this?"

He nodded. "And Shelly was there. She has a Glitter Marlin, too."

Frances hooted with laughter. "That's right! Otter! I am SO GLAD that was you and not me."

"Maybe it wouldn't have happened to you. Maybe you would have cut her off at the toilet."

Frances shook her head and sat down next to him at the table. "Baby, children are fucking insane. Four-year-olds are the childhood equivalent of the Joker. They'll mess you up just because they can. You're a great dad, and one day she'll appreciate the limitless possibilities you presented to her."

"Including people pooping in her mouth?"

"Yes. Plus we're definitely going to mention it at her wedding."

"OK."

She stroked his head. "Do you want a beer now?"

He nodded, banging his forehead gently as he did so.

———

A couple of hours later, as the evening grew darker, Iris stepped out of the shower and heard her phone ringing. Maybe it was the babysitter; she and Sara were planning on going out for dinner, to talk without Wyatt chiming in every three minutes. They were getting close to a decision about the film, about the baby, about the future. "Sara? Can you get that?" No answer. Frowning, Iris wrapped a towel around herself and went to the bedroom. Sara wasn't there, which made sense once she picked up the phone and saw her wife's name on the display.

"Hey, don't tell me you're too lazy to walk upstairs?"

"No, I'm in the street, outside." Sara's voice was hurried, low. "Come as quick as you can, OK?"

Iris looked out of the window. Sara, Michael, Frances, Charlie, Bill . . . What the fuck? All of them were standing in the street looking anxious. Iris turned and blindly put on whatever clothes she could find.

Rushing outside she called, "What happened? What's going on?"

Frances turned and said, "It's Theo. He's gone missing."

A police car turned onto the street, and Charlie raised his arms and waved like a drowning man.

Thirty-seven.

As Iris stepped out of the house, Anne pulled up in a taxi. Somehow she covered the ground to her husband without touching it. "Is he back?"

Charlie shook his head, reaching for Anne, pulling her close. "He was right there," he said, his words clear even from where Frances and Ava stood. "He was right there and . . ."

"Mom?" Lally appeared next to Frances. "Mom?"

Frances turned and looked down at Lally. "I'm sorry, baby, I'm really busy right now. We can't find Theo. Have you seen him? Is he maybe playing hide and seek?"

Lally shrugged. "I guess he's with Milo."

Frances frowned, and Michael started toward them, noticing the sudden concern on his wife's face. "Where's Milo, Lally? Isn't he in the house?"

The little girl shook her head. "No. He must have gone with Theo." She frowned suddenly. "He borrowed some of my birthday money. He has to give it back, right?"

"What birthday money, baby?" Michael picked her up and looked at her closely. "When was this?"

"A little while ago. I was watching *My Little Pony* and Milo came in and asked if he could borrow some of my birthday money and I said yes if he gave it back and he said he would and then Twilight Sparkle and Spike had a big fight and now they're not talking." She hugged her dad. "Do you want to come watch?"

He shook his head and watched his wife run into their house. Ten seconds later she was out again, her face white. He got to the cop just before she did.

———

Forty minutes later Paul Ramirez's squad car pulled up on the corner of the street, and he looked over at the gaggle of middle-class white people and sighed. No cop liked a missing kid. It always caused that twist in the gut, that fear that this was going to be one where a stranger had plucked a kid from the street and was even now doing unspeakable things. However, those cases were so rare Paul had never encountered one in nearly twenty years of being a cop, but what he did encounter all the time was kids running from their own parents. After some of those cases he almost wished for a stranger, someone whose evil was less . . . personalized.

He looked at the people standing there, already talking to another set of cops from his precinct and wondered if any of them had pushed this particular kid into running away. He examined the faces of the men briefly, as men were usually the ones who raped or beat or yelled, but he knew even as he did it that it was pointless. Evil was so good at hiding. He unlatched his seat belt and opened the car door. Kids were good at hiding, too. Hopefully it would just be one of those.

As he got closer he realized he recognized one of the women, although he didn't know her. He'd seen her at his daughter's school. She looked the same as she always did, a little unkempt, a little scruffy, a little overweight. Her jeans and hoodie were like his own uniform, and as consistent. There were several other women there, but only one was crying, so presumably she was the mom. That one was good looking, wearing expensive clothes and boots that would cost a week of his salary. It wasn't important, he was just used to gathering impressions. If the cops were there, it didn't matter who you were—and it certainly didn't matter what you wore. The shit had somehow hit the fan, and in those moments they were all the same.

His colleague turned and raised a hand. "This is Detective Ramirez. He's going to help us find the boys."

Boys, plural? He'd missed that detail. OK, that shifted things again.

"Shall we go inside?" he asked, after nodding all around. "I know right now you want to be out there hunting for your children, but we need to issue a more detailed alert and I'm going to ask you some questions."

Frances and Michael led him inside their house, with Charlie and Anne just behind. Several cops were already there, methodically searching every room. The first cops on the scene had asked for permission to search Anne and Charlie's house, and that search was long underway and nearly done. Then, when it turned out Milo was gone, too, a second set of cops had entered Frances and Michael's house.

"We often find the kids curled up behind a sofa somewhere," a cop had explained, trying to be reassuring.

"They're a little big for hide and seek," Michael had said, but inside he hoped against hope he was wrong, that they'd find them and he could yell at them and hug them and send everyone home and it would just be one of those days he and Frances could look back on and shudder. Rather than the day when everything ended.

"So," began Detective Ramirez, his notepad open on his knee. "Tell me about Milo and Theo. What's been going on with them lately?"

"Nothing," said Frances, speaking for the first time. This policeman looked vaguely familiar. "We've been getting along pretty well, to be honest. Milo's a good kid, an easy kid."

"And he and Theo are close?"

Frances turned up her palms. "They're in class together at school. We carpool together. We're neighbors. They hang out a lot. They play soccer together, you know." She paused, unsure of what to say and what not to. She looked over at Anne, who was sitting very close to Charlie, holding his hand.

Charlie cleared his throat. "Theo's been having a little bit of a harder time." He looked at Anne. "His mom and I have recently separated, and it's hard for the kids to understand."

Looking at them sitting closely together it was also somewhat hard for the detective to understand, but he took Charlie at his word. "Could he have gone to find you, Mrs. Porter?"

Anne looked lost. "He hasn't ever been to my apartment. He's not very . . . resourceful. I don't know if he could even find it."

"Where is it?"

"It's in the Palazzo."

"You said they play soccer. Are they in AYSO?" The detective smiled at the parents when they nodded. "Well, the Palazzo's across the street from the park, right? Maybe they know more than you realize."

Michael looked at the detective with increased hope. Clearly this guy was on top of it, maybe he'd find the boys in the park, maybe they were just fooling around. This wasn't possible, he knew it wasn't, because Milo wasn't that kind of kid, but then again he'd thought Anne Porter wasn't that kind of wife. Or, indeed, that Charlie Porter wasn't that kind of husband.

"Wait, what about her guy?" As he blurted it out he felt terrible for even mentioning it, but he couldn't have held it in. He turned to Charlie. "I'm sorry, Charlie. But what about the guy?"

Charlie knew what he meant, but he looked at the ground rather than at his wife. It was she who spoke to the detective.

"Michael means the man I was having an affair with." She shook her head. "He doesn't know the kids. I haven't spoken to him in nearly a month."

"This is why you are currently separated?" The detective might have been discussing the weather. All these were just facts to him; none of it had feelings.

All four of them nodded, answering the question.

"But the affair is over?"

Anne and Frances both nodded, and the detective looked at Frances for a moment before looking down at his pad again. "I'll still need his information, just to eliminate him."

"Of course."

The detective looked sympathetic. "It's very hard not to feel responsible when a child goes missing, but try not to panic just yet. Children sometimes wander off to the store, or to have an adventure. The fact that both boys are together is reassuring. It's much, much less likely they've been abducted." He paused. The next part could be delicate. "Having said that, is there anything in the relationship between them that causes you concern?"

Michael answered. "How do you mean? They are ten years old, they've known each other their whole lives."

"Children can be cruel to each other, sadly. Is it possible one of them is bullying the other? Or anything else?" The whisper of sexual abuse entered the room, and every adult felt suddenly guilty, whether they'd done anything or not.

The four parents in front of him shook their heads. "They argue over stuff like which *Star Wars* character would win in a fight with Superman, but neither of them are particularly aggressive." Charlie felt defensive. He added, "Theo's mad at me right now, but I don't think he'd pick a fight with anyone else." Suddenly he remembered the kid at school, and felt less sure of himself.

The detective looked at him curiously. "He's mad with you, but not with his mother?"

Charlie nodded his head, then put it in his hands and started to sob. Anne put her arm around him, pulling him closer.

Frances got up suddenly and went into the other room, returning to hand the detective a photo in a frame. In it the two boys were dressed for Halloween, one of them Iron Man, the other Thor. They had their arms around each other, laughing hard because she'd told them to act tough and in tensing for the photo one of them had farted. It was one of Frances's favorite photos, and suddenly she felt it was really important for the detective to see it.

———

Twenty minutes later the all-cars bulletin had gone out, photos of the two boys shared with every police station, squad car, helicopter, and individual officer instantaneously. When they'd last been seen, what they'd been wearing, the places they liked to go. Michael, Charlie, Sara, Iris, Ava, and Bill had set off, wandering the neighborhood calling and hunting. Extra police officers were on the way to assist.

Frances and Anne stayed at Frances's house, both clutching their cell phones, watching over Lally, Kate, Wyatt, and Lucas. The kids were on beanbags, watching TV and blessedly distracted. Kate knew what was going on, and had been very upset. Mostly she seemed upset her brother had left her behind, but now Mickey Mouse was taking care of it.

The two mothers sat at the kitchen table and drank tea, neither one of them saying anything because Frances wanted to scream at Anne that this was her fault, and Anne knew it. Outside it was dark. In another half hour it would be time to make dinner. Had to keep the children they still had alive.

Thirty-eight.

Milo was feeling particularly proud of himself. He knew the Hollywood sign was north, he knew his street was in the east of the city and that the soccer place was west of them, and he had successfully navigated himself and Theo all the way to the Palazzo without going wrong once. Beverly Boulevard was too trafficky, so they'd taken backstreets and it had been challenging, but he'd made it. It had turned out to be a whole lot longer on foot than it had been in the car, but still. No wonder he'd gotten his Boy Scout navigation patch.

Of course, he was starting to worry that his parents were going to be upset with him, but he thought he could explain himself to his mom. He couldn't let Theo go on his own, right? Theo was upset and angry and not at all good at navigation. He wasn't even a Scout. When they played Minecraft Milo was forever having to teleport Theo back to where he was, even though there was a compass right there on the screen the entire time. He couldn't have let him go on his own, that was all there was to it. He should have told his mom, though, but he'd thought it would be quicker than it had been, and that Theo's mom would call her once they arrived.

Theo was sniffling a bit. They had reached the point of the park nearest the entrance to the Palazzo, but now he was balking. Milo was trying to remain patient, and they'd zigged a bit and gone to a 7-Eleven to get candy. Now they were sitting on the wall opposite the entrance and waiting. Milo had noticed a grown-up man sitting a little way along the wall, and he was keeping his eye on him, just in case. The man looked over at them every so often, and once Milo caught him frowning. Milo knew not to talk to strangers; he wasn't worried.

"Why don't we just ask the guy at the gate?" he asked Theo.

"What if she's mad at me?"

Milo rolled his eyes. "You should have thought of that before. We're here now and it's taken a long time so we should go ask."

Theo looked at him. "Will you do it?"

"Yes," his friend replied, slightly exasperated. It was all very well when you started a plan, he thought, everyone's all brave then. But when it comes down to it . . . "Let's cross at the light, though."

The gate guard lowered his phone and looked impassively at the two ten-year-olds in front of him. "Yes?"

"We're looking for Anne Porter."

"Does she live here?" The guard had a list, but as it changed weekly he'd long ago realized there was little point trying to memorize it.

The boys nodded, and the guard reached for the list, licking his finger to turn over the pages. He found the name, and looked at the boys again.

"Shall I call the apartment?"

They nodded. He did so. He let it ring, but nobody answered.

"No answer," he said.

Milo and Theo looked at him. This was not an outcome

they'd anticipated. Theo looked at Milo, who shrugged. "We'll go wait for her," Milo suggested.

The guard was about to raise his phone again when a thought occurred to him. "You two are a little young to be out alone, aren't you?"

Milo nodded. "Yes, but it's OK." He looked across the street at the grown-up who was still watching them. "We're with him."

"You weren't sitting with him before." The guard might look like he spent all his time playing on his phone, but he had some standards. He monitored the environment. He kept tabs. Occasionally they had celebrities at the Palazzo, and he'd proudly thwarted paparazzi several times. "And he's there a lot lately, but I haven't seen you two before."

Milo just smiled at him, and turned to head back across the street. He was good at small talk, for a ten-year-old, because he'd watched his mom a lot, and she could talk to anyone. But he also knew that he didn't have small talk for this situation, and that a strategic retreat was probably the best option.

So, they went back to the wall and sat there. This time they sat closer to the grown-up, and Milo smiled at him as if they were old friends, and then looked over at the guard. He was watching, so Milo raised a hand and waved. The guard narrowed his eyes, but then his girlfriend texted him a picture of her boobs, and the little boys were immediately forgotten.

Milo sighed and looked at the grown-up, thoughtfully. He looked clean, normal, not like a homeless person. He looked a lot like the teachers at school, and Milo came to the conclusion that it was OK to say hello.

"Hello," Milo said. "We're waiting for someone who lives in that building. Is it OK if we sit here?"

"Sure," said the guy. "I'm waiting for someone, too."

"Is he out?"

"She," replied the guy. "Yeah, I saw her leave a while ago. I'm waiting for her to come back."

"I'm Milo," the little boy said, reaching out his hand, after checking the guard wasn't watching.

"Hi, Milo," the man replied, shaking his hand. "I'm Richard."

———

The first TV van showed up on Frances's block about a half hour after the bulletin went out to the police. Just the local news, of course, but it had been a slow week, and a live hunt for two missing kids was always good for ten minutes at the top of the hour. After the newspeople arrived so did *TMZ*, the celebrity newshounds: The word was that Sara Gillespie was somehow involved, and celebrities crying was broadcast gold.

When the TV lights had first brightened the side of Anne's face, where she sat in Frances's kitchen, she'd just turned away. But Frances had gotten up to see what was going on, and now she turned to the other mom and said, "Maybe we could show pictures of the kids on the news, and someone might see them?"

Anne nodded, and Frances went to get that same Halloween picture. When she stepped outside, the local news reporter approached her immediately, microphone in hand.

"Hi there, I'm Clarissa Romero, Channel 7 News. Any news about the missing children? Do you have a statement to make?"

Frances shook her head. "No news. They've been missing since this afternoon, but we're hoping they'll be found soon." She handed the reporter the photo, which was quickly handed back to a producer who got it on-screen in approximately twenty seconds.

The *TMZ* guy jumped in. "And is Sara Gillespie . . . ?"

"Sara's my son's aunt by marriage, yes. She's out looking for him now."

"And is it true that she and David Rapelli are having an affair?"

Frances looked at the reporter in bewilderment for a moment. "Who the hell is David Rapelli?"

"Her costar in the upcoming feature, *A Grander Canyon.*"

"No, of course she's not having an affair. You understand that two children are missing, right?" Frances and the news reporter both looked at the celebrity-seeking guy in the same way a bird looks at a slug: a mix of revulsion and an evaluation of the quickest way to eat it.

"Yes, of course," replied the reporter, beating a hasty retreat down the lawn.

Frances stared after him for a moment, then noticed Michael, Ava, Charlie, Iris, Sara, and Bill heading down the street toward them. The reporters followed her gaze and immediately scrambled their cameramen. There was an unseemly rush, and the crowd converged in a confusing melee of lights and microphones. Sara was used to it, but the others were alarmed.

"Please get out the way," said Michael, trying not to lose his temper, and looking around for a policeman to give them a hand. "We're trying to find our children, not film a reality show."

"Sara," said the *TMZ* guy, who'd been pushed aside by the best and brightest in entertainment. "Is it true that you and David Rapelli have been getting very close on set?"

Sara shook her head and kept moving.

"Is it true that you're making another movie together in China, and that he's planning on leaving his wife?"

Sara shook her head again, and added a frown for emphasis. "Is it true . . ."

Charlie leaned into the reporter's face. "I'll tell you what's true, asshole, my kid is missing. So get out of the way and have some respect."

The *TMZ* guy hung on. "Sara, do you have any comment about your missing nephew?"

Sara stopped, finally. "Yes," she said. "Milo, if you're out there, please call home and let us know you're OK."

Anne spoke. She'd come up behind the reporters and no one had noticed her. "My child is missing, too, Sara." The cameras turned to see her, and the lights revealed Anne looking pale and lovely standing next to a cop. *Ooh*, thought the reporters, *attractively grieving mother, fantastic*, and kept recording.

"I know, Anne," said Sara. "We're all thinking they're together, right?"

Anne didn't seem to hear her. "Yes. My son, Theo, is missing, and it's all my fault."

The local news reporter sniffed a story. "And why is that, Mrs. Porter?" She'd nailed that name, she thought. Thank God for her photographic memory.

"Because I cheated on his father and broke his heart."

Oh fuck, thought Frances. *She's lost it.*

"And why was that?" persisted the reporter. This was so much better than just a missing kid, this was classic entertainment, this was. Drama, pathos, inner pain, outer glamor. The *TMZ* guy pulled out his phone and started texting.

"Because I am a bad person, and I'm paying for it."

"You're not paying for it, Anne. Let's go inside, OK?" Frances pushed the reporter aside and took her friend by the arm. She lowered her voice. "Keep it together, this isn't helping us find the kids."

Anne shook her off. "No. You know it's true, Frances. You know it's my fault."

Frances said, "Anne, let's not talk about this in the street, OK? You don't want everyone to know your business." There was a roaring in her ears that reminded her of when her brother died, a sense that the world was turning upside down in a way that no one else could feel. How were they all standing so still when the ground was rolling under their feet?

Charlie joined them and took his wife's other arm. "Come on, Anne, let's go inside."

Anne looked up at him. "Charlie, you know it's my fault. I never should have cheated. I never should have let it happen."

"And cut to husband," said the producer inside the TV van. This was playing live, and the numbers were terrific.

The husband shook his head. "No, baby, it's my fault, too."

The *TMZ* reporter pushed in. "Did you have an affair, too, Mr. Porter?"

The news reporter turned to Michael. "What about you, Mr. Bloom? Were you involved in this affair? Is that why your child ran away?" She was *killing it* on the names this evening; she was a reporting *machine*.

Suddenly Frances Bloom lost her temper.

"No!" she shouted. "My husband wasn't involved. Neither was I, nor was Sara or Iris or anyone else on the fucking block." She pointed furiously at Anne, and then at Charlie. "She had an affair, and he behaved like a dick, and now the entire neighborhood is in ruins and why? Why??" Her face was red, her hair was sticking straight up, and she was about to go viral in the worst way. "Because it's more important for you to feel young and alive and sexy than it is to take care of your family and feed your kids and be kind to your husband and just show the fuck up for everyone else." She stepped toward the other mother, causing the camera people to zoom out as fast as they could in case she swung back and punched her in the face. "You're a selfish, selfish bitch, Anne, and if my son comes to any harm because of your affair I am going to rip your head off and piss down your gaping neck wound."

Then she turned and marched into the house, leaving everyone else standing on the lawn.

"And cut," said the producer in the van.

Thirty-nine.

"And then you broke up?" Milo licked his ice cream and looked at Richard with sympathetic eyes.

Richard nodded. He wasn't sure why he was confiding in this child, but there was something kind in his face that said it was OK. "We shouldn't really have been together in the first place. It was for the best."

"But it's still sad."

Richard nodded. "It will get better." He'd elected to go for a milkshake, and took a thoughtful swallow.

Milo said confidently, "My mom says everything gets better eventually, but that sometimes it takes a long time, and you shouldn't rush it." Of course, she had been talking about a twisted ankle, but he expected the concept was the same. He suddenly missed his mom, and wished he was home. She always smelled of cookies, she was always soft and warm, she was always there.

Theo was finishing his ice cream, but he chimed in. "My mom and dad just broke up. That's why I'm here."

"Oh yeah?" Richard frowned at him. "I'm sorry to hear that. My parents broke up, too, when I was your age. It's really hard."

Theo nodded. "I want to come and live with my mom." He looked at Richard. "Did you live with your mom?"

Richard nodded, thinking back to how tired his mom had always been. He'd never before considered how hard it must have been for her, and was suddenly ashamed of himself. He looked at these children, dealing with the same shit he had dealt with, feeling the same ache and not understanding how they could fix it. He realized losing Anne hurt so much because it was a fresh cut on a very old scar.

"Do your parents know where you are?" he asked them.

Theo looked at Milo, who licked his cone for a moment while he thought. Eventually he shook his head. "No," he said. "Theo ran away, and I wanted to make sure he didn't get lost, so I came, too."

Richard pulled out his phone. "Well then, you should probably call them."

———

It was Michael who answered his phone, and Michael who went to get the boys. Frances and Ava sat on the sofa, side by side, watching the play of police car lights and reporters' cameras on the inside of the curtains. Eventually Ava cleared her throat.

"Well, it was an effective image, even if it wasn't very pretty."

Frances sighed. "You don't think 'gaping neck wound' was maybe a little harsh?"

"Not at all."

"OK. That makes me feel better."

"Good." They lapsed into silence again.

"Are you going to ground Milo for, like, a year?"

Frances shrugged. "Maybe. Right now I'm just so overwhelmingly relieved he's in one piece and found that I'm ready to throw him a parade. Not a great parenting choice, but whatever."

Ava shifted a little on the sofa, inching closer to her mom. "You always make us feel like you'd be ready to throw us a parade at a moment's notice."

"I do?"

Ava nodded. "Yeah. You're very . . . supportive."

"How annoying."

"It is."

"Maybe if I were a little firmer with you guys Milo wouldn't have run away and you wouldn't be so angry with me all the time."

Ava looked surprised. "I'm not angry with you all the time."

"Yes, you are. Or you seem to be, anyway." Frances put her arm around Ava's shoulder, and tugged her closer. "I don't mean to be so annoying. I just never had a teenager before and I'm scrambling to keep up."

"That's OK. I've never been a teenager before, so we're in the same boat."

Frances took a chance. "Who is Piper? Is she the one who's making you unhappy?"

Ava was silent for a moment, then sighed and answered. "No, she's really just a girl at school. I thought we were friends, but then suddenly there was all this drama and now we're not friends." She closed her eyes, unseen by her mother, who nonetheless squeezed her. "It's very hard to know what's going on, you know? No one is what you think they are." She sighed once more. "Not even me. I don't know who I am anymore, and when I think I know I change again. It's very confusing. You and dad are the only ones who stay the same."

They sat there some more, saying nothing in a companionable way. These quiet moments are the mortar that holds families together, yet they often pass unnoticed. Frances reveled in them; it was her superpower.

"Do you ever feel like running away?" Ava asked her.

Frances shook her head. "Where would I go? Everything I love is here." She rested her cheek against Ava's hair, smelling— yet again—her shampoo on someone else's head. "Do you?"

"Yes and no. Yes, because I'd like to be somewhere else or someone else or sometime else. But no, because you'd just come after me." She looked at her lap, to hide the happiness she felt at that fact.

"I'm afraid so."

Ava straightened up and looked at Frances. "You know, I was worried about Theo until I knew he was with Milo. That meant they'd gone under their own steam, rather than being snatched by some asshole, right?"

"Sure. At least, more likely that."

"And Milo knows what I know, which is that you would never stop looking for him. You told us that all the time when we were little."

"I did?" Frances pulled a cushion over and hugged it, still a little freaked out by this day, despite her apparent calm. Luckily, Ava seemed sanguine, so that made one of them.

"Yeah. You said it over and over: If you get lost, stay where you are and wait. Daddy and I will be looking for you and we will never stop. If someone takes you, keep fighting, keep making noise and kicking them in the nuts, because we will be hunting for as long as it takes, and we will never stop." Ava smiled to herself. "I've never been scared of being alone, which I guess is a good thing because the chance of anyone wanting to date me with these eyebrows is remote."

Frances ignored the eyebrow comment. "Did I literally say nuts?"

Ava shrugged. "You may have. You must have told us five

hundred times. Ask Milo. You also went on and on and on about paying attention in parking lots, do you remember that?"

Frances ran her hand through her hair, which made it stand up like a radio antenna, unbeknownst to her. "I sound very boring. What did I say about parking lots?"

"You said," Ava mimicked her mother's voice, which was apparently like Daisy Duck's, *"they're looking for spaces, not children, so be careful."*

"Did I sound like I was on helium?"

"No, only in my head."

"OK." Frances had a headache. She couldn't believe she'd been so rude to Anne. Suddenly, though, she started laughing.

Ava looked at her. "Are you hysterical? Do I need to slap you?"

Frances laughed and shook her head. "No, I'm just laughing at the memory of your father's face."

"When you yelled at Anne?"

"No, just in general." She giggled. "His face makes me laugh. That's why I love it."

Ava raised her eyebrows, but her mom was still laughing, so she let it go.

————

Richard happened to be looking at the boys when the car pulled up in front of them, and when he saw the relief in their shoulders he suddenly got a memory of seeing his mother approaching the school gate at the end of the day: *I'm not forgotten. It's OK now.* A tall man got out of the car and came over to him, holding out his hand. Richard, still feeling about eight years old and strangely close to tears, managed to smile at him.

"I will never be able to thank you enough," Michael said. "I am so grateful."

Richard shrugged. "It takes a village, right?" He watched the man bend to hug his son, and then pull the other boy into an embrace, too. "Besides, it's nice to do something helpful for a change."

The man stood up and smiled at him as he shepherded the boys into the car. "My name's Michael Bloom," he said. "If you ever need anything . . ." He handed Richard his card.

Richard grinned at him. "Thanks," he said. "Glad I could help."

The car pulled away, and Richard watched it go. Then he turned and walked away himself, tucking Michael's card in his pocket, where it would be forgotten and washed away into fluff.

———

The smell of his mother's perfume always made Theo feel small. Throughout his life elements of it would drift across his path and take him right back to this moment and others like it, when the soft skin of Anne's neck felt more like home than anything ever would again.

He'd been worried his parents would be furious with him, but they seemed just very glad to see him, and even Kate had cried and held on to him as they sat together on the sofa. After a while his father pulled out of the snuggle and looked at him.

"Why did you run away, Theo? Will you talk about it?"

Theo nodded. A policeman had talked to him briefly, outside, after he and Milo had returned. He could tell the man was annoyed with Milo's dad for going to fetch them without telling the cops, but Michael had just shrugged and said he'd had no other thought but to get to them as quickly as possible. The man had looked at him thoughtfully and for a moment Theo had felt uncertain, but then the cop's face had cleared and he'd just led the two boys a little way away and squatted down.

"Is everything OK?" he'd asked. "Are you scared at home?" They'd both shaken their heads. "Why did you run away?"

"I wanted to talk to my mom," Theo had said.

"I didn't want him to get lost," Milo had said. "I'm a Scout, it's my job to help."

The cop had smiled a little bit at Milo, then looked at Theo. "Tell your mom and dad everything. Tell them what you want, tell them what you feel. They love you very much and they deserve the truth, alright?"

The two boys had nodded, and then the detective had stood up, ruffled Milo's hair, and walked off. Now Theo remembered his advice.

"I wanted to be with Mom. I love you, Dad, but I want you to be together again, I want it to be like it was before, even if she did something bad. I want you to accept her apology and let her come home so we can all be together." He looked at his family. "We are supposed to all be together, whatever happens."

"She can sleep in my room, if you don't want to share," added Kate. "It's fine. I can move my Beanie Babies." She looked serious. "I have too many anyway." Then she shook her head. "No, that's not true, but I can move them."

Charlie looked at Anne's face, the near-miss of the day washing away everything that had come before. They'd held hands and burned with fear, and the annealing had broken open a crack of possibility.

He smiled at her as if they'd never met, and she started to cry.

Christmas.

*F*rances was sitting in the living room, watching her kids decorate the Christmas tree, the old orange cat on her lap. She thought back to that morning in the tree lot: The kids and Michael were arguing about whether or not to get greenery for the front door, and Iris and Sara were trailing around after Wyatt, as he pointed to larger and larger trees. From this distance she couldn't hear what they were saying, but Sara kept shaking her head and Iris just looked tired and mildly green. The hormone treatments were making her nauseous, and Sara had stepped up to run the holidays. Of course, they'd be coming to Frances's house, as they did every year, but that was a week or two off yet. Hopefully Iris would feel better by then and able to eat.

Frances stroked the cat's head. Frances had seen Anne and Charlie unloading their tree the day before. They were still being a little too polite to each other, but at least they were all under the same roof, and the kids were doing better. Anne was sleeping in the guest room, but she was hopeful. They were seeing a therapist, all of them, and maybe it would work. And maybe it wouldn't. Not her problem.

Milo had taken his six weeks of house arrest and loss of computer privileges in stride, and he and Ava were getting on better since his transgression had led to both of them getting cell phones. The whole family had ended up staying offline for a month anyway, while the video of Frances losing her temper had enjoyed its fifteen minutes of fame. They'd ignored the media and after a week or two of leaving the phone off the hook it had all gone away. Frances knew it would haunt her on and off forever, but who cared? It had stopped the bitches at school calling her Saint Frances, which had always been annoying. As an additional bonus, the painful abyss of boredom occasioned by the lack of Internet had caused Ava to pick up her cello again and rejoin the orchestra. Proving once again that it's always darkest before the dawn, or that every cloud has a silver lining, or something like that.

Frances heard thumping down the stairs and suddenly Lally appeared, silently crossing the doorway on her way to the kitchen. She was dragging an enormous stuffed giraffe behind her, a giraffe Frances hated and had tried to get rid of many times. The neck, the body, the legs . . . The fucking thing took several seconds to clear the doorway, and Lally was exerting herself as she tugged it along. She appeared to have attached it to herself with—Frances swallowed—fur-lined handcuffs.

Michael looked up, ready to ask Lally if she was coming to help with the tree decorating. He saw the giraffe. He saw the handcuffs. There was the barest pause, then he looked at Frances. Almost imperceptibly she shook her head and watched her husband follow their youngest into the kitchen, hoping to head off further embarrassment. It probably wouldn't work, but she admired his willingness to try.

Still, it would be a funny story to tell Julie, who was hoping to be home before Christmas. The neighborhood would be together again, in all its imperfect, fractured, embarrassing glory. She'd just have to do her best to keep it that way. She stroked the cat and felt comfortable, even as he tightened his front paws and poked ten identical holes in her thighs.

Other
People's
Houses

Abbi Waxman

Discussion Questions

1. In this book the neighborhood plays an important role. What other situations create this kind of community, and how does seeing people every day change your relationship to them?

2. The central character, Frances Bloom, is someone who likes to help, because it makes her feel useful. Do you know someone like this? Do you find it easier to help or be helped?

3. Frances and Michael have a very happy but not very romantic marriage. Do you think that this will eventually drive them apart?

4. Anne Porter has an affair and nearly destroys her marriage. How important is sexual fidelity? Is it the most important element in a marriage? Can trust be rebuilt after a betrayal of this kind?

5. How much do children understand their parents' marriage? How hard is it to maintain privacy in a relationship once you have children?

6. Sara and Iris are experiencing communication problems in their marriage, although it's very strong. Have you gone through something similar, where communication breaks down for no apparent reason, and then becomes difficult to reopen?

7. Anne felt she was someone else in her affair, that it was something just for her. Ava also mentions a strong desire to be her own person, driving her own choices. How hard is it to balance a sense of self with responsibilities within a family?

8. Frances and Ava are navigating their changing relationship as Ava becomes more independent. Did you struggle against your parents or one parent in particular as you were becoming an adult? How do you think the experience of adolescence has changed since you were a teenager?

9. The title, *Other People's Houses*, alludes to the impression one gets of someone just by looking at them. How much can you really tell about someone based on their home, or the way they dress? Is appearance an expression of character, or armor?

10. Bill and Julie Horton are dealing with a challenging time in a very private way. What do you think are the advantages and disadvantages of approaching it this way?

Ready to find
your next great read?

Let us help.

Visit prh.com/nextread

Penguin
Random
House